THE PLAYERS IN
THE PALACE

DANNY LEHMAN—The man with the Midas touch. Out of a small-time coin dealership in Philly and cash-laundering scheme in the Caymans, he builds a fortune . . . and one of the most exclusive and most decadent casinos in Vegas. Now he has everything—if he only lives long enough to enjoy it.

SANDRA LEE—One of the best-looking women that money can buy. The first time she spots Danny Lehman at the tables, she knows she wants him. She means to protect him, look after him, take care of his every need. She's Danny's ticket to paradise.

SAUL MEYERS—An underworld banker who has his fingers on the purse strings of the Syndicate. He offers to bankroll Danny's deal in the desert and it's an offer Danny can't refuse. But when Saul does you a favor, you'd better be ready to return it . . . and more.

HENRY PRICE—He's a Wall Street power broker and a whiz at leveraged buyouts, hostile takeovers, merger arbitrage. Ivan Boesky's deals pale by comparison. Price has his eye on The Palace casino, and when he wants something he usually finds a way to get it—even if he has to dance around the SEC in the process.

EDDIE CORDOBA—Manager of The Palace, personally recruited from Beirut by Danny Lehman. He has ambitions, and he'll stop at nothing to see them through. Right now, Eddie wants to make it to the top, and Danny Lehman is all that stands in his way.

THE PALACE

PAUL ERDMAN

BANTAM BOOKS
TORONTO · NEW YORK · LONDON · SYDNEY · AUCKLAND

All the characters in this novel are fictitious
and any resemblance to actual persons, whether
living or dead, is entirely coincidental.

This edition contains the complete text
of the original hardcover edition.
NOT ONE WORD HAS BEEN OMITTED.

THE PALACE

A Bantam Book / published by arrangement with
Doubleday

PRINTING HISTORY
Doubleday edition published January 1988
Bantam edition / November 1988

ISBN 0-553-27538-0

Published simultaneously in the United States and Canada

Bantam Books are published by Bantam Books, a division of Bantam
Doubleday Dell Publishing Group, Inc. Its trademark, consisting of the
words ''Bantam Books'' and the portrayal of a rooster, is Registered in
U.S. Patent and Trademark Office and in other countries. Marca
Registrada. Bantam Books, 666 Fifth Avenue, New York, New York 10103.

PRINTED IN THE UNITED STATES OF AMERICA

O   0 9 8 7 6 5 4 3 2 1

PART ONE

1964 –1969

1

Danny Lehman's shop was, well, kind of shabby-looking, but it somehow belonged because it was just on the fringe of downtown Philadelphia, which is also shabby. Danny Lehman did not exactly exude class either. Class is something you're either born with or you're not, and Danny most certainly wasn't, which did not bother him in the least. His father had been in scrap until he went bust in the early 1930s, and Danny had maintained the tradition: he had started out with a pawnshop and had then moved up to a coin shop. Scrap, used coins: no class.

Danny was plump, usually sported one day's growth on his chin, and liked green sport shirts. He liked to bowl. He liked bagels. He liked his mother. He liked girls, in fact he liked them a lot, but for some reason had never married one.

In the fall of 1964 the guy who owned the shop next door, a travel agency, suggested that it was time for Danny to broaden his horizons. He could work out a trip to Europe for him, booking all the first-class hotels at cut rates since it was off-season, and would not even charge any of the usual commissions. After all, they were neighbors.

Never one to pass up a deal, Danny took him up on the offer. Almost immediately after arriving on the other side of the Atlantic, Danny was impressed by two things. The first was how he got taken every time hc had to change dollars into pounds, francs, or lire. It was the same in every hotel and restaurant bar none. By the time he hit Switzerland he had smartened up and decided to change his money at a bank *before* getting robbed at the hotels and the restaurants. He was disappointed to discover that the banks were offering rates that were almost as lousy. After all, they were banks, for God's sake, run by Episcopalians, or disciples of whatever type of God they worshipped in Zurich. Danny found out that Catholics were no better: in Milan they did the same thing; at the airport in Madrid, ditto. Danny figured that the money changers were taking an average of 5 percent in the middle for nothing more than giving him 375 marks in exchange for 100 dollars.

The other thing that astonished Danny was that nobody in Europe ever talked about the stock market. In Philadelphia, even in the bowling alley he frequented, everyone knew what the Dow Jones was doing, more or less. He could hardly believe it when somebody in Paris told him they didn't *have* a Dow Jones in Europe. What they did have, according to his French informant, a bartender at the George V who would talk to anybody to milk a tip, was a very highly developed interest in gold and silver. Coins maybe, Danny suggested, like the napoleon? It was the only French word he could pronounce with confidence. No, coins were for peasants and Americans, his financial adviser told him. The name of the money game in France, Switzerland, and Germany was bullion. That's where the rich Europeans had always put their dough. That's why they were still rich, and still able to frequent the bar at the George V.

Their reasoning was this, the erudite bartender went on to explain: every time there was a war, be it one of Napoleon's, World War I, or World War II, the governments of France or Germany or Italy would finance it by simply printing a lot of money. The inevitable result was that the value of everybody's paper money, be it marks, or francs, or lire, went all to hell. The smart Europeans, knowing that history constantly repeats itself, would begin trading in their cash for gold as soon as they saw the war clouds gathering. And when the war ended, in every instance they were among the few in society who had been able to preserve their wealth, in the form of that tangible asset gold, whose value had remained constant.

Later, after leaving a 25 percent tip, proving the bartender right once again, Danny figured that the only country that was at war right then was the United States in Vietnam. So maybe he should be thinking about getting into the gold business back home. The problem was that it was still illegal for Americans to buy gold in bullion form. All right, he concluded, then why not silver?

Danny asked around about who was number one in the silver bullion business in the United States. The answer was always the same: Engelhard Industries. When he asked foreign exchange, it was Deak-Perera. So with the help of a headhunter, Danny hired one of the best traders away from each. Soon every smart travel office in Philadelphia knew that the place to send people who needed foreign money before going abroad was the American Coin, Metals, and Currency Exchange on Broad Street: the new name that Danny had given his shop. And as the storm clouds started to gather over America's financial system as a result of the strain of the Vietnam War—giving birth to a new clan of doom-and-gloom merchants who had visions of the almighty dollar ending up in ruins, and who sought safety in, yes, bullion—well, the word spread that you could get good deals in Philadelphia.

Danny had a cousin in Trenton, New Jersey, who worked for a bank there. When he saw what Danny was doing in Philadelphia he suggested that Danny open up an office in Trenton, too, which he would be glad to run. Danny did. His cousin concentrated on the Jewish trade and it worked. The place was in the black by the third month.

Then Danny's cousin told him about a guy he knew in Boston who was a stockbroker and who was perfect for their type of operation: he was a big gun in the Catholic Church

up there, had built up a huge clientele among the parishio-
ners. Danny's cousin figured that on the Irish trade alone
they stood to do very well with a manager like that. Once
again, his cousin was proven right.

In Chicago, Danny went the Polish-Catholic route; in
Miami, he staffed the new place he opened up there with
Latinos; in San Francisco, he hired some Orientals. Just as
Aer Lingus and El Al had managed to build up the lucrative
North Atlantic trade by appealing to ethnic loyalties, and by
relying upon word of mouth among the faithful rather than
expensive advertising, Danny Lehman built up his currency
and bullion business by doing the same—and by offering
rates that beat every bank and every currency dealer in the
United States by 25 percent.

By the end of 1966, two years after Danny's historic trip
across the Atlantic, the American Coin, Metals, and Currency Exchange had spread to seven additional cities.
Danny Lehman's net worth was well into seven digits. In
December of that year, Danny went to Miami. He stayed at
the Fontainebleau Hotel. He had decided that it was time to
stop thinking about his business for a while, so every day he
went to the races at Hialeah, and every night he went to the
jai alai fronton. He loved to watch the horses by day and the
Basques by night, and he was excited by the atmosphere, by
the crowd. For it was this gaming crowd, the gamblers and
the bettors who seemed to enjoy life more than most people,
which fascinated him. They lived joyously for the brief moment of victory. They overcame stoically the more prevalent
brief moments of defeat. And they always came back.
Danny never bet; it was a sucker's game, he figured.

On December 23 Danny succumbed to the inevitable and
decided to check up on the local Miami branch of the American Coin, Metals, and Currency Exchange, which he had
opened about eighteen months earlier, and which was on the
main drag of downtown Miami, West Flagler. José, the
manager, was a Cuban. Danny, not being an early riser, got

there at about ten-thirty and had coffee with José in the back office. José said the place was making pretty good money in spite of the hard times. Actually, it was making damn good money. All of a sudden the rich Latin Americans had discovered how cheap the United States was compared to Europe, and were starting to come to Miami in droves to buy their mink coats, outboard motors, and Rolex watches. And they flocked to the American Coin, Metals, and Currency Exchange because the people there spoke Spanish and its exchange rates were better than those offered by any other bank or exchange office in town. The word had even gotten around São Paulo, Bogotá, and Caracas.

At around a quarter to eleven, a Cuban who worked at the coin and bullion counter entered the back office and mumbled something in Spanish, and immediately José got up, excused himself, and left, leaving Danny alone and puzzled. Danny went out to the shop proper and stood there watching a guy, definitely *not* a Latino, bringing in bags of coins, twenty-seven of them. Then José and the guy who was bringing in the silver—he could have been either Italian or Jewish—conferred, and a lot of hundred-dollar bills began to change hands. It took maybe ten minutes in all.

At eleven, José and Danny were again in the back room, each with new cups of coffee. Good coffee. Cubans know how to make coffee.

"Who was that?" asked Danny.

"Dunno" was the Cuban's response.

"Dunno?" asked Danny. "Then how come you didn't check out the coins, for Chrissake?"

"Don't have to," answered the Cuban. "They're always good."

Actually, there was not much to check. Either the coins were quarters minted before 1965, and thus almost pure silver, or they weren't. These were. With the silver bullion price on the rise, pure silver coins were starting to demand a premium, since they could be melted down and sold as bullion at a price higher than they were worth as coins in the monetary system. After 1965 the U.S. Government had started to smarten up and to use an increasingly smaller portion of silver per coin in the minting process; these new coins weren't worth melting down, at least not yet.

Danny mulled over the Cuban's answer for maybe a minute. "Always good, huh," he finally said.

"Yes."

"How often is always?" Danny then asked.

"Oh, about every ten days," answered the Cuban.

"How much's he bringing every ten days?" inquired Danny further.

"Oh, twenty-five, sometimes fifty bags."

"Always quarters?"

"Yes."

"Where's he from?" Danny asked.

José just shrugged.

"From around here?" Danny asked again.

"No," answered the Cuban.

They stopped here for a minute. Danny picked up his coffee cup and took a sip. So did José. They sipped some more. Then Danny continued with his interrogation. "So tell me this. Why'd he come here in the first place?"

"He came in with a customer. He had just one bag of silver the first time."

"A customer. Who's this customer?" asked Danny.

"A man who works at the jai alai place," answered the Cuban.

"What's his nationality?"

"Italian," answered José.

"When was that?" asked Danny.

"About six months ago," replied José.

"How much business in the meantime?"

"Let's see." José thought it over. "Something like four hundred thousand dollars."

"He let you know when he's coming?" Danny inquired.

"Well, he usually calls an hour beforehand," José answered.

"Who?" Danny asked.

"The same man" was the answer.

Danny paused and thought it all over. "Listen," he finally said, "next time he calls you I want you to call me immediately. Got it?"

"Yes, but I never really know in advance. Sometimes it's two weeks, sometimes maybe only five days," replied the Cuban.

"Doesn't matter. Just call me. I'm at the Fontainebleau. What time's he usually call?"

"Mostly between nine and ten o'clock in the morning."

"Okay. He calls you, you call me at the Fontainebleau, Room 756. Got it? Write it down."

José wrote it down. Danny took another sip of coffee, stood up, and left. Even on vacation, it was hustle that built a business. He went back to the hotel a happy man, an idea bubbling in his head.

On January 4, around nine thirty-five in the morning, the Cuban called Danny at the Fontainebleau to tell him he had received word that a new silver shipment would probably be hitting the store before eleven o'clock that morning. It took Danny just twenty minutes to shower and shave, and another twenty minutes to take a cab from Miami Beach to West Flagler. He went to the back room, where both José and a cup of coffee awaited him, and sat there with his employee chatting about the cold weather, jai alai, and the races.

Once more the counter clerk came into the back room and, in a hoarse whisper, told his boss that the guy with the silver bags was out there again. This time Danny Lehman and both Cubans walked out together. Danny stood immediately to the right and a little behind his Cuban manager as the customer brought in one bag after the other from the van standing at the curb. Every time the tall man, who was somewhere around six feet four inches, maybe even six feet six inches, shoved bag after bag across the counter, he looked first at the bag and then at Danny, silently asking himself, it seemed, who this new guy was and what exactly he was doing there. When the delivery was completed, José went through what was obviously a practiced ritual of weighing each bag, then writing down the weight on a pad. The posted selling price on the board behind the counter indicated that he was buying at $1.57 an ounce, selling at $1.67. Then he moved to the calculator, where ounces were converted to dollars. Having done all this, he wrote down the final number, circled it, turned the sheet around, and showed it to the tall man. The customer looked at the number, picked up the piece of paper, folded it, put it in his shirt pocket, and nodded his head. The Cuban went to the small safe located immediately behind the counter, opened it and pulled out a steel box, brought it to the counter, and put it down. It was full of one-hundred-dollar bills. He took out six packages with wrappers around them and, one by one, ripped off the wrappers and counted out singles. He used up almost all six packages. Then he reached into the cash drawer and extracted a fifty, a twenty, a ten, a five, and a couple of ones and laid them down beside the hundreds. He shoved the entire amount across the counter to the tall man, who put the bills into a very large, old-fashioned folding-type briefcase. Then he nodded again and turned to leave.

The number on the sheet of paper was $37,587.37.

"Sir," said Danny Lehman, just before the tall man had reached the door.

He paused, looked back, stared at Danny, and asked, "Who are you?"

José intervened immediately. "This is Mr. Daniel Lehman, the owner of this company. He's from Philadelphia, where our head office is located. We have branches in eight cities along the East Coast."

The tall man nodded again.

"I'd like to talk to you," said Danny.

"About what?" asked the tall man.

"I'd be interested in perhaps suggesting a special arrangement for you; a volume discount, if you would like to call it that," answered Danny.

The tall man said, "I'll let you know," and walked out.

Eight days later Danny Lehman was alone in his Philadelphia home watching the 76ers playing the Celtics when the phone rang at exactly ten o'clock. About two hours earlier he had hurried back from the bowling alley through a miserable, snowy Philadelphia winter night in order to catch the basketball game from the beginning. All he wanted at this moment was to watch the 76ers win, which they were doing. Then he wanted to take a good hot shower and go to bed. Now the damn phone was ringing. Danny Lehman, like everybody else, knew that ten o'clock phone calls rarely brought good news.

He turned down the volume on the TV, went to the phone, and barked, "Yeah," ready to slam the receiver down just as quickly as he had picked it up.

"Is this Danny Lehman?" came a voice.

"Yeah," repeated Danny. "What do you want?"

"I want to talk to you," the voice said.

"So talk."

"I've heard about you from a mutual friend to whom you introduced yourself in Miami a week ago. Do you remember?"

"Yes."

"I'd like to discuss the development of a business relationship, provided, of course, you're interested."

"I'm listening."

"Good. I'll be over in forty-five minutes." The phone went dead.

It was exactly a quarter to eleven when Danny's doorbell rang. When he opened the door, there stood a man about five feet six inches tall, the same height as himself. He was wearing a blue cashmere coat with a fur collar, and a fedora-type hat, and as he walked through the door into the hall-way, one could not help but notice his very shiny, pointed black shoes. The man said, "My name is Joseph Amaretto. I'd prefer you to call me Joe."

"All right," said Danny, "Joe it is." When Amaretto started to take off his top coat, Danny reached out to take it from him. But his visitor said, "No thanks, I'll hang on to it. This won't take long. No more than fifteen minutes."

Left with little choice, Danny led him into the living room. "Do you think you'll have time for a brandy?" he asked.

"I've never refused one yet," Amaretto replied, flashing a big smile.

Danny indicated that he should take a seat and a few minutes later returned with the brandy bottle and two snifter glasses. He poured a short one and handed it to his guest. Amaretto nodded his thanks, drank it, and quickly handed his glass back to Danny for a refill. Having received it, he settled back on the sofa, indicating that maybe they should get down to business. The social part of the evening was over.

"How many silver coins can you handle a month?" was his question.

Danny looked at him, raising his hands in a gesture meaning the sky was the limit, and answered, "Any amount you can come up with."

"How about five hundred bags a month?"

"No problem."

"Do you have the facilities for picking up quantities this large on a regular basis?"

"Where from?" asked Danny.

"We'll get to that," said Amaretto. "First the answer."

"The answer is yes. Anywhere on the eastern seaboard," replied Danny.

"I'm not talking about the eastern seaboard."

"Well, I can't say for sure unless you tell me exactly where this stuff is coming from."

"First let's clear something up," Amaretto said. "We know a lot about you. We like what we've found out. We would like to enter into a business relationship which will go on for quite a long time. Everything would be absolutely confidential, if you understand me. I'd also hope that we could expand the framework of cooperation to areas beyond silver coins."

The sentence might have been somewhat garbled, but Danny got Amaretto's message. "Fine with me," he said.

"You understand," Amaretto repeated, "that confidentiality is a primary requirement from our point of view."

"Perfectly," said Danny, this time with more accuracy.

Amaretto returned to the brandy, which he now sipped rather than gulped. "Fine," he said after the third and last sip. "The pickup place can be either Las Vegas or Reno, take your choice. Five hundred bags a month. What would you pay for them?"

"The price would be calculated from the closing quote on the London Metal Exchange. That's a bullion quote. We'd adjust it for bagged coinage. I'd give you the formula for your approval. There would be a charge of ten cents per ounce for transportation, handling, and insurance."

"Hold on," said Amaretto. "These coins wouldn't be presorted. And there will be dimes and silver dollars, not just quarters."

"We'll sort them out," Danny confirmed. "No additional charge."

The Italian said, "You have a deal. We'll call you in a day or two about the same time of the evening—here at home, if you don't mind. I'll tell you the exact time and place where you should make the pickup. Okay?"

"Okay as far as I'm concerned," said Danny.

"Fine." Amaretto stood up and put on his coat, which he had kept folded across his lap. He reached down for his hat, walked to the front door, shook hands with Danny, and walked out into the night. Danny stood at the open door and watched him go down the path, turn right at the sidewalk, and then move off at a brisk pace. There was no sign of a car, taxi, or limousine; in fact, there was no light or activity whatsoever outside. Danny watched him move fifty, one hundred, then two hundred feet down the street, and disappear. Shrugging, Danny turned around and went back into the house.

On January 21, 1967, a Railway Express van backed up to a warehouse in an industrial park in Reno to pick up three extremely heavy wooden crates. Three days later, they were dropped off at the warehouse of the American Coin, Metals, and Currency Exchange in south Philadelphia. After they were sorted and bagged, they were sold at retail throughout Danny's chain of outlets. The shipment brought in a quarter of a million dollars. Danny's profit amounted to approximately 17 percent of the sum. It was the largest single transaction that Danny had made in his business career. After all, he was literally a nickel, dime, and quarter guy.

2

Almost six months later, Joseph Amaretto returned to Philadelphia and again telephoned Danny, but this time at his office and in the morning. They arranged to meet for lunch at Bookbinder's, at the old Bookbinder's down near the water, not the other, newer one near downtown. Apparently Amaretto knew his way around Philadelphia.

Amaretto was with another man when Danny arrived. It was summer and Amaretto was wearing yellow slacks and a green sport shirt. But his colleague, who was introduced as Sam Sarnoff, had made no concession to the season: he wore a dark suit and an almost black tie with a gleaming white shirt. Sarnoff was also wearing cuff links studded with diamonds, which Danny figured were worth somewhere between twenty and thirty thousand dollars, per sleeve. Danny Lehman, like his father and grandfather before him, not only knew all about scrap metal and used coins, but also had an eye for precious stones. During lunch he questioned Sarnoff about the value of the diamonds. Sarnoff said, "Around fifty thousand dollars, both arms." He obviously appreciated the question, for it confirmed what Joseph Amaretto had said about Danny Lehman, namely, "The guy's got class."

The fish was excellent and the beer good. Apart from precious stones, the talk centered mainly on baseball: on the Phillies and the Dodgers. Danny Lehman rose even further in the estimation of his lunch partners when he confessed that he had been a secret admirer of the Dodgers since his boyhood days, when they played their home games not that far east of Philadelphia, and that he had remained a fan even though they were now based a few hundred miles west of Vegas.

It was a congenial sort of lunch, and it was not until a quarter to two that Amaretto burped, pushed back his chair, and said, "Danny, we've come here to break bread with you. We've been extremely happy with the way you've handled our silver coin business, and we want to express our appreciation for the confidential manner in which you've conducted these transactions. Our aim today is to tell you in person that not only do we want to continue our past business relationship with you, we'd now like to expand it. I think Sam would like to make a proposal to you. Sam?"

Amaretto's speech had sounded like a prepared introduction by a chairman of the board. That's exactly what it was.

"There is no reason to beat around the bush," began Sam Sarnoff, leaning across the table toward Danny. "What we have in mind, Mr. Lehman, is to seek your advice, your assistance, in redirecting the flow of funds arising from our silver transactions. To put it bluntly, our clients are experiencing difficulties in concealing cash receipts of this size. I'll explain it in a minute. But first"—and he paused—"first, we understand that not only do you deal in precious metals, but during the past couple of years you've also built up a business in foreign exchange. We assume that in such a business you must have extensive foreign bank contacts."

Danny looked at Sarnoff, nodded, and said, "Not exactly. They're more or less restricted to the Caribbean, although I'm not sure that's really any of your business." Then he stopped smiling. "I'm afraid, gentlemen," he said, while looking at Sarnoff, "that we're all going to have to be a lot more explicit with each other. Otherwise . . ." and his voice trailed off.

Sam Sarnoff looked at Joe Amaretto and Amaretto looked at Sarnoff, and their eyes must have confirmed an agreement to proceed. It was Sam who spoke. "Mr. Lehman, first I want to make it quite clear that we're acting as middlemen, or dealers, or perhaps a more precise word would be wholesalers. We're in essence a two-man operation. Now, what precisely do we do?"

"I've been wondering about that myself," Danny interjected.

"Why?"

"Just natural curiosity."

"Nothing more than that, I trust," Sarnoff said, glaring at him.

"What's that supposed to mean?" Danny replied, returning the glare.

"We're very, very allergic to people nosing around us."

"Who isn't?" Danny replied. "The Feds don't like anybody who deals strictly in cash. And I suspect that I've been in the cash business a lot longer than you guys, so cut the crap right now."

Again Sarnoff and Amaretto exchanged glances. Both nodded ever so slightly. Danny Lehman had apparently passed the final test. "You must know that skimming's a widespread practice in casinos in Nevada," Sarnoff said.

"When you talk about skimming, like everybody else I know that it goes on, but I'm not that familiar with Nevada casinos to know that it's widespread," Danny responded.

"Take our word for it. It is. And now we're coming to the heart of the matter, Danny, and why we have to be so careful about whom we deal with."

"We've already covered that," Danny said.

"All right. Our clients're involved in skimming in a big way. Their source: slots. Their problems: twofold. One, having skimmed, how to market the skim. And two, having marketed, how to hide the proceeds from the IRS and other interested parties. You follow me?"

Danny nodded.

"Okay. Thus far we've been devoting our attention exclusively to solving the first problem. Now what we propose to do today is mutually address ourselves to the second issue."

"Just how many suppliers do you gentlemen work with?" Danny asked.

"Eight," came the answer. "But the two principal ones—they're partners—contribute, I'd say, approximately 75 percent of the total."

Danny, frowning, mulled that one over, and then said, "They own these casinos?"

The visitors from out of town laughed. "Of course not. They *manage* these casinos or co-manage them," said Amaretto.

"So what you're saying," Danny said, "is that these clients have been hired to run these casinos and that they're running a skim on the side. And maybe the owner knows what's going on, and maybe he doesn't."

"Precisely" was the answer.

Danny Lehman was puzzled. "How do they do it? Skim, I mean, without the owners knowing?" he asked. "Don't they have auditors like in any other business?"

"I don't think you have to worry about that. That's a problem for the casino owners and, maybe, the IRS, right?"

"Sure, but you said that you have eight suppliers. Isn't it dangerous, if each one knows what the others are doing?"

Sarnoff gave the answer. "Your thinking's good, Danny, very good indeed. The point is that none of our suppliers knows that there are others. We deal with each one separately. As wholesalers, we collect the skim from Casino A, Casino B, and Casino C; we combine it, we box it, and we ship it to you for redistribution."

"Therefore," Sarnoff continued, "not only are they not aware of each other's existence, but also none of them knows of the existence of you."

Now a hint of a smile crossed Danny Lehman's face. He liked it. In fact, he liked it very much. "All right," he said, "you proposed that we address ourselves to problem number two. What is it?"

Sarnoff stretched his body into another position and leaned against the back of his chair. His hands lay flat on the table as if he were admiring his cuff links. He took a sip of his coffee and continued, "It's very simple. The men we deal with are all family men. They like to send their children to good schools. They like their wives to live in fine houses. They like to have motorboats. Some even like to have little airplanes so they can get away now and then and maintain their health. These things cost money. The problem, as I've already mentioned, is that the IRS is all over Nevada keeping an eye on these gentlemen. Thus they get the money from us, but *they can't spend it!*" Sam emphasized the last four words.

"So how can I help?" asked Danny.

"Well, like we said at the outset, we've heard about your foreign exchange operations, Danny," said Sarnoff. "You mentioned the Caribbean, which confirms what we've heard. In fact, we know that you go to the Bahamas quite often. We don't want to give you the impression that we are taking too deep an interest in your personal activities, but you know how it is: these things sometimes get brought to our attention, or at least to the attention of our friends. We figured from this that you might be able to help us, from down there."

They were very close to the mark. For what Danny had done was set up an arrangement with a bank down in Nassau, whereby it would conduct his offshore currency transactions for him, and channel them through what was essentially a mailbox bank of the same name that they controlled on the Cayman Islands, where the profits were left. That way there were no taxes due to anybody, anywhere, either in the Bahamas or in the United States. The Cayman bank apparently had no offices of its own but had been merely domiciled in the office building of a solicitor who worked for the Nassau bank. The only employee, if one could call him that, was a part-time accountant, a British national—British because they were much less susceptible to bribes than the locals—who flew over to the Cayman Islands from Nassau twice a year in order to fulfill the minimum accounting and reporting requirements set by the Cayman Islands' banking commission. Who *owned* these banks was never made exactly clear to Danny, but from his point of view it didn't matter. What did matter was that the Bahamas had stringent bank secrecy laws. On top of that, there was really no way that Danny Lehman could ever be identified with that mailbox bank, since he had never been to the Cayman Islands in his life, and intended never to go there either. So he decided to take the next step.

"You're right. I do have financial connections in the Bahamas. In fact, I work with a bank down there which is certainly able and, depending on certain provisos, may very well be willing to help you."

"All right," said Sarnoff. He was now excited. "First let me tell you that we sure appreciate your openness. You're just the way Joe told me you'd be, isn't that so, Joe?"

Amaretto smiled.

"What we propose, then, is this: from now on—and we'll provide you with the exact figures each time—we want approximately 75 percent of the proceeds from future silver sales to be directed to that bank of yours in the Caribbean. Now and then we'll request that your bank make a series of loans to two particular individuals. Their names will be given to you at the proper time. We'll suggest that these loans should be long-term, say twenty-five or thirty years; that they should not be collateralized; and that the interest charged to the borrower should be very high, since it is deductible. We anticipate that probably after a few years our clients, having duly made their payments on interest and principal might, no, *will*, want to pick up perhaps half the interest they've paid, but all of their payments on principal in, say, Nassau. We suggest the payout might be in the form of 'consultancy fees,' or whatever type of bookkeeping entry the bank might choose to get it off its books. This is the way our clients would like to finance the foreign travels in which they increasingly expect to indulge themselves in their golden years. Now our questions are these: do you think that the bank in the Caribbean with which you have that special relationship would have the facilities, one, to provide these loans now, and, two, to handle such confidential travel assistance services in the future?"

Danny answered their questions with a single word, "Yes."

The new arrangements were applied to the next shipment of silver from Reno. Twenty-five percent of the proceeds on the silver sales were returned to Amaretto and Sarnoff for cash payment to some of their Nevada clients; the other 75 percent was forwarded via Nassau to the bank in the Cayman Islands and credited to the accounts of the two clients.

Their names were Lenny De Niro and Roberto Salgo. Danny had to know because he set up their accounts. The signature cards went from the Cayman Islands to Nassau to Philadelphia to Nevada and came back, delivered by Amaretto in person. Before Danny forwarded them to Nassau he must have looked at the signature cards ten times. Danny reasoned that though these two men might be the biggest thieves in Nevada, there was no cause for him to worry. If they were ever going to present problems, they would be problems for Amaretto and Sarnoff.

Right?

Over the next eight months the coin volume coming out of Nevada suddenly stepped up appreciably, as did the balances credited to De Niro and Salgo. Then in March 1968 the first loans were made to the two new Nevada clients of that bank on the Cayman Islands. Again, it was through

Danny Lehman that the loan papers were forwarded, executed, and returned. The bank took a 10 percent fee up front and charged 16 percent interest on the thirty-year loans. The bank kept half of the interest and recredited the other half to its clients' accounts. The front-end fee the bank split with Danny Lehman. It paid it into his account in Nassau as a commission. Danny Lehman then did one more thing. He asked a friend of his to check around, for no real reason, perhaps, other than that the names Salgo and De Niro had set something in motion in his mind, to find out who was running the biggest casino operations in Nevada: the Sands, the Dunes, Caesars Palace, Raffles, the Circus; in other words the top operations. Mr. Lenny De Niro and Mr. Roberto Salgo, it turned out, were managing director and assistant managing director, respectively, of Raffles. Danny, who had never been in a casino in his life, also learned that Raffles, while not the biggest and not the best, was, perhaps, *the* casino in Nevada with the most unsavory reputation. A cautious man, Danny advised his friend to forget about the whole matter. The only two parties who could link Danny Lehman and the crooks who ran Raffles were Amaretto and Sarnoff, and an executive of a bank located on an obscure island in the Caribbean. Surely none of them were likely to talk. He was safe.

About three months later, Amaretto paid another midnight call to Danny Lehman at his home in the suburbs of Philadelphia. He delivered two large packages, each containing one million dollars in cash; paper money, mostly fives, tens, and twenties, with some hundreds. They were, he said, intended for deposit in the De Niro and Salgo accounts, respectively, and he had been told that further such cash deposits would be forthcoming on a periodic basis in the future. In all cases they would be hand-delivered by either Mr. Sarnoff or Mr. Amaretto.

In early 1969 Danny Lehman added up the cash flow, less

10 percent, that had passed through him to Mr. De Niro and Mr. Salgo: it amounted to just over twelve million dollars, or six million per annum, on average. Obviously they had moved well up from merely skimming slots.

3

On March 12, 1969, the board of directors of Raffles Inc. met in the company's corporate headquarters in the new part of Los Angeles known as Century City. The boardroom itself was wood-paneled, the board table solid oak, and the artwork on the walls subdued. The directors of the Wells Fargo Bank would have felt perfectly at home there. But it was the board of a Vegas casino, Raffles, that gathered there this day, and the seven members of that august body of that not quite so august corporation faced only two matters on the agenda. The first was a report by management on the company's activities and financial results for the fiscal year ending December 31, 1968; the second was an address by the corporation's general counsel on matters that had not been more closely defined on paper.

Where most companies are concerned, it is usual that the members of their board of directors gather for regular meetings at a reasonably early hour in the morning, say nine o'clock on the East Coast and maybe closer to ten o'clock on the West Coast. Not the board of Raffles Inc. It met at five o'clock in the afternoon. For most of its members tended to suffer from severe hangovers in the morning hours; then needed a late lunch to get them going; then a picker-upper around four-thirty—all this in order to brace themselves sufficiently for the quarterly fulfillment of the obligations incumbent on them as holders of high corporate office. Thus on March 12 the meeting had been scheduled

23

for five o'clock, but owing to late arrivals it was not until around a quarter to six that the chairman of the board picked up his gavel and smacked the oak table. This is something that board chairmen rarely, if ever, do to call a meeting to order. It was, however, a practice that Mario Riviera had decided to introduce in 1967, since it was the closest he would ever get to achieving, or at least publicly emulating, that station in life to which he most avidly and secretly aspired: being a judge. Once the members were finally seated, Chairman Riviera motioned to the two men who had been left standing at the foot of the long oak boardroom table to join him.

The two exchanged glances and just stood there for a while before slowly, deliberately, and, it seemed, provocatively moving forward. When they finally made it to the head of the table, instead of taking chairs they just stood behind the chairman with looks of surly arrogance on their faces. It was they, not the chairman, who now dominated the boardroom, their presence reeking of menace and latent brutality.

Turning to them, Riviera said, "Gentlemen, if you don't mind? I'd appreciate your sitting here, Mr. De Niro, and you there, Mr. Salgo." "Here" and "there" were to the right and left, respectively, of where Chairman Riviera was sitting. When the maneuvering was finally completed, a hush settled over the room. Chairman Riviera lost no further time. "I call this meeting to order. Our managing director, Mr. De Niro, has the floor."

De Niro rose. "I've been asked to come here to report on the results for the preceding fiscal year. The results were not good. In fact, they were very bad. We lost almost two million dollars. The final figure will be available from our accountants in due course. The loss this year will probably be higher." He sat down.

The first reaction around that oak table was profound silence. Then a movement of eyes began. First they looked

across the table, then moved up in the direction of the chairman, then down to the colleagues sitting near the foot of the
table. Nobody looked at De Niro. The basis for all this silent
eye-moving was a desire among the members of the board of
directors of Raffles Inc. to find one among them who could
come up with an appropriate response to the words that had
just been uttered by the thug now in their midst: Lenny De
Niro.

The spokesman who emerged was from St. Louis, the city
where the Western Pension Fund of the Teamsters' union
was headquartered, and what that union's representative
now said was to the point: "How the fuck is that possible?"

Lenny De Niro immediately got to his feet again and,
without the slightest hint of apology in his voice, said, "I
don't particularly like to be addressed in that tone. Understood?" He glared at the man from St. Louis for a full five
seconds. Then he continued, "All right. The explanation is
very simple. Business is lousy for everybody. It's just worse
for us. If I knew why, I'd fix it, wouldn't I?"

What De Niro was obviously trying to indicate was that if
market conditions in the gaming industry in the state of
Nevada were so adverse during the fiscal year of 1968, how
could a member of this board of directors have reasonably
expected him to pull off a goddamn miracle? The lack of any
signs of agreement around the board table seemed to indicate that such reasoning, such a line of logic, such an excuse, might have been appropriate had Raffles been part of
the shoe industry, even the trucking industry. But the gambling industry?

It was that same man from St. Louis, a Teamster, and
thus closely affiliated with the trucking industry, who again
spoke up. "I know the guys at the Sands," he said. "I know
the guys at the Dunes. They're not losing money, Lenny.
Something's wrong here. How the fuck can you lose money
when every game in the house's rigged against the jerks that
come into your place?" He was a huge, beefy man, and his

words came out in a rasp, the product, no doubt, of smoking cheap cigars, two of which were sticking out of the breast pocket of his off-the-rack brown suit.

De Niro answered in a steady voice, "I don't know exactly what you're trying to imply, George. I hope nothing. The whole country is in a recession, not just Nevada, not just Vegas. If you think you can do better, be our guest. Right, Roberto?"

Roberto Salgo just glared at the bigmouth from Missouri. At that point the door opened and in came a man in a pinstriped suit wielding a large attaché case, and obviously in a state of extreme agitation. This was a highly welcome interruption for Riviera, who, after all, had been responsible years ago for bringing in De Niro and Salgo as the operating heads of the casino. So it was with relief in his voice that Riviera stood up, both to offer due recognition of the entry into the boardroom of the corporation's general counsel and, at the same time, to say, "Gentlemen, I think the first part of the agenda has been covered. Let's move on to the second."

When the last syllable had left the mouth of the chairman, De Niro and Salgo looked at each other and then defiantly around the board table. Nobody, not even the director from St. Louis, was going to object to the chairman's proposal. So De Niro and Salgo got up and, with measured steps, disappeared out the boardroom door.

Their next stop was Harry's Bar, where both tossed down two back-to-back bourbons in silence, and simultaneously lit up two fine Montecristo Cuban cigars. Then, as if it was part of a regular ritual, both reached out and shook hands. After all, it had been no small accomplishment: they had managed, once again, to get away with a year of theft on a truly grand scale, an achievement which, by itself, gave no cause for special recognition in the United States of America in the 1960s. Tens, no, hundreds, of thousands had done the same. But what gave them cause for self-congratulation in that bar in Century City on March 12, 1969, was that they had stolen such vast sums, not from mansions in Beverly Hills or from customers of brokerage firms in New York, but rather from some of the biggest crooks not only in the United States, but in the entire Western world.

Upstairs on the seventeenth floor of the same Century City tower building that housed Harry's Bar, the general counsel had moved to the head of the table and taken the chair so recently vacated by Lenny De Niro. In contrast to his predecessor, he had arrived armed not only with mental notes, but with pound upon pound of documentation, which he proceeded to remove from his oversized attaché case. The very last thing he extracted from it was one single sheet of yellow paper.

Since Chairman Riviera did not seem to be in the mood to make any more introductions that day, the lawyer simply took command by holding up that piece of paper and talking. "Gentlemen, these are notes reflecting the precise key words of an oral and still totally confidential statement which was made to me two days ago by the Gaming Enforcement Division of the Casino Control Commission of the Sovereign State of Nevada. It's not exactly good news. The chairman of the Gaming Enforcement Division said, and I quote, 'It's known to us that three of the men currently on the board of directors of Raffles Inc. are acting in a "fiduciary capacity" for organized crime syndicates from three separate geographical areas in the United States.' End quote."

The room was once again very quiet. The dapper attorney then stretched his thin, rather bluish lips in the semblance of a smile and said, "That was not good news, was it? No. But now I have slightly better news." He paused for effect. "The chairman of the Gaming Enforcement Division also said that he did not intend, in his words, 'to reveal the identity of these individuals at this stage of the investigation.' He in fact further stated, and I quote, 'Maybe they must never be revealed by us.' End quote."

The mood in the room seemed to improve; it were as though a light had been switched on. But then the lawyer continued, quickly dimming that light.

"As always, I'm afraid, one must pay a price for better news, because, and now listen carefully, you guys," he said, slowing the pace of his delivery, and articulating each word with a threatening emphasis, "the only way that the names of these individuals will not be brought before the public—that is, the only way that Raffles Inc. and its one and only operating unit, the Raffles Hotel and Casino of Las Vegas, Nevada, will not end up being worth zilch—and again I ask you to listen very carefully, is if these three unknowns will voluntarily agree to divest themselves of their holdings in Raffles Inc. This has to be done within a reasonably short time, to be specific, within sixty days of this board meeting."

The lawyer then looked around the room and said, "All right, we need three volunteers. Who are they?" No one in the room moved.

"Let's try another approach, a fresh approach, one which I can only hope and pray will work for the sake of all of you. I stress: *all* of you. Because, believe me, *my* interests in this entire situation are limited and becoming more limited every minute. Let me suggest that perhaps the three unknowns in this room could, without prejudicing their positions because what transpires in this room this afternoon would go no further than the confines of this room—"

At this point the man from the Teamsters' union in St. Louis said in a voice that was equally quiet and threatening, "Sidney, get to the point."

"I will," the lawyer replied, "in my own way.

"Now," he continued, in an even more deliberate manner as if to rub it in, "it seems to me that the gentlemanly thing for these three particular individuals who are acting in a fiduciary capacity for outside interests to do would be to *buy out* the other four partners sitting around this table, the clean ones if I may so describe them; to buy them out at a fair appraised value. I'll arrange for the appraisal to be done. And to be done not within sixty days, but better yet within thirty days. Then these three unknown individuals who are acting in, and I again quote, 'a fiduciary capacity for organized crime' could fight their own fight with the fucking Casino Control Commission. Any thoughts on this so far, gentlemen, whoever you are?"

Silence.

"All right," said the lawyer, "I quit." He put the single piece of yellow paper back into his massive attaché case. He rose, nodded first to the chairman and then to the other members at large, strolled to the door, and disappeared.

The dilemma facing the men remaining in the boardroom was the fact that all were, in some way, shape, or form, operating as fiduciary agents for people who, by almost any definition, would be regarded as participating in organized crime. While all obviously knew that about one another, none of them knew what the Nevada Casino Control Commission's Gaming Enforcement Division knew. So why volunteer to divest if their name was not on the hit list?

Raffles Inc. was still alive, if not exactly well. Who could know what it might be worth if this current little problem was solved? To divest now, which was really just a nice word for selling out for a song, would be crazy. So there had been no sense in anybody standing up the first time, had there? The same logic applied to the second so-called solution that their ex–general counsel had proposed, namely, his suggestion for an internal takeover. Why would anybody throw good money after bad if he was among the three on the hit list in Nevada? They would close down Raffles Inc. anyway, wouldn't they?

Now, Chairman Riviera might not have had too great a knowledge of how to run a corporation, or too much style in running a board meeting, but he was able to recognize a situation that desperately called for a solution. He explained himself very clearly and succinctly. "We've got to find somebody who will buy this fucking company," he said, "and take *all* of us out." He then added, "Quick."

The man from the Teamsters' union decided to seek further clarification. He did so because the Teamsters had seven million bucks in Raffles Inc., in the form of unsecured loans. If Raffles Casino got closed down and became an untouchable, and if, as a result, this seven million never got repaid, it would mean personal trouble for him. For not only had he personally sponsored this loan in his capacity as a high official in the union's pension fund, which acted as the lender, but he had also personally taken a finder's fee on the loan from the borrower, from the hand of Chairman Riviera to be precise, of a quarter of a million dollars. If Raffles went into Chapter 11, and people started to sniff around . . . well, he had already concluded that there was no sense sticking his head in the sand; if he was going to be thrown into the Detroit River he might as well have it done in warm weather. So he decided to speak up then and there.

"Riviera. Who wants to buy a casino that's losing millions of dollars a year? Who wants to touch a situation which even the company lawyer has taken a walk from? Like nobody in his right mind! And so who's going to pay me back my seven million bucks? If the company can't, I'm afraid you guys, let's face it, have a moral responsibility here, especially you, Riviera." He hated to push a guy like Riviera this way, but there was not much left to lose, he reasoned.

"I've got a man who can sell this place," Riviera now stated, totally ignoring what had just been said. After all, who could blame a guy for being afraid of Jimmy Hoffa?

Led by the smartass Teamsters man, they all laughed.

"I'm telling you, I've got this guy who's a Hollywood agent. He's always selling crap to suckers."

The other board members looked at him. Hollywood

agents were the sleaziest of all merchants of deadbeat properties to be found anywhere on the face of earth. Everybody knew that. Middlemen from Lebanon, purveyors of tax shelters from Texas, even Swiss lawyers could not compete. So if there was a last chance for the sale, it had to be through a Hollywood agent.

They were right, although at first it didn't seem so.

4

The agent that Chairman Riviera had in mind was Mort
Granville. Mort Granville ran so true to form as a Hollywood agent that Riviera had to make five futile attempts to
get hold of him before Granville condescended to return his
call. One problem with Hollywood agents is that they have
no choice but to act in a totally stereotypical fashion; otherwise they lose their mystique, and if they ever lose that,
there'll be nothing there. Like Oakland.

Or to put it another way, *everybody* is overqualified for
the job of Hollywood agent. So when Riviera did finally get
hold of the wonderboy of Wilshire Boulevard, not only was
he asked to join him for lunch the next day, a great honor in
and of itself, but he was commanded to join Mort in his
booth at the rear of the patio of the Polo Lounge of the
Beverly Hills Hotel. Riviera ordered a Cobb salad and iced
tea, so Granville, feeling that such understatement could
hardly be left unchallenged, did the same. They had barely
ordered when Riviera blurted out the truth: he needed a
buyer, quick, for Raffles Inc., and the sellers were not too
fussy. The operative word was quick!

After Riviera repeated the word a second time, Granville
motioned to the Philip Morris–type bellhop and had a
phone brought to the booth. It was barely one o'clock in
California and so he got his man in New York without any
trouble or delay. The conversation, however, lasted two
minutes. Mort ended it by slamming the receiver down

without saying goodbye. That was the way he ended a lot of phone conversations.

"No dice," he said to Riviera. Then Granville continued, "Since you sounded so desperate I decided to start immediately at the bottom of the barrel. That was a guy from New York," and he went on to name one of the most prestigious investment houses on Wall Street. Mort had once met the guy at a party and then fixed him up with an aspiring singer from Hong Kong who had proceeded to feed him Chinese food and sleep with him, intermittently, for three days. He had dizzy spells for weeks afterward. They were due to his being allergic to MSG, he found out later with great relief. The next time he was in L.A., Mort had fixed him up with an Italian actress. She had given him the clap. But the guy still stayed in touch. Weird, even for an investment banker. The point was that Mort, despite these past "favors," had never asked for anything back. Thus the phone call.

"What'd he say?" inquired Riviera.

" 'Are you kidding?' that's what he said," the agent replied. "He also said, 'They're shutting Raffles down.' " Then Granville added, "Riviera, you might have told me about that shutting-down aspect of the situation. It's pertinent, you know."

"What now?" Riviera asked, ignoring as usual what he didn't want to hear.

"Don't ask me," replied Granville.

At this point the agent looked at his watch and, as if acting upon a printout that had appeared there, jumped to his feet, telling Riviera that he was already late for his next appointment. Riviera was left with the check and with the reality that the word must have already gotten out that Raffles Inc. was indeed dead, because if Mort Granville walked away from a deal that theoretically would have brought him 10 percent of anything, after just one phone call, there was probably no hope left in this world.

For Riviera this was not good because, in contrast to the

other members of the board, he did not act in, as the Casino Commission guy had put it, "a 'fiduciary capacity' for organized crime." In this case there was no fiduciary necessary. He *was* organized crime, where the southern half of California was concerned. Therefore the looming debacle would mean more than a mere loss of money; it would involve an irrevocable loss of prestige among his peers, and that could mean a lot more than the lousy five million dollars he had invested in the fucking casino in the first place. The fact that a shit-faced agent had just walked out on him, and just after a shit-faced lawyer had done the same, could hardly be viewed as anything less than a portent of what lay ahead.

Riviera should have had more faith in his fellowman. After all, the human race is not made up exclusively of agents and lawyers. Yet.

The next day Mort Granville, being an agent, and therefore being in touch with all that was trendy, decided to get into silver. Sure, he had heard that a lot of guys were doing it: like the anchormen around town; production types at the studios; entertainment lawyers; i.e., men who were always state-of-the-art–oriented. But it was not until that moment that he decided to go for it.

The final decision did not come as a result of any revelation as he drove his Porsche back to the office from the Beverly Hills Hotel. Rather, it had been spurred by such a mundane thing as a full-page ad he had seen that morning in the financial section of the Los Angeles *Times* announcing in a somewhat gaudy manner the grand opening of the first West Coast office of the American Coin, Metals, and Currency Exchange. By coincidence, about an hour later, when his secretary had brought in the mail, it had included an invitation to attend a cocktail party at the new coin place, which was going to be hosted by the man who owned the entire nationwide operation, a certain Daniel Lehman from Philadelphia. The explanation for the invitation, Granville figured, was that somebody must have sold the coin and metals guy a list of the names of L.A.'s emerging elite. In fact, his name came from a listing of everybody in L.A. who owned a Porsche.

As far as Mort Granville was concerned, with these new offices just three blocks up Wilshire Boulevard from his own office building, if it turned out to be a bummer, he would waste no more than a five-minute walk up Wilshire Boulevard and a five-minute walk back. Even an abortive trip by foot might do his body good because of the deep breathing he always practiced when walking. It was a good day to breathe, one of those days without even a trace of smog in the air, a day when you could walk up Wilshire Boulevard, see the mountains in the distance, and *have* to say to yourself with true conviction, "Thank God I live in Los Angeles!"

When Mort Granville got to the new branch of the American Coin, Metals, and Currency Exchange, the first thing he did was look at the store front. Not knowing a damn thing about coins, metals, or foreign currencies, what he looked at was the color scheme, and he liked it. There were those old collectors' gold coins, American eagles, displayed elegantly beside some bluish currency which, upon closer examination, turned out to be German marks. Mexican silver coins were laid out around some red and very large bills. When he squinted and took a closer look, it seemed to him that they were Swiss francs. What caught his eye most were the bars of silver bullion, the status investment Mort Granville had concluded he should seriously consider making, because though he was still "just" an agent, there was very little doubt in Mort's mind that within a matter of years or perhaps months he would become a producer, then a "major" producer. After that, his posting as head of a studio could not be far off. Looking ahead to the time when he would be running Columbia, or at the very least Twentieth

Century-Fox, it would be rather nice if when moving into his new offices he could have various bars of silver, preferably very large bars of silver, to put on the bookshelf behind his desk.

With this vision of the future in mind, Mort Granville entered the premises to be greeted by a fairly subdued crowd of perhaps a hundred people. He gave them a quick scan and came up with nobody of importance. Perhaps it was still too early for the entertainment lawyers and the financial planners.

It was then that a short, chubby, balding man grabbed his arm and introduced himself. "You look lost," he said. "I'm Danny Lehman. What do you think of this place? Interesting, isn't it? I own it and I'm damn proud of it. Let me show you around." It all came out in one breath as if memorized.

Mort Granville did not appreciate the laying on of hands, but somehow he immediately liked the little guy. Be kind, he thought. "Splendid place, Mr. Lehman," said Granville, as they moved from counter to counter, display case to display case. "You are not by any chance connected with Lehman Brothers in New York, are you?" This guy sure didn't *look* like it, but you could hardly go by that in L.A.

"No connection. And call me Danny," Lehman replied. "You're a coin collector?"

"No, I'm an agent."

"A real estate agent?"

Now, that was a very low blow, but when Granville looked at Danny's face he saw a type of innocence which indicated that this remark had hardly been meant in a vicious way. "No, actually I represent people here in the industry: like entertainers, actors, actresses, screenplay writers, you know, that sort of business. My name's Mort Granville."

This truly impressed Danny Lehman. For despite the fact that he was now a relatively rich man he had never in his life met anybody from this type of industry. This time his face expressed an obvious pleasure at having the opportunity to mingle with a man who mingled with the stars. Who knows, he thought to himself, maybe someday this simple boy from Philadelphia might be mingling with the same sort of crowd.

What he was thinking showed. Mort Granville, who appreciated any admiration from any source, decided to humor the little man further. "It seems that you're off to a good start here, Danny. How many shops have you got like this?"

"This is the seventeenth."

The agent's condescension visibly lessened. "And how long have you been in the coin business?" he now asked.

"About ten years" was Danny's answer.

"What's your turnover? You don't have to answer, but I'm curious about your type of business."

"About sixty million dollars this year, I estimate," answered Danny, nonchalantly.

"Sixty million!" Then as a further comment he whistled quietly through his teeth.

"Let me tell you, Mort, it's been a good business, but it's going to be a hell of a lot better in the future."

"Why's that?" asked Granville.

"There're two reasons. The war in Vietnam means the dollar's got to start going to hell sooner or later. Then everybody'll want to get out, won't they? Some'll want real estate, some'll go for other tangible things: paintings, that sort of crap. Some'll go to Switzerland to buy gold illegally. But the smart ones'll come to my place and legally buy Swiss francs, or German marks, or Japanese yen. The best of all, though, is going to be silver, especially if you're a bit of a gambler."

"Gambler? What do you mean by 'gambler'? Can you explain that gambler bit on silver?"

Danny did so at length, explaining that a lot of crazies were starting to get into this silver business. Not pension funds or Wall Street types, or banks, or insurance companies. The people who were going into the silver business were almost all individuals. And they were all doing it on an emotional basis. They were convinced that they, and they alone, knew what was coming. And the only way to survive it, they figured, was to trade in money for the real thing, for real coins, real bags of silver, real bars of bullion. The *real* crazies among the crowd were going into futures, buying silver on margin. Not the kind of margin you have to put up for stocks, but only 10 percent or even 5 percent margin. Leveraging to the hilt. That made for wild fluctuations in the market because one day they would double their money, even though the price had only moved up 10 percent. Then they would dump it and sell out, and the same thing would happen in the other direction: the price would move down 15 percent and in the process wipe out ten thousand speculators, all this within one week.

"So it's really just a roller coaster," Danny pointed out. "The stakes and the action are a lot bigger than you can find anywhere over there in Nevada. But that's what makes for horse races, which I love. That's also what makes the profits for people like me who're in the silver business, because it's like having a new type of bait attracting the same old suckers." Danny paused for breath. Then he finished his spiel. "Everybody's basically a gambler," he said, "and what we've got here is a new type of casino. You're a smart guy, you know in the end it's always the house that wins. Well, in the silver business I run the house, so I make a lot of money."

God must have sent him here, Mort's internal voice was saying. And if God also sent *me* here, He would want me to be open and honest. So Granville asked, "Want to buy a casino?" These were words that would lead to a total revolution of the gaming industry in the United States of America, but it did not seem that way at first. For Danny Lehman's reply to Mort Granville's question was "Nah, not really. I visited Vegas a few weeks ago for the first time, and you know something? That place has no class. It seemed to me, just looking around, for about forty-eight hours I guess it was, that those places are run by a bunch of amateurs. No public relations. What do you think of when you think of Las Vegas? I'll tell you: call girls, bad drinks, windowless rooms, sleaze. Right?"

Granville agreed.

"That's no way to push a product or to run a place of business, is it? People like clean places. Look at my place, how clean it is. Got me?"

"You may be right," said Granville. "But just because that's the way things are over there right now, that doesn't mean it can't change." Mort Granville could feel there was something here, maybe something big, something that had to be followed through as only he could do; something that would then end up as a really viable deal of which he would get 10 percent. Intuitively, to keep it going, his finger suddenly lashed out and pointed at a large silver bullion bar. "How much does that cost?"

"Four hundred dollars, give or take," came the answer.

"I'll take two," said Granville and whipped out his checkbook ready to close the deal on the spot. After an exact quote had been given by the counterman, Granville filled out the check and handed it over to Danny with his calling card. "Hold the silver for me, will you," he said. "I'll have it picked up later." Not too many people got mugged on this stretch of Wilshire in broad daylight, but you never knew. Better his secretary than him.

As Mort Granville turned to go, Danny Lehman's hand once again came down on his sleeve, but this time very, very lightly. "Just one question, Mort," said Danny.

"Yes?" and now that tingling that Mort had felt just a few minutes ago became more intense. "Yes?" he repeated.

"What's the name of that casino you have for sale?"

"Raffles," answered Mort.

The owner of the American Coin, Metals, and Currency

Exchange nodded and said, "I think you might hear from me."

It was three hours later when the party was finally over and Danny Lehman was able to head back to his hotel in a cab. It did not take him to the Beverly Wilshire, or the Beverly Hills Hotel, or even the newly opened Century Plaza. No, he roomed at the Westwood Holiday Inn. That was his style. Danny knew it and it did not bother him in the slightest.

Raffles. He was more than tempted and he admitted it. But it was risky. The temptation arose, naturally, from the fact that he knew something about Raffles that nobody else did: De Niro and Salgo. But the risk came from the same knowledge. He, Danny Lehman, was acting as a fence for the not insignificant amount of silver coinage that Lenny De Niro and Roberto Salgo, the co-managers of Raffles, had filched from their own casino over the years. If that was not bad enough, that type of grand theft was peanuts compared to what had started coming in recently in the form of bills. If the middlemen, Joe Amaretto and Sam Sarnoff, had lied to him and had indeed informed their clients about the identity of "their man in Philadelphia"—their man who was fencing the skim; their man who had also set them up with that bank in the Cayman Islands which was enabling them to make fools of the IRS—then he, Danny Lehman, might disappear for a minimum of thirty years, or he might just disappear, period, depending upon who got to him first. At some point a go or no-go decision would have to be made. It would involve the biggest such decision he had ever taken in his life. If he went ahead, he might really become somebody. Or, let's face it, he might blow everything.

But what was there to blow, actually? They've never let you have a real crack at anything. Coin stores! Big deal. When everything went bad in Philadelphia after his father's death and he'd had to spend his Easter school vacations with his grandma in Atlantic City, she did not talk to him about *coin* stores. Together they used to walk down the boardwalk, trailing behind the really rich people as well as the prostitutes and con men who were trailing them. "One day *you'll* be leading the Easter parade in Atlantic City," she would tell him.

Danny, though a very successful coin, metals, and currency man, had not restricted his education in money matters to these three areas alone. He, like almost everybody else in the sixties, had been lured into the stock market: first into mutual funds and then into opening a trading account at Merrill Lynch. He was familiar with such concepts as mergers and acquisitions and, in fact, had made good money on some merger arbitrage deals—Fred Carr's takeover of National General Insurance, Loews buying Lorillard, ITT bidding up the price of Hartford Insurance before absorbing it—so such determinants of the market value of a company as annual sales, net asset value, or price-earnings ratios were nothing new to him. Since he was an independent businessman, it was the last measure which always impressed him most. Who cared about assets if you could not make money out of them? Who cared about sales if they did not yield profit? No, when you bought something, you bought profit. Not just potential profit, either, in Danny Lehman's scheme of things; none of that blue-sky stuff. If you bought something, you wanted it to make money now and you wanted it to make a hell of a lot more money later. That's what capitalism according to Daniel Lehman was all about. He intuitively wanted an immediately positive cash flow, but *that* one even he'd never heard of yet.

So he mulled all this over in his head as he sat there on the sixth floor of a motel near the San Diego Freeway in the Westwood section of Los Angeles. The crazies these days were paying prices for companies amounting to twenty-five times earnings. Even dogs were selling at ratios of fifteen to one. Raffles, from the transparent eagerness of Mort Granville to get him interested, was obviously not just a dog, but a very sick dog. Therefore, ten times recent earnings would be the maximum to which a reasonable buyer would go.

He knew that six million dollars per annum, on average, had been stolen from Raffles during the past couple of years. It would seem logical that if Raffles was on the block to such a degree that an agent like Mort Granville would offer it to a man he'd met only five minutes earlier, you had to conclude that the casino was not only in deep trouble because it was losing money, but probably also in jeopardy where its license was concerned, because the whole place must be run by crooks from top to bottom. But, he reasoned, who cares about the licensing status? The guys who owned the place obviously wanted to get out, and to get out before the ax fell. Once they were gone, there would be no reason for the state of Nevada to quarrel with the new owner, since there was nothing wrong with Danny Lehman's reputation. On second thought, there *would* be nothing wrong with Danny Lehman's reputation so long as the De Niro–Salgo–Amaretto–Sarnoff relationship with himself remained as it was at this particular moment in time—unknown.

But back to the money angle. How big a loss was the casino showing officially? A million? Two? It was probably two million, maximum, Danny concluded, because Salgo and De Niro were not dumb enough to steal so much that the financial viability, the very existence of the casino, would be endangered as a result. That would amount to the killing of their golden goose.

So what were the *real* profits of Raffles? And based upon those profits, what was the value of Raffles? The calculation that Danny came up with was this: six million dollars' skim less the average losses per annum of the casino for the past two years, say two million, equaled four million, less the tax that would have had to be paid after depreciation, loss carryovers, and all, say a half million, equaled three and a half million, times ten, equaled thirty-five million dollars, which, realistically, would end up at, say, forty million. That's what Raffles Inc. was worth to Danny Lehman, subject to a look at their books, of course. Which raised a new problem: if he went back to that guy Granville and asked him for specifics on the financial status of Raffles, that is, if he asked for copies of the financial audits of Raffles during the last two or three years, invariably when this request was passed on to the people who owned Raffles his name would come up. In spite of the shape they were in, they were hardly going to hand that stuff out to just anybody. But then would come the moment of truth: if his name came up and rang no bells anywhere, fine. Then he would make an offer.

However, and this was a very big however, if the bells *did* go off, he would have to pull out of Los Angeles and stay out of Los Angeles for a long, long time. But think it all the way through, he said to himself. Who could possibly know of him and thus be able to ring those bells? Answer: four guys, none of whom had anything to do with the ownership of Raffles and none of whom wanted their boat to be rocked either. Since neither Amaretto and Sarnoff nor De Niro and Salgo would want to risk having him entangle them in anything, and so long as their paths, which had remained separate in the past, would also remain separate in the future, once this current brief interlude had ended, well, nothing would happen to him or them. Right? So . . .

At nine o'clock the next morning Danny Lehman rang Mort Granville at his office. Naturally Granville did not take the call, but he returned it six minutes later, a fact which if it had ever gotten out would have ruined the man in that town forever. Danny's request was simple. "Get me the financial statements."

The answer was equally simple. "I'll have a messenger over at your hotel with them within the hour. Where are you staying?"

The voice on the other end of the phone went a little quiet

when Danny mentioned the Holiday Inn as the place to which the delivery should be made. But then the cloud seemed to lift, since Mort Granville's twisted mind immediately came to the conclusion that he was dealing with a very cagey operator who understood the impact of understatement. First Riviera's Cobb salad and iced tea; now the Holiday Inn. Was this a new trend that he had failed to spot?

5

Exactly three days later the board of directors of Raffles Inc. reconvened. That something truly extraordinary was afoot was apparent from the time of day that this event took place: ten o'clock in the morning. The strain showed on the paunchy, sallow faces of the men there assembled. But in contrast to that late afternoon meeting a few days previously, there was a mood of guarded optimism in the air.

The chairman had personally phoned each of them to say that he thought he had found a "solution." Since nothing more was said, the normal reaction would have been unbridled skepticism. But they all knew that this time the chairman's reputation was on the line as it perhaps had never been before, and that if he was going to interrupt the daily pattern of their lives to the extent of calling a board meeting in the morning, then there must be something of true substance in the offing.

This guarded optimism, however, disintegrated immediately and totally when, after they had all duly gathered, the chairman walked in with nobody else but that hotshot Hollywood agent, Mort Granville, at his side. To them Mort personified precisely the opposite of substance. And when they examined the agent more closely and noticed that he had what could perhaps best be described as a perpetual manic grin on his face, the mood of the crowd in that boardroom was on the verge of turning ugly.

For they all knew Mort. How? Because Granville, along

with the rest of them, was a regular customer at that part of one of the bars just off the casino floor of Raffles known as "hookers' corner." Mort would invariably turn up once every other weekend, usually on Friday night when a new act was opening in the big showroom featuring one of Mort's clients, or a friend of one of Mort's clients, or somebody Mort would have liked to have as a client. The last class was, of course, the largest, for in spite of what Mort Granville thought about himself, the truth of the matter was that in the galaxy of Hollywood star agents, Mort Granville was not a supernova; rather, in the eyes of some, he more closely resembled a black hole.

"Gentlemen," said the chairman, "I think you all know Mort," and he paused here, hoping that no one would groan aloud, which nevertheless two did. The effect on Granville was nil; the manic grin persisted. "Mort," continued the chairman, "lay it out for them."

"I got a buyer, fellas," said Granville. "Let me tell you who he is: a guy from Philadelphia who owns a bunch of coin shops. I had him checked out. He's clean. He's got plenty of borrowing power. He's waiting outside and he's prepared to make an offer."

"What kind of an offer?" asked the Teamsters' union representative. "Nothing down and a hundred years to pay?"

Granville stared him down for a few seconds and said, "Why should I explain further, asshole? Let this man do it himself. His name is Danny Lehman. I'll get him."

Granville went to the door, opened it, stuck his head through, and motioned to Danny, who had been sitting there in the outside office eyeing the cleavage of the receptionist. It didn't bother her somehow, as this paunchy, balding little guy turned her on. So while she was fully aware that the man sitting across the room from her was copping, if not a physical feel, at least a series of highly targeted mental feels of that part of her anatomy she was most proud of, she refrained from shooting him a withering glance. Instead, she began sorting and resorting everything on top of her desk, a pattern of moves designed to display her anatomy from the most flattering angles.

Her thoughts were actually not too far off the mark, for Danny Lehman had been impressed by this leggy, bosomy blonde, just as he was impressed by Century City, by Los Angeles, by this whole new world of California. To the guy from Philadelphia it seemed almost unreal that these people from this town were willing not only to accept him as an equal, but to bow and scrape. To his credit, Danny Lehman was already perfectly aware of the reason why, the one and only reason why: money. He had money, they knew he had money, and they wanted his money. Therefore, they would do any fucking thing they had to do to get it: butter him up, deceive him, cajole, beg; you name it, provided that the end result was his money ending in their pockets. Which was absolutely fine with Danny Lehman, because already years ago he had figured out that anybody who had any illusions about life's being some kind of romantic, mystical journey was just asking for it, asking to be had. What life was really all about was money: making money, accumulating money. It all came down to the simple fact that all the best things in life, including romance, were for sale; and without money, no sale.

Danny had dressed up for the occasion. He had on a complete suit, a new shirt, a new tie, and new cuff links, which he had acquired the previous evening for a grand total of one hundred and forty-nine dollars. He walked to the head of the boardroom table, bowed his head slightly to the men present, and then shook hands with Chairman Riviera. The chairman beamed and seemed on the verge of putting his meaty arm around Danny's shoulder, as a further sign of his benevolence, before thinking better of it and saying, "It's a true pleasure to meet you, Mr. Lehman. We've heard a lot about you and we like what we've heard." Especially that he had a lot of money. "We're all eagerly looking forward to hearing what you have to say."

With that, Danny had the floor. "I guess you all know why I'm here," he began. "I want to make you an offer to buy this company. Mr. Granville here told me it's for sale. He's given me the recent financial statements and I think I know enough about the situation to come right to the point."

He then reached into the inside pocket of his suit jacket and pulled out a check. "Here, to show my good faith," he said, "is a cashier's check in the amount of five million dollars. I had it issued by my bank in Philadelphia in favor of Mr. Granville's company, which, he has informed me, will be acting as the agent in this matter. As I understand it, these funds will be put into escrow today at the Union Bank here in Los Angeles, provided we can agree on a deal." He paused, looked around the table, and sensed the latent greed present there. "This is my offer: forty million dollars." He paused again. He knew that he'd stunned them. It was only seconds later, however, when it was he, Danny Lehman, who would be stunned. In fact, beyond any doubt he became the most stunned man in the room. For during the pause he had created by throwing out the figure of forty million dollars for a casino in Vegas that was losing money, was losing its customers, and was about to lose its operating license, the door to the boardroom opened yet again and two men, both in their mid-fifties, entered the room.

For a moment they just stood there while the chairman, obviously angry, stared at them and seemed on the verge of losing control. Then he backed off. "Would you mind taking a seat back there. We'll get to you in a minute. All right?"

The two intruders chose to remain standing. It seemed to dawn on the chairman that their lack of manners might offend the man who had just made an offer of forty million bucks for what up to now had been an unsalable property. So rather than risk giving the impression that they were anything but just one big healthy, happy, and prosperous family, he quickly addressed himself to the visitor from Philadelphia.

"I do hope, Mr. Lehman," he said, "that you will pardon this interruption. However, these two gentlemen are the managers of our casino operation in Las Vegas. That's Mr. De Niro on the left and Mr. Salgo on the right. They are, if I may say so, the best—the very best—in the business. And very punctual normally. Their plane must have encountered fog."

Visibility that day at both the Vegas airport and LAX was a hundred miles. But this guy, Riviera figured, was from Philadelphia, so how would he know that? The chairman now beamed at his two revered employees and said, "Gentlemen, this is Mr. Daniel Lehman, who has come here to discuss the possibility of assuming the ownership of our corporation. This would mean, of course, that should we achieve a meeting of minds today, he would replace me as the chief executive officer of this company. In other words, he would be your new boss."

Danny watched the two men with the utmost care. His hope was to detect absolutely no sign of recognition. For had there been just the *slightest* hint, the merest *passing* flicker of mental recollection of the name Daniel Lehman, then it was time to stop fishing, to cut bait, and to get out. Quickly!

But there was nothing. Absolutely nothing. In spite of this apparent reprieve, Danny could hardly help but focus his mind on the fact that the situation that had now arisen was nothing less than outrageous. For there, no more than thirty feet away from him, stood two men, De Niro and Salgo, who he knew for a fact had been involved in a massive looting of the revenues of the corporation he was now trying to buy. What was even more grotesque was that he, Danny Lehman, was the man who not only had been fencing that loot, but who had also, through his Bahamas–Cayman Islands connection, arranged for the return of the stolen money to the thieves in the form of "legitimate" loans. And yet there they stood: calm, self-assured, cocky; proof positive that the middlemen, Amaretto and Sarnoff, had done precisely what they had promised him, namely, keep his name, his identity, completely concealed. The question now was: if he moved toward consummation of this deal; if he gained control of Raffles Inc.; if he therefore became the boss of Lenny De Niro and Roberto Salgo—what would be the reaction of Joe Amaretto and Sam Sarnoff? He had been through this thought process before, Danny recalled. Then he had concluded that it was an imponderable but hardly insurmountable obstacle. Now, he reasoned, it would once again very quickly and very simply reduce itself to money. If money could buy Raffles Inc., money could just as surely buy Amaretto and Sarnoff.

But to ensure that the waters that seemed still would remain still, Danny decided to address a few choice words to those two men who, when one came right down to it, represented not only a threat to this deal but quite obviously a threat to the future of Danny Lehman as a surviving member of the human species. So he looked toward the far end of the room and made a statement. "I'd like to go on record right here and now that, should this transaction go through, I fully intend to keep you both on as the senior management of our casino operations. In fact, I'd greatly welcome it if both you, Mr. De Niro, and you, Mr. Salgo, would not only stay on in your current capacities, but would also agree to enter into the negotiation of a two-year employment contract which would guarantee to me that a smooth and mutually profitable transition could take place between one ownership group and the other ownership group."

Danny was very nervous, and the way his words had just flooded out reflected that. But nobody seemed to notice. Where De Niro and Salgo were concerned, his words evoked no response whatsoever. No smiles of gratitude; no signs of eagerness to please the new boss. Nothing. They just continued to stand there stony-faced and silent, and vaguely threatening.

Well, fuck them, Danny thought, and turned to whisper a few quick words in the chairman's ear. The words took immediate effect, for Riviera then said, "Lenny. Roberto. I think that Mr. Lehman has made things very clear. The matters that remain concern the board alone. Do have a good trip back to Vegas." Given little choice, the pair left the room having spent a total time there of just over three minutes. Everyone seemed relieved.

The rest of the meeting was perfunctory and tedious. All that really happened was that Danny Lehman said he intended to give the sellers a one-year note for the balance of the purchase price. He insisted that the note be nonnegotiable, since, as he put it, he did not want to find himself owing money to anybody but people of the highest repute. He then suggested that it might be appropriate if he were to leave the room to allow the board to consider his offer and to formulate an appropriate response.

Ten minutes later they called him back in. Their response was simple: too little up-front cash, especially if that note was nonnegotiable; and the maturity of the note itself was way too far out: six months was the maximum that would be acceptable. In summary, what they wanted was fifteen million dollars cash now and the remaining twenty-five million in 180 days. Instead of starting to haggle, Danny referred the matter to their mutual agent. Mort came up with the not exactly original suggestion that they might split the difference down the middle, that is, ten million cash and a nine months' or 270 days' note. Both the seller, as represented by Riviera, and the buyer, in the person of Danny Lehman, pounced upon this marvelous idea with an alacrity that would have appeared suspect to even the most naïve of observers. For both the buyer and the seller were convinced, no, more than that, *they knew for a fact,* that the other party was being taken to the cleaner's.

To seal the deal before anything new could possibly come up, Danny Lehman immediately handed over his five-million-dollar check to the agent and stated for all to hear that his lawyer would show up in two days from Philadelphia, with another check for an equal amount. He then suggested to Riviera that, following this, his attorney would contact the Raffles attorneys and start working out the details. Riviera wrote down the name and number of Raffles Inc.'s new law firm for Danny. That was it. Danny shook hands all around and left.

Once the door had safely closed behind him, everybody in the boardroom started to talk at once. The impossible had happened. The Teamsters man even went up to the chairman and pounded him on the back. All the while Mort Granville just stood to one side, his manic grin becoming ever broader as the realization sank in that within a matter of days he would become a millionaire. Then, just for a fleeting moment, one that lasted barely five or six seconds, the grin subsided and a cloud passed across Mort's face. The cause of this very temporary consternation was a question which, in a truly inexplicable fashion, had come into Granville's mind; namely, was it fair to take a nice, dumb little guy like Lehman for such a ride, one that would inevitably wipe him out?

But the response to this disturbing thought was immediate and obvious: nobody had forced Lehman to do this and maybe, who could tell, the little guy might get a little fun out of it during the next couple of months before either the losses or the authorities closed the place down. Although, Granville concluded, upon further reflection it was highly doubtful whether during such a brief period he was going to be able to get forty million bucks' worth of fun!

* * *

Danny had gone directly to the bank of elevators, passing the leggy, bosomy receptionist without looking at her, without even giving her a passing thought. Likewise, seventeen stories down, he had hurried past that Italian restaurant with its cute little bar without even noticing that it was there. For Danny's mind was engaged, fully engaged, with one subject and one subject only: money; his money, in fact all of his money and a lot more. Not that there was any doubt in his mind that this was anything but the best deal that he had ever made in his life, or perhaps would ever make in his life. No, he was not worried about the forty million dollars he had to put on the line. What he was already subconsciously trying to work out was what this forty-million-dollar investment would bring to him during the next two, five, or ten years. Danny Lehman sensed that in this particular instance, past was by no means prologue. If, no, *when,* this was all worked out, his past would be discarded forever. Forgotten. Buried. But it would be an orderly burial, starting, he thought, right now.

He found a cab across the street in front of the Century Plaza Hotel. Once at the Westwood Holiday Inn, he got on the phone to his lawyer in Philadelphia. The lawyer listened for a while; first about the need, the immediate need, for another five million dollars in cash. The news produced no words, just a grunt. Then he was told about the thirty-million-dollar note. That produced an even more emphatic grunt. When, finally, the attorney was told that the note was due in 270 days, he spoke for the first time. "Danny—I'm saying this as a friend and your lawyer for the last ten years—are you sure you know what you're doing?"

Danny ignored the question. He reminded his attorney that he was fully equipped with his power of attorney and that he should go back to the bank and do what he had to do, i.e., get the second five-million-dollar cashier's check, and then get on a plane for Los Angeles. There was really no sense in any more talk on the phone. "Just get on the plane when you're done," he said, "and take a cab to the Holiday Inn on Wilshire in Westwood."

The lawyer managed to get a 5:30 P.M. plane the next day out of Philadelphia and arrived in Westwood around nine o'clock that evening, California time. When he walked into Danny's hotel room he first dropped his overnight bag and briefcase to the floor and reached into the inside pocket of his jacket for his wallet, from which he then proceeded to extract the cashier's check and hand it over to Danny.

"Danny," he said, "let me tell you straight and emphatically: I think you're making a terrible mistake here. You're throwing away, on some whim, everything you've built up. Frankly, I don't get it." There was true worry in the man's voice, and the reason for it came out in the words that followed.

"I know you're a clever businessman, we all know that. But you must realize I had to give the bank everything you've got as collateral, including your house, to get this second check. The bank likes you, likes your business, but after this, let me tell you, you now have zero credit available to you in Philadelphia, and my guess is that the same holds for any bank in the United States. You're borrowed to the hilt. You understand that, don't you?"

"It figures," Danny responded.

"Okay. So now let's go on. You've got to come up with thirty million dollars for that note, and not in ten years, or in five years, but in 270 days. Now tell me, how the hell do you expect to be able to do that?"

"I'll find a way," answered Danny. "That's my job. Your job is to close this deal and to close it quickly."

"All right," said the attorney. "You're the boss, Danny. But I'm telling you, you'll get ruined as a result of this. I look at you as a friend, and I have for years. I hate to see this happen to you. Why? Can you at least explain to me why you are doing this?"

Danny refused to answer. Although he knew, in a way, in a way that was becoming clearer by the hour. If Riviera, Mort Granville, or hoods like De Niro and Salgo could do it, then Danny Lehman could do it a hell of a lot better and a hell of a lot quicker. He had probably already wasted five years of his very valuable time, out of sheer ignorance of how easy it was! No lawyer could possibly understand that. Nothing was ever easy in their minds. So Danny just stood silently as his lawyer stooped to pick up his briefcase and his overnight bag.

"What's the next step and when?" the lawyer asked. He then added, immediately echoing Danny's thoughts, "These things tend to get complicated, you know."

"I'll make the arrangements," said Danny, "and then call your room."

As it turned out, there were no complications. The new attorneys of Raffles Inc. drew up the contract, which had but one new element in it, namely, that the buyer would be regarded as being in total default should the note not be paid in full within thirty days of maturity. Danny's attorney, Benjamin Shea, did everything possible to get this taken out in the hope of leaving the whole default question as vague as possible. But it was that or no deal.

At this juncture in the negotiations he spoke on the phone with Danny and pleaded with him to take the second option—no deal—so that they could get the hell out of there and go back to Philadelphia where they both belonged. They could still get out more or less intact, he explained, because there was no question that he could retrieve the ten million bucks from that escrow account. Maybe the Los Angeles attorneys and that agent would try to play games, but he would get it back. Then they could walk away from this thing before promising something that they simply could not fulfill.

But Danny refused to listen. "I'll take care of that note,"

he said. "Please do what I'm asking, Ben. I know what I'm doing. And if it goes wrong, you're on record as saying it would."

Benjamin Shea was undoubtedly a friend, and considered him one also, Danny reasoned, but fear of malpractice had already spread from the medical to the legal profession, a fear that transcended all other emotional attachments, even blood relationships. Hence, lawyer off the hook, the contract and note were signed, and the resignations of the board of directors of Raffles Inc., the en masse resignations, were submitted and notification thereof forwarded to the Nevada Casino Control Commission. At the same time, the credentials of the new owner of Raffles Inc. were forwarded to the commission, along with the names of the three men who would form the nucleus of the board of directors of Raffles: Daniel Lehman as chairman; as vice-chairman, Benjamin Shea, lawyer from Philadelphia; and as company secretary, of all people the agent from Los Angeles, Mort Granville. Finally, an application was made for an operating license for the casino in the names of the new parties.

It was decided that it would be better if the latter submission to the Casino Control Commission be made in person, so it was on March 27, 1969, that Benjamin Shea went to Las Vegas to perform that final act which gave Daniel Lehman control of the Raffles Casino and Hotel of Las Vegas, Nevada. After the Nevada officials had gone through Shea's submission, they were so happy with the solution that was immediately getting Raffles out of mob control that they gave him a temporary operating license on the spot and, in essence, guaranteed that he would receive a permanent license in no more than sixty days. The lawyer had wanted Danny to come along with him in order to, as he pointed out, "at least look over the place that you have bet your life on." But Danny refused. So at the same time the lawyer was catching a PSA flight from Los Angeles to Vegas, Danny Lehman was boarding a United flight to Philadelphia.

* * *

By nine o'clock the next morning, Danny had made a series of telephone calls: to the Provident National, to the Philadelphia National, and to the Mellon National Bank over in Pittsburgh. In all three cases he arranged an interview with one of the bank's senior loan officers, and since he indicated that some urgency was involved, he managed to get both meetings with the Philadelphia banks set up for that same afternoon, while the meeting with the man from Mellon was agreed upon for lunch the next day in Pittsburgh.

By one o'clock that next day Danny knew exactly where he stood. He had just paid ten million dollars down and given a thirty-million-dollar note for a property that no bank in Pennsylvania would accept as collateral for a loan of any type or any size. In none of the three cases did they even get to any discussion of property values, of profitability, of cash flow. Once the niceties were taken care of, the conversation that followed over lunch with the senior loan officer from the Mellon Bank in Pittsburgh was typical.

"Mr. Lehman, if you don't mind let's discuss business. I'd like to say that we have run a check on your operation over there in Philadelphia and we like what we have seen. Now, what can we do for you?"

"I'm trying to finance an acquisition," Danny had replied.

"We do that kind of business, of course. What exactly are you trying to buy?"

"Well, it's a little outside the field I've been in during the past ten years."

"I see."

Pause.

"It's a hotel complex."

The man from Mellon responded, "We have done a lot of hotel financing, in fact more than a few Hiltons in the state of Pennsylvania. We've even financed a few abroad. Where is the hotel?"

"Well, it's in this country. In the West."

"I see."

"To be more precise, it's in Las Vegas. Nevada," he added, as if to pinpoint that city more exactly in case the banker was not quite sure where it was.

"What's the name of the hotel?"

"Well, it's actually not *just* a hotel. It's also a casino. Raffles. Raffles Inc. I've arranged to purchase Raffles Inc."

"Sorry, Mr. Lehman, I'm afraid that's out."

"But let me tell you—"

"Sorry, Mr. Lehman, as I said, that's out. The Mellon Bank does not finance casinos or the acquisition of casinos. For obvious reasons."

The day after Danny's meeting in Pittsburgh, Benjamin Shea was back in Philadelphia to report that everything had been accomplished with remarkable smoothness in Las Vegas.

"The meeting with the Casino Control Commission people could not have been better, Danny," Shea said, as they sat in the dark living room of Danny's house. "They were not just helpful, but downright solicitous."

"How come?" Danny asked.

"You want me to tell you straight?"

"You always do."

"All right. It had nothing to do with their welcoming you to Vegas because of your being Mr. Clean or something. To be sure, it was made quite clear that they approved of you, me, and the entire new slate of directors. But let's face it, Danny, they reached that conclusion pretty damn fast. And that's what bothers me. I could not help but detect a sense of *urgency* in getting the transfer of ownership of Raffles over and done with as quickly as possible. And now my opinion as to why. Ready?"

"Go ahead."

"Because they know there's something basically wrong

with the casino itself. Financially wrong. And they don't want Raffles to get into a jam and cast a cloud over the viability of the entire gaming industry in the state, scaring off investors. The whole financial condition of Nevada is directly linked to the continuing success and further growth of the gaming industry. And they're planning on you using your money—money which you have not yet got, I might add—to bail out Raffles and thus them."

"So you think I've bought a lemon."

"A very big forty-million-dollar lemon."

"Maybe. Maybe not."

"Look, Danny. I'm not sure how, but I'm willing to try to get you out of this deal before it ruins you."

"Thanks, Benjamin. But I'm staying in. End of discussion. Okay?"

The two men just sat there in silence during the next few minutes. Then Shea spoke again. "Okay, Danny, you're the boss. But the least we should do is get to work and at least try to finance that note as soon as possible. Do you want me to try to start scheduling a few things?"

"No," said Danny. "I'll take care of that myself."

For the next thirty-two days Danny Lehman never showed up in his office on Broad Street. Instead, he kept to the neighborhood in which he lived, a working-class neighborhood, just like the one he'd grown up in. His house was even furnished the same way as his parents' had been, with heavy furniture, thick curtains, and an old-fashioned kitchen. His cleaning lady came in every afternoon except Sundays to take care of the dishes, if there were any, to make Danny's bed, do the laundry, dust. Despite the fact that he was "staying home," Danny seldom saw her. He was out taking in a matinee at the movies, or having a beer or two with the boys at the bar next door to the bowling alley. At night he watched sports on television. Not once did he return his attorney's phone calls, at least a dozen of which had been registered on his answering service as the days and weeks passed. Danny had gone into a defensive crouch: thinking, weighing up, calculating, hoping, but coming up with nothing. For the first time in his life Danny was going through the process of thinking before acting, and it was getting him nowhere.

6

At the end of April 1969, the doorbell rang at Danny Lehman's house at ten o'clock precisely. Danny, as he had been doing night after night, was sitting in his living room, alone, naturally, and thinking. That note was due in 230 days. The doorbell rang again and again. Danny, who had not even checked with his answering service for five days, was determined to let the thing ring until whoever it was went away: probably his lawyer coming to tell him yet again what a fool he had been. After the sixth ring, Danny decided that this problem also was not going to go away by itself. When he opened the door, he was not overly surprised to see it was Joe Amaretto.

"Please excuse me, Danny. I really didn't want to intrude on your privacy. But I've tried to phone at least seven or eight times. . . ."

"No excuses necessary," Danny said. "You know you're always welcome. Come on in. Let's start with a cognac." This time there was no overcoat or hat to be taken care of. It was an early spring in Philadelphia, and a touch of warmth still lingered in the evening air. The room remained silent, neither man saying a word, as Danny went through the ritual of getting the cognac glasses and then filling them a lot fuller than he normally would have done. It was Courvoisier, a gift. He sat down across the coffee table from his guest and asked, "Do you want to start, Joe, or should I?"

"Maybe I'd better," said Amaretto.

He reached for the huge briefcase he always carried and laid it on top of the coffee table. At first he was going to open it, but then decided to just let it lie there. "There is another half million here, Danny, all big bills this time," he said, "to be processed as usual, with the exception that the entire amount is to be loaned to a new guy. I've got his name written down here." He reached into his jacket pocket and then handed over a small, folded piece of paper, obviously some kind of hotel stationery. Danny unfolded it. The name of Mr. Rupert Downey had been typed on it. That was all. Danny then refolded the paper and handed it back to Amaretto, who, for the moment, appeared not to know quite what to make of this. But he immediately found out.

"I'm sorry," Danny said, "but you'll have to find somebody else to help you out on this one, or, for that matter, any future ones. The last shipment was the last shipment, if you know what I mean. I'd have contacted you, Joe, but I've been busy and I've had things, you know, on my mind during the last month. So I'm really sorry that you had to make this trip to Philadelphia and waste your time with those phone calls, and then have to come over here in the middle of the night, but—"

"We understand, Danny," said Amaretto. "You see, we've heard."

This was hardly a surprise to Danny. Even *The Wall Street Journal* had run a half column on the sale of Raffles.

Amaretto paused for a moment before he continued. "We've heard, Danny, but frankly we don't quite understand." Then he added quickly, "When I say 'we,' don't misunderstand what I'm talking about: I mean just the two of us, me and Sam Sarnoff, because believe me, Danny, this thing has remained strictly, I mean strictly and exclusively, confidential."

Danny broke in, "I know, I know, Joe. I appreciate it,

believe me, I appreciate it. But what's this about not understanding?"

"Well, if you've gotten control or are getting control of Raffles the way the word has it, how come you're sitting here in Philadelphia? How come, you know, you're not in Vegas, taking over that place from those goddamn crooks?"

"It's too complicated to explain at the moment, Joe, but as long as we are on the subject, what are you going to tell Salgo and De Niro? And this new guy. What was his name again? Rupert Downey? Who the hell is he anyway?"

"We don't know and frankly don't care. It's just a name that Salgo and De Niro gave us."

"All right, but I'll ask you again: what are you going to tell Salgo and De Niro?"

"The truth. That our distributor in the East has folded up, gone out of business, and that we've tried to find a new one, unsuccessfully. That we've concluded that it's probably going to take a while to find a new one."

"Any thoughts on how long?"

"Oh, probably months," replied Amaretto.

Danny nodded. "I like that answer. I like that answer a lot."

Then Amaretto became very serious, leaned forward, and asked, "Now, what about those guys in the Caribbean that have that bank down there that's made those loans to De Niro and Salgo? If push comes to shove, are you going to be able to keep their mouths shut as to where this money came from?" There was a touch of fear, not just anxiety, in Amaretto's voice now.

"I think so," said Danny. "In fact, I'm pretty damn sure so, but you can never be certain."

Amaretto winced. "Maybe you should talk to them," he suggested, "soon."

"You're right," Danny replied. "I'll do it tomorrow, early tomorrow."

"Our names never came up with those guys down there, did they?" Amaretto asked.

"No, never; never mentioned," replied Danny.

"And it'll stay that way, I hope?"

"It will definitely stay that way."

"So I think we understand each other. I think we agree, don't we?" Amaretto asked.

"I think so. I think we've never met, isn't that right?" asked Danny.

"That's exactly right."

Amaretto got to his feet and then picked up his oversized briefcase, still unopened, still apparently very heavy. "I'd better take this with me," he said, grinning for the first time.

"What are you going to do with it?" asked Danny.

"Give it back to De Niro and Salgo," replied Amaretto. "It's their problem now because I think I know what I'm going to tell them. In fact, I *know* what I'm going to tell them: that not only have they lost their distributor in the East, but they're going to lose their agents in the West. Danny, Sam and I are going to get out of this business right now."

"Take it easy," Danny then said, sensing that the man's fear was developing into a latent panic; he'd seen De Niro and Salgo and he understood why. "To make it easier for you to get out I'll do that last deal for them. Leave the money here."

"Thanks," Amaretto replied, the relief flushing his features. He eased the briefcase back onto the table. As they walked out of the living room toward the front door Amaretto suddenly stopped and said, "Danny, I've got to ask you something. It might sound like prying, but I'm going to ask it anyway."

"Go ahead."

"Well, you know De Niro and Salgo are going to keep stealing, don't you?"

"Of course."

"So how are you going to stop them?"

"I don't know yet."

"Now listen, Danny, I'm going to give you an opinion for what it's worth, even if you didn't ask for it."

"Go ahead," said Danny.

"The only way you're going to be able to stop it's to kick out not only De Niro and Salgo, but also the next six guys under them. That's one big pack of thieves."

"You may be right."

"The problem is, Danny, you try that and they'll get you, you must know that they'll get you. They are so entrenched there and they're so fucking greedy and so fucking arrogant that they think they own the place. They're so fucking stupid that they don't even know that if they keep stealing at the rate they've been stealing, then the place is going to go belly up. They can't figure that out. But believe me, if you try to reason with them, or kick them out, or, worse, if you try, you know, to get them into trouble with the authorities, they'll *kill* you, Danny. I swear to God, they'll *kill* you. And if they find out about us, they'll think we put you up to this and they'll kill *us.*" It was the first time Danny had ever heard Amaretto speak with such desperation in his voice.

"Now let me tell you something else," Amaretto continued. "As I just said, I've decided that Sarnoff and I, about a week or so from now, are leaving. We're not only leaving Nevada, we're leaving the United States for a while. And when we come back to Reno, we're going to get into an entirely different kind of business, and we're never going to set foot in a casino again. You'd be well advised to do the same, Danny. Because you can't beat these guys. Nobody can."

With that he turned, opened the door, and left. He also left a chill behind that had nothing to do with the weather. It was caused by the long shadow of two men in Las Vegas.

* * *

Just before noon the next day, Danny called the First
Charter Bank in Nassau and contacted his man there, the
one in charge of, as they so nicely put it, "special projects."
He started off by explaining that something new had come
up, and asked whether they could chat about it on the
phone. He was informed that he would get a call back in
about thirty minutes.

When the call did come precisely thirty-two minutes
later, his Bahamian partner apologized profusely but said he
had reason to believe that there was a tap on the bank's
lines, a completely illegal tap, one that had been put in under the auspices of both the Securities and Exchange Commission and the Internal Revenue Service. The problem, he
said, stemmed from some of the trust arrangements they
had set up with a string of American clients, especially a
bunch from Northern California. It appeared that a hotshot
district attorney in San Francisco had gotten some sort of a
court order that allowed them to go after these clients any
way they wanted. American judges, it seemed, could unilat-
erally extend their courts' jurisdiction to wherever they
wanted, including the Bahamas. Cheeky, but not something
the Bahamas was likely to go to war over. Thus the precautions.

It was somewhat startling to hear all this explained in an
impeccable Oxford accent, one that Danny knew for a fact
was by no means phony, since his Bahamian partner, by the
name of Montague Davies, was in fact a product of both
Eton and Oxford—a law graduate of Oxford, to be more
precise. The man had decided to pursue his postgraduate
career in a warmer climate and from Nassau's Bay Street
had proceeded to specialize in the establishment of legal
façades for the most sophisticated types of white-collar
criminals.

"Now, what's the problem, Mr. Lehman?" he asked, thus

turning from apologies to business as usual, at least business as was usual for him.

First, Danny explained, he had one more loan to be arranged for those parties in Las Vegas, the ones from whom the funds had been coming and to whom the same funds had been going back via that subsidiary bank in the Cayman Islands, the bank through which he, Montague Davies, always made the "arrangements." It would be the last one. Whether or not Montague Davies, the First Charter Bank of the Bahamas, and/or the First Charter Bank of the Cayman Islands wanted to continue a relationship with those clients was, of course, entirely their business. All that Danny was concerned about, all that he really wanted, was the ironclad assurance that in the future, as in the past, no mention whatsoever would ever be made of his name.

"It's understood, old chap. Consider it done," answered the Englishman.

"But if they ask at some time?"

"The Bank Secrecy Act forbids us from making any unauthorized disclosures to third parties regarding the affairs of our clients. We regard you, Mr. Lehman, as a very valuable client and have for years. We are most appreciative of the high volume of foreign exchange business that you direct to us, and hope that it will continue in the future. Does that put your mind at ease?"

"Completely. Thank you," said Danny. "Now for something else, as long as we're both on the line. I'm in the process of buying a hotel-casino complex in Las Vegas. To be precise, I've really already bought it with ten million down and a thirty-million-dollar note, which will come due in just under eight months. It's a 6 percent note by the way. I want to raise some money to cover that note. I'd agree to what I think you British call a 'floating charge' on the entire property. What I'm looking for is a loan for around five years. I'd be willing to pay a very nice finder's fee to a party such as yourself if you could introduce me to a lender. I'd also be willing to pay a nice setup fee, front end, to such a lender, and I'd be prepared to go as high as 10 percent interest, even 12 percent."

"I think I fully understand what you're after," said Montague Davies, a bit too dryly for Danny's liking.

Undeterred, Danny plunged on. "Now, I guess you know why I'm asking you. I've found out that no bank, in fact no lender I know of in this country, will touch anything to do with the gaming industry. So my question is really this, Mr. Davies: is your bank interested?"

"Theoretically, yes. But it's too big for us, Mr. Lehman. We are not that large an institution. We're a merchant bank, not a commercial bank. We're not Barclays or National Westminster, you see. Our principal activity involves arranging financing, not providing it. In any case, we certainly would not be in a position to lend thirty million dollars on any one transaction, all the more so in the United States and especially to a firm in the type of business that is subject to rather extraordinary surveillance. We have, as I have already explained, enough trouble in the States. We have to think of the clients we've already got. And we wouldn't want to do anything that would, you know, provoke the Americans even further, so that they might tend to come down on us like a pack of wolves. You must understand that."

Danny said, "Yes, of course, I certainly do. Well, I'm sorry I brought it up but I thought that maybe—"

Then the Englishman cut in. "However, I do think that perhaps we still may be able to be of some service to you in this matter. We do have associates, friendly parties, with whom we work very closely in our little bank in the Cayman Islands, the one that has been able to service your clients, or should I now say ex-clients, from Las Vegas. They are people who, I believe, understand the industry that you've become involved with. I think they would at least hear you out on a proposition. Are you interested in pursuing this, Mr. Lehman?"

"Who and where are they?"

"Well now, I don't think I can exactly tell you *that*, but I will tell you *this:* they are represented in some matters by a man, an attorney, in Miami. If you'll agree I will let him know about this matter and will give him your name. You understand: your name will be mentioned. And if he is interested he will call you. Is that agreeable?"

"Yes," answered Danny.

"Just one thing, one more thing," the Englishman said. "I believe at the outset you did mention that there would be a substantial finder's fee involved should we be able to develop something for you. I trust that you will remember us should something happen?"

"Don't worry, I will," replied Danny.

"Thank you so much, Mr. Lehman. As usual it's been a pleasure doing business with you. Goodbye, sir, and good luck!"

The line went dead.

7

Ten days later, during the first half of May, Danny got the phone call. It was brief and to the point.

"I'd like to speak to Mr. Daniel Lehman," said the voice at the other end of the phone.

"Speaking."

"A mutual friend in the Caribbean told me about your special project. We're interested in it. Are you free tomorrow?"

"Yes."

"Good. Take Eastern Flight 741 to Fort Lauderdale tomorrow morning."

Pause. "All right. Where do we meet?"

"Don't worry, I'll find you." Click.

The big break? The much sought-after partner . . . ? Danny chose not to spell out the word.

The airport in Fort Lauderdale was not much to look at in 1969. For the most part its buildings looked like leftover World War II barracks, and the baggage claim area was nothing more than an open shed. About the only place today where you encounter similar outdoor baggage claim areas in the United States is Hawaii: Maui or Kauai.

Flight 741 of Eastern was not even half full, since May was definitely off-season. Within twenty minutes of landing, the sixty-odd people who had been fellow passengers with Danny Lehman all seemed to have found their baggage, and after another five minutes they had all disappeared into cars, cabs, vans, and buses. This left Danny a completely solitary figure standing uncertainly on the curb adjacent to the Eastern baggage carrousel. Another five minutes passed, and then another. Stoically, Danny just stood there. Then a brown Chevrolet Impala suddenly appeared at the curb in front of him. A man leaned over from the driving seat and asked rather quietly through the open window on the right, "Are you Lehman?"

Danny answered, "Yes."

"Might as well get in, then."

Danny first opened the back door and threw in his overnight suitcase, closed the door, and then climbed in beside the driver. The man held out his hand and said, "My name is Saul Meyers. A pleasure."

Danny took his hand, and said, "It's mutual." Then he added, "I appreciate your picking me up personally."

"Well, I don't do it often, I can tell you that. But for you, Mr. Lehman, nothing but the best." He gave Danny a wolfish smile. *That* got Danny worried.

Then they drove off. They headed toward the Port Everglades area and then turned south on Highway 1, drove for maybe four or five miles, and then turned left, heading toward the ocean. In the final stages of the trip they passed through an uninhabited wilderness area. It seemed rather strange for these parts. Danny assumed it was probably a swamp that had been partially filled in and then abandoned as too remote for commercial property development. The road itself was almost brand-new. It was paved, and it was leading toward what appeared to be either a medium-sized high-rise hotel or a condominium complex—one that stood in rather splendid isolation on the very edge of the swampy meadow and the beach.

As they approached the structure, it became apparent that it was completely surrounded by a high fence topped with barbed wire. The newly paved road narrowed down between cement walls, ending at an imposing barrier flanked on both sides by guardhouse structures, both manned. As they drew up, uniformed guards with revolvers at their hips came out, approached the car, and carefully scanned the interior of the vehicle from both sides, in spite of their obviously knowing whose car it was and who was driving it. Then one of them asked, "Are you all right, Mr. Meyers?"

The answer: "Fine, everything's fine."

Both guards nodded. One went back into his bunker and the barrier lifted. The other waved them through. They were met at the entrance to the building by a doorman who immediately summoned a young Latino to take care of the car. They walked through the revolving doors and again were met by two uniformed and armed security people. Again the same question was asked: "Everything all right, Mr. Meyers?"

And it drew the same answer: "Fine, everything's fine."

They entered an extremely elegant hallway, the floor Italian marble, the ceiling high, and antique furniture lining each wall. After about twenty paces they went up ten steps and passed into what appeared to be a lounge area. The centerpiece was a huge circular seat designed to take at least thirty guests. It was now two-thirty in the afternoon and there was absolutely nobody in the huge room except the bartender clad in a white bow tie and a red jacket—maybe his idea of what a bartender would wear in an elegant English club, something that was as far removed in atmosphere and decor from this building between Fort Lauderdale and North Miami Beach as any place possibly could be. But he didn't know that.

"You must be thirsty," stated Meyers, who up to now had said very little to Danny Lehman except for making the usual remarks about the flight, about Eastern Airlines, about how early it had gotten hot that year and yet, in spite of the heat, for some reason the humidity had stayed fairly low. Florida talk.

"Vodka and tonic would go down great," said Danny.

Mr. Meyers held up two fingers to indicate that they would both have the same. Once the drinks had been served, Meyers said to the bartender, "Jimmy, I'd appreciate it if you'd hunt down a couple of cigars for me. You know the brand I smoke, and take your time, take your time."

Jimmy nodded, took a couple of swipes at the bar with a towel, and then disappeared.

"Well, Mr. Lehman, I suggest that you call me Saul. May I call you Danny?"

"Certainly."

"Okay, Danny, I know what you're here to talk about. You've bought yourself a casino, if I've been informed correctly?"

"Yes."

"In Vegas, they tell me."

"Right."

"Why would anybody be selling a casino in Vegas? Almost all of them're money machines, aren't they?"

"Almost all of them. That's right."

"But not this one?"

"Not this one, or at least on the *surface* not this one."

"I see. And you know what's going on under the surface, is that right?"

"Correct."

"What's the name of the casino?"

"Raffles."

"It figures. That's what we thought. That dumb bastard Riviera wouldn't know how to make money if somebody handed him the goddamn United States mint. Okay, tell me more."

Danny Lehman told him more. In fact, he told him everything, all except for the details about *how* he had come to know that the profitability picture of Raffles was radically better than it appeared on the surface. He waited for Saul

Meyers to insist upon his going into it further, but he found out that there was nothing to worry about.

"How you know all this, Danny, is your business. All I can assume is that you are telling us the truth, because it won't do anybody any good, especially yourself, if you're not, will it?" It was put as a statement, not a question. Danny had noticed that a lot of big-money guys had a habit of putting statements in the form of questions. "Now you want us to refinance you so that you can meet your obligations on that note, which must be coming due now in just under eight months. Am I right?"

"Yes."

"Okay. Now I'm going to offer a suggestion. Take it as just that: a suggestion, and not an offer. Okay?"

"Fine," said Danny, sensing that this was either going to be "it," or . . .

"Now, assuming that your figures are right about the basic profitability of the situation out there at Raffles, and for the moment leaving aside any discussion of *why* such a large proportion of the profits has been, shall we say, diverted, but further assuming that you must somehow know how you're going to solve that problem, we'd be willing to consider helping you. However, I think you must know that we regard this as a real high-risk situation."

"I recognize that," said Danny.

"The key part of this is that we might be prepared to lend you, let's say, thirty or thirty-one million dollars for five years at 10 percent per annum interest, involving a straight-line amortization," continued Meyers. "But listen carefully: I think that rather than looking at this as a loan, you'd be better advised to consider it a convertible debenture or, let's say, a loan with warrants attached. Let's be even more precise. If you can't manage the situation, and if you can't make any of the payments—and we'd expect payments every six months, again on a straight-line amortization basis plus accumulated interest—we'd want to have the option to take over your complete equity interest in Raffles for the remaining face value of the note. Do you understand?"

"Not exactly."

"All right, let me run through it again. Let's assume we make the loan tomorrow. Let's say that six months from now you were able to make the three-million-dollar payment. Then six months after that you also made the second three-million-dollar payment. But six months after *that* you couldn't. Follow me? Fine. Well, that would then mean that we'd take over your interest in the casino and you'd be out the original ten million bucks cash down payment, plus the two three-million-dollar payments that you made to us. Do you understand?"

"Yeah, I understand. I don't think that I'd be willing to go for a deal like that."

"I'm not asking whether you would or wouldn't. I'm not done. Do you want to hear me out further?"

"Go ahead."

"We'd expect that even in the event that such a default occurred, you'd remain on as the titular owner and chairman of Raffles, along with your entire board of directors. And that you all would stay on for at least one full year until arrangements could be made by my principals to prepare for an orderly transition of personnel which would meet the needs of the Nevada Casino Commission. And that from beginning to end you'd keep all this to yourself." He stopped there.

"Look," he continued, "we don't want anything to go wrong. What lender does? But if you had to stand in for us for a while, then don't worry, Danny, we'd pay you well, take care of you for a long time. But the fact of the matter is that you'd be out at least ten million bucks of your own money and probably a lot more. As I said, it's a high-risk situation."

"Anything else?" asked Danny.

"Well yes, it's not something that would be part of any

contractual agreement, you understand. It'd be more a gentleman's agreement to the effect that should everything work out for you, as we all hope and expect it to, with the result that in five years you are home scot-free, then if at some time, who knows when, I or some of my principals would come to you and ask for a favor, and at the moment I have no idea what that might be, but if we came and said, 'Hey, Danny, you know we scratched your back a little bit back in '69, so maybe you could help us out a little bit in '76,' well, we wouldn't want you to forget us."

"Makes sense," said Danny. "In fact, it'd be understood, but let me ask you a few things."

"Anything."

"If I decide more or less to accept your proposition, how soon could these funds be made available?"

"Within thirty days. Maximum."

"And who'd be the lender?"

"I don't know, but most probably a corporation domiciled in the Netherlands Antilles. That would be the same party that would get the option, or warrants, or whatever, depending upon how we formulate this."

"Why the Netherlands Antilles?"

"Because of the double taxation agreement with the United States: no withholding tax applies on interest or dividend payments made from the United States. That keeps the IRS out of it."

This was all news to Danny Lehman, but Saul Meyers was rising steadily in his estimation. "And who owns this company?" Danny then asked.

"A Dutch bank."

"I see. Then you mentioned, if I heard correctly, thirty-one million dollars."

"Yes."

"But I only need thirty million."

"No, you'll need thirty-one million, and I'll explain why," continued Saul Meyers. "There'll be the finder's fee for our mutual friend in the Bahamas. I think five hundred thousand dollars would probably be fair. Okay?"

Danny nodded.

"And I think that the same amount would probably be fair where my particular services are concerned."

Danny again nodded.

"Don't worry," Meyers added, "my principals will be fully aware of both of these commissions. I think they'll be appreciative of the fact that you saw fit to cover these expenses, rather than calling upon them either to assume or to partially assume the usual cost of doing this kind of business."

Meyers paused and then asked, "So what do you think?"

"I think I'm going to have to think about it."

"Fair enough," replied Meyers. "How about another drink?"

Right then the red-coated bartender called Jimmy came back with two Partagas cigars and handed them to Meyers. "Do you smoke these things?" asked Meyers.

"Today, yes."

The two men lit up, set to work on fresh vodka and tonics, and got to talking about the upcoming Joe Frazier fight, when two bronzed young women entered the room and came up to Meyers. "I'd like you to meet two friends of mine," he immediately said to Danny. "This one's Laurie and that's Rita.

"Say hello, girls. This is my friend Danny."

They both gave him a big smile. Laurie took the barstool on Danny's left while Rita took the one on Saul Meyers's right. Meyers then ordered four more vodka and tonics. Danny found himself talking about Philadelphia, about Joe Frazier, about jai alai. And the girls seemed to think that their old friend Saul Meyers had finally come up with a really nice guy for a change. Then, around four o'clock, Danny glanced at his watch.

"What's that all about, Danny?" asked Saul. "No sense

looking at the time. What I thought was that the four of us could go on to dinner and make an evening of it. There's lots of room here at the inn for you, Danny."

Laurie, who by that time had firmly hooked her arm around Danny's, gave him an especially hard squeeze when the last words were spoken, as if to emphasize that nothing in the world could give her greater pleasure than to spend the next twenty-four hours with him. But Danny Lehman shook his head. "Thanks, Saul, thank you, girls, but I'm afraid I'll have to take a rain check on that. And believe me, I want to take a rain check on everything!" And now he squeezed Laurie whatever-her-name-was with a strength born of sincerity. "I've got some business to attend to that's already waited too long," he added. "And like I told you, Saul, I'll be thinking about it."

Meyers was disappointed. "Don't take too long, Danny. We don't like to be kept waiting, you know."

Fifteen minutes later Danny was back in the brown Chevrolet Impala, but this time it was the young Latino parking attendant who was at the wheel. He drove him in complete silence to the Fort Lauderdale airport, dropping him off, upon Danny's instructions, in front of United. Danny got out, and then opened the back door of the Impala in order to retrieve his bag. He thought he saw two men in a car that had just slowly passed the Impala looking at him through the back window with more than just incidental interest. As he walked into the terminal there was an alarm bell ringing in the back of his mind. But he ignored it, and it silenced itself as he found himself hurrying for a flight that would take him to the Miami airport, where he would have to change to get United's Flight 201, headed for Los Angeles, but with a stop in Las Vegas, where Danny Lehman intended to get off. If anybody *had* had him under surveillance up to this point, they would sure as hell have a tough time following him any farther.

At the check-in counter they told him that they expected

boarding to start in approximately five minutes. So Danny decided to make a quick phone call. When he got hold of the reservations desk at Raffles, he asked for a top-of-the-line room, told them he would probably be there for three nights, and asked them to leave a message for either Mr. De Niro or Mr. Salgo, or preferably one for both. They should be informed that a Mr. Daniel Lehman expected to be arriving at McCarran Airport on United Flight 201 at around eight o'clock, and that he requested the pleasure of their company for either a late dinner or a drink.

Flight 201 from Miami was a dinner flight, but Danny waved off the stewardess's offers of both food and drink. He had already had enough to drink at that bar during the past couple of hours, and his nerves were such that he definitely was not hungry. So while the rest of the people in the first-class section were eating, drinking, and reading, Danny just sat there thinking. He liked that guy in Fort Lauderdale: Saul Meyers had a nice way about him. He liked those girls, too, especially that one that he had drawn—Laurie. Laurie. He had to keep her in mind.

But going back to that Meyers fellow, the one thing that had seemed puzzling was why Meyers had never really pressed him on how, or why, he was so sure he could make a go of Raffles. Meyers must have found out that the casino was in trouble, not necessarily in trouble with the Casino Control Commission, but in financial trouble. Yet Meyers seemed to have had no qualms about the thirty—or rather, thirty-one-million-dollar loan.

And then it dawned on Danny. Out of outrage over his own stupidity he banged himself on the head with the palm of his left hand, causing the stewardess who was walking up the aisle to give him a strange glance. It was obvious that they *knew;* they *knew* about De Niro and Salgo. After all, Meyers's principals, whoever they were, were friendly parties, close to that bank in the Cayman Islands that had made those phony loans to De Niro and Salgo. So that meant the

club of insiders who knew the truth about what was going
on at Raffles had expanded from Amaretto and Sarnoff to
himself, then to the English banker in Nassau, and now,
quite obviously, to the friendly parties, whoever they were,
associated with the Cayman bank, and finally to their attorney in Fort Lauderdale, Saul Meyers. The club that had
started out as a cosy little three-man conspiracy now seemed
to be developing a membership that would soon challenge
the Trilateral Commission in numbers. The more Danny
reflected on this, the less comfortable he became.

Maybe this whole trip had been a mistake from beginning
to end. Maybe he shouldn't have raised this issue with that
Englishman in Nassau in the first place, causing him to
bring up the name of Raffles with those principals of his,
who, in turn, had brought in Saul Meyers, who might or
might not be having him tailed. Which raised yet another
question: if *they* knew all about De Niro and Salgo, was it
not inevitable that De Niro and Salgo would somehow find
out all about *him?* Could it be that word had already somehow started to leak back to the crooks running Raffles, word
that this guy Lehman already knew too much? And if it
had, was this the most clever thing for him to be doing right
now?

The stewardess was coming back up the aisle again and
this time saw what seemed to be an expression of deep concern on Danny Lehman's face. They had encountered a little turbulence over New Orleans, and maybe, she reasoned,
the man's a little queazy about flying. Normally she avoided
conversations with single males beginning to approach middle age like the plague, but somehow this one, although a
little pudgy and obviously not too tall, seemed like a nice
guy. And there was something sexually attractive about
him. It was impossible to say what, but there was no doubt
in her mind that he would be one hell of a lot of fun in the
sack.

There seemed to be something about Danny Lehman that

even attracted women back when he had brushed them off. They didn't seem to mind! So repeatedly during the rest of the trip she dropped by to offer him a drink, to suggest a snack, to give him some peanuts, to ask if he wanted something to read. But Danny just sat there. He never read. Well, almost never. Now and then he read the sports page of the *Philadelphia Bulletin.* He also read *TV Guide.* But that was about it. After all, you could hardly make any money while reading, could you? So why waste the time?

The next time the stewardess stopped at his row, she bent down to ask, "Mr. Lehman, are you sure you won't have something to drink? We still have quite a bit of time until we arrive."

"Okay," said Danny. "Bring me a beer, any kind of beer."

After she brought him the beer she sort of draped herself over the back of the empty seat beside him and asked where he was going to stay in Vegas. When he told her Raffles she raised her eyebrows, since he hardly looked like the type who would go to such a place.

"How long are you going to be there?" she asked.

"Oh, I guess three nights," Danny answered.

"Actually, you know," she said, "I go on to Los Angeles. But then I've got the next couple of days off." She continued, "Come to think of it, I haven't been to Vegas in over half a year."

All of a sudden Danny felt expansive. "I'll tell you what I'll do," he said. "You give me your name and address, and not this week, maybe not even this month, but pretty soon you'll hear from me and you can go to Raffles for a day, or two days, or even a week anytime you want to. Bring a friend; girlfriend, boyfriend, who cares. And it'll be on the house. How's that?"

The stewardess now undraped herself. "Gee," she said, "how could you arrange that?"

"You'll find that out when you hear from me."

She never did. Danny *meant* what he said. But soon, very soon, there were other things on his mind.

When Danny emerged at the arrival gate at McCarran Airport he looked around, half expecting somebody to be there. Nobody was. Down at the baggage claim area again, he took a couple of scans. Still nobody. The queaziness that had attacked his stomach in the airplane over New Orleans gradually started to return. And fifteen minutes later it got a lot worse. For when he walked into Raffles—skirting the casino floor and going directly to the reception counter—and mentioned his name, the girl looked at him in a rather odd way. Then she went to the back of the office, returned, and said, "Mr. Lehman, I am afraid we don't have a reservation in your name. How do you spell that again?"

"L-E-H-M-A-N, first name Daniel."

"Well," she said skeptically, "I'll check again."

When she came back she had a little white slip of paper in her hand. "Sorry about the delay, Mr. Lehman. Now we've found it."

He filled out the registration form, informed her that he would be there for probably three nights, gave her his American Express card, and waited while she made an imprint from the card. He walked over to the bellhop who was ready to take him to his suite. "I'm expecting a message," Danny told him, "from one of the executives here at the casino. Either Mr. De Niro or Mr. Salgo. Where would such a message have been left?"

"Let me check, sir," said the bellhop. He went back to the reception desk and returned immediately. "I'm afraid there are no messages, sir."

Danny followed the bellhop over to the elevators at the far side of the casino and went up all the way to the second floor. The room he had been given was immediately adjacent to the elevator bank. As they walked in, from the smell of it, it was also right above the kitchen. When he looked

out of the tiniest of windows, all he saw was an immense
ventilator funnel. He also heard the blast. He turned immediately to the bellhop and said, "This won't do."

The bellhop just shrugged, indicating he had nothing
whatsoever to do with such matters.

"Stay here," Danny said. "I'll call down to reception and
get this changed." He called down and was informed that
the hotel was fully booked. His was the last room they could
make available, and it was implied that he should appreciate
the fact that Raffles had decided to make any space available
for him at all.

He gave the bellhop a five-dollar bill and sat down on the
bed. All of a sudden he felt hungry. He'd had neither lunch
nor anything to eat on the plane. Maybe, he thought, this
was a sort of compulsive hunger because of the situation
that seemed to be developing. But still, it was better to eat
something. Danny was no health freak, but he believed in
taking care of himself. So he picked up the phone and called
downstairs again, this time to room service. A salad and a
steak was all he wanted. Plus some coffee. That was it.

Ten minutes went by. Twenty minutes. Half an hour. No
food. He called down to room service to complain. They
assured him that somebody would be up within five minutes.
Half an hour later, he called down again, got the same assurance, upon which he told them to take the goddamn food
and shove it. This time he slammed down the phone. If it
had not all been so damned ominous it would have been
funny, he thought. There he was, the guy who owned this
fucking hotel lock, stock, and barrel, and he couldn't get a
decent room, not to speak of a decent meal. In fact, he
couldn't get a meal, period, decent or not!

Now what? he asked himself. De Niro and Salgo, that was
what. Get to them, fire them, kick them out *right now,* that
was what. But first he had to find them, which would hardly
be possible if he sat around that room any longer, listening
to the ventilator while inhaling the fumes from the kitchen.

He found out immediately that it might not be that simple. For as he closed the door on Room 202, embarking on what he had already mentally labeled his search and destroy mission, he noticed two men standing in the area in front of the elevators immediately adjacent to his room. They watched him. They were both big, very big, and both had on blue suits. They were not talking; just standing there. In fact they were just standing there looking at him. He rang for the elevator and as he went in he noticed that both were continuing to track him. Then one reached for the walkie-talkie unit that was clipped to his belt and started talking in a low voice. When Danny reached the main casino floor, a full story below, he decided to have something to drink, this time something a little stiffer than beer. So he left the elevator and headed for the bar next to the baccarat tables.

The casino floor, he noticed as he walked, wasn't exactly crowded. At least half of the blackjack tables were not operating. There were people at maybe one out of five slot machines. As he approached the baccarat area, he saw that it was totally deserted. To get to the bar itself you had to take a step up, passing through a gap in the brass railing that separated this particular bar area from the main casino floor. Some sort of headwaiter was standing there. He asked Danny whether he preferred the bar or a table. Danny thought a table would be better, and commented to the effect that this bar seemed to be by far the most popular area in the whole casino.

"Well, that's not too hard to understand, maybe," the man answered. "This place is what they generally refer to as hookers' corner. Look around and you'll see what I mean."

After Danny had taken his place at a very small table against the wall he did look around, and it didn't take a great deal of imagination to figure out where that name had come from. There must have been at least fifteen young ladies there; some of them, Danny noted, were very young indeed, but this was somewhat compensated for by the fact that there were also a few who appeared to be awfully old indeed.

The crowd in the casino seemed to be picking up a bit. In fact, immediately to the right of the bar area there was even some action at the baccarat tables. Danny ordered a bourbon and water, and as the waitress brought it back he noticed that the two gorillas he had seen outside his room on the second floor were now talking to the headwaiter. The three of them were standing about ten yards away. Twice while they were talking all three looked directly at him. Of that he was sure.

While this was going on, it seemed that all fifteen ladies, young and old, in the bar area were simultaneously sizing him up. And every time there was eye contact between one of them and Danny, however inadvertent, immediately the lady in question flashed as big a come-on smile as she could muster. Danny decided that it was probably not the worst idea in the world, but also decided to spend a little time picking and choosing before making up his mind.

So for a while he just sat there surveying the vast casino floor. The crowd he estimated at probably six or seven hundred people. He checked some of the physical characteristics of the place, and it did not take much more than a cursory glance to note that the carpeting was shabby, that the pit bosses were bored to death, that most of the waitresses one could perhaps best describe as slovenly. Out of the corner of his eye Danny noticed that the bar's maître d'hôtel, or whatever one called such a man in such a bar, was slowly making the rounds of the place with a word here and a word there to each of the hookers. Once he had moved on, as if by magic they had transferred what was left of their interest in Danny Lehman to other targets. Eye contact was reduced to zero. Then, as if to add further insult to injury, the maître d' slapped down a RESERVED sign on all three tables surrounding Danny's, leaving him there in splendid isolation, or perhaps "quarantine" would have been a better word.

The maître d' then disappeared, probably to report back to the gorillas. To say that Danny was starting to develop a severe case of paranoia would have been a definite understatement. For right then he remembered hearing that above the ceilings in these casinos there were catwalks from which everybody in the place could be observed through peepholes, or through the phony mirrors up there. He envisioned De Niro and Salgo just above him, sitting there and laughing their asses off. Let them laugh, Danny thought, as long as they're laughing about what's happened so far.

Then he was momentarily diverted, because even in that crowd, which was now up to probably a thousand customers, you couldn't help but spot the statuesque figure of the woman approaching: in her early twenties, at least six feet tall, and dressed in a perfectly cut black suit and white blouse, with stunning hair, she approached the bar area with a stride that indicated that she knew who she was: the most attractive woman, by far, in the casino.

When she took the single step up into the bar area, the slit in her skirt opened to reveal legs which, although Danny just caught the briefest glimpse of them, sent a stinging sexual shock through his system. The fact that they were black heightened her overall aura. She was about to take a seat at the bar when her eyes moved, met Danny's, and stopped right there. He maintained the contact and so did she. With no hesitation whatsoever she came right over and sat down. "Honey," she said, "you seem to like to be alone. If I'm bothering you, just say so."

"You know something?" Danny exclaimed. "You are the most gorgeous creature I have seen in one hell of a long time." She smiled a broad smile, reached over, and patted his hand, then left her hand on top of his and said, "Honey, you don't look so bad yourself. My name's Sandra Lee. What's yours?"

"Danny. Danny Lehman. That's my name, and I sure as hell would like to buy you a drink." He waved a waitress over. She seemed fidgety as hell as she took Sandra Lee's order for a champagne cocktail, but nevertheless she brought it back without saying a word.

"I haven't seen you here before," the black girl said. "Where are you from?"

"Philadelphia."

"Did you come in here on one of those junkets?"

"No, by myself," Danny answered.

"Uh, I like that." The hand that had been holding his now moved below the table to make an exploratory feel. Danny, who was hardly inexperienced in these matters, felt a shiver that he hadn't felt in weeks, no, months; in fact, since this whole damn thing with Raffles had started in that new shop he had opened on Wilshire Boulevard. He had been so mesmerized with the forty million bucks he had put on the line that he had reverted to a state of total inactivity in other areas, which he now realized had even extended to sex.

"Look," he blurbed out, "I hope you don't mind my saying so right away, but I would sure like to fuck you!"

"Honey," she answered, "I think you found yourself the right girl. You're staying here, aren't you?"

"Yeah."

"Show me your room key."

He fished it out and laid it on the table.

"You stay right here, Danny boy," she then said. "I'll be ready in a minute, okay?" She then got up and headed, Danny assumed, toward the ladies', to make sure that everything was in place that she normally had in place when she got down to business.

She was gone at least five or six minutes before she returned, walking this time with a brisker and somewhat firmer stride. She sat down, leaned as close to Danny's ear as possible, and said, "Man, I don't know who you are, and I don't know what you're up to, but you're in trouble, baby!"

"You got the word, too," Danny replied, also in a very low voice.

"I got it," she said.

"So why're you still sitting here?" Danny asked.

"Because nobody tells Sandra Lee what to do, that's why."

This time it was Danny Lehman who moved his hand under the table to grasp her thigh through the slit in her skirt, which, upon further exploration, seemed to extend almost up to her hip.

"Would you like a word of advice?" she now asked.

"Yes," Danny answered, and he really meant it.

"Get the hell out of here!" she warned.

"I'm not sure that would be the end of it," Danny replied.

"You're probably right," she said. "When Sid and Gino have an interest in you . . ."

"The two gorillas in the blue serge suits?"

"That's them," she answered. And they both just sat there for a minute.

"I've got an idea," she said.

"Whatever it is, I'm for it," Danny replied. For he had already concluded that he was in a no-win situation.

"Come on, honey," she said, and suddenly got up, grabbed her purse, grabbed Danny's hand, and began to lead him out of the bar and straight across the middle of the casino floor. They were quite a pair: the tall, gorgeous six-foot-two-inch black whore moving through the crowd as if she owned the place, and the five-foot-six-inch plump, balding guy trotting along beside her. Out the main casino doors they went. The black girl handed the parking attendant her valet ticket, the car was whipped up in front of them within a matter of minutes, and she climbed in on the driver's side while Danny joined her from the other side. His door was not even closed when she put the car in gear and they took off with a roar of the engine and a screech of tires. She was proud of her white Thunderbird convertible.

"Hold on," she said, as they turned out onto the Strip and as she gunned it up to a speed of at least fifty miles an hour within thirty seconds. Ten minutes later they approached the downtown area of Las Vegas; she turned into a cross street and then very soon they were in a rather run-down residential neighborhood.

At this point he finally asked, "Where are we heading?"

"My place, honey. It's like I told you: I don't like people fucking around with me, so if it can't be your place it's going to be my place. Okay?"

Damn, Danny thought, two of the most enticing pieces of ass being offered to him within a span of less than half a day, and he was going to have to pass on both of them. Life was becoming increasingly unfair. Then he said, "Sandra, look, sometime later I will explain all this, but would you mind just taking me to the airport instead? I don't like to cut and run. I've never done it in my life. But I don't like *these* odds one bit." She slowed the car down, looking over at him. Danny continued, "I'll take care of these monkeys in my way and in my time. Until I'm able to, I sure as hell don't want to get you in trouble."

She had now stopped the car at the curb. "I already am," she said, "but don't worry; Sandra Lee can take care of herself. The one I'm worried about is you. Why, for God's sake, are you fooling with this crowd?"

"Because they've got something I own and I want it."

"What can be worth that much?"

"It's not what's *it's* worth. It's what *I'm* worth. If I can't beat these stupid crooks at their stupid games, then I can't beat anybody. But suspect I can, and I think that after I do, it's going to be *them,* and a lot of lot of other people, who are going to think twice before they start fooling with *me.* Do you understand?"

"I think I do," Sandra Lee replied. "Though I don't know why at this point."

"Well, next time, and by God there definitely will be a

next time, I'll explain further. At your place, my place, or both."

She'd heard that one before. Yet . . . She gunned the car into a U-turn. Fifteen minutes later they turned right into the access road to the airport terminal. Danny extracted five one-hundred-dollar bills from his wallet and reached over to put them on Sandra Lee's lap.

"What's that all about, honey?" she asked.

"Just a little gesture of thanks."

She turned to him and flashed an enormous smile. "Danny Lehman," she said, "you've got class. I like you. I like your guts. I like what you just said a few minutes ago."

He smiled back at her and laid a hand on hers. "You'll hear from me. You can count on it."

She would, and she would not be disappointed.

When he got to the American Airlines counter, walking slowly and deliberately and looking straight ahead the entire way, he asked for the next flight east. When the girl at the counter suggested he would have to be a little more specific, he just told her to tell him when the next American flight was headed east. She didn't even give him a funny glance, since in Las Vegas you got all kinds of queer requests. "There's one leaving for Chicago in exactly twelve minutes. Gate 7. You want a ticket?"

He gave her his American Express card and, after a wait which seemed interminable, was finally handed a ticket.

"You'd better run," she said, "fast."

When he got to the gate they were closing down the counter. He waved his ticket at them, and they waved him toward the tunnel leading to the waiting DC8. *Now* he took one last glance back into the terminal. Two very large men in blue serge suits were trotting in the direction of Gate 7, though still a good fifty yards away. Immediately after he stepped into the plane the stewardess slammed the door. He sat down in the very first row and fastened his seat belt, and almost immediately the plane jerked as it was towed away from the gate. About four minutes later they were airborne.

Five minutes after that, Danny Lehman's breathing gradually returned to normal, but not his mental state. "I'm going to beat those bastards if it *kills* me," he said in a low mumble to himself. Then for some reason the old Jack Benny joke occurred to him, the one about "Your money or your life," coming from a stick-up artist holding a gun to Benny's head. "Lemme think about it," had been Benny's reply.

Well, before he, Danny Lehman, could give the same answer he first had to have the money. But that meant going the Fort Lauderdale route, the route that led from Saul Meyers to Montague Davies in the Bahamas to the Cayman Island bank and those close associates of Davies and Meyers who knew all about the casino business.

When you went that route, what was the final destination?

That was precisely the question put to him the next day by his attorney and the still-reluctant vice-chairman–elect of Raffles Inc., Benjamin Shea. "You know the answer," Shea said immediately, and added, "so don't do it, Danny." And before Danny could get stubborn and begin to plant his feet in concrete—Shea knew his client—he continued, "I've got excellent contacts at Mercier Frères."

"What's that?" Danny asked, despite himself.

"An investment bank."

"Forget it, Shea. Banks don't lend money against casinos. We've been through that, remember?"

"It's an *investment* bank, Danny."

"So what?"

"As you know, they invest *in* companies, raise money *for* them, and not just lend money *to* them."

"So?" Danny wasn't in the greatest of moods.

"Well, it can't hurt to talk to them."

"About what?"

"The thirty million you need."

"I need a loan, not a partner."

"You think what they're offering you in Fort Lauderdale is just a loan?"

Mercier Frères was not just "an" investment bank. It had been started in Paris in the nineteenth century and by now had been established in both London and New York for nearly a hundred years. Though Mercier had been founded later than Lazard Frères, it was that merchant bank which Mercier had tried to emulate from the very beginning. Now, almost a century later, the partners of Mercier were still keenly aware that their bank was Avis and Lazard was Hertz, but none would ever admit it out loud.

Henry Price was one of their three managing directors, the one responsible for all of their operations in North America. He was Groton, Harvard, a Fulbright scholar, on the board of governors of the Council on Foreign Relations, the board of directors of IBM, the board of elders of the Episcopal Church. *Summa summarum,* he numbered among the one hundred most powerful men in the United States.

Price was forty-nine and was, by any standards, a very fine physical specimen. When he was in France, which was often, invariably someone there would remark that there was an uncanny resemblance between him and Giscard d'Estaing. Both were very tall, and rather thin, and looked down upon the world with a great deal of skepticism that was often taken, and correctly so, for disdain. But where Giscard would look down upon his world of politics from the Élysée Palace on the rue du Faubourg St.-Honoré, Henry Price ruled his world of finance from the offices of Mercier Frères, at times from their original site on the Boulevard Haussmann, more often from the merchant bank that they maintained under the same name in Moorgate in the

City of London; but usually from the offices on Wall Street, from which Mercier Frères ran their American investment banking activities.

Mercier Frères was not as fast-growing as Salomon Brothers, not as large as Goldman Sachs, not as snooty as First Boston, and certainly not as aggressive as Lehman Brothers. Lazard Frères was the house that it resembled most closely. And, inevitably, the next comparison that was made was between the two "stars" of these two institutions: Felix Rohatyn of Lazard and Henry Price of Mercier. Rohatyn was the more flamboyant of the two, the one who enjoyed publicity. He liked to see his name on articles expressing rather radical opinions concerning the economic future—or lack thereof—of the United States on the editorial pages of *The Wall Street Journal,* which had the circulation, or in *The New York Review of Books,* which lacked circulation but made up for it by having the type of readers that Rohatyn felt were sufficiently bright to appreciate him. It was said that Rohatyn had political ambitions; that he wanted to become the architect of America's economic and financial policies, just as Henry Kissinger now was of its foreign policy. The similarities did not end there. Both Kissinger and Rohatyn came from Central European origins; both were first-generation immigrants consumed, probably to a very healthy degree most of the time, by ambition.

Not Henry Price; ambition, politics, and Central Europe were all foreign to this man, but especially ambition. At forty-nine, if he was consumed at all it was by a desire to gradually abdicate his position in that American corridor of power which, like the Eastern shuttle, runs from Boston to New York to Washington. Spurred on by a disastrous divorce, he was determined to rebuild his private life into one that would offer everything that was new, different, and satisfying. He had recently acquired a farm in Virginia and at the annual meeting of the principals that year had stated that while he would remain on as managing director at

Mercier indefinitely, he would henceforth devote his attention only to special projects; to new ideas.

So on May 27, 1969, he received Daniel Lehman and his attorney, Benjamin Shea, for lunch in one of the dining rooms on the tenth floor of the Mercier Frères building on Wall Street. He did so because Shea was a nephew of one of the firm's other partners, but also because of the nature of the proposal.

He regretted his decision the very first moment he saw Lehman. Which was a pity, because the project, a casino, was both new and intriguing. Nobody at Mercier Frères had ever considered getting involved with the gaming business. In fact, as far as Price knew, nor had anybody at Morgan Stanley, or Lehman Brothers, or Goldman Sachs. Even the brethren in London who would try anything—the more daring merchant banks such as Hambros; Hill, Samuel; Guinness Mahon; or even S. G. Warburg—had never thought of casinos. In itself, this made the idea intriguing.

The menu that day consisted of melon, cold salmon, and a chocolate mousse. When port was offered with the melon, it was obviously a first for Danny Lehman. It was, therefore, also obvious to Henry Price that it would be a waste of time to try to engage the man in small talk. So he got right down to business.

"I assume that Mr. Shea has told you about our firm, Mr. Lehman?" he asked.

"Yes. You raise money, you don't lend it."

"Precisely. We help corporations place their new issues of stocks, bonds, notes. And so forth. Usually we place these instruments with the general public. Sometimes we do private placements. What exactly did you have in mind?"

"I need thirty million dollars."

"For how long?"

"Five years."

"If I understand your situation correctly, you need the funds to complete the purchase of a casino in Las Vegas."

"That's right. Raffles."

The cold salmon arrived. So did a bottle of Sancerre. Price grimaced when Danny downed most of the wine in one gulp.

"I'll tell you bluntly, Mr. Lehman, that we have never been involved with casinos before. So it would be very difficult for me to present a case to my colleagues unless I could demonstrate that the borrower is extremely sound. After all, the question that is always asked first is: how will the loan be repaid? I assume you've brought along the financial statements." The last sentence was addressed to Benjamin Shea, but it was Danny who answered.

"They won't tell you much."

"Really. And why not?"

Lehman could hardly explain that the true earnings of Raffles were much higher than those reflected in Raffles' P&L statements, since, for years, management had been stealing millions. So he said, "Because financial statements cannot tell you about the future. And that's what counts."

"I agree. Tell me about that future."

Danny did, in a monologue that lasted twenty minutes. The chocolate mousse arrived, and Danny was still going on.

"When the Atlantic City casino gets operational, the profits are going to be phenomenal. Do you know how many people live within a hundred miles, a hundred and fifty miles, two hundred miles of Atlantic City? Tens upon tens of millions! I know, since I've done my research, Mr. Price. Benjamin, show him the numbers."

Lehman's attorney withdrew a fifty-page report from his briefcase and handed it to Price, saying, "Mr. Lehman asked me to commission this demographics study."

"You see?" Danny said, as Price started to flip the pages. "And a large percentage of those people can hardly wait to start gambling *legally*. That's the point. Today they have to travel thousands of miles to Nevada in order to do that."

While Danny continued to speak, he watched Henry
Price as carefully as the investment banker had been watching him. After Price had handed the study back to Shea,
Danny could see the banker's eyes begin to glaze over. He
should have known better than to come here. A Henry Price
was as much out of his depth in Danny Lehman's world as
Danny was in Price's. He should have been blunt with Benjamin Shea before this unfortunate meeting had been scheduled in the first place. White shoes and casinos did not mix,
and they never would.

Lunch ended abruptly when Henry Price looked at his
watch. It seemed he had a plane waiting for him. He mumbled something about a farm in Virginia. By two-thirty Price
was airborne in his firm's Learjet. An hour later he dis-
embarked at National Airport, where a limousine was waiting to take him to his farm, a three-hundred-acre spread
near Middleburg that he had bought six months ago for $1.7
million. Henry tried to visit it every other weekend. For
three reasons: the solitude, the horses he stabled there, and
the woman who usually spent her weekends with him.

Although *he* referred to Natalie Simmons as his fiancée,
she never called him anything but a "good friend." He was
New York, she Georgetown; Middleburg was his escape
from Wall Street, hers from the art gallery where she
worked in Washington, D.C., a city where they also spent
weekends together.

It was during one of his stays in Paris last year that he
had met her on the curb outside the entrance to the Ritz. It
was April and it was pouring. He had just missed his limousine, which had to circle the block one more time. She was
frantically trying to get a cab and failing miserably, beaten
every time by the Parisian mob.

So, out of nothing more than sympathy for a compatriot,
he offered her a lift. The last time she could recall even
considering a "lift" was in high school, but this handsome

man in his slate-gray topcoat, who carried a rolled umbrella and spoke with a mid-Atlantic accent, could hardly be suspected of any motives other than kindness. And the alternative was simply giving up meeting her girlfriend for hot chocolate at Rumpelmayers, and she was damned if she was going to let a bunch of rude Frenchmen do *that* to her.

A couple of hours later, as both were returning to the hotel, they ran into each other again in the lobby. They had a drink in the bar, dinner at Lasserre, and champagne at the Crazy Horse Saloon, and, to the utter surprise of both of them, ended up in her bed at three in the morning. She kept her white nightgown on the entire time; he apologized when it was over. They tried it again the next night and this time her hand actually guided him into her. She did that very rarely. He had hardly expected it. The result was that both of them climaxed very quickly, and in contrast to the previous night, he stayed for breakfast and they shared both the *Herald Tribune* and *Le Monde,* and, eventually, their own war stories.

The biggest war in his life had been with his wife and it had just ended in divorce. That was one reason why he was spending more time than usual in Paris: to try and forget her once and for all. Natalie's disastrous relationship had also just ended, fortunately, as she explained, this side of marriage. But it had been a very close call.

After Vassar, she had come over to Paris to study the history of art at the Sorbonne. The semester had barely begun in 1967 when she had met, and fallen completely in love with, a young man from Basle who was working in Paris for CIBA, the Swiss chemical concern. After one month they shared his apartment, and three months after that he had proposed marriage. Upon his insistence they had gone to the American embassy in Paris to determine what his status would be should she decide to return to the United States "someday," as he had put it. No problem, they'd been told. He would automatically be issued a green card upon pro-

ducing documentary evidence that they were indeed man
and wife. It would be a matter of weeks. That evening they
celebrated, leaving her so exhausted that she slept in the
next day while he went to work. Sex had never been her
strong point anyway, although he seemed to think of little
else. Out of boredom, she took a look through his desk. And
there was an entire folder of his correspondence with Du
Pont. They were highly interested in him and willing to pay
him a salary that was, she knew, triple what he was getting
from CIBA. The catch was that they required that he have
permanent residence status: a green card. The last letter in
the file was one in which he explained that the green card
was no longer a problem. He would have one within thirty
days.

She had gathered together her belongings within thirty
minutes and walked out. She had not seen the jerk again.

After Natalie had finished her story, they had gotten
dressed. Price was about to leave for the office when she
asked him to take the day off and join her for an afternoon
at the Louvre. He immediately agreed. Her passion for art,
he soon found out, had become very specific: women painters, and the appalling lack of appreciation they had been
shown, even in France.

They spent most of the next two weeks together, and by
mutual agreement decided to see if it would work beyond
Paris. She'd had enough of the Sorbonne, Paris, and, in fact,
Europe, and would be returning to the United States in the
summer. To do what? Maybe work in a gallery in New
York, or Boston, or Washington, D.C., with the idea of one
day owning her own. She wasn't quite sure. She eventually
ended up in Georgetown, in a small town house that she
bought with funds from her trust. Her great-grandfather
had been one of the founders of General Mills, so money
was no problem. Her college friends who met Price at the
occasional dinner party she gave in Georgetown that summer wondered what this twenty-four-year-old woman saw

in a man of forty-eight. She knew. He filled a major vacuum in her life, as she did in his, and neither had any ulterior motives whatsoever, neither money, nor status, nor, most important, green cards. The arrangement even allowed her to play housewife now and then, a role she loved to play as long as it lasted only forty-eight hours maximum. When that mood hit her, she usually arrived at the Virginia farm for their prearranged weekend well before Price did, and worked with the kitchen staff in planning the meals.

So she was waiting on the veranda when the limousine pulled up. The first thing Price did before kissing her was to hand her a bag full of art books from Scribners and a box full of chocolates from Belgium.

"For the farmer's wife," Price said.

"Not quite," she said, and then added, "but you are a dear, Henry. And you are also early."

"It's because I walked out of my own luncheon at the bank."

"What drove you to that?"

"It was a who, not a what: a little grubby fellow from Philadelphia. Ghastly man."

"What made you invite him in the first place?"

"The usual: his attorney is a nephew of a partner."

"What did he want?"

"Money. To buy a casino. In Las Vegas."

Natalie Simmons responded, "From *you?*" She giggled. "How ridiculous."

"Well, not entirely," Price replied. "He's got an idea. About Atlantic City. He became almost lyrical when he got onto the subject. He thinks it's a natural place for casino gambling. He's figured out how many people live within a hundred miles, two hundred and fifty miles, of the Boardwalk, that sort of thing."

"How many do?"

"About fifty million. Even more, I think. In any case, a hell of a large chunk of the American population."

"All dying to gamble?"

"Exactly."

"And he would make Atlantic City into a Las Vegas East?"

"Precisely."

"Even the people who live in New Jersey don't deserve that!" she said.

"That's debatable. In any case, they don't deserve *him*."

"Hardly the Right Stuff, eh?"

"Exactly. In fact, the perfect description of the man."

"Never mind," she then said, reaching over to pat his hand, "you'll never see him again."

"That's for damn sure," Price responded.

This was precisely the same thought that was going through Danny Lehman's head at exactly the same time. He had just arrived in Fort Lauderdale courtesy of a National Airlines flight from La Guardia. There was also a limousine waiting for him. In it was Saul Meyers. He was sitting in the back of the black Lincoln that was parked at the curb next to the baggage carrousel. "So you've made up your mind," Meyers said as Danny climbed in and joined him. Danny nodded.

"We thought you would," Meyers continued, and added, "You won't regret it."

He made it sound believable. Almost.

PART TWO

1969–1980

8

Two weeks later, on a day that was hot as hell in Philadelphia, Danny Lehman got to the office just before eleven o'clock. He was sweating profusely as he stepped through the doors of the American Coin, Metals, and Currency Exchange World Headquarters, as the not too discreet sign said on the building that housed it. The only problem was that the building, and the company, in fact the whole damn thing, now essentially belonged to the bank who, against that collateral, had advanced him the ten million dollars he had used as a down payment on the casino. Though, to be sure, now that Fort Lauderdale had come through he had been able to pay off the note and now owned that casino lock, stock, and barrel.

In retrospect, buying it had been easy; taking possession was proving less so. Much less so. And if he did not get possession soon, very soon, the Fort Lauderdale mob would take possession of him. But he had made a decision in principle: to wait it out. To wait for an opening. He had no intention of walking into that den of thieves again unless he could walk in with artillery heavy enough to blow them away. The situation was taking its toll. Danny's appearance had changed markedly during the past month. He was fifteen pounds lighter and 10 percent balder. He told everybody that the weight loss, at least, was fully explainable and was due to his having taken up tennis. He had not only taken up tennis; he had become a tennis fanatic in thirty days flat, spending up to three hours a day taking lessons, practicing alone, and even venturing into a few matches with other neophytes. He knew it was escapism, but what the hell.

"Mr. Lehman, somebody is trying to get hold of you. Frantically! We tried everywhere. The service said you left an hour ago." It was his general manager, normally not an excitable type.

"I played a little tennis before coming in," Danny replied. He was still sweating to prove it. "Who is it?"

"A Mr. De Niro. That's all he said. He'll call again in five minutes, you can be sure."

"All right. I'm going up to my office. I'll take care of it." He said it calmly, but his stomach was churning at a furious pace. De Niro calling *him!* This could be it. He worked out of a small office suite on the third floor, reachable by either a creaky old elevator or a very steep staircase. Danny took the stairs; it built up tone in his leg muscles. His secretary was standing inside the door of the tiny reception area waiting for him. "That man is on the phone again," she said.

"I'll take it inside. No visitors until I say so." He picked up his phone while still standing. "Yes?"

"Is this Lehman?"

"This is Daniel Lehman, yes. Who's this?"

"Lenny De Niro. And Roberto Salgo is standing right beside me."

"What do you want?"

"There are some other people standing right beside me, too. From the FBI."

"I see. And?"

"They're trying to raid the place!"

"And?"

"For Chrissake, man, it's your place. I'll put them on the phone and you tell them to get the fuck out of here and to stay the fuck out of here until our lawyers get here to protect our rights."

"What lawyers are you talking about?"

"Look, Lehman, you own this place. You've got lawyers. So tell these guys to get the fuck out of here or you're going to—"

"Hold on there, De Niro. I'm not going to do anything of the sort. If the FBI's raiding the place, they must have a reason. When you find out what the reason is, call me back. Okay?"

And Danny hung up. Had his new "associates" intervened?

Half an hour later, his secretary stuck her head around the door, very carefully. "It's Las Vegas again," she said.

"De Niro?"

"No. A man who says he's from the FBI," she replied, and her expression showed she was scared. She had heard, everybody in the building had heard, that Mr. Lehman had gotten involved with some casino in Nevada and that something had gone very wrong. She liked her job and she liked her boss. It seemed as if both might be in danger.

"Put him through," Danny said.

"Mr. Lehman?" It was a deep voice that came over the phone.

"Yes."

"My name is William Smith. I'm the special agent in charge of the Las Vegas office of the Federal Bureau of Investigation." He spoke with a southwestern type of accent, probably from Oklahoma. It was the same sort of semi-drawl that airline pilots affect. "Mr. Lehman," Smith continued, "we'd appreciate it if you'd come to Las Vegas right away."

"If you think it's necessary," Danny answered without hesitation.

"We've established that a flight is leaving Philadelphia in just about an hour from now, and from what we've been told, there's space on it."

"Which airline?"

"TWA Flight 62."

"I'll be on it."

When the plane was about forty-five minutes away from Las Vegas, a voice over the loudspeaker asked that Mr. Daniel Lehman please identify himself to one of the stewardesses. When he did, she told him that the cockpit had been informed by the "authorities," as she put it, that they wanted him to disembark first. Two men would be waiting for him. When the door slid open at the airport and Danny stepped out, there were three men, not two. The oldest among them stepped forward, reached into his pocket, and produced what looked like a small leather wallet. He opened it and showed Danny his badge.

"Mr. Lehman?"

"Yes," replied Danny. The badge bit had impressed him.

"I'm Special Agent Smith. William Smith. Let's go."

Smith did not waste any time. He had no sooner started walking down the long corridor leading to the terminal exit when he started working on Danny. "We assume you're here, Mr. Lehman, in order to cooperate with us?"

"Your assumption's correct," Danny answered.

"What is your relationship with Mr. De Niro and Mr. Salgo?" the special agent asked.

"None. In fact, less than none," Danny replied. "As you must know, I assumed ownership of Raffles a number of months ago. But up until this point I have not interfered in any way with the management of the casino here in Las Vegas. This was not by choice, Mr. Smith. To put it very bluntly, the management, specifically De Niro and Salgo, locked me out."

The agent nodded his head as they continued to walk at a fairly brisk pace, and said, "That confirms exactly what we've heard."

Danny was glad that he was in such good shape as a result of his tennis playing and stair climbing. Once outside,

Smith and his colleagues went directly to a gray Ford parked rather majestically where no car was ever allowed to park. They were watched by an airport cop who was obviously resentful of this higher police authority which had temporarily occupied a piece of his territory. The two younger FBI men got into the front seat, while William Smith and Danny Lehman took over the back.

As they pulled away, Smith turned to Danny and said, "Now let me explain the exact nature of our problem. We've obtained a search warrant for your place from a federal judge, but it has been successfully challenged, at least temporarily, by the shyster lawyer, if you'll excuse the expression, that De Niro and Salgo came up with about one minute after they talked to you on the phone. In fact, thinking of it now, they must have found him before that, because De Niro had barely hung up before this guy walked into the executive offices of the casino. Well, we really had no choice but to walk out."

"Why?" Danny asked. "And what were you searching for?"

Smith chose to ignore the second question. "The warrant is not specific enough and, frankly, it's because we *think* we know what we are after and even where it is, but we're not sure."

Danny was getting increasingly confused the more Smith spoke, and it showed.

"Don't worry, Mr. Lehman, we've got the place watched from the front, from the back, and from the top. We know every senior employee in the place; every one of our men has studied their pictures, and, as far as we know, so far nobody has gotten out with anything. Now, that does not mean that if and when we get in we're going to come up winners. There are probably a lot of good places to stash something in a casino. Nonetheless, we are pretty sure that if we have access to the entire casino, and sufficient time, we'll come up with what we want, which will be all we'll need to rid you of De Niro and Salgo for a long time."

"What exactly is that?" Danny asked again.

"I think that at this point, lest somehow what we do and say here may later be interpreted in court as entrapment, or in case it may be implied that for completely selfish and personal motives the two of us got together—colluded—in order to nail De Niro, Salgo, and all their pals—for those reasons I think it best I do not answer your question at this point. If I do, maybe this whole thing could get thrown out of court later. So if you don't mind going on faith a little bit longer—"

Danny broke in. "What do you want me to do?"

"You own the place. If you invite us in, there is no power on earth that can stop us. Right?"

Danny thought it over. "I guess so." He did not appear convinced.

Special Agent Smith then tapped the shoulder of his colleague sitting beside the driver in the front seat, and said, "Harry, let's have it." The young man produced a piece of paper and handed it back over the seat.

"This looks a little formal," Smith said to Danny, "but as I have already indicated, we can't be too careful in these matters. Now, all that this essentially says is that you, Daniel Lehman, as the principal owner, chairman of the board, and chief executive officer of Raffles Inc., which owns the casino and hotel in its entirety, hereby authorizes the Federal Bureau of Investigation to enter your premises and to have complete access to the entire property for a period of forty-eight hours starting . . . and we will fill in the date and exact time right now if you agree to sign this, Mr. Lehman."

Danny reached inside his jacket pocket for his pen. "Where?"

"Between the red X's."

Danny signed.

* * *

When they pulled up in front of Raffles it was not the
doorman who came forward but two more FBI agents
dressed in almost exactly the same way as the two young
men who were now emerging from the front seat of the gray
Ford. As they walked up the broad stairs to the doors at the
main entrance, they were met by an elderly guy, in his sixties, who held up his hand like a traffic cop and said,
"Smith, stop right there! If you've got a new warrant, show
it to me. If you haven't, back off!"

Smith said, "I've got something better than that. This is
Mr. Daniel Lehman. He owns this place. Here, read it." He
handed over the piece of paper that Danny had signed in the
car. When the man was done, Smith didn't wait for him to
give it back; he grabbed it back.

"Okay, fellas," he said to the four young FBI types, who
were now all standing in a huddle off to the right, waiting.
"In we go."

As they went through the door, Smith asked Danny,
"Where's the counting room?"

Danny replied, somewhat shamefacedly, "Frankly, I
don't know." So everybody stopped on the terrace overlooking the casino floor. Smith then said to one of his younger
men, "Go down there, get a pit boss, and bring him back."
The agent returned with a man who stood there with a completely blank look on his face.

"Could you please tell me where the counting room is?"
Smith asked.

The man's arm went up, he pointed to the rear of the
casino, and he said, "All the way back"; then added, "Anything else?"

The FBI man did not bother to answer this question; he
just said to his entourage and Danny Lehman, "Follow me."

The counting room was indeed right at the rear of the
main casino floor. It was really nothing more than a big
square box slapped against the rear wall, and apparently

constructed not of Sheetrock and plaster but of materials of substantially greater width and strength. Upon closer inspection, what it really resembled was a kind of blockhouse, which the interior decorators had tried their best to disguise by decorating it in garish colors, and with even more garish murals. Mounted into the front walls were thick glass windows with what looked like bank tellers standing behind them. The entrance to this bunker was a single door off to the left, a door that also had a narrow, thick plate-glass window mounted at eye level. It was obviously the only means by which one could gain access to the counting room.

Special Agent Smith stepped forward and thumped on the door with his right fist while at the same time tapping as sharply as possible with his left knuckles on that plate glass.

A woman's startled face suddenly came into view.

"Open up!" yelled Smith. He held up the leather wallet containing the badge and emblem of the Federal Bureau of Investigation of the United States of America, flat against the windowpane.

"I can't," came back the woman's muffled voice, the voice of a person who was scared out of her wits.

The agent now took Danny Lehman's arm and drew him to his side. "Tell her," he ordered Danny.

"My name is Daniel Lehman," he said, "and I am the new owner of this place. In that capacity, ma'am, I request that you open up this door immediately."

By this time there were tears starting to run down the cheeks of the face that was staring out at them. "I couldn't," she whined, "even if I wanted to. I don't have a key to unlock this door."

"Who does?" yelled Smith.

"I'm not authorized to say," she answered.

This made more than a little sense, since the knowledge of who had the key that would open the door that led to one of the largest accumulations of cash in the United States would inevitably have been too tempting for some of the more daring crooks of this world to resist using it for selfish purposes.

The agent now turned back to his entourage and said, "Jack. Harry. You stay right here. Nobody goes in. Nobody comes out. The rest of us are going upstairs." Smith now knew where he was going. He led them around about a quarter of the circumference of the casino main floor to an elevator that had been placed very discreetly down a short corridor. It was a single small elevator with no sign indicating where it led to. It was so small, in fact, that there was barely room for the four men in it.

Smith punched the button marked "3." When they got out, there was a sign with an arrow indicating that the executive offices were right ahead. Smith said to Danny, "I think it would be appropriate if you would lead. Just go straight down this corridor to the office at the end. My bet is that De Niro and Salgo are both in there."

When Danny got to the end of the corridor, instead of knocking on the door he just opened it and walked in. The FBI man had been right. De Niro sat behind the huge desk at the far end of the room; Salgo was sitting on a sofa off to his right. Both had in front of them large glasses filled with what was obviously a lot of whiskey and very little soda. De Niro stood up in violent anger and let fly, ignoring Danny. "Smith! You've been told once to get the fuck out of here, you and all of your creeps. Apparently none of you understand English too well, so I'm going to have to tell you again: get the fuck out of here. Now! If you don't I am going to arrange to have you removed, physically removed, right now. Do you understand that?"

Smith didn't say a word.

De Niro turned to Salgo. "Where is your goddamn lawyer?"

"He said he wanted to wait downstairs at the front entrance because he thought this might happen," Salgo responded.

"Well, get the senile bastard up here," De Niro commanded.

"Oh no, Salgo. You sit right where you're sitting." Smith stepped forward and produced the same piece of paper they had shown the attorney downstairs. It was becoming increasingly apparent that the attorney had been wise enough to leave the casino as unobtrusively as possible and head back to his office, if he had an office.

"Read it," the special agent said as he gave De Niro the document that Danny had signed in the car. De Niro read it and handed it over to Roberto Salgo. In the meantime, nobody in the room said a word.

Then Smith broke the silence. "We'll need all the keys."

"Why?" De Niro asked.

Then it was Danny Lehman who spoke. "All the keys. All of the casino's keys, which are now my keys; and specifically right now, the keys to the counting room."

"We don't have any keys," De Niro answered.

One of the young FBI men stepped forward and whispered something in Smith's ear. Smith listened with a slightly impatient frown, looked sharply at De Niro, and asked, "Who's your chief accountant here?"

De Niro just looked at him.

"All right," said Smith, "if you want to play it that way it's fine with us. Everybody stays here." With that he left the room and a minute later came back with a young, extremely good-looking secretary in tow. Smith pointed at the telephone on De Niro's desk and said, "Young lady, I want you to call the chief accountant and tell him to come to this office. Right now."

The secretary was obviously a tough nut, since in contrast to the woman down in the counting room, she was not intimidated in the slightest. Nevertheless, she did as she was told. Then Smith told her to go back to her desk, which she did. A few minutes later a very agitated man in his late forties walked in. He looked at De Niro. He looked at Salgo;

he looked at Danny; and then at the FBI crew, not knowing
exactly who he should address his first words to. He didn't
have to worry in that respect, since the chief FBI honcho
moved right in front of him and, with his face about six
inches from the newcomer's face, said, "That man behind
me is Mr. Daniel Lehman. He owns this place, as you know.
He wants the keys, all the keys to everything in this fucking
casino; he wants them right now and he specifically wants
the keys to the counting room. Where are they?"

"Rupert," said Salgo, "not one syllable to these guys." He
punched each word out with increasing emphasis.

Special Agent Smith ignored Salgo, stepped back from the
newcomer, and addressed Danny. "Mr. Lehman, I would
like you to meet the head of the accounting and auditing
department of this casino, Mr. Rupert Downey."

An alarm bell went off in Danny Lehman's head. Rupert
Downey? Rupert Downey? He knew the name. How in the
world was that possible? Then he remembered: this was the
guy who had received the last loan that was processed from
his home, through the Caribbean, and back to Las Vegas.
The money had come from the briefcase full of cash that
Amaretto had left on his coffee table that night. Easy,
Danny told himself. As he watched Rupert Downey's face,
there was nothing, absolutely nothing, to indicate that Downey, who was now starting to tremble, had even the faintest
clue who he was. This was another one he owed Joe
Amaretto and Sam Sarnoff.

Just to make damn sure, Danny stepped forward, shook
hands with Downey, and said very quietly, "I'm Danny
Lehman, Rupert. I think you understand what's happening
here. I want you to know that I'll try to be as helpful as I
possibly can when this whole thing is over. So I would
greatly appreciate it if you'd agree to Mr. Smith's request."

Now Downey's face began to twitch. He didn't dare look
in the direction of either Salgo or De Niro when, in a voice
even lower than that used by Danny, he answered, "Come

with me." Danny followed him out of the room. Everybody else stayed. When Danny returned with Downey he pointed to a bundle of keys the accountant was carrying. "I think I've got exactly what we need."

Smith looked at De Niro and then at Salgo and said, "You've got a choice: you can stay here or you can come with us." Both men decided to go with the FBI.

It took the elevator two trips to transport everybody down to the casino floor, but once they were reassembled they moved like a wedge in the direction of the counting room. When they got there, Downey stepped forward to unlock the door and then stepped back to allow Smith and everybody else, including De Niro and Salgo, to move in ahead of him. Smith had said he knew what he was after and where it was. Obviously, they were now all inside the "where."

The counting room itself was the size of a small bungalow. It had been partitioned off into three sections. The first was the entrance area into which they had now all stepped. Straight ahead of them was the second area, a room about twenty feet by twenty feet. Everything inside was totally visible, since the upper halves of the partitions were all glass. In the center was a large table. Around the table stood five women. In the middle of the table was a pile of cash. One woman had a stack of bills in front of her and was counting them at an amazing speed. When she was done counting she handed the bills to the woman beside her, who did the same. Apparently they counted out loud. Then the bills were handed to a third woman, who ran them through a counting machine, which also wrapped them. Then a fourth woman took over, but it was not quite clear what she was doing; it appeared that her function was to take the information that was printed on the wrappers around each of the stacks of bills that had just emerged from the counting machine, and to record it in a ledger. The fifth and final woman was obvi-

ously there to put the now counted, wrapped, and recorded
stacks of bills into containers, which were then sealed.

On the wall behind the counting table was a row of metal
racks, obviously mobile, since all were mounted on wheels
with rubber tires. The racks had two tiers. On each tier
there were three metal boxes, and these boxes were, in turn,
chained to the rack itself. The first woman approached the
racks and produced a key that opened the padlock on the
chain attaching the metal boxes to the metal racks. She then
lifted a box off the rack and brought it to the counting table.
She turned it upside down, and out of it tumbled another
large pile of money, which the woman on her left now
started to count, and thus the whole procedure started all
over again.

Everyone just stood there in silence taking it all in until
Smith turned to Rupert Downey and asked, "Where are
your safes? Are they in there?" And he pointed to the counting area they were all watching.

"No," replied Downey, "in the other room."

"All right, that's where we'll go."

It required a new key to get into the other room, and
Downey had it with him. This room was slightly larger than
the one where the counters were so busy. It represented the
nerve center of the casino, housing both the money bank
and the data and information bank supporting the gaming
operations. There were rows upon rows of filing cabinets,
containing detailed financial information on all clients of
any significance. At the front was a type of banking counter
with thick bulletproof windows facing the casino floor.
There stood the tellers who were visible from the main floor.
There were two slits in the glass: one at the bottom of each
window and one cut into the middle of the glass, allowing
for verbal communication between the men standing behind
the counter inside the counting room and men who approached the counting room from the outside—usually one
of the pit bosses, one of whom was standing there now.

"What's he doing?" Danny asked Rupert Downey.

"That's where the pit bosses bring the markers," the auditor said. "The people in here then check our files to see if the customer's credit is still good. In essence a marker is just an IOU. They, plus the cash and the chips, constitute our 'inventory,' all of which is stored in this room."

"But exactly *where* are they stored?" Smith asked.

Downey pointed to the right side of the room. "There." He indicated a wall of steel doors.

Smith now looked at Danny and said, "I think that's what we want to look at." He then turned back to Downey. "How do you get into those steel cabinets?"

Downey replied, "With a key and a combination."

"Well? Let's get started," Smith commanded.

Downey moved forward, produced yet another key, inserted it into the lock, turned it, quickly spun the dial next to the key five times in alternate directions, and then slid open the large steel doors. Behind these doors, on the left, were two huge safes mounted one on top of the other, and, to the right of them, four rows of safety-deposit boxes and drawers, just like those one sees in the vaults of banks.

"How do you open those safety-deposit boxes?" was the next question that Smith put to Downey.

"It takes two keys, as usual. Our key and the boxholder's," Downey replied. "I'll demonstrate it," he continued. "Box number seventeen," he said, "is my box."

Downey reached into his pocket for his key chain. Then he sorted through the keys he had brought down from the office until he found its match. He inserted the two keys into box seventeen. He then drew out a metal tray and started to hand it over to Smith, who backed away from it as if the auditor were offering him a box full of rattlesnakes.

"No, no," Smith said, "this has to be done correctly."

Downey turned to Danny and then back to the FBI agent, and said, "Sir, I don't mind at all if you look through this. These are just personal documents, that's all. I would feel relieved if you did so."

Smith continued to look reluctant but nodded his agreement. Downey put the metal tray on a table in the middle of the room. Smith stepped forward to the table, lifted the lid of the tray, and began very gingerly to finger through its contents. It was quite obvious that there was nothing in the tray except insurance policies, some bank statements, and what looked like a will. When Smith, in a practiced drone, described what he was finding in the tray, it was not only disappointment that registered on the faces of the men from the Federal Bureau of Investigation, but suddenly a growing concern. Danny sensed that perhaps this whole thing was in the process of blowing up in their faces.

This might be very embarrassing for the FBI if it proved to be the case; for *him,* however, it could have truly disastrous consequences. For Danny could not help but remember the last words Amaretto had spoken to him in Philadelphia. "If you try to get them into trouble with the authorities," he'd said, "they're so fucking greedy and so fucking arrogant that they'll kill you, Danny. And then they'll kill us."

If the other safety-deposit boxes contained nothing more than this, if De Niro and Salgo were not caught red-handed, they could simply walk away from it all, and who on earth could stop them?

The agent in charge of the Las Vegas office of the FBI was watching Danny, and he must have sensed the train of thought in the man's mind. So once again he took charge and now addressed himself to De Niro, who was just standing there, smirking. "All right, Lenny, your turn."

"For what?"

"Look, do you want to do this the easy way or the hard way? We look now or we look later. You know damn well that I can get a search warrant, if not within an hour, at least within days, and in the meantime, if necessary, Mr.

Lehman is going to stay right here and is even going to sleep here should it take that long; isn't that right, Mr. Lehman?"

Danny nodded his agreement. Why not? His neck was already in the noose.

"So," Smith continued, "it's up to you; make up your mind."

De Niro continued to smirk. Suddenly he said, "All right," to everybody's surprise and steadily mounting apprehension.

"Which is your box?" asked Smith.

"Not box," answered De Niro. "Drawer. And not drawer. Drawers, plural."

"Okay. Which ones, plural. Answer!"

"One, two, and three." And they were big drawers. That produced a noticeable increase in tension in the room. Nobody had that many insurance policies.

De Niro continued, "Roberto there, he's got three, four, and five, don't you, Roberto?"

Salgo nodded. That took care of all the drawers right there.

"You've got your keys with you?" Smith asked.

"Yes."

"Well, use them," Smith said.

De Niro looked at Smith and then spoke in a sharp voice. "Let's stop right here for a minute. I'll do this my own way, okay? In my own time. Right?"

Danny's apprehension mounted. Either De Niro felt it necessary to prove what a dangerous bastard he was through bravado to the end, or he, Danny Lehman, had pulled the pin on a grenade that was going to be a dud. Worse yet, it might prove to be a grenade with a timer. Nobody, especially De Niro and Salgo, was going to get blown up here today. But when the timer ran out in maybe a month or a year, it was going to have a very lethal impact on two other men in that room: Rupert Downey and Danny Lehman.

Nobody challenged De Niro, so he continued. "I want to explain something first. My colleague, Mr. Salgo, and I have indulged ourselves in a little bit of the action here during the past couple of months. I know, we all know, that's against the rules, but as you all also know, nobody pays any attention to those rules. What I'm telling you now is that Roberto and I have spent more than a few hours at the baccarat table and we've been lucky. Very, very lucky. And if you don't believe me, you can check it out with the guys running those tables. Their names are . . ."

It's a dud, was Danny's first panicky thought. These guys simply can't be beaten. The FBI's conclusion was obviously exactly the opposite. In a thickly sarcastic Oklahoma drawl, Special Agent Smith interrupted De Niro. "Okay, okay, Lenny, we can get to the names later."

De Niro said, "Roberto, give me your keys." Salgo did as he was told. De Niro said to Downey, "Give me your fucking key, too, asshole." Downey also did as he was told, his face absolutely ashen.

"I want everybody to remember that I'm doing this voluntarily," De Niro then stated. Having had the final word, he stepped forward, manipulated the keys, pulled out drawer number one, and put it on top of the table. Then drawers two and three. Then four, five, and six. He gave Downey back his key with the words "Here, asshole," and smiled at the rest of the group. "Gentlemen," he said, "be my guests."

Danny Lehman had, to put it mildly, a lump that felt as big as a basketball in the pit of his stomach. This whole thing, he thought, is going to be a bust. De Niro is making fools out of the entire Federal Bureau of Investigation. I never should have listened to those guys in the first place when they asked me to come here from Philadelphia. Those boxes are no doubt either empty or full of old newspapers.

Smith looked grim. He walked over to the table and raised the lid on the first drawer that De Niro had pulled out of the steel cabinet. He looked into it, and what he did next startled everybody in the room: he took the drawer, raised it, turned it upside down, and with a quick move slapped the metal bottom. What tumbled out were bills, stacks of bills, all hundreds and fifties. He took the next drawer and did the same thing with the same result. As he grabbed the third one, one of his younger associates said, "Stop it for Chrissake, Bill, that's fucking evidence!"

Smith looked even grimmer now. He addressed De Niro: "Okay, asshole, we've got *you*. Nobody, but nobody, will buy that horseshit about the baccarat table, and I don't care if every employee in this place swears to it. You're even dumber than we thought." Up until that point all of the employees in the counting room had tried to ignore as best as they could what had been going on, but now their activities ceased entirely. Smith reached inside his jacket pocket and produced what appeared to be a printed card. "Abiding by the Miranda decision . . ." He started to read De Niro and Salgo their rights.

When he was done, he motioned with his head, with the result that two of the younger agents stepped forward and handcuffed De Niro and Salgo. "Take them downtown," Smith said. "All right, one more thing," he continued, after the co-managers of Raffles Casino had been led off. "I want to go into that place where those women are counting that money and look at something. Who's got *that* key?"

One of the men who had been standing at the counter trying to go about his own business now stepped forward. "I've got the key, sir, but I'd like to ask that you alone step in. You can understand that we have to be very, very careful about these things."

"I understand that," Smith said. "We'll do it your way."

Everybody shuffled back out into the small hallway in front of the glass-enclosed room that contained the five women, the metal boxes, and the piles of cash. Smith went in alone. Although it was impossible to hear a word of what he said, it was quite obvious what his instructions were. All action stopped in there; the five women and Smith got together and started to pull the metal racks holding those chained metal boxes away from the wall. The FBI man crawled behind them on his hands and knees; he seemed to find what he was after almost immediately.

When he came out he just said to his colleagues, "It's exactly what we thought. I think we can go back to the office now, fellas." To the employees he said, "Okay, everybody, back to work. Tell them"—he pointed to the women in the counting room—"they can do the same."

Smith turned to Danny Lehman. "I suggest you come with us so we can give you a full explanation. I think you'll find what we are going to tell you, how can I put it, of great interest, great interest."

Danny said, "Do you mind if I do that a little later, say, tomorrow?"

Smith smiled at him. "No problem, Mr. Lehman. In fact, I thought you might want to have a little time to sit down and start to enjoy things around here. It's all yours now."

Danny returned the smile. "How about if we begin right now with my inviting everybody, all of you guys, for a drink. All the liquor around here belongs to me, too."

Smith laughed and actually patted Danny on the back. "Mr. Lehman," he said, "we'd love to more than I can tell you, but I think you understand we can't do it during business hours."

Danny got the message. "Mr. Smith . . . or may I call you Bill?"

Smith answered, "Bill it is."

"Why wait until tomorrow? How would it be if we reconvene here after business hours, say around eight o'clock tonight, so that you can start at the beginning and lead me all the way through this thing."

Smith liked the idea. "It's a deal. I'll call you when I get here." But then he thought of something. "Where will I be able to reach you?"

"Hookers' corner," Danny answered.

Smith grinned. He liked that. He then issued one final command. "Mr. Downey"—the accountant now looked as if he needed a doctor—"I think you'd better come with us, too."

Downey looked at Danny as if asking for help. Danny was embarrassed. First he looked away; then he walked away. And as he was walking, he was hit by a very disturbing thought: there but for the grace of Amaretto and Sarnoff go I!

9

Danny headed for the elevator to the executive offices on the third floor. The smartass secretary was there to greet him when he reached the door that led to the general manager's office.

He looked at her for a few seconds and then said, "I'm going to ask you to do something, and if you want to do it, fine; if not, that's also fine. All right?"

The woman nodded uncertainly.

"I want you to round up some boxes: wooden boxes, cardboard cartons, whatever's around. Okay? Then I want you to round up a couple of girls to help you. Is there a secretarial pool around here somewhere?"

"Yes, sir, it's in the back."

"Good. Get two or more girls from the typing pool, and then I want all of you to collect everything, and I mean everything, you find in De Niro's office, and everything you find in Salgo's office, and put it in those boxes. Do you understand?"

"Yes, sir," she answered.

"Now, before you do that, I want you to call the head of security around here, whoever he is, and tell him to come up here. Could you do that right away?"

The secretary made the telephone call and then disappeared to attend to her various roundups. Danny decided to take the chair behind the secretary's desk and, while he was at it, to take a quick run through her papers. None proved very interesting. About five minutes later, a rather heavyset swarthy man came hurrying up the corridor. He saw Danny behind the desk and didn't approve of what he saw.

"What are you doing sitting there, and who the hell are you anyway?" he demanded.

"My name's Lehman, Danny Lehman. I own this place. What can I do for you?"

The impact of his words was immediate and devastating. "I'm terribly sorry, Mr. Lehman. I'm head of security. You asked for me, apparently."

"I did. I also asked some of the young ladies up here to pack up all the belongings of De Niro and Salgo. I want them stored somewhere secure under lock and key, and when it's done, I want you to tell me where the place is and then give me the key."

"When?" the man asked.

"Right now. Wait in De Niro's office. Nobody goes in but the girls. Nothing comes out that isn't in boxes. Right? I don't want one item missing, do you understand?"

The man didn't say a word. Instead he just disappeared into the general manager's office, closing the door behind him very, very carefully. Then, gradually, Danny Lehman started to return to normal. He'd had enough of confrontations to last him not only for the rest of the day, but for the rest of the year.

Forty-five minutes later the offices of De Niro and Salgo had already been totally sacked and packed. The head of the casino security force and the tough cookie who was De Niro's secretary jointly presented him with the key which, they explained, would open the storage room on the basement level adjacent to the underground garage, Storage Room G. By this time Danny had seen more keys in one day than in any other day of his life, and was sick of the sight of them. Nonetheless, he accepted this last one graciously and then addressed a few more words to the pair standing in front of him.

"First, I want to thank you. Second, I want to tell you that you're both fired. I'm going to have paychecks ready for you within the next half hour. I'm going to include in that final paycheck an extra month's salary in both of your cases. I'll arrange that you can pick them up at the cashier's counter downstairs. Now I want you both to pack up your things, and I want you and those things out of this building in no more than one hour from now."

Danny then turned his back on them and walked into the general manager's office, which was now bare of everything but a desk, a chair, a coffee table, a couple of sofas, and some empty bookshelves. He picked up the phone and asked to be connected with the assistant manager in charge of room reservations. Once again he said, "This is Daniel Lehman." Then: "I'm not sure if you know who I am."

"Yes, sir, I do," the man on the other end replied. "Yes, sir."

"Tell me, what is the best suite in the house?"

"It's Suite 1515, sir, in the tower."

"I want it to be ready for occupancy within thirty minutes."

"Sir, I'm afraid it's already occupied by a very important client who is, I might add, a close friend of Mr. De Niro."

The word had apparently not reached the reservations desk. "Well, kick him out. I want all of his stuff out, and the room ready to go within thirty minutes. Do you understand?"

"Yes, sir."

About forty minutes later, Danny was lying in the bathtub in Suite 1515 of the Raffles Casino and Hotel, singing loudly and badly. He never got too far with any given song, since, after just a few bars, he remembered the tune but not the words. No matter, he told himself. Danny Lehman had beaten them. Danny Lehman had arrived. Danny Lehman was happier than he had ever been at any time in his life. Because he now knew that it was just a matter of time before he got this money machine under control; just a matter of time before he would start to produce profit upon profit, starting a process which, he knew, would make him richer than all the people in the Lehman family combined, back through generation after generation to the old country and, beyond that, back no doubt to Palestine.

Atlantic City! For months now he had barely had time to think about Atlantic City. And it would still be a while before that project could be moved front and center. First he had to clean up Raffles. But after that: imagine what Atlantic City could be once again! No, not *could* be, *would* be. An instant money machine on a scale that even Henry Price could not imagine, because the Prices of this world had run out of dreams. But not Danny Lehman. Now that the nightmare was over he would have time to indulge in daydreams again. Because he'd won.

At eight o'clock sharp, bathed and shaved but dressed in his normal style—a pair of brown slacks and a yellow sport shirt—Danny Lehman was back at exactly the same table in the same bar as he had been just a month previously. Now as then, he sat in splendid isolation, since RESERVED signs had been put on all the tables surrounding his. But this time they had been placed there at his instruction, placed there by a maître d' whose demeanor exuded a humility, a docility, and a subservience so pronounced that Danny decided then and there not to fire the guy; at least, not to fire him that day.

Just a few minutes later, William Smith arrived. He greeted Danny with a big open smile and a very firm and enthusiastic handshake. "I'm off duty, Danny, and if you don't mind I'd like a double vodka martini with a twist and tell them to forget the vermouth."

Danny decided to follow suit and told the maître d' to get two of them. The man arrived back with the drinks so quickly that it was surprising that the speed of his movement didn't result in a meltdown of the ice cubes. Smith downed most of his in one go, flashed another big grin at Danny, and said, "Are you ready?"

Danny answered, "I'm ready."

"All right. Here we go. From the beginning." He paused. "De Niro and Salgo have been skimming this place for years. That's hardly an unknown practice in this town, but the word was out that these two guys were going at it in a very hot and heavy fashion. You're obviously brand-new at this business and you probably were not aware of the talk that had been going on around here. It proved, if anything, to *understate* the situation. We've now counted the cash we found in those safety-deposit drawers in the counting room, and just so you'd know, I wrote down the exact figure on a piece of paper."

He now pulled it out of his pocket. "Here are the grand totals: De Niro, five hundred and sixty-nine thousand four hundred dollars. Salgo: four hundred and eighty-seven thousand six hundred."

"I'll be damned!" Danny exclaimed. Which required a bit of acting. In actual fact, the numbers added up almost exactly, based upon what had been coming through Philadelphia via Amaretto up until just over a month ago.

Smith continued, "Now, we have no way of ascertaining over what period of time these two men accumulated these amounts. But our suspicion is that it was probably over no more than a couple of months. So you can see, Danny, this has been a very big operation indeed. From what we have been able to determine, it started out on a really small-time level, almost on the level of petty theft when compared to the amounts we are talking about today. It seems that initially these two geniuses were raiding the slots, stealing silver quarters and silver dollars and peddling them through some fencing operation that we still haven't been able to track down. There's a big missing link there. But that's getting off the main track."

Let's hope it stays on that sidetrack, Danny thought.

"Okay," Smith continued, "what they figured, and I guess correctly so, was that the controls in the counting room were simply too good and complete for any large-scale theft to escape the attention of the accountants around here. That changed, and I'll come to that in a minute. But anyway, in the beginning it was silver."

"How?" asked Danny. "How did they do it?"

"Well," the FBI man answered, "now that you own and run this place, it's the sort of thing you'd better bone up on." He continued, "As is usual with so many of these types of crime, it was so simple that it's hard to believe it worked, in retrospect. The answer lies with the people that constructed this place six or maybe seven years ago. The counting room was originally built in exactly the same position and in the same way as it stands today: nothing more, really, than a big concrete bunker slapped against the rear wall of the casino building. What somebody did—and God knows who authorized it, but somehow it must have arisen from a demand of the building inspectors, trying to conform with the building code in regard to precautions against fire—was put a fire door in the damn counting room, a door that led directly onto the parking lot at the back of the building. Now, you probably don't know this, but there is an absolute rule laid down by the Casino Control Commission of the state of Nevada from the very beginning that there can be only one method of access, one door and one door only, leading into, or, more pertinently, leading from the counting room of any casino in this state."

Smith was right. Danny had no idea that there was such a rule. In fact, he was totally ignorant of all the rules, not just this one. Out of this realization, which just now began to dawn on him, an idea started to develop. But for the moment he let Smith continue.

"What I suspect happened is that the guys who owned this place knew about that door. I don't mean De Niro and

Salgo, and I don't want to mention any other names here because I don't think they're going to come up in this investigation. As you must know, the guys that owned this place, the guys you bought out, were men of not exactly impeccable credentials. What I think happened is this: one, or more, or all of them saw the opportunity, the latent opportunity one could say, inherent in having a fire door in such a wonderful place. And instead of having the construction corrected, they had the thing plastered over, or at least more or less plastered over. Now, what I suspect further is this: those guys never used that door, but at some time, and our guess is it must have been two or three years ago, either Salgo or De Niro, we'll never know how, found out about this door and started to use it."

Smith stopped there for a moment to finish his second drink, but then continued, "I've already mentioned that we think they started out on a truly penny-ante basis."

"How?" interjected Danny.

"Well, what happens in this casino where the slots are concerned is that they're emptied out every twenty-four hours. What they do is wheel those carts—those metal carts you saw in the counting room—from machine to machine, and dump the coins into the metal boxes, which are then chained back to the cart so nobody can snatch one and run. This is done at four in the morning, because that's when the level of activity in casinos, not just this casino but every casino in general, is at its lowest ebb. You can understand why you'd want to do it at this time because it'd be rather embarrassing if too many people were there to witness the amounts of their money that the casino was carting off to its counting room. There's nobody in there counting at that time in the morning. The first shift of women counters, the ones we saw in there, arrives at eight o'clock in the morning and works until two, and the second shift works until eight o'clock in the evening, and that's when at least the counting activity in the counting room is shut down for the day. Okay so far?"

Danny nodded.

"What De Niro and Salgo would do is this: they'd go into the counting room, since they've got all the keys and combinations, and they'd unchain some or maybe all of the boxes. Then one of them would cart the metal containers out through that fire door and dump some of the contents onto a pick-up truck or whatever was parked back there, no doubt leaving a sufficient quantity in each box in order not to raise any suspicions. Then the stuff would be moved off and, as I said, would later be sold through some fencing operation, probably out of state. While one guy was raiding the counting room, no doubt the other was in the other section of that place where the credit files and everything are stored, creating a diversion, or in any case distracting the attention of anybody that was still in there at four o'clock in the morning."

Smith emptied his glass and then continued. "After all, whoever was there at that time of night would probably be as low as you can get on the organizational chart of this place, and there, 'visiting' him, would be one of the two guys who runs the place. Who's going to even consider blowing the whistle on any suspected hanky-panky under those conditions. Right?"

The more Danny listened to the FBI man, the more that idea was growing in his mind.

"Anyway, I'm sure that whether it was De Niro or Salgo who was doing his thing in the counting area, he worked in the dark, so it was really not very difficult to pull off, even on a regular basis. You've seen the physical setup there. But there's a limit to how much you can do with this sort of operation, because to a substantial degree the movement of coinage inside a casino is circular, if you know what I mean. The customers buy their rolls of coins from the cashiers; they then lose them to the slot machines; the slot machines are emptied out every twenty-four hours and the drop is brought to the counting room. It's counted, and the coinage is recycled back to the cashier. So, as I said, there is a limit to the amount of money those two guys were able to take out of circulation, and I think they reached this same conclusion at a fairly early stage. But what was still available to them was the fire door, provided that somehow they could find a way to circumvent the auditing system in regard to the really *big* money floating around in this casino, namely, that generated at the gaming tables.

"Am I going on too long?" Smith asked Danny.

"Hell no," Danny replied. He really liked this guy Smith. And he could tell that the feeling was mutual. And, despite himself, Danny was fascinated with the story Smith was telling. It was, in fact, the mirror image, seen from the inside, of the same story he'd been following for years from the outside, through the periodic visits of Amaretto and Sarnoff to Philadelphia. *Déjà vu* was the phrase they now used for that, Danny thought.

"Okay. Now, I don't know if you noticed, but there is really no way to get around the controls in the counting room. The women in there count out loud and this count is picked up by a microphone and recorded. Likewise there is a camera, in fact three video cameras, trained on that room. Again, all the activities are put on tape. Well, the audio and video tapes go to the auditing department and are used to verify the results recorded in the ledger accounts. Right? So how do you get around it?"

The question had perhaps been asked in a rhetorical manner, but the answer suddenly flashed into Danny Lehman's mind and he blurted it out. "Downey! Rupert Downey!"

"Precisely," said the FBI man. "Once they had the chief auditor in cahoots there was no problem. All they had to do was change the numbers in the ledger that they received from the counting room, and at the same time lose or make inaudible and unviewable those portions of the tapes covering the period of time for which the count was to be falsified. Once they had 'fixed' the exact amount, out the fire door it went. This time no truck was necessary. Either De Niro or Salgo would just fill up his pockets at five o'clock in the morning and walk out the back, and that would be it. One would disappear into the night while the other was putting up the smoke screen. So when it got to this point, the operation was literally unstoppable. When you've got collusion between the managers of a place like this and the auditors, then the sky's the limit. And De Niro and Salgo, I guess, were determined to aim for just that: the sky."

"But why were they stupid enough to keep that amount of the skim in the safety-deposit boxes?" Danny asked. "Why didn't it go out the fire door immediately?"

"Well, that's the sixty-four-thousand-dollar question. And we don't know the answer. All we do know is we got a tip from somebody, and we don't know who it was. It was by telephone. It might have been somebody inside the counting room or somebody out on the casino floor, or even somebody upstairs in the executive office. Or maybe somebody on the outside who's got somebody on the inside. But it certainly came from a person who was out to get the asses of De Niro and Salgo and their buddies. The informant tipped us off to the effect that there was a lot of money accumulating in some safety-deposit boxes in this casino. The same source gave us some—I might as well be honest—most of the information about who was involved and what they had been doing. But back to your question. Why did they keep that amount of money here?" Smith stopped for a minute, and then said, "What follows, you understand, is pure conjecture.

"Okay. What we suspect is this: that the fencing operation De Niro and Salgo had been using for some years folded. Or perhaps they had a falling out with the people who had been fencing for them. But in any case, the pipeline got plugged all of a sudden. Got stopped up. They nevertheless kept stealing, but they were probably afraid of keeping the steady accumulation of new cash around at home or elsewhere. I mean, there are lots of crooked people around who might have stolen it!" Smith laughed at his own joke, and Danny joined him.

"Furthermore, I think these guys had developed such a degree of overconfidence that they didn't think twice about keeping this amount of money in their safety-deposit boxes until they found a new pipeline to a new fence, or unplugged the old pipeline to the old fence."

"But how can you prove it?" Danny asked. "They claim they won it all at the baccarat tables."

"All right. I told you it was just conjecture. And between you, me, and the fence post, we can't prove a damn thing. Because, let's face it, they must have been spreading lots of joy among the baccarat dealers."

Danny privately thought that they were the next ones who had to go.

"But not to worry. We brought the IRS into this case just about an hour and a half ago. We explained our problem to them and they confirmed to us, in fact absolutely guaranteed, that the Treasury Department is going to go after these guys for criminal tax evasion, which no doubt extends over a period of years and obviously amounts to millions of dollars. As you know, the IRS doesn't normally have to prove anything. They'll just take the amounts that we found, over a million, extrapolate back, and come up with some number that is so staggering that it would mean that these guys would go to the slammer for the next twenty years at least. They'd probably get off a lot easier if they had just killed a few people. Or maybe I should say if they had killed a few more people, going on the rumors that have been floating around these two guys for years now. But all this we're hardly going to admit. As far as they will ever know, we've got the goods on them for grand theft on a monumental scale. Our story is that after we've arranged for them to get fifty years, then we'll turn them over to the guys from the IRS, who will get them for another twenty years. In the end, no doubt, we'll make a deal, as much as I hate deals. But we won't have the evidence we would need to take it all the way in a court."

"What about Downey?" Danny asked.

"Well, that's different. I kind of think that we should make a deal with him right now if he turns state's evidence. Wouldn't you agree?"

"Yes," said Danny. "For sure. I feel sorry for that guy."

"Don't," replied the FBI man. "He's a crook just like the rest of them. So that's it, Danny. . . ."

"Wow," said Danny. "Would you care for another drink?"

"With pleasure."

When the second round came, the two men just sat there in silence for a while, savoring the moment. Then the FBI man said, "When I was walking in, one of the fellows told me that you fired the head of security here. Is that right?"

"That's right," Danny replied. "In fact I want to talk to you about that." His idea was now a certainty.

"No need to talk to me about that, Danny. I have no doubt that if there was anybody else here who was also involved in this operation it must have been him. We'll get to him in due course."

"I didn't mean that at all, Bill."

"No? Sorry."

"I might as well be rather blunt. I'd like you to take over as the head security man of this place. I'd pay you very well and you'd have a completely free hand. I'd ask you to do just one thing initially and that would be to clean this place out from the top to the bottom. Anybody, and I mean anybody, with anything in his background, with any funny connections, in fact with anything suspicious at all, I would want out! Because what I intend to do is to start this place all over again with an absolutely clean slate, and then I intend to keep it that way. You know there's this myth going around that the very nature of the gaming business dictates that casinos can only be run successfully by crooks: gambling, prostitution, crime, criminal operators . . . they all go together, in fact, have to go together. Well, I'm going to prove them wrong.

"Secondly," Danny continued, "I want you to teach me the rules of the game here, and how everybody tries to break them. Do you want to help me?"

Bill Smith did not hesitate. "You're goddamn right I do, Danny. Give me three months. I've got a few things to take care of first, not the least of which are De Niro and Salgo."

"Three months. You've got it. Are you willing to shake on it?"

"Yessir, Mr. Lehman."

"Okay, Bill, thanks, and we'll be in touch. In fact I'll have a contract drawn up this week."

"You're on," said Smith as he left.

After Danny had lost sight of Smith he suddenly realized they hadn't exchanged one word about salary. And the more he thought about it, the better he liked it. Smith trusted him to be fair, to be correct. When his luck had turned, it had turned completely!

It was now approaching nine o'clock on that evening of June 9, 1969. And hookers' corner was starting to fill up with hookers. In contrast to the last time Danny had sat there, however, not one of them cast even a passing glance in his direction. But there was no apparent change in the level of activity on the casino floor. It was then, exactly then, that Danny decided what had to be done.

He started to raise his right hand to beckon the maître d', but it had barely risen six inches above the table before the man was already scurrying in his direction. "Bring me a phone!" Danny ordered. And the maître d' not only brought a phone, plugged it in, and placed the instrument in front of Danny, but also picked up the receiver and placed it gently

in Danny's right hand, which was still six inches above the
table. Then the man retreated, facing Danny in a position of
obeisance that would have been more fitting in Riyadh at
the king's palace than it was in Las Vegas at hookers' corner. But it was a scene that further confirmed the validity of
the idea that was starting to grow at an almost explosive
rate in Danny's mind.

It took the hotel operator ten minutes to finally track
down Danny's hotshot Hollywood agent. All that Danny
said to Mort Granville was that he'd appreciate it if he'd get
on the next plane to Vegas. Granville agreed immediately.
The next call was to his Philadelphia lawyer, to whom he
gave exactly the same instructions.

He had just replaced the receiver for the second time
when somebody patted him very gently on the head from
behind. He tilted back to see who had dared pull such a
stunt. And when he did, all he could see, at least initially,
was a white sweater filled with two of the most shapely
breasts that Danny Lehman had ever observed, at least from
that angle. But then he saw above that marvelous sweater an
even more marvelous face. A black face.

"Sandra Lee!" he exclaimed. "You're exactly the right
thing at the right time."

The woman leaned down and kissed him first on the forehead and then firmly on his lips. "Your place or mine?" she
asked.

"Mine," Danny replied immediately.

"And what about," she continued, "you know, about that
problem you were having the last time we saw each other?"

"Solved, baby," he replied. Then he remembered that
those two goons with blue suits were probably still on the
payroll. But that, he thought, could certainly wait. After all,
a man had to set priorities in life.

"So where's your place?" the woman asked.

"I'll show you right now."

He got up and took her hand, and again, as last time, this

incongruous pair began to work their way across the casino floor. But this time, instead of heading for the exit, they headed for the elevator bank in the hotel tower. As Danny walked beside this woman he was, if anything, more impressed than before by the regal manner in which she carried herself, looking first left, then right, upon the motley crowd, more than a few of whom stopped to gaze. Now, as before, her style of dress could not have been more simple: a white cashmere sweater and a narrow black skirt, slit almost up to the hip, but worn in a way that was highly suggestive, yet at the same time perfectly discreet.

When Danny led the way into Suite 1515, the first thing that Sandra Lee did was emit a low whistle. "Honey," she said, "I knew you had class, but I didn't know you had *this* much class." She then turned to him and nearly smothered him with a bear hug into which she put every ounce of pressure she could muster from her long, lithe black body. "Sweetie, I think what you need now is a good piece of ass."

With that she stepped back and pulled off her white sweater with one swift movement. She wore no brassiere because it was obvious that what had been beneath that white sweater needed no support. She then opened four buttons at the side of the black slit skirt and, again with a swift, sure movement, stepped out of it. It was now apparent that Sandra Lee was not in the habit of wearing any underwear at all.

"Now I am going to do you, Danny," she said. With the same sureness she soon had Danny undressed and on the bed, where she proceeded first to arouse him with a tongue that seemed never to stop, and then to fuck him with a style, imagination, and vigor that left Danny Lehman as drained as he had ever been in his life. And when she rolled off him for the last time, she said, "Honey, let's eat."

Lying on her stomach with her long legs and high heels in the air, heels that for some reason she had decided to put back on, she picked up the phone and ordered a complete menu that began with Iranian caviar, moved on to onion soup, and ended up with roast pheasant. When she was done she put her hand over the phone, and asked, "Danny, what do you drink?"

"It's got to be champagne, the best they've got. This is my big night. The first that I've had in many a month. So get the best."

She returned to the phone and said, "Send up a bottle of Cristal. No, make that *two* bottles of Cristal. Two bottles and two ice buckets and listen, honky, I want that up here within five minutes or it's going to be your ass!" And she slammed the phone down and laughed like hell.

Danny loved it. He started to giggle, which got her going even more, and when they both finally got over it, he said, "Sandra Lee, I like you. I like your style. I think we're going to get along just fine." Then: "We'd better get some clothes on before that champagne arrives."

"Fuck the clothes," said Sandra Lee. "All we are going to do is turn the thermostat up, and if somebody doesn't like it, screw him."

The champagne arrived in less than five minutes, and it was Sandra Lee who went to the door to let the waiter in, still simply clad in gold earrings and high heels. But Danny couldn't do it. He was from Philadelphia, after all. So he waited in the bathroom until the delivery had been completed.

"Come on out, you chickenshit," called Sandra. He did, and when the food arrived they both went through exactly the same performance. Then the two of them spent the next couple of hours eating and drinking and fooling around a little bit, then drinking and eating some more. Around midnight Sandra Lee suddenly made a proposal. "Danny," she said, "I don't want you to get bored. I've got a girlfriend, in fact she's my roommate, and her name is Shirley-Anne. Why don't I call her up and ask her to come over and we'll make a little party of it?"

She did, and later the two black hookers and Danny Lehman were all sitting in the bathtub in Suite 1515 of the Raffles Hotel and Casino. They were drinking from their fourth bottle of Cristal champagne, which had been delivered by a waiter who wouldn't have exchanged jobs with anybody that night, especially when he entered the room with the third and fourth bottles, as well as two additional ice buckets, to find not only one tall black naked woman there, but now a second, dressed in exactly the same way, except for the fact that she wore neither earrings nor shoes.

"Girls!" Danny suddenly asked. "If you owned this place, what would you do with it?"

"For one thing," Shirley-Anne said, "I'd sure as hell put in a much bigger bathtub. Man, I'm wedged in here so I can hardly breathe, much less move."

Danny reached down and put his hand between her thighs, explaining that he was going to try to unwedge her, a move that got all of them giggling again. But then Danny said, "You're right, you're absolutely right. What else?"

"Are you asking *me* again?" Shirley-Anne said.

"Yes."

"Mirrors. You've got to have mirrors all over the place, don't you. It's more fun that way."

Again Danny said, "You're right."

"What they should do," the black woman continued, "is make this look like a very elegant cathouse. That's what the guys want when they come here, isn't it? And so do their wives if they get taken along. But they don't want to come to a cheap whorehouse like this goddamn place. It's got to be like an expensive French or Italian whorehouse. Aren't I right, Sandra Lee?"

"You're absolutely right, honey, but why are you asking all this?" Sandra asked Danny, as she gently began to massage him below the sudsy waves.

"Because I think I probably forgot to tell you girls something. I bought this place a couple of months ago."

"You bought what, honey?" asked Shirley-Anne.

"This place, Shirley-Anne. Raffles. The casino. The hotel. Everything. It's mine now."

Sandra Lee suspended her massage, extracted her hands from the suds and put them on both sides of Danny's head, pulled him even closer, and said, "Danny boy, I knew it, I just knew it; you're something special!"

The phone rang, and when Danny dripped his way across the room to pick it up it was his Hollywood agent reporting in. Six hours later it was Sandra Lee who took the phone when it rang again, since Danny Lehman was out cold, having been totally saturated with both alcohol and sex. She told the man who claimed he was Mr. Lehman's lawyer from Philadelphia the same thing that Danny had told his Hollywood agent, namely, "Mr. Lehman's busy right now. Call him this afternoon, but not too early this afternoon." In fact, all three of them slept until 3 P.M.

The next day Danny Lehman was installed behind De Niro's desk and was explaining to Benjamin Shea and Mort Granville, the two charter members of his board of directors, everything—almost everything, since he left out Sandra Lee and Shirley-Anne—that had happened during the previous forty-eight hours. When finished, he expressed his conclusions very succinctly. "What all this proves is that this casino operation has always been profitable in the past. But when you look around, you can't help but wonder for how long. If things around here are run in the future the same way as they've been in the past, this place is going to go broke fast, even with De Niro and Salgo gone. It's quite obvious that Raffles is rapidly losing its clientele. Who wants to gamble in a place with lousy service in a building where the paint's peeling? This casino's got to be rebuilt from the ground up, and that's exactly what we're going to do. I'm going to close this place down at the end of the week. I'm going to fire most of the employees. I'm going to hire the best goddamn architect and the best goddamn interior decorator that I can find. And we're going to redo it from scratch."

Neither Granville nor Shea wanted to say a word, it seemed, so Danny continued. "And I'm going to do something else. I'm going to change the name. I've been thinking about it for some time now, and what we need is a name that expresses class. We want this place to be a place that people are going to fight to get into, because it's going to be, you know, like a private club, not for everybody, not for the masses, but something exclusive, a place with a reputation like a Maserati or a Rolls-Royce, and the name's got to express all of that.

"Last night I spent six hours looking around this town. I was in and out of every big casino here. And the only place that even comes close to what I'm talking about is Caesars Palace. The place was packed! So I asked around why. It's all due to a guy by the name of Cliff Perlman. Everybody says he's a genius. He created Caesars Palace and in the process established new standards for the entire casino industry. So why not copy success? I'm going Caesars and Perlman one further.

"What we are going to call this place is"—here he paused for dramatic effect—"the Palace. That's what we're going to call it. *The* Palace. Because it's going to be *the* gambling palace, not just of Vegas and not just of the United States, but the gambling palace of the whole goddamn world. Our place, our Palace, is going to be to the gambling business what Buckingham Palace is to royalty: top of the league. In one word, it will have *class!*"

10

Exactly one week later, the Raffles Hotel and Casino closed its doors for good. True to his word, Danny fired almost two thirds of the casino's employees outright, and the rest of them were told that when the casino reopened, possibly, just possibly, they might be kept on.

Danny then decided that what he needed most urgently were two things: an architect and more money. The architect he found almost immediately. He had heard about a man up in San Francisco who was a friend of the Shah's, a confidant of the Kennedys, an architect to the people who ran the world, a man who built elite structures for the elite. Danny flew up to San Francisco to meet him and immediately told him what he wanted: a palace in the desert of Nevada, a palace to top all palaces. Not, he stressed, just a copy of Caesars Palace, but something on a much higher plane: a place that *reeked* of splendor and exclusivity.

Danny confessed that he didn't know exactly how to go about it, but he'd heard that this man knew about desert palaces because of the work he did in places like Iran and Saudi Arabia. It was true. Then Danny mumbled something about structures he had read of in such places as Persepolis, Jidda, and Riyadh. The architect knew of them, but he wondered if it would be altogether appropriate, and he tried to put it as discreetly as possible, to use as models structures that had been essentially inspired by the Muslim faith. Well, that stopped Danny for a while, since he hadn't really thought about it from that angle. His inspiration had come from the *National Geographic* magazine, which his mother subscribed to for him. As the conversation progressed over a fish lunch at the Washington Square Bar and Grill in the North Beach part of town, the architect gradually brought him around to the concept that what he really wanted was a palace, yes, but a modern palace filled with exclusivity *and* decadence. He suggested that though Danny had been right in searching for the correct motif in antiquity, he had probably gone a thousand or so miles too far east. The best model for Danny's purpose in all of the ancient world was still that of Rome, he said. Cliff Perlman had been right when he had used the specifically Roman motif for Caesars.

Then he continued, "But what you need is *real* fountains and baths, *real* marble and *real* statues. Not kitsch like they've got at all the other places in Vegas. Let me make a suggestion, Mr. Lehman. Go to Rome, go to Pompeii, visit Herculaneum, tour Sicily and look at Syracuse and Agrigento, and you will see what I mean." Then he added, "But to make it work we'll have to add neon lights and air conditioning and wall-to-wall carpeting."

Danny was already convinced. Would the Shah hire a dummy? Then came the real question. How much would it take to re-create out of the old casino the ultimate Roman palace with neon lights that the architect envisioned? "Twenty-five million dollars minimum, but my guess is it will cost forty million before we're through" was the answer.

"How much would you need to start?" Danny asked.

"Twenty million, Mr. Lehman. In the form of an irrevocable letter of credit. After all, you're not exactly General Motors." It would be a very hot day in San Francisco, the architect had already concluded, before he ever saw that kind of money from this guy.

* * *

The first thing Danny did when he got back to Las Vegas was to go to a phone booth and put a call through to Fort Lauderdale. Meyers was not in. Then Danny had a better thought. Why give those guys any big ideas that he, Danny Lehman, really needed them?

He went back to the hotel, called his attorney, and instructed Shea to put the American Coin, Metals, and Currency Exchange on the market. He told him he wanted a quick sale. He realized that this would not allow him to get the maximum price, but he was now convinced that he was on the right track in Las Vegas and that time was of paramount importance. If he ever went back to Fort Lauderdale for more money it would be for some really big money—Atlantic City money.

Between now, Las Vegas, and then, Atlantic City, he had to prove himself, on his own. A letter of intent was signed ten days later. A New York conglomerate agreed to buy Danny out for a total consideration of twenty-two million dollars cash, a price well above anything Danny had expected to get. After paying off the loan he had taken out in Philadelphia in order to finance the initial cash down payment on Raffles, he would still be left with a hefty bank balance. Armed with that, or at least the documented promise of a hefty bank balance when the transaction was completed, Danny managed to negotiate a twenty-million-dollar revolving line of credit with a Los Angeles bank, or at least his lawyer from Philadelphia did. Days later, Danny was issued a letter of credit for the same amount.

When his bank in Southern California called the architect's bank in Northern California informing them of this fact, the temperature in San Francisco was ninety-two degrees, the hottest day of the year. The architect was impressed! A Shah this Lehman fellow wasn't, but to produce both the twenty million and the hottest day of the year that quickly: not bad.

The reconstruction of the casino and hotel began on July 15, 1969. Three days later, Danny Lehman, who by this time had reached a stage of total exhaustion, decided to take some time off. He would go to Rome as the architect had suggested. And while he was in Europe, he would also look around at some of the casinos in that part of the world. For Danny had a feeling in his gut that he might find something, maybe the missing elements in that grand design which he sought, just as only five years earlier he had discovered the entire foreign exchange business, something which, after all, had just netted him twenty-two million dollars!

When three days later the man in charge of the reception desk at Claridge's looked up to find a short, pudgy American wearing a wine-colored sport jacket over a pink shirt with white tropical trousers above brown loafers, and beside him a six-foot-two-inch negress clad in a green dress with a décolletage that ended well down into her midriff, he knew that somebody had made a terrible, terrible mistake.

"Your name, sir?" he asked.

"Lehman. Daniel Lehman," the American answered.

"One moment, sir," the man at Claridge's replied. He went into the office to check the list of those clients' names deemed acceptable for lodging by the management of Claridge's, because he knew that nobody, but nobody, could have been granted a reservation if his name wasn't recorded there. And how did one get one's name registered in the beginning? Only upon the recommendation of somebody who was already there, naturally.

Lehman? Lehman? Of course. There was the obvious reason for this unfortunate mistake. Someone had surely mistaken this man for one of the partners of that prestigious firm of Lehman Brothers in New York. George Ball had been at the hotel just last week. Or was it a mistake? One could never be absolutely sure where Americans were concerned. The assistant manager, clad in tailcoat and striped trousers, went back to check. "You are, sir, I believe, from Lehman Brothers, the investment bank in New York, are you not?"

"No. I'm from Las Vegas. But it was a bank, my bank in Los Angeles, which promised to fix me up with a room in London. I borrowed twenty million dollars from them, and so they got me a hotel room here."

It was now decision time for Claridge's: to kick out a couple who looked like a pimp and his whore and risk a confrontation that might never end, causing discomfort for the other guests who, as they came and went, were already casting curious glances in the direction of this unique pair—or to check them in as quickly as possible and hope that they would stay in the room and out of sight during their stay. The assistant manager decided on the latter course of action, and within minutes Danny Lehman and Sandra Lee were in a suite on the third floor, one that was going to set Danny back two hundred pounds a night, but he didn't know that yet. It was a curious mélange of Victoriana and art deco that is uniquely Claridge's.

"Do you like it, honey?" Sandra Lee asked.

"It looks awfully goddamn old-fashioned to me," Danny replied. "It reminds me of something my grandma might have liked. Man," he added, "the British are sure behind the times."

Sandra Lee, of course, checked out the bathroom next, but she was delighted at what she found. "Come here, Danny. Look at this stuff. My God, the fixtures must be fifty years old. And look at the old mirrors, the marble! It's beautiful. I love it!"

"Beautiful? Are you kidding? It looks a bit seedy to me. I'll tell you something. I was afraid to ask that guy downstairs how much the room would be, but boy, if they charge me more than fifty bucks a night for this, I'm sure as hell going to complain."

They took a nap, but by six-thirty that evening Danny

was ready to go. "Honey, I'm going to call the front desk," he said, "and ask them for the names of the best casinos in this town."

"You don't have to do that," Sandra Lee answered.

"Why not?" he asked.

"Because I know where they gamble here. Since they don't have casinos, they do it at clubs. I not only know the names of some clubs, I even know where they are. The best one is Crockford's. It's off Pall Mall. The other one is Les Ambassadeurs. It's a restaurant and nightclub, with gambling thrown in. That's where the very upper class go to have their fun. It's opposite the Hilton."

While she was speaking, Lehman watched her, his eyes growing ever wider with amazement. When she was done, he expressed just that. "How in the world do you know these things?"

"Honey, what you mean is how in the world could a black hooker from Las Vegas know anything about London, England. Isn't that right?" It was right and they both knew it. "Well, Danny, if you want the truth I'll tell you," Sandra Lee said. "I've got a client from London. He always stays at the Sands. He is in the insurance business, with Lloyd's, if I remember correctly, which also happens to be here in London, my dear. About a year ago he did very well at the Sands and I sat beside him the entire time. The next day we both flew to London. He put me up in the Savoy and every night we dined exquisitely and danced and gambled, and that's how this big black hooker from Las Vegas knows a few things she probably shouldn't."

"Ahh, come on, cut it out, Sandra Lee. I didn't mean it that way."

"I know you didn't mean it that way, but that's the way it came out," she answered.

"I'm sorry. What matters is that we know where we want to go tonight. What was the name of the first one again?"

"Crockford's. But it's not that simple. You can't just go

there. Like I told you, in London these casinos are private
clubs. You have to be a member to get in, or"—and she
paused—"you have to know a member who will vouch for
you."

"And do you think your friend would do that?"

Sandra Lee smiled. "For me, yes. For you?" She spread
her hands, but then burst out in a giggle. "Of course he
would, Danny! I'll call him, or at least I'll try to call him. I
don't think he's in London that much of the time. But who
knows, we might be lucky. I'll give it a try, okay?"

She went to her immense black purse and pulled out a
very thick, well-thumbed notebook, which Danny eyed with
some awe and more than a little discomfort.

She read his mind immediately. "Danny, this isn't just
where I keep my telephone numbers. I keep everything in
here that I want to remember: recipes, restaurants, the
names of records I want to buy. All sorts of things worth
remembering for a lady," she said, letting just a little mocking smile cross her face.

Danny liked the answer. In fact, he liked the answer a lot
because it seemed honest and rather sensible. He liked girls
who played it straight.

"I've got two numbers," Sandra Lee went on. "One here
in London and one in a place somewhere outside called
Amersham. I think I'll try the second first." She did, and
she got the man she sought immediately. They chatted back
and forth for a number of minutes, and when she hung up,
she said, "Danny, we have to get dressed in a rather spiffy
way. My friend—his name's Douglas Penn—will be picking
us up 'within the hour,' as he put it. Now I'm going to put
on something very black, and I would suggest—if you don't
mind, Danny, I would strongly recommend—that you put
on that blue suit of yours with a white shirt and a striped tie.
You know, the one I gave you just before we left."

"The tie? Are you sure?"

"The tie, Danny."

Douglas Penn looked exactly the way an upper-class Englishman should look. He was tall. He was thin. He carried an umbrella and he wore a waistcoat. He had red cheeks and he spoke with both a slight stutter and a slight lisp. He drove a Bentley aggressively, so he covered the distance between Claridge's and Crockford's in less than a quarter of an hour.

Crockford's was housed in a huge, rather unassuming stone mansion, and though a club, it was hardly in the class of an Athenaeum or a White's. There was, however, a substantial overlap of their membership lists. That meant that one could have lunch in the hushed dining room of the Athenaeum with one's banker, bishop, or member of Parliament, and then have dinner in the very lively atmosphere of Crockford's, perhaps with a chum from one's years at Oxford, or more probably with one's mistress, or with someone one hoped might become one's mistress.

At Crockford's they greeted Douglas Penn like an old friend and not an eyebrow was even slightly raised when he introduced Sandra Lee and Danny as his guests. A quick look around downstairs indicated why: the posh restaurant there was crowded with a mixture of types and races. Here a Chinese person, there a Pakistani. At one table a group of young Arabs in full desert dress, there a colored gentleman in tribal robes dining with a young girl who looked as if she was playing truant from her English boarding school. It was London at its best.

"Now," said the host, "should we eat here and then go upstairs, or should we go upstairs and eat later at Les Ambassadeurs?" Mr. Penn looked at Sandra Lee and Sandra Lee looked at Danny Lehman.

"After the flight, neither of us is particularly hungry right now," Danny said, "so let's go upstairs if that's where the gaming takes place."

"So be it," replied Douglas Penn.

They walked up the stairs and entered a foyer in which a

number of people were gathered in front of what looked like a cloakroom, which, upon second glance, was hardly its function anymore, since there was a man behind the ledge who was accepting not overcoats but money. To be more precise, money was being handed over from the outside and chips, very large chips by American standards, were being returned from the inside. It was not just the size of the chips that was in stark contrast to what Danny was now used to in American casinos; the crowd stood in equal contrast. For almost everybody up there, from the money changer in the "cloakroom" to the "host" who now greeted them, and especially Douglas Penn, in an especially effusive manner to the "guests": all were dressed in a manner which, at least from an American point of view, one would consider as formal. Most of the men were in black tie, and more than a couple of winged collars; the women, for the most part, wore full-length gowns, enhanced by what appeared to be extraordinarily expensive jewelry. Crockford's no more resembled a Vegas casino than did Claridge's a Holiday Inn. In fact, Douglas Penn had explained to them in the car, no one, but no one, referred to an establishment such as Crockford's as a casino, it was a club with gaming privileges, which prompted Sandra Lee to say to Danny, "I told you so."

The upstairs itself was divided up into three large rooms, each the size of very large living rooms, and a fourth, smaller one, which functioned as the bar area. Two of the gaming rooms were devoted to roulette and what appeared to be bridge games, of all things, and the other room to a game that was quite obviously the one that was providing all of the action. There were three tables in that central gaming room and all of them were going full blast. In fact, around each table, which seated a dozen people, there was a full row of spectators standing behind the seated players, sometimes two deep.

"What's going on there?" Danny asked as he stood in the foyer, still observing the scene from a distance.

"Chemmy," answered Douglas Penn.

"What?" Danny asked.

"Chemmy, my dear chap. That's the word we English use for chemin de fer. Foreign languages have never been our strength, you know," explained Douglas Penn.

Danny still looked puzzled, since his French was not weak, it was nonexistent.

"You call it baccarat," continued the Englishman; "that's from *baccara,* which is also French, named for the town of Baccarat, where the crystal is made.

"I see," said Danny, who didn't know anything about crystal either, and who still understood very little about gaming. To save him any embarrassment, Sandra Lee intervened. "You know, Danny," she said, "they tried to make it the big game at the Sands. It was Toni Manzoni who introduced it there. He's one of our local Cubans. It was a bust when they started it, and it's been nothing else ever since. It's too complicated."

"My dear," the Englishman said, "you are half right. I've been to the Sands." He was too discreet to mention with whom. "And I agree fully with what you just said about it being a bust there. But I can't understand it. Chemmy is definitely not complicated. You Americans don't know what you're missing. Baccarat, chemmy, chemin de fer, I don't care what you call it: it's the most exciting game in the entire world. Come watch and listen for a while. You'll agree with me, Mr. Lehman, I assure you."

All three of them moved up to the middle table. It was a long table shaped like two horseshoes facing each other, or to some people's eyes it was shaped more like a kidney. In the indenture sat a dealer. Around him, to his right and left, sat nine players. They seemed to be starting a new game because there was an immense number of cards on the table—312, or six decks to be precise—upon which the dealer was focusing his attention. They were shuffled and then stacked and then shuffled again and then stacked again, and put into a wooden container shaped somewhat like a shoe, which is exactly what they call it in the United States. In Europe they cling to the old terminology and call it the *sabot,* which means exactly the same thing. And it is the path of movement of this sabot, which travels slowly and counterclockwise as it is passed from player to player till the game is over, which gave rise to the original name of this game, namely, *chemin de fer,* the French term for a railroad. It was a railroad that could provide a very fast ride to both the promised land and to disaster, as subsequent events soon demonstrated.

At the table in front of them, with the six decks of cards now in the shoe, the dealer looked around at his audience of nine people and asked, "Ladies and gentlemen, what am I bid?" Somebody called out a hundred pounds, the next a hundred and fifty, a third, a woman, three hundred; and then a swarthy fat man, who seemed to be of Egyptian origin, bid one thousand pounds with an air of finality that immediately proved justified. For it stopped the bidding. "I don't follow," Danny now whispered to his English host.

"In chemin de fer the person who bids the highest initial bet gets to act as the 'bank.' He can continue to act as the bank as long as he continues to win. When he loses, or decides he's had enough, he passes the shoe to the person on his right, who becomes the new banker. The cards in one shoe are dealt down to the last seven or eight cards. Then they shuffle up again, and the bank is auctioned off anew. Remember: the holder of the shoe is always the banker. And all the other players can only bet against him. So now it will be everybody against that Middle Eastern gentleman."

The Egyptian who had been willing to put up the largest amount of money in order to act as the bank now pushed ten chips, denominated at one hundred pounds each, into the center of the table. The dealer counted them and then pushed the sabot to the Egyptian, now officially the banker, and the action began. It was amazingly quick and amazingly simple. The Egyptian drew one card from the box and slid it across the table to the croupier. The card remained there face down. Then the Egyptian drew a second card and, without looking at it, slid it partially under the shoe from whence it had come. Then he drew out a third card and again slid it across the table to the croupier, who again let it lie there face down. Finally a fourth card was extracted from the shoe and likewise partially shoved under the wooden sabot immediately in front of the banker.

The croupier, still not turning them over, took the two cards in front of him in the middle of the table and pushed them over to a woman seated immediately to his left. She took them in hand, looked at them carefully, and then put them back down on the table, again face down, and passed them back to the croupier. Danny Lehman, who was getting impatient, leaned over to his English companion and asked in a hoarse whisper, "What was that all about?"

The Englishman leaned back and told him, "It was about nothing, absolutely nothing. It is just courtesy, a formality. This game is a pure matter of luck. No skill at all is involved, absolutely none. That woman has no more influence on the outcome of this game than the man in the moon, or for that matter that Middle Eastern type or even the croupier. It's simple luck where all of them are concerned."

Danny Lehman grunted, and it did not seem to be a grunt of approval. The pointless ritual completed, the croupier now took the players' two cards and turned them face up. They were a king of spades and a five of hearts. The king of spades equaled zero and the five of hearts its face value.

"*Cinq,*" he called out. He then nodded to the Egyptian, who drew his two cards from beneath the shoe and turned them over. They were a three of diamonds and a five of clubs: a total of eight.

"*Huit,*" the croupier called out and added, "*La petite.*"

The next move was that the croupier quickly proceeded to rake all the players' chips from in front of each of them and added them to the banker's pile in the middle of the table. He then slid the four used cards through two slots, the banker's cards through a slot on his right and the players' two cards, or those that had been dealt to him in his role as agent for the other players, through a slot on his left. This done, he nodded to the Egyptian.

Danny Lehman again whispered, this time rather loudly, to the tall, slim Englishman beside him, "What happened?"

The Englishman raised his hand just slightly, indicating that Danny had somewhat exceeded the tolerated level of decibels, and answered, "The banker, the Egyptian, had a five and a three, which equals eight. The croupier, acting for the rest of the players, drew a king and a five. In this game, all the face cards count zero, so the players' king and the five added up to five. The whole point of this game, in fact the one and only point, is that he who gets closest to nine wins." He continued, "As you saw, the Egyptian got closer with his hand, totaling eight, than did the players with their hand, totaling five. So he won."

"That's it?" Danny asked.

"Almost. If after the initial two cards are dealt neither hand totals either eight or nine, then a third and final card is dealt to both, according to a fixed set of rules. The hand with three cards with a total count closest to nine then wins, regardless of the total, unless they tie. That's the whole game. The only other thing that you have to know is that no hand can ever total more than nine. For instance, if a hand contains two cards, say a six and a five, which would otherwise total eleven, in chemin de fer and baccarat you drop the first digit so that the eleven becomes a one; or a fourteen becomes a four. A three-card total of twenty, for example, ends up as a zero, as far from nine as you will ever get. It's the simplest game in the world. It's also the most exciting game in the world. Now just watch!"

The Egyptian dealt a card to the croupier, one to himself,
the second card to the croupier, the second card to himself.
The croupier pushed his two cards across the table, this time
to an elderly, very distinguished-looking man dressed in
tails, who in turn gave them but a cursory glance and
pushed them back to the croupier, who then turned them
face up. This time the players' cards added up to seven; the
Egyptian's cards again added up to eight.

"Huit," the croupier again called out, and again added,
"La petite."

"What did he say?" Danny asked.

"Eight, verifying that the banker has won again. And *'la
petite,'* indicating that it was a 'natural,' meaning that the
banker's hand wins automatically. No more cards need to be
dealt."

There was no doubt that the Englishman's interpretation
of events was correct, since the croupier now raked in all the
chips that had been bet in front of the eight other people
sitting around the table, and once again pushed them onto
the pile in the center of the table. The Egyptian then proceeded to win three further times in succession, each time
with a natural. Each time the bank money in the middle of
the chemin de fer table again doubled: from four thousand
pounds to eight thousand, then sixteen thousand, and finally
thirty-two thousand pounds sterling. The murmur around
the table had increased to a quick chatter when the pile had
grown to sixteen thousand. But now at thirty-two it had
grown to a sharp hum, very muffled, to be sure. Although
the two other chemin de fer tables in the room were still
going full blast, neither had a single spectator around them
any longer. All attention was focused on the center table,
and on the Egyptian who just sat there saying not a word,
sipping from a glass of champagne once in a while, and
puffing incessantly on a dark, ugly-smelling cigar, a habit
that seemed to have been lifelong from the stained appearance of his teeth.

But now he stopped both the sipping and puffing and just sat there in an almost comatose condition. All eyes around the table and from the rows behind were on him, and quickly the room became almost totally silent. Even the players at the other tables seemed to sense that something very big was about to happen. Finally the banker moved to reach into his pocket and pull out what looked like a card.

Danny could not contain himself any longer. He again leaned over and asked, "Now what the hell's he doing?"

The Englishman replied, "He's probably got a system. Maybe he's checking the odds. By God, if I were he I would get up and leave!"

The Egyptian did not get up and leave. He nodded at the croupier and then the croupier nodded at the players around the table, soliciting once again their bets against the thirty-two-thousand-pound bank. But suddenly the center of action shifted. A young man in Arab headdress, who had thus far not even participated in any of the action, now spoke out in a very soft but highly distinctive voice. "Banco," he called.

Danny had watched him on different occasions out of the corner of his eye because, although the man had a large pile of chips in front of him, all one-hundred-pound chips, he had just sat there, betting nothing, drinking nothing . . . just chain-smoking Gauloise Bleu cigarettes. Now his single word galvanized the room to the point of evoking gasps from a couple of ladies in the audience, no doubt more theatrical than real, but certainly adding to the fun. Again Danny nudged his English companion and asked, this time with rising excitement in his voice, "What's happening?"

"That Arab chap has just preempted everybody. Any player can do that anytime by calling out 'Banco.' He's preempted on all other bets that the other players could have made against the Egyptian. Now it's the Arab against the Egyptian. It's going to be the bank's thirty-two thousand pounds there on the table against the thirty-two thousand

pounds which that Arab chap is now going to have to come
up with. Watch and you'll see what I mean about this game.
Just keep quiet and watch!"

The Arab motioned to the croupier; he, in turn, motioned
to another official of the gaming room, who walked over to
stand behind the Arab and then leaned down to listen to
what the Arab wanted. The man nodded, went back to the
foyer, and returned immediately bearing a large number of
chips of a quite different color. He handed them to the Arab.
When the Arab pushed thirty-two of them onto the center
of the table, it was obvious to all of the participants and
spectators that they were denominated at one thousand British pounds each—the equivalent of two thousand four hundred dollars each. This meant that the grand total that was
now in the pot at the center of that chemin de fer table at
Crockford's in London on that warm summer night was the
equivalent of almost one hundred and fifty-four thousand
dollars. Or calculated in yet another way, one that was quite
appropriate considering that there were now only two men,
both from the Middle East, involved, the pot was the equivalent of sixty-six thousand, six hundred barrels of oil. Remember, this was 1969.

By now one could notice just the slightest hint of perspiration on the brow of the Egyptian as he began to deal the
cards from the shoe. When the cards were turned face up,
the player's hand consisted of a three of hearts and an ace of
diamonds. In chemin de fer an ace counts as one, so the
player's hand totaled four. He signaled that he needed a
third card. In front of the banker there were a five of clubs
and a king of hearts. His total was five. First the player had
to draw.

The perspiration on the Egyptian's brow was becoming a
full-fledged sweat, and in fact a couple of drops of water
now began to roll from his forehead to his cheek and then
dripped down onto the green baize that covered the table.
He drew a card and shoved it across to the dealer, who

immediately turned it up. It was a four. A four of hearts. The room was now completely silent. All action at the other tables had completely ceased.

The banker had the option of drawing a third card or not. He hesitated and then drew the next card. The last card. The bank's card. Slowly the Egyptian turned it up. It was another five of clubs. Zero. The bank had lost. Finally and massively.

The dealer, having taken 5 percent of the chips from the pot for the house, swiftly pushed the remaining chips over to the soft-spoken Arab on his left. The room was by now totally still as everybody watched the Egyptian. He was still sweating profusely. But his color had not changed, his hands were still steady as he lit up a new cigar, and his voice was firm as he ordered more champagne. He obviously intended to stay. "Bravo," said Mr. Penn. And he was seconded by at least half a dozen other voices. This Egyptian knew how to play the game.

The object of their admiration now passed the shoe containing the cards to an old dowager sitting to his right. Then he requested more chips, this time in a loud voice. He wanted thirty-two thousand pounds' worth. He then stared at the young Arab, and his gaze remained fixed on him for a full half minute.

Suddenly Danny Lehman had had enough. "You're right," he said to Penn. "You're absolutely right. There is no game in the world that even comes close to this. Let's go."

The next stop was Les Ambassadeurs, where they dined and danced, and then went upstairs to the gaming tables of that establishment. It was the same thing all over again: roulette and chemin de fer, but, as at Crockford's, it was the chemin de fer tables that attracted all the attention, and it was at these tables that tens of thousands of pounds were changing hands every ten or fifteen minutes. It was there that Danny again noticed that at the end of play the croupier was always extracting a certain number of chips and placing them in front of himself.

"Why's that?" he asked Douglas Penn.

"Oh," the Englishman said, "the house always collects 5 percent from all winning banks."

Danny made a mental note of that. True, it needed even further simplification to go over really big in the States. But there was now not even the slightest doubt in Danny's mind that chemin de fer—or baccarat—and The Palace were meant for each other. Just one day in Europe and he'd already found what he wanted. When they got back to Claridge's, Danny told Sandra Lee that he'd had enough of London. There was no way that their visit there could possibly be further improved upon. It was time to celebrate, and leave.

So he picked up the phone and ordered a bottle of Bollinger champagne and caviar for two. Then he called British European Airways and booked two seats on the 10 A.M. flight from Heathrow to Frankfurt. His next stop was going to be Baden-Baden. If he had learned this much from the lazy Limeys in just twenty-four hours, imagine what he might pick up from the industrious Krauts!

11

They collected a mercedes from Hertz at Rhein-Main Airport, picked up the main north–south Autobahn which runs along the border of the airport proper, and headed in the direction of Freiburg im Breisgau and ultimately the Swiss border. About two hours later they came to the Baden-Baden exit and, within minutes, found themselves in one of the true garden spots in all of Germany.

One enters Baden-Baden via the Lichtentaler Allee, the Champs-Élysées of southern Germany. It is a broad boulevard lined with huge trees and gardens full of rhododendrons, azaleas, roses, and zinnias. The lush vegetation is more Mediterranean than Central European. And it was, in fact, a Roman emperor, Caracalla, who gave the town its first big start. However, it was the warm springs, not the vegetation, that attracted the health-conscious Caracalla, who apparently spent most of his time building spas. The Emperor also set the tone and established the social standards for visitors to Baden-Baden. The more plebeian types were definitely not welcome. It was to become and remain a playground for the very rich for almost two millennia, for Romanovs and maharajahs, Habsburgs and various Princes of Wales. The final centerpiece was added in the middle of the nineteenth century with the reconstruction of the Kurhaus, the oldest casino in Greater Germany, in the style of Versailles. There, until World War I, one played with chips of gold and silver.

The girl behind the Hertz desk, no doubt inwardly amused at the embarrassment she would inevitably cause these singularly common Amis, had recommended Brenner's Parkhotel on the Lichtentaler Allee. As they drove the Mercedes up to the entrance of this palatial establishment, which was surrounded by immense, impeccably kept grounds dotted with statuary and ponds, to any outside observer it would have been obvious that this pair was even more out of place there than they had been at Claridge's. But apparently quite oblivious to the grandeur of it all, the two of them simply walked into the place, blithely in Danny's case and gamely where Sandra Lee was concerned, and requested the best accommodations the house had to offer. They got what they wanted: a superbly appointed suite of vast proportions, overlooking a huge swimming pool area that had been built as an almost perfect replica of a Roman bath.

It's all starting to come together, Danny thought as he opened the french doors leading from their bedroom to the terrace overlooking the magnificent pool and grounds below.

Sandra Lee had gone down to the lobby just to look around. So Danny decided to stay out on the terrace for a while, taking in the late afternoon sun. About half an hour later Sandra Lee was back and joined him out on the terrace.

"Fabulous, isn't it, Danny?" she said.

"Yeah," Danny admitted, and then went on, "but you know something? This is the first time I've ever been in Germany. I never wanted to come here. Not that I ever thought of it that much, but I'm a Jew. And this may sound stupid, but you know the girl at that Hertz counter in Frankfurt, and the people downstairs, somehow I had this feeling they knew I was a Jew. And they knew they had to be nice to me, or at least appear to be nice to me. But I'm just as sure they don't like us any better now than they did thirty or forty years ago."

"Ah, come on, honey," said Sandra Lee, "that may be true of some of the old guys around here, but I don't believe for a minute that any of the young ones feel anything but shame for what their parents did to your people. Look, it's the same way with us blacks, except it wasn't the Germans that were doing us in, it was the Americans. But that's also changing. You can't forget that stuff, but please don't let it get you down. We are here in a beautiful hotel in a beautiful town. So loosen up. Let's enjoy ourselves. We're on vacation."

"What've you got there?" Danny then asked, pointing at a small paper bag in her hands.

"A book," she answered.

"You read German?"

"No, dummy, they've got a whole section of English paperbacks at the newspaper stand in the lobby."

"So what did you get?"

"One I had to read in college, and now I am going to read it again. Not because I have to, but because I want to."

"College, what college?"

"Mills College."

"Where's that?"

"In California. In the Oakland hills."

"What kind of college is it?"

"A women's college. Liberal arts. Very fancy."
Silence.

"Now, honey, you were wondering what a black hooker was doing at a fancy women's college, weren't you?"

"Ha ha, and you were the one who told me not to be paranoid about the past," Danny replied. "Look, I'll forget about what the Germans did to me if you forget about whoever it was that did whatever they did to you, okay?"

"I'll tell you what I was doing at Mills College: I was there on a scholarship. It's a very liberal school. They believe it is good for the upper-class girls to mingle with, you know, with us."

"So what happened?"

"I left, after my sophomore year. I couldn't stand it. I don't mean I couldn't stand the school. It was wonderful. But I didn't have a nickel to my name. I had a scholarship and I still had to wait on tables. I just couldn't put up with the condescending attitude of those prissy young bitches."

"So what did you do?"

"I went back to Los Angeles to try to make some money."

"Well, you've been making money, a lot of it. So quit bitching."

"I'm not bitching, Danny. I am trying to explain."

"Well, then stop explaining if it bothers you. What did your parents have to say when you left this college?"

"I don't have parents. Most black girls don't have parents. They have *a* parent. My mother was sick, absolutely sick."

"What does she say now?"

"We haven't talked in three years." Then she continued, "What about your mother? Is she proud now that her son owns a casino in Las Vegas?"

"My mother is seventy-five years old. She knows absolutely nothing about either Las Vegas or casinos. She lives in the past but is perfectly content with her life."

"What do your brothers and sisters think?" she then asked.

"I don't have any brothers and sisters."

"That's too bad."

"Maybe. On the other hand, I like to be alone. I've enjoyed being alone since I was a kid."

"Now, come on. Didn't you have any friends?"

"Of course I had friends. In fact, the best time of my whole life was when my mother used to take me to Atlantic City from Philadelphia. My grandmother lived down there and she had a house right on the beach. There was a whole gang of kids, local kids. From the time school was out in June until it started again on Labor Day we had the best time. Most of them were Italians. Italians know how to have fun. You know, it's difficult for us Jews to have fun, then and now. I think we simply think too much."

"Ah, come on, Danny, don't let this place get you down. I've got an idea. Let's go down and have a drink. That'll pep us both up."

"Nah, I don't feel like it. I think I'll just sit out here on the terrace for a while longer. Why don't you go and read your book?" He did and she did. About an hour later it was starting to get a bit chilly on the terrace, so Danny finally came inside. Sandra Lee was lying on the bed, reading.

"What's the book called?" Danny asked.

"The Gambler."

"Who wrote it?"

"Dostoyevsky. You know, he also wrote *Crime and Punishment.*"

"Why're you reading that stuff?"

"Because I remembered that he'd written this short novel about casinos. It all took place in Germany, so since we're here I thought I'd reread it to really get into this place. Probably other people do the same. That's why they've got it here."

"What's it all about?"

"It's about a Russian. He's a compulsive gambler."

"What the hell was a Russian doing gambling here in Germany?"

"It was about a hundred years ago, Danny."

"So what's so interesting about a compulsive gambler anyway? Most gamblers are compulsive."

"I guess that's the point. This guy destroyed himself. He landed in jail. He lost his girlfriend and ended up absolutely ruined."

"So?"

"So? So? I mean it has something to do with what you're doing, doesn't it? Let's face it, Danny, whether your mother knows about it or not, you're now in a business that destroys people."

"That's no concern of mine," Danny said, now getting just a little bit peeved and showing it. Sandra Lee decided not to answer. She just raised her eyebrows and went back to Dostoyevsky.

Then she looked up again. "What about the slots? You know who plays those: the cabdrivers, the waitresses, women who work in factories. They come to Vegas for one night and blow everything they've saved for the last couple of months. I mean, is that terrific?"

"Nobody forces them. When they come to Vegas, they have a good time. That's it. A casino isn't there to make anybody rich, especially the cleaning lady or the cabdriver. A casino, at least an American casino, a Las Vegas casino, *my* casino when I've got it fixed up the way I'm going to have it fixed up, is there to provide illusions; to invite dreams, to allow these people to get away from their crummy cabs and from the crummy factories and their god-damn lives and come over to a palace in the desert. That's all I'm going to give them: a palace in the desert. And so they spend five hundred or a thousand dollars. They'll get their money's worth. Because for twenty-four hours or forty-eight hours they'll live a life of class. In my casino I won't care who the hell they are. Everybody who works in my place is going to treat everybody, even the worst bum, in a classy way. And that goes for a Mexican bum, a Chinese bum, or a white or black bum. Now tell me what the hell is wrong with that?"

"And what if these bums end up like this guy in this novel, this Russian, and wreck their whole lives?" Sandra asked.

"Forget about your book which is a hundred years old

and come back to reality. Look, a guy like that what's his name . . ."

"Alexis."

"Okay, this guy Alexis, he's a compulsive type, I'm sure. If he hadn't ruined himself gambling, he'd have ruined himself drinking, or, these days, ruined himself on drugs."

Sandra put the book down and was silent for a moment, but then said, "You may be right Danny. But that doesn't—"

"Of couse I'm right. Look, I don't want to hear this moral crap. I mean, what about the stock market, for God's sake? Or what about the commodities markets? What about all those people who are trying to make a fast buck in real estate? That's gambling! The only difference is you can't compute the odds when you do that. In a casino you take five minutes out and ask around and you can find out exactly what you're getting into. Strictly mathematics."

"You think that waitress is going to sit down and read a book on the mathematical odds before she sits down in front of a slot machine?" She added, "Shit!"

"Look, Sandra Lee, I'm telling you that I'm not interested in waitresses and I'm not really interested in slot machines. That's why we're here in Europe. I've got this idea that the real profit doesn't lie there like most people seem to think. I've got the very definite impression that the way to get really rich in this business is to concentrate on the rich. Leave the little fish to the other guys. I'm after rich guys. So who should care if they end up like bums? But let's stop this, for Chrissake; let's get dressed and see how they do it here in Baden-Baden.

"I don't expect to see too many Russians, do you?" he added with a mocking smile.

"What's that supposed to mean?" Sandra asked.

"Well, I don't like these deep discussions, but I'll tell you something: I'll bet there are about twenty million Russians that would give their left arm to be able to get out of that

country and come over here and lose their life's savings on a
weekend. Look, that's what free enterprise is all about: the
excitement of being able to make a lot of money or lose a lot
of money. Now, if you're a Russian, like what's his name
again?"

"Alexis."

"Alexis. I'll bet if he lived in this century and spent his
life driving a tractor in Siberia, this guy Dostoyevsky sure as
hell wouldn't have written a book about him, you know
what I mean?"

The casino in Baden-Baden was a bust. Danny sensed
that from the moment he stepped into the building. It resembled a mausoleum, not a place where you had fun. From
the marble floor to the heavy curtains to the hush that per-
vaded the place, there was nothing that Danny Lehman
found even remotely attractive, including the people, most
of whom looked like visiting farmers. They actually had to
pay admission to get in! And once they got in they walked
around the place in the same way they had been walking
around other tourist attractions earlier that day.

The only tables that had even a semblance of any action
were the roulette tables, but when Danny checked out the
stakes, he saw that the average bet was five marks! Less than
two dollars!

"Where are all the princes?" he asked Sandra Lee as they
walked through the place. She was, as usual, drawing the
envious glances of everyone from the croupiers to the visiting farmers. "Back in Russia driving tractors," Sandra replied.

They went back to the Brenner's Parkhotel and had some
Wildschwein with Preiselbeeren and Spätzle and a good bot-
tle of Mosel wine, ending the meal with a delicious piece of
Schwarzwälder Kirschtorte and finally a bottle of Sekt, the
German version of champagne. By ten-thirty they were up
in their suite.

"Say," Danny said as they undressed. "I'm going to stay up and take a look at that book of yours, okay?"

"Go ahead," Sandra said.

At two o'clock in the morning, when he had finished reading the book, Danny leaned over and shook Sandra Lee, who had been in a deep sleep for hours.

"What do you want, Danny?" she asked, suspecting that she knew full well what he wanted.

"Nothing. Just wanted to tell you that, as usual, you helped again to make this little trip worthwhile. Baden-Baden, the way it is now, stinks. But the way it was—that's something else. What I'm going to do is find the right people, and when I find the right people I'm going to give them exactly what this Russian guy Alexis was looking for: excitement, high stakes, a feeling of being part of the elite. Class. I'm going to get the same types to come to Vegas. He's got a count in that book. He's got those upper-class Englishmen. He's got a general. He's got them from all over the world. They all came here because the stakes were high and the atmosphere was right: not lousy five-mark chips, but gold florins. Not fucking nobodies, but aristocracy!"

"To hell with it. Go to sleep." She leaned over and gave him a pat, and then they both went to sleep.

The next day they caught a Lufthansa direct flight from Frankfurt to Beirut. The plane was barely off the ground when Danny ordered a bottle of champagne, real champagne, to celebrate having left German soil. Danny had concluded that there was nothing Jews could learn from Germans except that they should stay away from one another.

12

There was a message waiting for Danny when he checked into the St. George Hotel in Beirut. It could hardly have been more brief. "Call me at 702 555 9977 after 7 P.M. my time." And it was signed "William Smith."

Sandra Lee watched his face as he read it. "Not good, huh?"

"What time is it in Vegas?" Danny asked.

"It must be either nine or ten hours behind this place. So my guess would be around two or three in the morning." Which definitely put it after 7 P.M.

The first thing Danny did in their room after the bellhop had left was to get the telephone operator. This being Beirut, he figured that it might take a day or two to get through to the States. But Lebanon, at least in 1969, though in the Middle East was not really of the Arab world. It thought of itself as the Switzerland of the eastern Mediterranean, and its phone system lived up to that forced comparison. The head of the Las Vegas office of the FBI was on the line in less than thirty seconds.

"It's Danny Lehman. What's wrong?"

"Oh," and there was relief in Smith's voice. "Look, I found out where you were going to be from your attorney, Mr. Shea. I hope you don't mind."

"Of course not."

"I'll make it brief. De Niro and Salgo got out on bail the day you left town. Just like we expected."

"Yes," Danny said.

"Well, the day after that, two guys got killed. Their names were Amaretto and Sarnoff. Joseph Amaretto and Sam Sarnoff."

The missing link, as the FBI man had put it, was no longer missing.

Danny turned ashen. Sandra Lee was watching him and moved in his direction, but then changed her mind and disappeared into the bathroom.

"Ever hear of them?" Smith then asked.

"No," answered Danny, and there was a quiver even in this single syllable.

"I didn't think so. We're pretty sure we know why they got killed. And who did it: the who being Roberto Salgo."

"Shit," Danny said, with a fervor that came from being scared.

"Yeah, I know how you must feel. They were no doubt fencing for De Niro and Salgo. They worked out of Reno. Our office there has known about them for years, but never really came up with anything that we could nail them for. Which, frankly, didn't really bother anybody that much, since they were small-time. At least, we thought they were small-time."

Danny just listened.

"De Niro and Salgo no doubt figured out that somebody must have informed on them, and then they came up with these two guys."

"Were they?" Danny asked. "Working with you, I mean?"

"No. We had an informer. I told you: the one who phoned us. But it couldn't have been either of the dead ones. It was an insider. A casino insider. We'll never know who, I'm sure."

I'll bet Fort Lauderdale knows who, Danny thought. But he said, "Then how do you know it was Salgo who killed them?"

"We don't know for sure. But Salgo was seen with both of

them at a bar in Reno two nights before their bodies were fished out of the Truckee River. The bodies were kind of mutilated, I should add."

"So is Salgo back in jail?" Danny asked.

"No. No way we could do that. Zero evidence. Which brings me to why I called you, Danny."

He does know something, Danny thought. I'm going to be the evidence.

"I want you to be very careful," Smith then said. "Salgo hasn't been seen since. If I could find out where you were with one phone call, I'm sure he and De Niro can do the same. They still know everybody at the casino."

"Why me?"

"You got them arrested. You ruined them; you and whoever informed on them in the first place. They think they took care of the latter up in Reno, and got away with it. Now if they try to get you over there in the Middle East, there's not a damn thing we can do about it either. There's nothing we can do to prevent it, and, if they succeed, there's no way we could go after them. Lebanon is, to put it mildly, a bit outside our jurisdiction. We could contact their law enforcement people through the embassy. But I'm sure those Arab cops are not going to care too much if some visiting Jew thinks he's in danger of getting knocked off by some American mob types, if you know what I mean."

"Yeah," Danny replied. First surrounded by Germans; now Arabs. Then he said, "Is it going to really be much different when I get back? If they've been crazy enough to go this far already, what's to stop them from staying crazy enough to get me, no matter how high the risk?"

This time it was the voice on the other end of the phone that remained silent. Then: "Not much, Danny. Even when I'm working for you, that's one thing I couldn't guarantee. There are lots of bad ones in this town, hell, that's obvious, but very few who act irrationally. It's part of the business.

Right? But anybody who goes out and kills just like that
. . . well, it's scary. So be careful."

"I will. And thanks. I'll be back in a couple of days."

When he hung up, Sandra Lee was coming out of the
bathroom, wrapped in a huge white towel. "Come on,
honey. I've got a bath ready. It'll relax you, and I'd say, by
the look of you, that you need relaxing bad. So maybe we
shall have to do more than just soap your back." She did
more. Afterward he told her every detail of his conversation
with William Smith. Then she gave him some valuable advice.

It was around six in the evening when the phone rang,
startling both of them. Incoming phone calls in Beirut could
hardly bring anything other than more bad news. "I hope
this is Danny Lehman," the man on the other end said, in a
voice that seemed to combine a variety of accents.

"It is."

"This is Eduardo Cordoba. I run the Casino de Liban and
I just heard that you had arrived in Beirut. Welcome!"

"Who told you?" The question was, of course, not unre-
lated to what he had just heard from the FBI. Any unsolic-
ited phone call would now have to be regarded with suspicion.

"That's part of our business, isn't it? But to put your
mind at rest, it was the concierge at the hotel. You apparently inquired about our casino; he then automatically let
our people know. For a small gratuity, of course. But please
accept my apology if I'm intruding."

"No, no problem," said Danny, for it was true. He had
asked the concierge while waiting to be checked in.

"When your name came up, I, of course, recognized it.
We heard about your taking over Raffles. I thought I'd like
to welcome you to the fold by inviting you for dinner this
evening. On the off chance you might accept, I've already

taken the liberty of instructing one of our limousines to pick
you up at the St. George at eight. I do hope you'll come."

"With pleasure. I'm with somebody—"

"I know," interrupted Cordoba. "The concierge also told
me. We are all waiting to meet her!"

It was a Rolls that pulled up at eight on the dot in front of
the St. George, and there were whiskey and gin beside the
ice bucket on the bar in the back, ready to go. Plus a dozen
canapés topped with black caviar. There was a bottle of
almost frozen Stolichnaya to go with that.

The drive from Beirut to the Casino de Liban takes about
an hour, and it is a spectacular one. The farther north one
goes, the wilder the coast becomes, as the rocks rise above
the sea. It is comparable to Highway 1 in California, especially where it runs high above the Pacific between the Russian River and Mendocino. The car was air-conditioned, but
Sandra Lee asked the driver to turn it off. She wanted to
take in the Mediterranean evening air. It was still very warm
but, amazingly, not humid.

The casino itself is perched on a huge rock formation
overlooking the sea. It stands in splendid isolation. And it is
a splendid structure, combining the Middle Eastern with the
French, as is only proper in a former colony, or mandate, of
France. Eduardo Cordoba was waiting for them at the entrance, which led to a huge high-ceilinged hall. The gaming
facilities were off to the left; the dining and entertainment
rooms, to the right. There were tons of marble and acres of
rugs and carpeting. "First dinner, then the show, if you
agree. I know that to invite you Americans to watch our
show sounds, let us say, presumptuous. But I am willing to
take that risk, if you agree."

His English was near-perfect, but hints of both French
and Spanish accents were discernible. His was an attractive
voice, and Cordoba was an attractive man. He seemed to be
in his mid-forties. He was at least six feet tall, but probably
no more than 160 pounds, a lean man whose most striking

features were his black eyes and his hair of the same color. He was dressed in an old-fashioned pinstripe suit, and his tie could have been one of a Guards regiment. His manner was that of a good-natured sport, but his eyes, to which one was drawn, were coolly appraising. Sandra Lee had been attracted to him from the very beginning, and it was she who now took Cordoba's arm as well as Danny's and said, "Honey, we will do anything you say. Provided . . ."

"Provided what?"

"That we get some very cold Dom Pérignon very quickly."

The champagne was cold, the dinner superb and served with an elegance that matched anything that Lasserre, or Grand Vefour, or Tour d'Argent could have offered that year in Paris.

The show that followed was absolutely spectacular. It was set in an amphitheater that had more Greek than Roman influence. The show opened with a belly dancer and a flaming sword–swallowing act, which did not bode well for what might be coming later. But then, all of a sudden, the performance took on a dramatic nature. The stage tripled, at least, in size and now there were elephants and camels and Arabian horses apparently coming from all sides. Then, from above, immense chandeliers, golden chandeliers, three of them, began to descend, and from each chandelier hung six nude women, all completely coated with gold. When they reached stage level, there was suddenly the sound of rushing water, while at the same time short walls, obviously hydraulically powered, began to rise, sealing off what once had been the aisles in front of the semicircle of seats nearest the stage. Soon filled with rapidly flowing water, they became canals along which floated an entire procession of golden swans, each bearing two golden showgirls, plus an assortment of monkeys, parrots, and other exotic birds.

"This is the damnedest thing I've ever seen!" Danny exclaimed.

If Beirut was the playground of the rich of the Middle East, where one could do what one chose without religious or social restraints, then the Casino de Liban was the centerpiece of that playground. It offered to the elite of the Middle East what many of them wanted: European women, American cocktails, and, as Danny soon discovered, English-style gaming where huge sums of money could be won and lost without anybody really taking any notice—and all this in an atmosphere of French congeniality combined with the Middle Eastern penchant for extravagance.

Again, of course, it was at the baccarat tables where all the action was to be found. Even the stakes on the tables at Crockford's paled by comparison. As if reading Danny's mind, their host started very quietly to identify some of the men in the room. "That man over there, for example, the very dark one with the pointy beard. He is a famous Saudi Arabian prince. He comes to Beirut every three months and spends every single evening of his stay here at the casino. Those four women behind him at the chemin de fer table change every time. But they are usually Danish.

"The man next to him," Cordoba continued, "the old one, he is Turkish. He owns mines there. He comes once a year and stays only three days, usually. His sons come more often. The man on his right, he's also a prince, but an Italian prince, which, you must appreciate, is not quite up to Saudi Arabian standards. But nevertheless . . . His wife is Brazilian. She is still eating, most probably; she is very fat. But she also owns an awful lot of coffee in Brazil, as the old song used to say."

"Which song?" asked Sandra Lee.

"You're too young for that," Danny answered, and then asked Cordoba, "Where on earth did you learn the words to that song?"

"I went to a prep school in Santa Barbara, California. During the war. My father was in the diplomatic corps of his country and was stationed in Washington for much of the time when I was a child. Then he was posted to Berlin. They left me in the States. Our country, by the way, was Argentina."

"What is your country now?" Danny asked.

"None," Cordoba answered. And then continued, "That man next to the Italian is from Israel. He is with, or works for, the Israeli Aircraft Corporation. He's an arms dealer. Works out of Beirut. Comes here once a week. Usually drops a couple of thousand pounds each visit. He's a terrible gambler. Also a very unpleasant man."

"That surprises me," Danny said.

"What surprises you?"

"That an Israeli would be allowed to live here, much less deal in arms."

"Beirut is an open city. Lebanon is the most liberal of countries, the most multireligious of societies. We have a million Muslims, to be sure, but also many hundreds of thousands of Christians, many tens of thousands of Jews; we have Copts and Jehovah's Witnesses and Old Catholics and—everything else. Even Israelis who deal in arms.

"Everybody is safe here—even the most rich. You will notice we have no armed guards here in the casino," Cordoba continued. "You will see no military people on the roads, because we essentially have no army. And the only police you will see are directing traffic. It is like Switzerland."

"You love it here," said Sandra Lee.

"Yes. Very much. And now it is all going to collapse. Nasser is losing control. There will be war, and the Palestinians will take over this country. And it will all be over. Very quickly." Then abruptly: "I expect you both must be very tired after your trip. If you agree, I will ask your driver to take you back to Beirut."

Both agreed spontaneously and, in Sandra Lee's case, with an audible sigh of relief. As he walked them to the Rolls, Cordoba made two remarks. "Danny, I would like to

have a further word with you in private and about private
matters. My private matters. Could we do that over lunch
tomorrow?"

"With pleasure. Why not at my hotel? Say twelve-thirty?"

"Done. One other thing. A man has been asking for you
for the past two days. In Beirut. And twice here at the
casino. We don't know his name. He was obviously accus-
tomed to dealing in cash only. Dollars. He brought a bundle
with him to the casino. But he had bad luck the first night
and ran out. He then had some funds wired to us. They
came from a bank in the Cayman Islands, but he's American. I thought you might like to know this. Perhaps we
might be of some help in the matter if, that is, it is a matter
that should be dealt with. In any case, I have told the people
at the St. George to keep an eye open. They will take good
care of you."

And then he disappeared back into the Casino de Liban.
Sandra Lee, who had heard it all, said nothing. But she held
Danny's hand during the entire drive back. She knew that
both had the same name in mind.

Salgo.

The St. George Hotel had a wonderful outside terrace at
the rear, looking out onto the beach below and the Mediterranean beyond that. The crowd was always a mixture of
local Beirut society, almost exclusively Christian, and tourists who for the most part were French or Arab, and mainly
from the financial elite of their respective countries. The
women were also of two classes: the wives of local men, on
average in their forties and overdressed; and mistresses, on
average in their twenties and underdressed (in terms of
quantity, not quality)—these being the companions of the
foreign visitors. Race and color went truly unnoticed; jewelry, shoes, décolletage did not.

As it was a weekday, the ratio of women to men at lunch
that day on the terrace was at least three to one. In fact,

Danny Lehman and Eduardo Cordoba were the only men lunching together. The St. George was a place reserved for pleasure, not business.

"It doesn't exactly look like this country is anywhere near falling apart," Danny said, once their Campari and sodas had arrived.

"It's because you can't see them from here," Cordoba answered.

"Can't see what?"

"The camps. The Palestinians. Hundreds of thousands. Hussein kicked them out of Jordan; no other Arab country wanted a gang of troublemakers like they are. So they've invaded Lebanon. And this country is neither willing nor able to do anything about it. One of these days they are going to try to take us over." And Cordoba's hand traced a semicircle, taking in the elegant high-rise buildings that rose up from the sea: some banks, some hotels, some condominiums.

"That is why I asked if we could lunch together," Cordoba continued.

Danny waited.

"Let me tell you more about myself. I spent my childhood and youth in your country. But then, after the war, we lived in Paris. My father was at the embassy; my mother became, as usual, involved with the local society. I ended up enrolled at the Sorbonne, but, as so often happens, I spent my time with the girls, drinking, even dabbling in drugs, although that was a long time ago, and gambling. I don't know how much you know about the Paris gambling scene, but if I may explain very briefly?"

"Please do."

"It could hardly be a greater contrast to what you are used to in Las Vegas. Your casinos there have always been wide open for everybody. In France that was not true for many decades. Laws were designed to protect the workers, the poor, from the 'vice of vices.' Casinos were banned

within a sixty-mile perimeter of Paris. The only exceptions
to this ban were the 'big' games—baccarat and chemin de
fer—which were tolerated, *provided* they were strictly limited to private clubs, clubs which were reserved for the elite,
those who could 'afford to lose.' Where the clubs are concerned, or *cercles,* as they are known in France, gaming was
supposed to be only a small sideline, a way of providing a
diversion from the main purposes of these establishments.
The main purpose of, for instance, the Cercle Anglais, is to
foster Franco-Anglo cooperation. The Aviation Club sup-
posedly only has members who are pilots. All this, of
course, amounts to hypocrisy on a scale of grandness that
only the French could manage. To sum up briefly, there are
sixteen such *cercles.* The most luxurious of these is the Cercle Concorde on the Champs-Élysées; the place where the
big action has always taken place was, and still is, the Cercle
Haussmann. I began working there in, well, let's think now,
it must have been in 1952. My parents could not understand
it. But in 1952 Paris was still a very drab place, especially
for someone who considered himself a hot-blooded Latino. I
found the excitement I thought I needed at the Cercle
Haussmann, and spent the next eight years there. Then I
moved to London. Not Crockford's, but nevertheless a place
that came close."

"Why?"

"Why did I leave Paris?"

"Yes."

"Well, in 1960 new ownership moved in at the Cercle
Haussmann. One referred to them, one still refers to them,
though never in their presence, as the 'Corsicans.' They took
over one club after the other. Their names are wonderful:
Raffali, Benedetti, Mondolini, Francisci. Believe it or not,
they all come from a few villages in southern Corsica situated within half a dozen kilometers of each other. They
wanted their own people in. But don't misunderstand. I left
in friendship. In fact, I consider some of the members of

those families to be among the best friends that I have in this world. We help each other solve problems. You know? In this business, problems tend to move from casino to casino, from country to country, and, today, from continent to continent. Some of us long ago recognized that mutual protection was necessary. The Corsicans are good at that sort of thing."

"And after London?"

"I spent a couple of years at Monte Carlo, and then came here to manage the Casino de Liban. I've been here five years now."

"And you're ready to move again," Danny then said.

"Yes. Could you use me?"

"As you said yourself, Vegas is another world."

"Ah yes. But it is in a world which has gotten very, very small. The high rollers don't care where they gamble. In your desert or beside my beach: it's the same to them, as long as they can find the action they seek, and as long as they are treated in the manner in which they expect to be treated. And justifiably so. They find action here or in London and also at the Cercle Haussmann; they also find the same standard of service in all of these places. Why go elsewhere? They don't and they won't, unless they can find bigger action and better treatment somewhere else. Provide it in Las Vegas, and they will come to you. More than that: you provide what they want and *I* will bring them to you."

"Define action."

"Simple. One word. Baccarat."

"That's it?"

"That's it."

"What else?"

"Credit. For the big ones, almost unlimited credit. And no interest on these credits. Ever. No matter how long they remain outstanding."

"What else?"

"Attention. Someone who will fulfill their every whim

when they are in town. Someone who gets to know them so
well that they anticipate that whim before it even becomes
one. Suites, girls, booze, airplanes, yachts, limos, everything.
All on comp. No questions asked. Just no drugs. That's
out."

"Baccarat. Credit. Comp," Danny said.

"That's it. Plus having somebody who knows who they
are."

"And that's you."

"That's right."

"How many are there?"

"A couple of thousand really big ones. But the number
keeps growing. Especially in places like Hong Kong and
Mexico where nobody pays taxes."

"They can support a casino?" Danny asked, skeptically.

"Yes."

"How many of that couple of thousand do you know?"

"Five, maybe six hundred."

Danny did some calculations in his head, paused, and
asked, "How soon would you be ready to move?"

"You give me thirty days' notice; I'll be there on day
thirty-one."

Danny Lehman had already made up his mind. He knew
it was impetuous: he had barely met the man. But . . .
"One more very important question."

Cordoba interrupted. "I know what you're coming to: am
I clean enough to be licensed in Nevada?"

"Beyond any shadow of any doubt clean enough?" Danny
asked.

"Yes," Cordoba said.

"You're absolutely sure?"

"Absolutely."

"Then you've got a deal. Consider that thirty days as
starting from right now. Unless you want to talk about, you
know, what kind of a deal . . ."

Again Cordoba interrupted. "Not necessary."

"Shall we order lunch?" Danny then asked.

"Frankly, Danny, I'm not hungry. My stomach's nervous. This was important for me. Do you mind if I pass?"

"Of course not. I think I'll just stay here a while longer. I'll call you before we leave. You're sure, now, about our deal?"

"I'm sure." Cordoba extended his hand to Danny and left.

Danny sat down and was pondering whether or not to order lunch when Sandra Lee appeared at the doorway leading from the hotel to the terrace. She had a frantic look on her face, and when she spotted Danny and came to his table, the look did not change.

"What's wrong?" Danny asked, rising to meet her.

"Sit down," she hissed. "He's at the bar. I was sitting inside having tea when he walked in. He saw me. And he saw me recognize him."

"When?"

"About ten minutes ago. I was petrified. Did I make a mistake coming out here? He must know I came to find you." She was trembling. "I'm afraid, Danny. If he kills you, he's going to have to kill me."

"Where do you get this kill stuff? That's George Raft movie crap."

Now her expression changed, from one of fear to one of fear mixed with anger, maybe even including a tinge of hatred. "Look, don't give me any of that innocent act. Your business is nasty. It's run by nasty people. Don't try and con me. Con yourself if you want. But not me. Now what the fuck are you going to do? Salgo is not here to visit the Roman ruins up in those hills back there."

"I'll go talk to him," Danny said.

"Don't!" And this was said with vehemence. "Stay away from him. I told you that yesterday. Don't go near him and don't let him get near you."

"How? He's not going to disappear."

"Talk to Cordoba. He came here for a job, didn't he?"

"How did . . . ?"

"It was kind of obvious. He wants out of this place, and you're the solution."

"You're right. I hired him."

"So call him. Explain the problem. Now!"

"I can't now. He's on his way back up to the casino."

"So call him in an hour. In the meantime, let's get out of here." She left ten Lebanese pounds on the table and almost dragged him to the stairs that led down to the path to the beach. Instead of going toward the water, she left the path and moved across the lawn to the broad boulevard that bordered the Mediterranean, crossed it, and headed into a street that led up a hill. Danny literally trotted behind her. Two blocks and five minutes later they were inside the Inter-Continental Hotel. In contrast to the St. George, this hotel was completely new and totally modern. Its lobby could have been that of the Inter-Continental in Geneva, Frankfurt, or Hong Kong. The only clue to where it was located was that in the middle of this lobby there was a swarthy man in Turkish costume pushing around a cart bearing an immense brass urn from which he drew coffee when any of the guests he offered it to chose to partake of the "freebie," which many did, since freebies of any kind are, to put it mildly, an extreme rarity in the Middle East. Sandra Lee was one of the takers. With a tiny cup in each hand she then carefully moved to the rear and installed herself on a sofa that offered a view of the entire sweep of the lobby, including the front entrance. Danny had no choice but to join her. He reached for one of the coffees.

"First get a newspaper," she said, "a French one. Then coffee."

He got a two-day-old *Figaro* from the newsstand and rejoined her.

"You read and sip that godawful coffee. I'll watch. At three on the dot you call that Cordoba."

At three he did just that, and the conversation was brief. "That man you said was looking for me—he's at the bar of the St. George, or at least was there an hour ago. His name is Salgo. He's trouble."

Cordoba said nothing.

"Perhaps very big trouble," Danny then added.

"Big enough trouble to affect your casino operation?"

"Yes."

"Were you seen together?"

"No. Sandra Lee saw him. That's all."

"Where are you?"

"At one of the phones in the lobby of the Inter-Continental."

"Give me the number."

Danny did.

"Stay there." No more than seven minutes later the same phone rang. "He booked himself into the St. George at noon," the Argentinian said. "Let me suggest something. First, is Sandra Lee with you?"

"Yes."

"Good. In fact, perfect. Go to the front desk of the Inter-Continental in about five minutes. I'll have a room arranged for you in my name. Sign nothing. Just pick up the key and go to the room."

"And what will happen?"

"Some friends of my Corsican friends happen to be in town. *Pieds-noirs.* This place reminds them of their old homeland, Algeria, although some of them miss the violence. So I'll actually be doing them a favor. All right?"

Danny said nothing. Then: "All right."

Roberto Salgo was sitting at the bar of the St. George Hotel, waiting. Now that he was so close, he was getting increasingly impatient, even though it had been only days ago, after he had cut off Amaretto's fourth finger as De Niro held him down on the floor of the RV in the desert outside of Reno, that the man had screamed out Danny Lehman's name. Salgo had gotten so goddamn mad that he had taken the meat cleaver and, in one go, taken off what was left of the entire hand. In the end, when they had dumped both Amaretto and Sarnoff in the river, there were a lot of pieces missing from both bodies.

"Gimme another one," he said to the bartender. It was his third bourbon and soda. It had been so easy to track down the son of a bitch. Raffles had always referred its clients to the same travel agent in Vegas, because he and De Niro had always gotten a kickback on all the commissions, and free trips to anywhere on earth they wanted to go. Lehman had used the same agency, and now he knew why. The black bitch! She no doubt took *her* clients there, and for the same reasons.

The owner had delivered him a printout of their itinerary in the parking lot of the Dunes. From the look of intense fear on the man's face, there was no chance that he would ever talk about it, or even dream of doing so. The dilemma now was the black bitch: she'd recognized him. He was sure of it. But had she been stupid enough to tell Lehman? After all, she must know what would happen to her if she did. Christ, she'd been working Raffles long enough to know all about him and De Niro. Right?

"I'll be right back," he told the bartender and walked to the bank of house telephones in the main lobby of the hotel. He picked up one of the phones and asked, "Could I please have Mr. Lehman's room?" He let it ring three times and hung up. Still there, he said to himself, so she must not have told him.

"Check," he said. He paid it in dollars and, forgetting about any change, hurried back into the lobby and out of the door.

"Do you need a car, sir?" The man stood beside a Cadillac limousine, with dark windows. He had seen at least a dozen such cars in Beirut. The Arabs obviously went for them.

"Naw," Salgo said, and then he changed his mind. "How much for a grand tour of Beirut?" He looked at his watch. "Say for about two hours, and then back here." That should be about the time that Lehman and the black bitch would be back in their room, getting a little rest before preparing to go out for dinner. He knew the habits of tourists.

"A hundred dollars," came the answer.

"You got it," Salgo replied.

"If you sit up front beside me," the chauffeur said, "I can better explain Beirut to you. That is," he added with a show of humility, "if you don't mind."

"Hell no," said Salgo, although he never would have agreed to do it in Vegas where they knew him.

The dark-complexioned man, who spoke with a French accent like so many natives of the Lebanon, which, after all, had been a French protectorate for many years, opened the car's front door for Salgo, closed it behind him, and then scurried around to the other side and into the driver's seat. He moved the car swiftly away from the curb.

"I suggest we first go north for a bit," the driver said. "The coast is very beautiful. Like parts of the Riviera in France. Or," he added, "Corsica, where my family comes from."

Five minutes after they had left the outskirts of Beirut, following the same route that Danny Lehman and Sandra Lee had taken the night before on their trip to the Casino de Liban, the smoked-glass panel that separated the backseat from the driver's compartment slid back very slowly, very quietly. Just as slowly and just as quietly two gloved hands appeared, holding a length of piano wire.

With one swift move, the wire was looped over Salgo's head and then drawn across his throat. It took a good fifteen seconds before the violent thrashing of Salgo's body ceased.

Then the garroting of Roberto Salgo, Corsican-style, was completed.

Ten minutes later, the driver turned left off the main road and followed a dirt track that took them to the very edge of a cliff overlooking the rocks below and the Mediterranean beyond. When the Cadillac came to a halt, two swarthy men emerged from the backseat. They expertly removed all the clothing from Salgo's body and put it in the trunk of the car. Then they threw the body onto the rocks seventy feet below. The incoming tide was already beginning to cover them.

The driver, who had been watching all this while smoking a cigarette, looked at his watch. *"Cinq heures,"* he said. *"Alors, allons donc avoir un apéritif."* He drove the Cadillac back to the main road and headed north once again. At the next village they pulled over in front of a primitive sidewalk café. While they talked about soccer, two of the Corsicans had Pernod; the third, a Perrier.

At eight o'clock the next morning the phone rang in Room 1137 of the Beirut Inter-Continental Hotel and Sandra Lee took it. "It's Eduardo Cordoba."

"Yes?"

"You can go back to your suite at the St. George. Maybe wait an hour or so, so it looks like you're returning from a morning stroll."

"But—"

"Nothing more needs to be discussed. Tell Danny that I will cable him in Las Vegas when my travel plans firm up. In the meantime, *bon voyage* to both of you."

"Thanks, Eduardo."

"You're welcome."

Beirut Airport lies south of the city on a flat, dusty strip of land between the mountains and the sea. Sandra Lee and Danny boarded Middle East Airlines Flight 11 to Rome at noon the next day.

By one o'clock Danny had finished his third vodka martini and ordered a fourth.

"Is that smart?" Sandra Lee asked.

"No," Danny answered.

"What's bothering you?" she asked.

"Salgo."

"Why? He's gone."

"And those two other guys, too."

"Those two in Reno?"

"Yes."

"So what? From what Smith told you, Salgo killed them. Now with a little help from your new pal, Eduardo, we . . ." She decided not to finish that sentence.

Sandra Lee remained silent for a few minutes, and then said, "What about De Niro?"

"What about . . . De Niro."

"He's still alive and well."

"Maybe. You leave him to me." Now he was getting a bit aggressive.

Sandra Lee decided to shut up for a while. In the meantime, Danny was into his fourth martini. "You're wondering why I'm doing all this, aren't you?" he suddenly asked.

"Maybe. I mean, is it worth getting killed for, for Chrissake?" she answered.

"Maybe it is," he replied. After a few seconds: "Didn't expect that answer, did you. Hah!" Then: "Look, I've got one hell of an idea. The biggest. The best ever!"

"Sure. Baccarrat and *real* Roman baths," Sandra Lee said.

"Naw, not that. Well, that, too. But I mean the *biggie*. Atlantic City. You know what I'm going to do? I'm going to single-handed—is it handed or handedly?—never mind; I'm going to remake Atlantic City into the hottest place on the East Coast. I loved Atlantic City when I was a kid. Did I ever tell you that?"

"Yes, Danny."

"I used to stay with my grandma. We used to go to the Boardwalk and to the shows on the steel pier. It was great. The best times I ever had in my life." He picked up his glass again. "Then the politicians moved in and cleaned the place up, as they say. They wrecked it is what they did. It's a terrible place now. Well, not much longer. I'm going to put it back on the map. And nobody's going to stop me. Not the mob, not the bankers, not the pussyfoots like my lawyer. I'm going to build the best goddamn casino in the world in Atlantic City before I'm done. And then if you want to have a good time in Atlantic City again, you'll be able to. You want to drink, make a fast buck—come to Atlantic City. Do you know that there are over fifty million people living within a two hundred-and-fifty-mile radius of Atlantic City? With nothing, nothing to do? Did you know that? No, you didn't, did you? Now let me tell you something else. I told all this to a guy called Henry Price. You never heard of him, did you?"

"No, Danny."

"Well, he's a hotshot on Wall Street. Really big. Understand?"

"Yes, Danny."

"Well, I told him just what I'm telling you now. And do you know what the bastard did? He looked at his watch, and threw me out!"

"The son of a bitch!"

"Exactly. And now, Sandra Lee, we are going to show them all: Henry Price, the fucking mob, everybody, that two little nobodies, like you and me, can . . ." He rambled on. And on.

Over Brindisi he fell asleep.

Two hours later they landed at Fiumicino Airport. Sandra Lee reminded Danny that the original purpose of the trip had been to take a look at the Roman ruins.

"Fuck the Roman ruins," he said, and they went over to the Pan Am counter and booked a direct flight to Los Ange-

THE PALACE 189

les. So Danny saw no Roman ruins. In fact, later he never
even remembered seeing the airport at Rome.

The next day Danny had the worst hangover of his life.
But when he entered the casino grounds of the "old Raffles
place," as it was now known, the first person he asked for
was the architect. For the next three hours they pored over
the plans. Danny sensed immediately that the architect had
come up with exactly what he wanted. The Palace would be
a place where even Caracalla, or whatever the hell his name
was, would have been more than happy to take a bath. But
Danny was sure that guy Alexis would feel right at home.

But there was still a loose end: De Niro. Danny decided
that it was one that, if left alone, could prove fatal to everything that was now falling into place. So early the next
morning he summoned William Smith, who still had a while
to go with the FBI. It was Smith who directly broached the
subject the moment after he arrived in the executive offices
of the casino, about the only part of the entire building complex that was not under renovation. "Did Salgo turn up in
Beirut?"

"Not that I know of," Danny answered.

"Funny," said the FBI man. "We managed to track him
as far as Rome, and it seemed like a cinch that he was
headed directly for you."

Danny shrugged and then asked, "What about De Niro?"

"He's still in town. Never left town, from what we know.
Still living in his house on the north side with the wife and
kids, playing the good citizen."

That clinched it for Danny. Try as he might, he simply
could not get Lebanon and Salgo out of his mind. For the
truth was that he, Danny Lehman, had killed that man. No
matter how indirectly, no matter how much it was justified,
no matter that it was in self-defense, he had had a man
killed. That simply could not be allowed to be the first step
down a road that would lead God knows where. Because he

knew what would happen to De Niro if he was brought to
trial for murder the way things stood now. They would sentence him to life, and in seven years he would be out on
parole. And out to get Danny, just like Salgo had been.
Except that now De Niro would be doubly motivated. And
then what? He'd have to send for the Corsicans again. And
after De Niro, who would be next? Not only that: what if he
got caught? Danny had to admit it: *that* was what ultimately
scared him most. It was one thing to take such a fucking
risk five thousand miles away in Beirut where nobody
seemed to care. But here in America, if you were caught for
being involved in murder, they punished you, no matter
what. He wasn't even sure if they had a death penalty in the
state of Nevada. Danny then concluded, The very fact that
whether they do or not is now important to me is nuts! Uh
uh; no more of that stuff.

So he said, "Look, I've been thinking, especially after
your phone call in Beirut. I've got nothing, absolutely nothing, to gain from pushing this thing any further. You
know?"

"I agree."

"What if we decided not to press charges?"

"You mean the casino?"

"Yes. Could he be convinced to leave town then? For
good?"

Smith puzzled on that one for a full minute. "Probably,
except for the IRS; they press their own charges."

"What if they get paid what they think is due them?"

"That's something else."

"How much is involved?"

"Well, we've talked about it vaguely. They're thinking in
terms of a couple of million dollars' unreported income. So
you'd have the tax on that, the penalties, and the interest on
both. Million bucks would probably do it. If it was a cash
settlement."

"A million for De Niro, or for both De Niro and Salgo?"

"Million each."

"Would they drop the criminal charges if they got the million? Got it now?"

"My guess is that the IRS would drop both the criminal and the civil charges. Such good shape they're not in. De Niro and Salgo are going to keep claiming that they won all that stashed cash at the baccarat table and that it all happened very recently. With those two guys dead up in Reno, it's going to be damned hard to prove otherwise. That goes for us as well as the IRS. So they might be very happy indeed to get their money and close this thing out. If they do, we'll follow."

"Can you find out. Today?"

Smith did. And the IRS confirmed what he had thought right down the line. De Niro was picked up at seven that evening in one of the casino's limousines and brought back to the gaming establishment he had run for most of its existence. Danny and his attorney, a very uneasy Benjamin Shea, were waiting for him in his old office on the third floor. Danny indulged in no small talk whatsoever. He told De Niro he wanted to make him an offer and that it was not open to any discussion. All he wanted to hear was a simple yes or no.

The offer: first, the casino would withdraw its complaint against him and would urge the federal authorities to drop their charges against him. Second, the casino would grant him a one-million-dollar "golden handshake," provided the funds were put into an escrow account and designated for tax settlement purposes, this to take place with the full knowledge and agreement of the IRS. If the authorities all agreed—and there was no reason to believe they would not; in fact, quite the contrary—that would allow him, De Niro, to leave town permanently, in fact to leave Nevada permanently, to begin establishing a new life for himself and his family. This new life would have nothing to do with the gaming industry in any form, in any place, or at any time.

These were the only conditions. But they were absolute conditions.

Yes or no?

De Niro knew that being persecuted by the IRS was about the worst thing that could happen to any American. It was, after all, the IRS, not the FBI, who had finally put Al Capone away. They had no fucking regard whatsoever for the rights of anybody, especially those they had designated as targets, for reasons that had nothing at all to do with taxes. They would, he knew, hound him publicly, to make an example of him, to keep him in a state of perpetual fear. The IRS would haunt him literally to the end of his life. So he accepted the offer with an alacrity that appeared genuine beyond any doubt.

Salgo's name never came up, but De Niro obviously knew. For after the deal had been struck, as he turned to leave what had been his office at the casino for the final time, the emotion reflected in his last glance back at Danny Lehman was one of neither thanks nor fear. It was one of deep, black rage. He left town exactly thirty days later.

The loose end had been taken care of.

Or had it?

Danny Lehman wasted no further thoughts on De Niro. As usual, he became completely absorbed in the project at hand, the conversion of Raffles into the casino of his dreams.

Two years later, in the summer of 1971, The Palace opened its doors, and became an instant smash success. During the next five years, Danny Lehman spent almost all of his waking hours, day and night, inside The Palace, making sure that it stayed that way. He lived alone in the penthouse, which had been especially designed to suit his tastes, so the less said about it the better. For a while Sandra Lee shared it with him, until one day, for the first time in their relationship, she asked a favor of him.

"Danny," she said over breakfast one February morning in 1972, "you don't even know I'm here anymore."

"What was that?" he'd replied, since he was absorbed, as usual, in poring over the latest computer printouts of the casino's financial results.

"Now listen to me for a change, Danny! Would you do something for me?"

"Sure. Name it." He had stopped reading.

"I want you to let me work the baccarat tables. I want to become a dealer."

"Why?"

"I want to be independent."

"You don't have to do that, honey. You know you can have anything you want. Just ask."

"I don't want to have to ask. I want to do it on my own again. Okay? Believe me, Danny, I won't let you down." He'd never heard her plead like this before. It was embarrassing.

"Sure," he said. "Look, I'll talk to the dealers right away. When do you want to start?"

"Tomorrow."

A month later she moved out, explaining that it was never good when an employee fucked the boss on a regular basis. She didn't let Danny down. Quite the opposite. She was soon so good, so attentive to the regulars, that the high rollers started to come from as far away as London and Hong Kong to spend an evening at Sandra Lee's baccarat table at The Palace.

During the rest of the decade, they drifted even further apart, as Danny Lehman's attention increasingly turned to Atlantic City. By the last year of Jimmy Carter's term in the White House, Danny's new casino on the East Coast was fully operational. As a result, Atlantic City was in the process of being reborn.

By 1980 Danny Lehman had finally arrived.

PART THREE

1980

13

Nineteen eighty was not the best of years for the United States, but nobody noticed that in Las Vegas. Good times in Vegas are strictly defined by the number of overnights at the hotels and the aggregate win of the casinos. Both were up in 1980. So who cared about the rest of the country? For The Palace it was truly a banner year; the casino was in the process of grossing over $500 million, netting $35 million, returning, therefore, $1.75 profit on each of the 20 million outstanding shares that The Palace Inc., the parent holding company, had issued when it had gone public in 1973, allowing Danny to pay off the note and consolidate The Palace's financial situation, at least temporarily. Its shares were quoted on the New York Stock Exchange.

So who cared about hostages in Iran or inflation at home? If anybody in the entire state of Nevada did, it was not Danny Lehman. If there had been any problem at all for Danny during most of the years of the Carter presidency it had been the fact that Wall Street and the investors of America had for four years steadfastly refused to recognize The Palace for what it was, a real money machine. So its shares had sold—even in the best of times when the Dow was flirting with 1000—at only nine times earnings. As late as 1977 you could have bought into The Palace for a lousy two dollars a share, meaning that Danny Lehman, who owned exactly 10,312,000 shares of The Palace Inc., could claim a personal net worth of only $20 million. In retrospect, he probably would have been worth a lot more if he'd stuck to the currency and bullion business, especially since silver was heading from $4 toward $40 an ounce and gold from $150 to $800—while The Palace's stock seemed stuck forever at $2.

But all that changed in 1979. The Palace Inc.'s common had suddenly soared to a peak of $35.25 on August 17 of that year, putting the price at over one hundred times earnings, meaning that Danny's stake in his own company was suddenly worth just over one third of a billion dollars. Wall Street had come around, suddenly and massively, for two reasons: it finally recognized the past, and it anticipated the future.

The past was represented by the magnificent casino-hotel-entertainment complex, the world's largest, which Danny had produced out of the decay of the old Raffles operation in Las Vegas. His formula had worked magic: the Roman motif, baccarat, unlimited interest-free credit for the high rollers, and the high rollers themselves. The Palace had become their place, just as Eddie Cordoba had promised that summer day in Beirut in 1969. And just as Danny had thought from the moment he had been caught up in the action at Crockford's in London, it was that American version of chemin de fer—baccarat—which had attracted them to the American desert. Amazingly, it was also the baccarat tables that would contribute well over 60 percent of the total casino win that The Palace would chalk up in 1980. To be sure, The Palace had become one of the biggest credit institutions in Nevada in the process: it now had as much as $30 to $40 million in outstanding "advances" to its clients at peak times. As in Saudi Arabia, no interest was ever charged. But as with Bank of America in San Francisco, write-offs due to defaults were infrequent, averaging less than 2 percent. Eddie Cordoba saw to that, sometimes with the help of his "Corsicans," but occasions requiring their intervention were extremely rare, in any case a lot rarer than

outside skeptics would ever have believed, Why? Because
the high rollers all wanted to be able to come back to the
new Mecca of the gaming world someday, so they paid their
debts voluntarily.

But what really made the difference, what set The Palace
apart from every other casino in Vegas and, for that matter,
in the world, was the attention its management lavished on
its clientele, and the entertainment it offered clientele and
visitor alike. Visitors now came from all corners of the
world to have fun, for The Palace had the reputation of
being Hollywood, Disneyland, Wimbledon, the Hock-
enheimerring, and Madison Square Garden all in one. It was
the Casino de Liban magnified, not tenfold, but one hun-
dredfold.

That was the past and the present. The future that beckoned, a future that had just begun, was Atlantic City. The
high rollers and baccarat might have been Eddie Cordoba's
contribution; Hollywood, Disneyland, and Madison Square
Garden might have been Mort Granville's; but Atlantic City
was solely and exclusively Danny Lehman's baby, from the
moment of conception to that of realization. The hotel-casino on the Atlantic coast had now been in full operation
only six months. What had startled Wall Street was that it
was not only already in the black; it was ten million dollars
in the black! Result: high rollers and baccarat in Vegas, plus
instant massive profits in Atlantic City, added up to a success unparalleled in the history of the gaming industry.

And all this was only the beginning. Danny Lehman had
just announced his decision to build a second hotel-casino in
Atlantic City, and the land had already been acquired. Not
that he was standing still in the West: Danny had simultaneously embarked upon a program that would double the capacity of The Palace in Vegas by 1982. He had just bought a
hotel-casino complex on the south shore of Lake Tahoe.
What Howard Hughes had tried to accomplish in the 1960s,
and miserably failed to do, Danny Lehman had attempted

in the 1970s, and was now achieving to a degree that was truly astounding. He seemed virtually unstoppable.

Even Henry Price could no longer ignore the phenomenon. For the details of Danny's success were highlighted in a report by Mercier Frères, the international investment bank, a copy of which Price had taken with him from New York to his Virginia farm one summer weekend in 1980. As usual, Natalie Simmons was at the farm with him. "If he is a latter-day Howard Hughes, then why does he need you?" she asked.

Henry Price, who had been reading parts of the report aloud, took his time to answer. "Because something must be in the process of going wrong."

"How do you know?" she then asked.

"Look at the share price. Thirty-five dollars last summer. Twenty dollars now. Short interest growing steadily. Nobody on the street seems to know why. I suspect that Mr. Lehman might, however."

"But why is the firm trying to bring you into this?"

"Because it seems that he asked for me."

"You mean Lehman?"

"Yes."

"He sounds like a very grubby little man."

"He is, my dear. I've actually met him. Don't you remember my telling you about him? Maybe not. It was eleven years ago. In any case, 'grubby' was precisely the word I remember using to describe him then."

Natalie was now watching Price closely. "And in spite of that, you are seriously considering it." Her attitude on the matter was made quite clear from the tone of her voice. Her tone was not by any means a harsh one, it just conveyed a certain anxiety, which she then reinforced with the following words. "I suggest, Henry, that before you really get involved, even in the slightest, you consider your own reputation. After all, it is not just this man Lehman. It must be everybody in the gambling business. All grubby, and no doubt all crooked, if you ask me."

"Gaming," he said.

"What?" she asked.

"Gaming," he repeated. "They prefer that you call it gaming, not gambling. It sounds better."

"How silly."

"Perhaps. But just remember that every two-bit stockbroker in New York now calls himself an investment banker."

"Ah yes, but the difference is that you *are* an investment banker. And bankers and gamblers should not be seen in public together, in my opinion."

"Maybe. Maybe not. One must be realistic. Let me read what our hotshot analysts at Mercier Frères have to say." He picked up the report again. " 'We estimate,' they say, 'that domestic legalized gambling is running at an annual rate approaching thirty billion dollars per annum, and that the inclusion of the underground gambling pool, principally sports betting, raises the ante to a ninety-to-one-hundred-billion-dollar market annually, a size sufficient to rank gambling as'—and now listen carefully, my dear—'as the *third largest United States industry.*' "

"Amazing. You've made your point."

"Quite."

"But it's not really that, is it?"

"No, probably not."

"You want to shock a few people."

"Maybe."

"You want to do whatever has to be done to bail this grubby Lehman fellow out of his overextension or whatever, and then be able to say to everybody back in New York or over in Paris, 'See, Henry Price can still pull off his stuff wherever he wants, whenever he wants, if he chooses to.' "

"Perhaps."

"And assuming you do, what will you really have proven?"

"Nothing, *really,*" and the emphasis showed that he was becoming rather peeved.

"Let's face it," he then went on, "what happens to Mr. Lehman and The Palace will hardly alter the course of Western civilization, will it? It's meaningless."

"Then why do it?"

"To use that tired phrase yet again: because it is there, my dear."

"May I come along?"

Price now smiled for the first time during the conversation. "Aha," he said, "you see! You too!" She almost never accompanied him on business trips. She said it was because she had to keep her eye on her Georgetown art gallery. But he knew that it was also because, despite the fact that they had been "going together" for more than a decade now, she didn't like it when strangers gave her a certain look when it was explained that, no, she wasn't Mrs. Henry Price, but rather Miss Natalie Simmons.

"All right, I'll admit it. I *am* curious. But also I don't want you to have to stay in that ghastly place all by yourself, assuming you are really going to go there."

"Of course I'm going, so start packing. Two medium-sized suitcases should do."

"You mean now?"

"Well, yes. Lehman is sending his Lear to pick us up at four at National Airport."

"You told him already that I would be coming along?"

"In fact, I did."

"You know something? I like that. After twelve years you're still full of surprises." Natalie came over and gave him a peck on the cheek and then disappeared up the stairs.

That evening, a Lincoln was waiting for them on the tarmac about a dozen yards from where the plane parked at McCarran Airport in Las Vegas. The driver, not a regular driver but one of Bill Smith's security staff, first settled them

in the backseat and then retrieved the suitcases from the
airplane and put them in the trunk.

"Welcome back to Las Vegas, sir," the driver said as they
started to pull through the steel-mesh gates onto the public
roadway.

"Well," said Price, "when you say 'back' in my case you
are referring to a long way back. The one and only time I
have been here was in 1962, and then only for a few hours."

"And you, ma'am?" the driver asked.

"Never been here at all," was her answer, stated in a tone
of voice that indicated that conversing with drivers was not
one of her regular habits. So he decided to shut up and
drive.

If one could pick an ideal moment to arrive in Las Vegas
for the first time, it would have to be at early dusk during
late summer. The heat still shimmers on the desert floor, but
beyond, and not that far beyond, lie the mountains, which
take on a blue, then a purple hue as the evening light becomes increasingly diffuse. Then, suddenly, one is confronted with the Strip: and the dramatic natural scene fades
behind the lights of the Sands, the Dunes, MGM Grand, the
Silver Slipper, the Flamingo, the Golden Nugget, Caesars
Palace. The casinos seem to get brighter and brighter, and
closer and closer together, the farther down the Strip one
goes. And they blot out totally any lingering romantic
thoughts about deserts or mountains.

"My God," she said. "Look at this!"

"Isn't it something?" he said. "I had no idea what had
become of the place. I seem to remember it as a small town.
This makes the bright lights of Broadway look like a joke."

A mile later they halted at the brightest intersection of all:
on one corner the MGM, on another corner the Flamingo,
on the third corner Caesars Palace. But on the fourth corner, bathed in a greenish-bluish light emanating from the
enormous fountain on the grounds in front of it, stood The
Palace. The sign that said so rose fifty feet high, broadcast-

ing the name with a light display of such intensity that the sunglasses Natalie still had on were not even out of place.

"My God," she said again. "I thought I'd already seen everything, but this place beats them all."

The driver decided to break his long silence. "That's what everybody says about The Palace, ma'am. There's only one of them, isn't there?" It was obviously the prime object of local pride. The Palace was to citizens of Las Vegas what the Golden Gate Bridge was to the San Franciscans: not just a tourist attraction but a monument, a true landmark.

When they pulled up under the immense cantilevered canopy, two doormen rushed up to the car, obviously having been alerted to the fact that one of Bill Smith's men would be bringing in a VIP of the highest order. Inside the casino-hotel proper there was a scene that verged almost on bedlam. The casino floor was jammed; the noise level, fifty decibels plus. All tables, every single one, were going full blast. And the area that contained this manic scene seemed to be measured not in square feet but acres! Though it seemed hardly possible, what one's senses were confronted with inside The Palace was even more astounding than the neon dazzle one faced outside.

Like two people who had just landed on the moon, and whose initial reflex was to take it all in quickly lest it should suddenly disappear, neither Henry Price nor Natalie Simmons said a word as they proceeded the fifty-odd yards from the entrance to the hotel reception area. The minute the doorman mentioned Price's name at the desk, an assistant manager came out to greet them personally and, waiving all formalities, asked them just to follow him; their accommodations, it seemed, were ready and waiting.

The accommodations were one of the four suites on the twentieth floor of the new tower. They defied description. The living room was built around a fountain. Beyond the fountain was a statue, a replica of Michelangelo's *David*, not quite full-size, but at first glance it seemed so. To the right of

David there was a circular bar equipped with everything one
needed, including a live bartender. Beyond the bar was a
dining room of immense proportions. The candles on both
the buffet and the dining table, twenty-four in number, had
all been lit. The entire main section was partially ringed
above by a balcony. One reached the balcony via a semicircular staircase. Upstairs there was a suite within a suite,
again one of extraordinary size reflecting equally extraordinary taste: a blending of ancient Baghdad and modern
Anaheim. For instance, the sunken bath was made from
mauve marble.

"Never in my entire life . . ."

"Darling, nor in mine."

When Natalie Simmons had finally taken it all in, she
asked, "But do we have to stay here?"

"We hardly have a choice, but then why not? This probably will never happen to us again. Let's lie back and enjoy
it."

"But it's absolutely outrageous," she said. "Look at the
color scheme!"

They both shook their heads and began to giggle, while
Natalie sat down on the circular bed, watching her image in
the lighted mirrors above and around the bed. Then she
opened the soft gauzelike curtains that encircled the bed, so
as to be better able to reappraise the entire suite. The so-
called color scheme was one of oranges upon greens upon
purples upon pinks, but to call it garish would not only have
been an understatement of vast proportions, it would also
have been unfair. For as ludicrous as it all appeared when
seen through the eyes of "civilized" Easterners, who were
used to the best that New York or Paris or Rome had to
offer, The Palace had not been built to please *them.* And it
was Henry Price who said just that. "Darling, this is probably not for us to judge and most certainly not for us to put
down. This man Lehman undoubtedly knew exactly what
he was trying to accomplish here. I suspect he wanted to

provide adults with the counterpart of Disneyland, and I think he has succeeded to a remarkable degree. But I think I could use a fairly stiff drink."

"Make that two," Natalie answered, "but first tell me: must we dress for the occasion or may we go as we are?" And again she giggled.

"I think we will chance it and go as we are."

At that moment he noticed that lights were blinking on the many telephones scattered around the place, so he picked one up, and when connected with the message desk was informed that Mr. Daniel Lehman was expecting them for dinner at nine o'clock in the Florentine Room, and that dress would be formal. After he had hung up he turned to Natalie and said, "Well, my answer was premature. I fear that, contrary to all expectations, we will indeed have to dress for the occasion. I do hope that you have brought some evening clothes along."

She had. "And what is the occasion, if I might ask?"

"We have been beckoned to dinner by Mr. Lehman."

"You mean you were invited via the message desk?" she asked.

"Well, my dear, this is a new and strange country. As Goethe once said, *Andere Länder, andere Sitten.*"

The Florentine Room, The Palace's most elegant dining room, had nothing garish about it. It had been designed as a replica of the Tour d'Argent in Paris, and rather successfully. It suffered somewhat from the fact that the view was not of Nôtre Dame and the Île de France but rather of the parking lot and, beyond that, a vacant lot. But copies can hardly ever be expected to live up to the original totally. The ambience, at least one's initial impression of it, was not enhanced by there being three armed guards at the entrance to the restaurant, who, however, immediately let them pass when Henry told them his name. They had barely stepped into the room when a man about five foot six inches tall, slightly on the plump side, immaculately groomed and just as immaculately tailored, and smiling a smile that could only be described as very broad, open, and friendly, came up to them.

"You're Henry Price," he said. "We've met before, if you recall."

"I do recall," replied Price.

"You've done us all a great honor by coming over here today, and I hope everything so far has met with your approval. If there's anything, anything at all you need, just call my office. My secretary knows you're here. Tell her what you want and you'll get it."

"It's all fine. And we're delighted, simply delighted to be here," Price responded. He almost meant it, since Danny Lehman was obviously trying his damnedest to be a gracious host. So why not be agreeable? After all, there could well be a great deal of money to be made here.

Danny's eyes then turned to the young lady at Price's side; she appeared to be in her mid-thirties, in contrast to Price's sixtyish appearance. It was very apparent that Danny approved of what he saw, and he said as much. "Well now, Mr. Price, tell me who this young lady is, and before you do let me warn you: I like beautiful young women, but I promise you that she is going to be, beyond any doubt, the most beautiful woman in this room tonight. And we have some pretty good-looking women coming, I can tell you."

"Mr. Lehman," said Henry Price, "please meet my fiancée, Natalie Simmons."

Danny took Natalie's hand in both of his and gave her a smile which, if anything, was still broader and even more open. "If you don't mind, Mr. Price, I would be honored if your delightful fiancée would join me at my table this evening." Without waiting for an answer from Henry Price he turned to Natalie and asked, "Would that be all right with you, Miss Simmons?"

"I would be delighted," she answered, although her voice indicated more than a small measure of, not hesitancy particularly, but rather a feeling of having been taken back by the abruptness of it all. Danny Lehman noticed nothing, naturally, and once again took hold of her hand and said, "Come. I must introduce you to some of my friends who will be joining us for dinner this evening."

The first friend was Eddie Cordoba. Eddie, Danny explained, ran The Palace. Then he introduced an Englishman, Chapman by name. He was, he declared, the owner of the Lotus auto racing team. Next in line was an Argentinian, a friend of Cordoba's. And so it went on until finally she spotted Henry Price again across the room. She made her excuses to Danny and hurried to Price's side.

"What are all these people doing here?" she immediately asked.

"It seems," he began, "that there is going to be a Grand—"

At that moment there were three loud claps, and when everybody turned to see what was going on, it was Danny Lehman who clapped again. "It's time to eat, folks, so let's sit down."

Natalie had drawn the place of honor, to the right of Danny Lehman. To her right sat the Argentinian, a Mr. Reutemann according to the engraved place cards, who explained why all these people were gathered together. "You see," he said, "we are having a race here tomorrow and Mr. Lehman has put on this dinner party for some of the owners and drivers. I guess you could best describe it as a pre-race get-together."

"And where is this race going to take place? Out in the desert somewhere?" she asked.

"No," answered the Argentinian, "actually, in the parking lot."

"The parking lot?"

"Yes, the parking lot. You see, Mr. Lehman and Mr. Cor-

doba decided last year after having watched the Grand Prix
in Monaco that it would be rather nice to have one here.
They couldn't put it on, or at least couldn't *quite* put it on in
the casino, so they decided to stage it in the parking lot."

"But how on earth can you convert a parking lot into a
Grand Prix race circuit?"

"With about two million dollars," Reutemann answered.

"You must be kidding." She noticed he wasn't. "Then
how does one park from now on?"

"No real problem. It's only taken them three days to put
it up, and they tell me it will only take them one day to rip it
down. So it won't cause that much difficulty. Now tell me,
Natalie, isn't it, you are coming to watch me race tomorrow,
aren't you?"

"Well no, no one has said anything."

Reutemann then leaned across her to address Danny Lehman. "Danny," he said, "Natalie insists upon coming to the
races tomorrow. You've fixed her up, haven't you?"

Danny shook his head and said, "No, but it will be done
right now." He waved a finger at Cordoba, who immediately
sprang up from his seat to come over and, having received
his instructions from Danny, left the room directly. He was
back three minutes later. "Everything has been arranged,
Miss Simmons," he said. "The necessary credentials will be
delivered to your room in the morning. My suggestion is
that you come to the track around eleven o'clock. That way
you can choose the spot you want before the race starts."

The dinner was excellent by the standards of any country.
Surprisingly, nobody drank much, even though the white
was a superb product of France and the red, a 1978 Jordan,
California's finest. At ten-thirty, Danny Lehman stood up to
say that the party was over and in a courteous but strangely
abrupt fashion said good night to everyone at the table, including Henry Price and Natalie, and disappeared from the
room.

Henry immediately came over, put his arm around Natalie, and, leading her out of the dining room, asked, "Darling, shall we go down to the casino and try our hand at something?"

"Please, no," she said. "I hope you don't mind terribly if we call it a night. I think I've had already too much of this sort of thing. Let's go upstairs and see if our personal barman can serve us a nightcap."

"I don't mind it at all," he answered with disappointment. "In fact, I've had quite enough myself."

They proceeded back to the tower suite, which was now *sans* bartender, so Henry did the honors. Within a short time they found themselves beneath the sheets, and also beneath the immense circular mirror that reflected their immense circular bed. The entire room was bathed in a pinkish sort of light from a hidden source, and presumably controlled by a switch that was also hidden, so well hidden that they were not able to find it. This did not bother Henry; he went to sleep right away. Natalie, however, could not; and, for one of the few times in her life, rather regretted that the man beside her was, well, not insisting. Even the light would not have bothered her, though she did prefer to do it in total darkness. She did not find the sight of *it* exactly aesthetic. But somehow, that night, she had the feeling even *that* would not have bothered her. How to explain it? She speculated for a few minutes and then came up with the answer: either it was the Latin machismo of the Argentinian racing driver, and she giggled, or, and this surprised her, perhaps it was the way Danny Lehman had insisted upon touching her from the moment he had first laid eyes upon her. All through dinner he had found a way to touch her that was apparently very casual, yet somehow intimate. Anyway, it was all rather ridiculous, she told herself, and after glancing up at the mirror one more time, she turned away from Henry and drifted off to sleep.

14

It began with what sounded like a series of staccato sputterings, which soon merged to become a growl, a growl that quickly became a howl, and then a roar.

"Henry. Are you awake?"

He was now. He looked at the bedside clock. It was 7:30 A.M. "What's going on?"

The roar was now interrupted, or perhaps a better word is "superseded," by a series of fierce, ear-splitting whines, now building up, now fading. And all this was permeating a room on the twentieth floor, one that was still bathed in a faint pink light, and that appeared to be as hermetically sealed off from the rest of the world as possible.

"It's outside," Price then said.

"Obviously," she replied, sliding out of bed. She first tried to find a way to open the curtains, and God knows what else that stood between her and the window, but failed completely. Nothing budged. So she ducked under them, slid open the window, and looked down upon a huge racetrack, surrounded by a series of grandstands and bleachers, around which at least twenty racing cars were pounding at what she could tell were ferocious speeds, even from that height.

"Henry!" she screamed. "You've *got* to see this."

Henry, sleeping naked as usual, crawled under the curtains and was soon crouched at her side, equally stunned by the scene below. "Christ!" he exclaimed. A few minutes later his arm went around her shoulder and then descended almost immediately to her left breast. His right hand came around to take her right hand and pull it to his erection. She had no choice but to grasp it. Then, reluctantly, her hand began to move, first slowly, but then more quickly and intently.

"Honey," he said, "let's go back to bed." But she just kept going.

"There," she said soothingly, looking neither at him nor, most definitely, at *it*.

Then chimes sounded, so loudly that one could hear them above the bedlam outside. She pulled her hand away immediately and, flushed with embarrassment, ducked back out into the bedroom. "It's somebody at the door," he said, reemerging behind her.

"I'll see," she said. "You're not dressed." She put on a rather flimsy robe over her nightgown and quickly descended the semicircular marble staircase to the living quarters below. When she opened the door, it was to find Danny Lehman, tennis shorts and all, waiting there with a huge package in his arms. Again he greeted her with a huge grin. "Gee," he said, "I hope I'm not too early."

"No, not at all. I mean, with all that noise out there we've been up for at least an hour," she lied.

"Look," he then continued, "I've got your credentials for the race and I brought something else I thought you might like. May I?"

"Of course," and she led him into the living room.

"Here," he said. He proceeded to rip open the package and hand her two huge jackets, obviously his and her versions of the same design.

"What are they?" she asked.

"Racing jackets. Special editions. We only made twenty of them."

They looked like the sort of thing that Canadian hockey players wear when trudging through the snow to and from the rinks in northern Quebec. Made of shiny satiny material, they were predominantly fire-engine red, with black stripes down the arms and, in huge letters on the back: THE PALACE GRAND PRIX—1980.

"Try it on," he said. As she struggled to do so, both her robe and nightgown ended up in a total state of disarray.

"Let me help you," said Danny, ever the gentleman. After he had gotten her arms through the sleeves, he then fumbled for the zipper, finally had it, and then drew it slowly up to her chest, giving her breasts a very careful examination in the process. By the time he was finished, he and Natalie were only inches apart. He stepped back and, without looking down at her body again, said, "It looks terrific on you."

He then reached into his pocket and handed over two badges. "Put them on the jackets. They'll get you anywhere you want to go down there. I look forward to seeing you around eleven." And he turned and left.

Trembling, Natalie slipped out of the jacket and slowly went back upstairs where Henry Price was waiting, still naked. "What was that all about?"

"Tickets for the race. And jackets for both of us to wear that are simply unbelievable," she answered.

"Let me go down and look," he said.

"In a minute, Henry," she replied, reaching down again to grasp what remained of his erection. When she took it into her mouth a couple of minutes later he was so surprised and excited that he came within ten seconds.

She'd never done *that* before. Maybe there was really something to Las Vegas.

At eleven o'clock precisely, Natalie Simmons and Henry Price entered the elevator at the top of the Palace tower. It was a slow descent to the main lobby, stopping on almost every single floor until the elevator had reached its weight limit. The routine was the same at each stop. The gaming *cum* race fans, almost all men, stepped in, looked at Natalie

Simmons and then at her racing jacket, and either silently, or in three cases out loud, said the only thing one could say, "Wow!" The guy that got in on the sixteenth floor went one further. "I'll give you five hundred dollars for those jackets." When neither Natalie nor Henry said a word, he added, "Each!"

Rather than get into any detailed conversation, Henry just shrugged and said, "Sorry," and the elevator, this time, headed straight for the lobby. When they had managed to push their way through the crowd in the casino, already going full blast at 11:00 A.M., and out of the back entrance of the casino, normally used for access to the parking lot, they were met by a deafening silence, and by a very long line leading to the gates of the track itself. Almost immediately a scantily clad young lady came up to them, gave the badges with their blue ribbons and the letter *A* a quick glance, and asked Henry where they would like to go.

"What are the choices?"

"That badge, sir, will get you anywhere you want to go."

"Where are the cars?" Natalie asked.

"In the pits for the final checks."

"We couldn't actually go there, could we?" Natalie asked.

"Anywhere you want" was the answer.

And a few moments later they found themselves on the narrow strip separating the track itself from the pits, in which the crews were really doing nothing but standing around having their pictures taken. They had been there but a minute when Eddie Cordoba appeared, as if by magic. "Mr. Lehman asked me to see to your needs," he said. "May I suggest that we say hello to a couple of the drivers, and then, perhaps, have a glass of champagne?"

They went first to the Saudi Leyland cars to meet Alan Jones and Carlos Reutemann, who vaguely remembered having met Natalie the evening before, then over to the Brabham piloted by Nelson Piquet and, at the insistence of Henry Price, who seemed to know more about this than either Natalie or Cordoba expected, to meet Mario Andretti, who was driving an Alfa Romeo 179C for the Marlboro team. "We've served as advisers to Alfa in Milan on various occasions," Price said. "In fact, it was upon our advice that they got back into racing."

They ended up in a roped-off area at the finishing line, where a boxed lunch consisting of Iranian caviar, gravadlax, and cold pheasant awaited them. Men in white jackets were serving Moët et Chandon to counteract the heat, which had already built up to the low nineties.

When the race began, it was the incredible noise that impressed the pair from the East Coast the most. But then, to stand behind a thin concrete wall, only waist-high, and be able to lean over and look at a Grand Prix racing car coming at you at a couple of hundred miles an hour and passing within feet of where you were standing—and then another and another—was, as Henry put it, "a rather uncommon experience." It was over in two hours, and it seemed that nobody really cared who had won, except for Reutemann and his team, who were the victors. Within thirty minutes of the end of the race the crowd of fifty thousand was gone and a crew of construction men were already starting to rip down the grandstand.

Inside the casino the unreality of it all was further magnified. For on passing through the doors one left the heat, the blinding sun, the dust, and the rowdy atmosphere of the sports crowd behind, and suddenly found oneself in a perfectly controlled, sixty-eight-degree, dust-free atmosphere: a world of dimmed lights and the muffled background noise of coins jingling in slot machines. It seemed that almost every one of the fifty thousand who had attended the race, paying up to two hundred and fifty dollars for the privilege, was now in the casino.

"That man Lehman is a genius," Price said as he and Natalie walked from the "new" casino, which had been built at the base of the new tower, to the vast area of the "old" casino. They passed thousands of people whose main aim in life now appeared to be to find a place at a blackjack or craps table and come out a winner, just as Reutemann had in the Grand Prix.

When they finally got back to their suite, it was to find the message lights on the telephones blinking. Again it was an invitation to dinner. Another black-tie event, but this time in Palm Springs. Someone would pick them up at their room at six-thirty. It was optional, the message said, whether they packed an overnight bag or not. There would be accommodations waiting for them in Palm Springs; a plane would be available if they chose to come back to Vegas.

The same man who had picked them up on their flight in from Virginia knocked at the tower suite at exactly six-thirty to escort them to the limo. The plane that awaited them at McCarran was a Gulfstream II, the luxury liner of the private airways. It was the ever present Eddie Cordoba who was standing next to the plane greeting the dozen or so passengers, all of whom seemed to arrive at the same time. They were all strangers, so Natalie and Price kept to themselves. The trip from Vegas to Palm Springs was short and dramatic: straight up over the sharply rising mountains, and then straight down into the valley that contains the Springs. On the ground it was a repeat of the scene in Las Vegas: a fleet of black limos ready to transport each of the couples in air-conditioned privacy.

The common destination was the Palace-owned villa, built in the Spanish style, surrounded by plush green lawns, and overlooking the obligatory immense pool area. It was there that they were all gathering, and it was there that Daniel Lehman was greeting the guests as they came down the steps. Naturally a mariachi band was playing in the background, and just as naturally a team of Mexican waiters was circulating with the champagne and caviar canapés. To say that Danny greeted everyone effusively would not even begin to describe the enthusiasm he displayed. What did not seem particularly appropriate was that the guests did not seem worthy of such effusiveness. To Price and Natalie they looked like rich retired butchers with call girls. The men had paunches in every case, and all smoked cigars. Two thirds of the women were blond.

Before Price and Natalie had quite made it up the receiving line to Danny, the Mexican band burst out in a very brassy version of "For He's a Jolly Good Fellow," and Danny went up to the microphone in front of the band, accompanied by someone who looked like the president of the butchers' union: an old guy, probably over seventy, but one who was still built like a linebacker, and who had a blonde in her mid-twenties in tow.

"Listen, everybody," yelled Danny, once the band had stopped. "This evening's a surprise party for a man you all know and love, and who deserves this celebration more than anybody I know in the whole world. He's a man who is all heart. Somebody once asked me who I'd turn to if everything went bad, when everybody was walking away. You know what I mean?" A lot of nods. They knew, it seemed.

"Well, the man I named was this man." And Danny put his arm around the seventy-year-old hulk, and squeezed. "So let's hear it for Mannie!" he then yelled.

He got the applause he wanted. Mannie just stood there grinning, and then held up his arms in the boxer's victory salute to himself when the band this time began a Tijuana version of "Happy Days Are Here Again." Then a parade of waiters suddenly began to come down the steps from the main house, each carrying a tray of delicacies that would make up the buffet dinner. The crowd of about fifty murmured appreciatively and began consuming exotic pâtés, marinated seafood, and clams cooked in a superb combination of herbs, in a manner that indicated that they were quite used to this sort of cuisine.

"Casting pearls to the swine, wouldn't you say?" These

words came from Eddie Cordoba, who stood behind Natalie as she helped herself to some clams. She was too startled to reply. "No offense, I hope," Cordoba continued. "It's just that sometimes it's hard to stomach even for me."

"Who are they?" Natalie asked.

"Shall we all sit together and perhaps I can explain," replied Cordoba.

The three of them found a table as far away from both the buffet and the band as possible. No sooner had they sat down than a waiter filled their glasses with a 1978 Meursault-Perrières. He returned a few minutes later to ask which red wine they preferred, a 1969 Lafite or a 1959 Latour.

At the tables around them, the wine seemed to disappear almost as soon as it was poured, and the volume of noise began to build up in spite of the fact that they were outdoors. A few of the blondes let out a screech now and then. Then Danny Lehman suddenly materialized at their table. He spoke directly to Natalie. "Great that you could come. How do you like the place?"

"It's marvelous," she answered.

"I hope you're staying the night. You've got the best of the bungalows if you do."

"No. It's so kind of you, Mr. Lehman. But we decided to go back. This is all still a bit . . . strenuous for us, isn't it, Henry?"

"It is. Overwhelming."

"Henry," Danny then said, abruptly. "Could we talk tomorrow morning?"

"Sure."

"Eight o'clock all right? My office?"

"Perfect."

Danny was then accosted by one of the blondes, who almost dragged him off toward the area where the dancing had begun. He looked back at Natalie with a feigned look of helplessness and disappeared.

"He's something, isn't he?" commented Cordoba.

"Yes," answered both Natalie and Henry. And both meant it in their own ways.

"Now," said Natalie, "tell me. What is this place?"

"This"—and Cordoba's hand traced a circular movement—"is one of the establishments which The Palace keeps for its clientele, those high rollers you've no doubt heard about. There's this place, then there are the yachts, plural, one in Miami, the other in San Diego. Then there's La Costa, and the place in the Catskills, and . . . well, there's one more, but I forget where it is at the moment."

"But who are these clients?"

"From all over the world, usually. But not tonight. This is strictly for our American friends."

"And who is the guest of honor?"

"Mannie?" he replied, and then just sat there thinking for a minute. "Mannie has been coming to The Palace once a month since I've been here, and that's been, what, ten or eleven years now? Anyway, Mannie used to just come to shoot craps. After all, that's what all his friends play, or at least used to play. And a lot of his friends are here tonight. Mannie was originally from St. Louis, I might add. Now he's from"—and again his hand traced a semicircle—"from these places.

"Anyway," Cordoba continued, "about ten years ago I introduced him to baccarat. He loved it from the first minute, because it's fast, very fast, and you don't have to think. Ever." Cordoba leaned over the table toward Henry Price and said, now in a much softer voice, "Mannie drops an average of two million dollars a year at the baccarat table. Every year except this year. So far this year it has been almost five million. He dropped a very, very big packet a month ago, the weekend of the big fight."

"Amazing," said Price.

"Let me suggest something," Cordoba said. "Hang around for another fifteen minutes. Then I'll have your car ready to take you back to the airport. Our plane is there waiting. It'll start to get a bit crude soon. And I think you might . . ." His voice tailed off. "Now please excuse me," he said.

Cordoba walked over to the dance floor and retrieved Danny from the blonde; then both of them disappeared in the crowd. Five minutes later Danny once again climbed onto the podium and the band stopped. "Mannie," he said. "Where are you?"

Mannie staggered onto the dance floor, supported by two young ladies. "Mannie, I've got something I want to show you, and everybody! Follow me!"

Danny stepped back down to the dance floor, pushed one of the ladies aside, and, taking Mannie's left arm, led him, and the parade of guests that followed, up the stairs toward the main house. But rather than entering, he followed the walk around the left side, leading toward the circular driveway that wound around the inevitable fountain, as spectacularly lit as the neon "signature" of The Palace. He shooed the second blonde away, and then, with Mannie, walked up to a red Rolls-Royce Corniche that stood alone in all its splendor. Danny raised his hands to silence the crowd and then spoke in a voice that all could hear. "Mannie, happy birthday!" And he handed over the keys of the Corniche to the huge, aging man. Tears began to stream down the man's face. He embraced Danny, then Cordoba, who stood beside Lehman, then a third man, who Henry later found out was one of Danny's partners, a man by the name of Granville. Then all four stood together with their arms around one another. The ceremony ended almost as quickly as it had begun. The crowd moved back toward the dance floor, lured by the sound of the Mexican band. Cordoba found Price and Natalie and took them over to a waiting limo. "How did you like the last little scene?" he asked, as he opened the back door of the car for Natalie.

"Truly touching," she answered.

"Glad you thought so. Mannie will lose the cost of that Corniche in less than two hours tomorrow night." He grinned and closed the car door behind them.

Half an hour later they were airborne, heading back to Vegas, alone in the Palace's Gulfstream with the two pilots. "Henry," Natalie said, once they were up.

"Yes."

"Maybe it's better we go back to Virginia."

"Yes, I know what you mean."

"Let's. We can get our things at the hotel and just leave."

"No. That wouldn't be fair."

They sat in silence for the next five minutes. "What kind of people are they?" Natalie asked. Henry Price just shrugged. But Natalie knew that he was bothered, perhaps deeply bothered, by what he had witnessed.

"Look," he then said, "Lehman knew it. You noticed he did not introduce us to a single one of those people."

"Thank God. But then why invite us?"

"Maybe to show that one client, the birthday boy, covered the total cost of today's extravaganza in the parking lot. Even with the Rolls thrown in. If that was Lehman's point, he made it, at least as far as I'm concerned. You could not help but wonder how much the other twenty-five guys who were there this evening 'contribute' on an annual basis."

Then he added, "Don't worry, dear. I'll be careful tomorrow. If I don't like what I hear, we'll be on a plane before lunch."

15

Henry Price rose at six-thirty the following morning. Without waking Natalie, he left their suite, went down to the pool, which was totally deserted, and did his normal fifty laps. Then it was back up to the suite, where he showered and shaved and, finally, put on what Natalie called his banker's uniform, a pin-striped suit. Ready for work, he headed for Danny Lehman's office.

When Price left the small elevator that led to the executive offices of The Palace it was exactly eight o'clock in the morning, and he was amazed to see the place bustling with people and activity. Somehow, he thought to himself, one had the idea that everybody in Las Vegas probably started work around ten, or even eleven. Danny Lehman was in the hallway waiting for him. As Price walked up, he looked at his watch. "Eight on the second. I knew it," he stated. "Now, do you want the grand tour, or would you prefer to get right down to business?"

"Business," Price replied.

Henry Price knew only too well the value of grand tours. Invariably when he visited a company for the first time, one that needed either his money or his services in obtaining some, the first day was totally wasted with a tour of their bricks and mortar and whatever was contained within: assembly lines where automobile firms were concerned; laboratories if the company was in either pharmaceuticals or electronics; vaults and computers if it was a financial institution. On one memorable morning, when visiting a rubber company, he had been forced to watch women dressed in white testing prophylactics mechanically. That was outside Tokyo. In London, the chairman of the board of an office machine company there had personally picked him up at Heathrow in the company Rolls, since the chauffeur had suddenly been taken ill. They needed a hundred million dollars, and it was thought that when Price saw their magnificent new plant on the outskirts of London, Mercier Frères would simply thrust the funds at them. For an hour and a half the chairman, Price, and the Rolls wandered around an industrial park somewhere off Western Avenue, searching, asking directions, searching again. They never found it. Needless to say, the company also found no lender in Henry Price.

"Then let's look at the numbers," Danny said.

Price immediately agreed. He was a numbers man.

"I'll bring in our financial man. His name's Matthew Kelly."

Kelly was a man of very few words and masses of computer printouts. He presented page after page of statistics to Price, and Price either nodded or grunted, after which they moved on to the next set of numbers, or he asked a very brief question and got an immediate equally brief answer. Danny had quietly left the room and returned after fifteen minutes bearing two cups of coffee. After having placed them on the coffee table in front of the two men, he left again. When he returned for the second time an hour later, Kelly was in the process of packing up and leaving.

"What're you doing, Kelly?" Danny asked, visibly disturbed.

"Mr. Price said he doesn't need me anymore, sir."

"At least for the moment, Mr. Kelly," Price added.

Danny's expression brightened. His financial man left.

"Well, what do you think?" he then asked Price.

"You need a quarter of a billion dollars rather badly."

"Exactly."

"You've overdone it a bit in Atlantic City, I'm afraid."

"For the moment, yes. In the long run, no."

"What's the long run in your business?"

"Two years."

Price laughed. He liked the answer. "Why are your banks not willing to carry you that long?"

Danny shrugged. "Because they're banks, I guess. They gave us a construction loan. The construction's done, with the usual overruns. They want their money back."

"That's all?"

"As far as we know."

"How's Atlantic City done thus far?"

"On schedule."

"I saw your projections. You expect to gross two hundred million this year, if I recall the number. And to net 10 percent. Right?"

"Yes."

"What will be the combined cash flow next year of both the Nevada and New Jersey operations?"

"Sixty million."

"Assuming you net twenty million in Atlantic City."

"Right."

"If I arranged to get you that quarter of a billion for five years at 15 percent it would be a rather tight squeeze, wouldn't it? If Atlantic City somehow didn't quite pan out, I mean."

"Yes, it would."

"That's no doubt why the banks want out," Price stated.

"Probably," Danny answered. "They're worried that Atlantic City won't be able to support all the new casinos that are about to open: Bally, Caesars, Boardwalk, Claridge, Playboy, Resorts International, Ramada Tropicana, Golden Nugget, Harrah's. It's a long list."

"Will it?"

"Of course it will. Just look at the demographics. There

are fifty million people within a day's drive of Atlantic City. We've just scratched the surface so far."

"Some of the people on Wall Street seem to disagree."

Danny shrugged, but said nothing more.

"What kind of a kicker could you offer Mercier Frères' clients?" Price then asked.

"What would Mercier Frères expect?"

"We would want the notes to be fully convertible."

"That's pretty steep."

"You've got a risky situation here."

"At what price could the conversion rights be exercised?"

"That would take some study. I don't think that would present a big problem. Normally it's 20 percent above the market price at the time of the closing. We're investment bankers, not thieves."

"What else?"

"Immediate representation on your board."

"Who?"

"Probably me."

"Where will the money come from?"

"I'd put together a private placement syndicate. In Europe. We might put up some of the money ourselves. In any case, you would be dealing only with us. Nobody else. Now or later."

"How soon could you put such a deal together?" Danny then asked, this time after a substantial pause.

"Oh, say within two months."

"That quickly? What about the SEC?"

"No problem if we do it all outside of the United States, which is what I would intend to do. That, plus the fact that our name would be on it." Then Price added one further condition. "We would, of course, require absolutely and on a contractual basis that you would remain with this company as its chief executive officer during the entire term of this loan, Danny. We'd also expect that you continue to supervise Atlantic City. We know you personally got it off the ground; now we'd want you to keep it there."

"Henry, you couldn't keep me *away* from Atlantic City. That place was my idea and that casino is my baby." Then he added, "The conversion aspect bothers me. I've personally controlled The Palace absolutely from the very beginning. I don't believe in partners."

Price had an immediate answer: "If, and I emphasize the 'if,' we exercise the conversion rights it will only be because the combination of your leadership and our money has produced the success we both fully anticipate. After that we will be the most silent of silent partners. We exist to make money, not run casinos."

Danny nodded and asked, "Assuming we proceed with this, how long would it take you and your bank to come up with something concrete? You know, like a written proposal or whatever you call it."

"A week. How long would it then take you to get your board's approval?"

"A day," Danny answered.

And again Price laughed. It was hard to get one up on this guy.

"One more question," Danny then said. "How would we handle the publicity on this?"

"Easy. There will be none. When it's all done we'll place a couple of tombstones in the *Journal* and the *Times,* and after those bare-bones announcement ads, no further comment."

"Why? Are you still reticent to have your bank's name identified with our business?"

"Not at all. We always do it that way."

This time it was Danny who grinned. Both men then rose from behind the coffee table. "I'll need a little time to think about all this," Danny said.

"Take all the time you need. Now I have a request."

"Name it," Danny replied.

"Do you think I could get in a little tennis this morning?"

"Sure. Would you like to play with one of our pros?"

The thirty-two-year-old pro was waiting on the court half an hour later. An hour after that he was surprised to find out that his opponent on the other side of the net had actually caused him to work up a mild sweat. Some of those old geezers could really surprise you. And this guy was a fucking banker. No doubt that was why Danny Lehman had asked him the favor. On the other hand, it was comforting to know that even a rich bastard like Lehman had to kiss somebody's ass. The old guy must be *really* important, the pro concluded. So he let him win a game.

Danny Lehman liked to walk when he had something important to think about. At nine o'clock in the morning The Palace was not exactly going full blast, so he could walk and think without having somebody stop him every dozen steps or so to say hello. By ten-fifteen he had made up his mind. So he took the elevator to the top of the tower and rang the bell outside the door of Price's suite. It was Natalie who opened it.

"I guess he's not back yet," Danny said, suddenly embarrassed.

"He's playing tennis," she said.

"I know."

"Come in for goodness' sake."

She was wearing white shorts and a white blouse, the top button of which was open. Danny looked at the desk and saw the stationery on top of it. "I'm interrupting," he said, ready to back right out of the room.

"Not at all. I was just catching up on a few letters. I need a break. I've got some coffee going in the kitchen. Would you join me? I'm sure Henry will be back soon. He's been gone for almost an hour already."

Damn good legs, too, he thought as he watched her disappear. And he also liked the short blond hair. She was quite a number. He sat down on the sofa, and when she returned with the coffee and leaned down to serve him, the second button on her blouse popped open. I'd better be careful, he thought. If I even *think* about fucking her, that guy Price is bound to notice and I'll blow this whole deal. He crossed his legs and he could have sworn that she was watching his crotch while he did so. Settle down, boy, he told himself, and then said to her, "You're an artist."

"No, no. I own an art gallery, that's all. In Washington. I first worked there, then bought it. Are you interested in art?"

"Definitely. Especially statues. What kind of art are you into?"

"Women painters, predominantly. It's the specialty of my gallery."

"You mean like Grandma Moses?"

"Kind of, yes. Although actually most of our painters are early-twentieth-century Europeans. Names like Paula Modersohn-Becker, or Suzanne Valadon." She saw that he was drawing a complete blank. "Now let me warm up that coffee for you," she said, and this time when she reached down to pick up his cup the *third* button gave way and Danny was faced with a luscious white cleavage.

Exercising self-control that he never thought possible, Danny said, "Here, let me." He stood up, reached across the table, and, one by one, as she stood there frozen to the spot, did up her buttons.

"There," he said, hoping that the trembling of his hands had not been noticed.

As if by telepathy, Henry Price chose that moment to walk into the suite, and Natalie turned to greet him, cool as a cucumber.

"Darling, I've been discussing art with Mr. Lehman."

While showing me your breasts, Danny thought, though he said, "Yes, and very interesting it was, too. Now tell me, was Joey nice to you?"

"He was. In fact, he let me win a game," Price replied.

"Do you mind if I get back to business for a minute?" Danny then asked.

"Not at all," replied Price.

"I've decided to accept your two hundred and fifty million dollars at 15 percent for five years," Danny said. "I don't like the conversion aspect, but I can live with it."

Price moved forward to shake his hand as Natalie retreated to her desk on the other side of the room. "Wonderful," he said. "I'll get right on the phone to New York. Then I think you should send that man Kelly up here. We're going to need a lot of data and documents from you people. I think he's probably the best qualified to help us there." Then he added, "If you agree."

Of course Danny Lehman agreed. New York was also enthusiastic, to put it mildly; 15 percent interest with conversion rights at a premium of 20 percent of current market, which would mean twenty-four dollars a share, and all this from a company in solid financial shape and one with a brilliant future: Henry Price had outdone even himself. In fact, it was a situation of such merit that the partners of Mercier Frères unanimously agreed that they should keep part of the deal for their own investment account through either London or Paris. And it was obvious that they would have to ration the outside allocations of this one very carefully. The Europeans had *never* been given an exclusive shot at a thing like this. It was agreed that the whole matter should be left in the hands of Price: he should decide which European banks to invite in; he would make the presentations personally. And the sooner the better, before Lehman, or somebody on his board, had second thoughts; i.e., before they decided to check out Kuhn, Loeb or Lazard or Salomon Brothers for a better deal.

It was with some reluctance that Price agreed to his role in all this: running around Europe putting together yet another syndicate was not his idea of semiretirement. But he could hardly turn it over to anybody else at this point. Furthermore, it could hardly take very long. Unless . . . unless there was something somewhere in The Palace's financial woodwork that had not yet come out; something that could explain why Danny Lehman was so immediately ready to accept the terms he had proposed. The only thing that made him uneasy came up when he was going over the draft of the "History" section of the private placement prospectus that The Palace's financial man, Kelly, was helping him put together.

"Now, you say here, 'In the spring of 1969 Mr. Lehman assumed control of the company, then known as Raffles Inc., and three months later took on the position of chairman and chief executive officer.' "

"Yes," Kelly answered.

"Why the delay between 'assuming control' and becoming CEO?" Price asked.

"I believe that there was some kind of a conflict between Mr. Lehman and the senior management."

"Was that before your time here?"

"No, I was here, but not privy to that type of information."

"I see. Well, I don't think anybody in either New York or Europe is going to raise the issue. But there's one they might raise, and it's not covered here."

"What's that, sir?"

"Where did Mr. Lehman get the financing allowing him to 'assume control'?"

"He sold his old business in Philadelphia."

"I know that. But where did the rest come from?"

"I don't know. I'll have to ask Mr. Lehman."

Price made a quick decision. Despite his reservations, there simply was no sense in introducing some new element at this point, one that might for some reason upset Lehman, and thus rock the boat. This was a deal that every house on Wall Street would leap at. He intended to close it as quickly as possible. "Hold on. I'm not sure it's pertinent. After all, the SEC is not going to have to pass on this. Again, it was a long time ago and really has nothing whatsoever to do with the current status and outlook of the company."

"I agree. But still, I could ask Mr. Lehman and—"

"No. Let's drop the matter. Now, back to the balance sheet. Accounts receivable. They seem awfully high. What's the reason?"

Boring stuff, but it had to be done. And three days later it was done. And at five o'clock on the evening of that third day, Price announced to Natalie that they would be leaving the next morning for the East Coast, and then, almost immediately, for Zurich. Then they would return directly to Las Vegas, provided everything could be worked out.

"I'd rather not come with you, Henry," she told him. "As you know, the Swiss lost their charm for me a long time ago. Do you mind if I just stay here for a few days until you return?"

"Of course not. But why here? I would have thought you'd prefer going back to your Georgetown house."

"Actually no. I'm rather enjoying myself. I think I might even rent a car, visit the Hoover Dam, take a spin in the desert."

When he left for the airport at six-thirty the next morning he decided not to wake her. In fact, he sensed that she again needed what she called "space"; better he let her be for a few days. He would call her from New York.

16

Natalie didn't get up until noon. She had awoken around eight and realized that Price was gone. It didn't bother her; quite the opposite. She then decided to rent a car for the afternoon. She picked out a red Cadillac convertible. Why not, she told herself. When in Vegas . . . She went to the dam, took the guided tour, and returned to the hotel around five o'clock, hot and dusty.

While she was taking her bath in a replica of Pompeii's finest, she thought to herself, What I need now is the calming effects of a very dry martini, ice-cold and straight up. But what on earth does a lady alone wear during the cocktail hour at The Palace?

She decided on a little black dress, which would probably turn out to be the only little black dress at The Palace that evening, but what the hell, she thought as she emerged from the elevator into the vastness of the casino, I'm probably also the only one in this place that has ever heard of Paula Modersohn-Becker.

Next problem: which bar? The one that was supposed to resemble a circus tent? The one that was built like a Viking ship? The one featuring country and western? She kept walking and was suddenly confronted with a bar that was built like a bar, looked like a bar, and had no music. Furthermore, she noticed with comfort, it was also a bar in which there were a number of other women sitting by themselves. Good for them! She took a step up, passing through a gap in the brass railing that separated the area from the main casino floor, and was greeted by the maître d', who scrutinized her and, failing to recognize her, said nothing and just proceeded to show her to a table well off to the right. Then he seemed to decide that he should say *something,* so: "I thought you might want to watch some of the big action. It usually starts to happen right about now."

A girl in a slave costume took her order, and when the drink arrived, Natalie decided to just settle back, take in the scene, and wait for the promised action to take place.

Just minutes later, it was clear that whatever it was, was going to happen in the area immediately to her left, the one that was roped off from the rest of the casino. Four terribly elegant Chinese women had suddenly appeared and taken their places at the long gaming table that was situated not more than five yards from where Natalie was sitting, though one step down and separated from the bar area by the brass railing. Nonetheless, it was so close that Natalie could not help but hear that the foursome were chatting in Chinese, not English. Then one by one they were joined at the table by what looked like an Italian count, then by what must have been a New Jersey truck driver, followed by a housewife, no doubt from Orange County, and finally by two fellows, both in yellow pullovers, who, she thought, were definitely from San Francisco. As striking as the group was, it and its components were pushed into the background when the person who was obviously the croupier walked up to the table and took charge.

She was dressed in a classically cut suit, had perfectly styled hair, stood at least six foot tall, and was perhaps in her early thirties, but a woman who moved in the knowledge that she was the most attractive woman in the place, even a place that by now contained a couple of thousand people, maybe a third of whom were female.

She was soon joined by two men, both in black tie, one on her left and one on her right, and finally, in the background, yet another man, also in a tight-fitting tuxedo, who took his place in a high chair as if ready to begin judging a tennis match. But though surrounded by these three white men in formal attire, it was the black woman in her dark suit and white blouse who was in charge. She was the one who gave the signal that the game was to begin, handing three decks of cards to each of her colleagues and retaining two more decks. They then all began to shuffle their cards. After recollecting the now shuffled eight decks, she stuffed them into a shoelike container. Then came a couple of mysterious moves. First the black woman inserted what looked like a plastic joker into the shoe. Then, for whatever ritual reason, she extracted the top card from the shoe and turned it over. It was the eight of diamonds. She put it into a slot in the table in front of her, and then extracted eight additional cards from the shoe and put them into the same slot. Finally, she handed the shoe to one of the Chinese women, the one sitting to her extreme right, who immediately proceeded to take over by starting to deal around the table. The dealing done, the bets were placed, some cards were turned over, and, to Natalie's surprise, it was all over within two minutes. The Chinese woman ended up with all the chips, and her three friends chirped with happiness. Seemingly unaffected, she simply returned to the shoe and started dealing the next game. The bets were again placed. The cards were turned up. The winner was declared by the black woman. Another two minutes. Natalie didn't have a clue what was going on, but it was clear that vast sums of money were changing hands at a speed that was simply appalling.

Two martinis and forty-five minutes later they changed dealers at the number one baccarat table at The Palace, and Sandra Lee headed for her regular early evening drink. She had noticed the white woman in the little black dress watching her almost incessantly while she had been calling the cards at her baccarat table and decided, for no real reason, to ask if she could join her. A lot of customers liked that: a baccarat caller was big stuff in any casino, and to be seen drinking with one brought the prestige of being considered a high roller, since nobody but high rollers ever dared go near the baccarat tables.

"Do you mind, honey?" she asked, looking down at a now somewhat flustered Natalie Simmons.

"No, not at all. In fact, how very nice of you. I guess you must have noticed: I've been admiring you from afar."

"Yes. Aside from all the staring, you have no idea how you stick out in this particular crowd." Her eyes moved around the bar area.

Now Natalie became truly disconcerted. She knew she didn't perhaps fit in her Givenchy and Charles Jourdan satin pumps, but . . . The black woman read her mind perfectly. "No," she said and then giggled, "it's not what you're wearing. It's just that it's obvious that you intend to keep it on, that's all."

Natalie still couldn't figure it out.

"This's known as hookers' corner, ma'am, and, for reasons known only to himself, Steve put you at the table which has the largest turnover in the place; I'd say probably twenty tricks a night at two hundred dollars a pop originate right from where you're sitting."

Instead of blushing, or showing even the slightest annoyance, the white lady in the little black Givenchy seemed to love it. "Oh boy," she said, "wait until I tell this to Henry Price!" She thought of that first night they had been together in Paris. How she had, well, not exactly hated to have to do it, but still . . . and no doubt it had showed. Maybe it still did. A hooker she was not cut out to be. But to hell with it, there are other things in life. Right?

"You're sure I'm not bothering you?" her visitor then asked.

"No, please stay. I was just reminded of something."

"You just mentioned a man's name. You're thinking of him, I'll bet."

"Actually, yes."

"Now the question, the one that I'm immediately asked by men, is how did a nice girl . . ."

". . . like you end up in a place like this?" said Natalie.

"That's it. You want to know the answer?"

"Only if you want to tell it."

"Why not? It's got two parts. First, I got kicked out of Mills College. Second, I started sleeping with the boss."

Natalie never even raised an eyebrow. "That's actually rather commonplace. Except the bosses are usually stock-brokers or regional sales managers or congressmen. At least you must have picked a fun boss."

"Do you know Mr. Lehman?"

Natalie had not expected *that*. "Oh my," she said. "I really didn't mean to pry."

Sandra Lee leaned across and patted Natalie's hand. "It's not exactly a secret. Anyway, we don't really see that much of each other anymore. Haven't for years. Danny's been too busy, I guess. And during recent years he's been spending most of his time in Atlantic City. So I guess it's the old 'out of sight, out of mind' thing where I'm concerned." Sandra Lee paused and scanned the bar area. "Oh, oh, more company."

Natalie was about to turn to see what she meant, but what she meant was already at the table, totally overlooking Natalie and glaring down at the black woman. "I've told you at least a dozen times, Sandra Lee: I don't want you hanging around this bar on your breaks. It gives a bad impression. You're a dealer, not a goddamm hooker anymore."

"Fuck you, Cordoba," was her answer. Then, to Natalie: "Pardon the French, dear."

Eddie Cordoba looked as if he were going to have a fit right there and then. Then Natalie intervened. "How very nice to see you again, Mr. Cordoba. Do join us, if you have a minute. I'm afraid that Henry has left for a few days. I'm sure he would've wanted to thank you for all the arrange-

ments you made for us the other night over at Palm
Springs."

Cordoba was instantly transformed. He reached down to
take Natalie's hand and now, ever the charming Argentinian, implanted a Continental kiss between her second and
third knuckle. "How very, very nice to see you again, ma-
dame. This calls for a small celebration." A wave of his
hand brought Steve, the maître d', who in turn brought an
ice bucket containing a bottle of Dom Pérignon. He was
followed by one of the slave girls bearing three glasses.
When they were filled, Cordoba raised his, looked first,
rather pointedly, down at Sandra Lee, and then at Natalie
Simmons, and said, "Peace." And sat down.

Then, addressing Natalie, he said, "The word is that Mr.
Price and Mr. Lehman are getting along very well."

"Yes, they are," Natalie replied. "But don't ask me anything about business. When they start talking in terms of
hundreds of millions of dollars I'm way out of my depth."
Turning to Sandra Lee, she said, "My major at Vassar was
art history."

Cordoba interrupted. "Excuse me, I'm afraid I'm out of
my depth now. And I've got some work to do. One of our
most important clients from Mexico City is coming in
shortly. Mr. Lehman insists that I personally take care of
him. It's been a great pleasure to see you again." He rose
from the table, bowed to Natalie, ignored Sandra Lee, and
left.

Sandra Lee's eyes tracked him until he had disappeared
into the crowd now milling around the periphery of the
casino floor. Only then did she again address Natalie Simmons. "What's your fiancé do?"

"Henry's an investment banker."

"Yeah. It figures." She paused, and then continued, "I
know it's absolutely none of my business but I'm still going
to say it: be careful of that man, especially if your fiancé is
going to bail Danny Lehman out."

"Bail him out? Of what?"

"Honey, everybody in this place knows that Danny Lehman made a big mistake going into Atlantic City the way he did. It's eaten up all his time during the past year, and word has it that it has also eaten up most of the profit from this place. That the money guys, the banks or whoever, have him by the balls and are getting panicky now that everybody and his brother is about to open up a casino in Atlantic City. What they're saying is that the six-month joy ride that Danny had as a result of his being the first one to open up there full-time is about to end with a big bang. So the greedy bastards have told Danny that either he gets them their money back or they move in and Danny moves out. Cordoba, who's been running this place almost single-handedly since Danny's been tied up in New Jersey, can hardly wait. He's got the furniture movers on standby. He probably measures Danny's office once a week to make sure his new rug will fit."

"I see," said Natalie.

"I hope so. When you told him your friend and Danny were talking about hundreds of millions of dollars the guy actually turned white. I'm not kidding. You yanked that new rug of his right out from under Danny's desk where he thought he'd be sitting in a few weeks."

"So what can he possibly do about it?"

"It's not just Cordoba. He's gotten to be very palsy with one of the guys, one of the key guys, on the board of directors of this place, one that used to be a Hollywood agent. You can imagine how loyal he is to Danny! He and Cordoba are cut from the same cloth, believe me. I see them huddled together right here, two or three times a month. Muttering among themselves and laughing. Not when Danny's in town, though."

"Have you told Mr. Lehman about all this?"

"Danny wouldn't listen if I did. First, he's been so successful it could be he now thinks he's invincible. Second,

Mort Granville and Eddie Cordoba have conned him into believing they worship the very ground he walks on. But third, and no doubt least important, like I told you, we don't see each other in that way anymore." She paused and then said, "Let's face it, Danny Lehman's become a very big man. So he now associates with people like *you*." For the first time there was bitterness in her voice.

"I don't understand," Natalie said.

"You will in a minute. What Cordoba said was absolutely right. Sandra Lee is nothing more than an ex-hooker: a *black* ex-hooker. Danny Lehman fixed me up as a dealer a long time ago. And since then we've gone our separate ways."

She looked at her watch. "Gotta get back to work. It's been nice chatting with you." She got up to leave.

"Please wait just a minute," Natalie said. "I've got an idea. Are you free for lunch tomorrow? We could eat up in my suite."

The black woman hesitated. "What time?"

"Is one o'clock all right? I'm in 2001. In the tower."

"I'll be there," Sandra Lee answered, all hesitancy now gone. "I can't believe it: the two of us girls at lunch. I think I might wear a hat." She giggled, leaned down and kissed Natalie on the cheek, and left.

At one o'clock the next day—but one o'clock in the morning—just five hours after Cordoba had strode away from hookers' corner, he also showed up for a rendezvous; one that was, however, strictly for the boys. And it took place out in the desert, a good hour's drive northeast from Las Vegas, in the Valley of Fire where the red stalagmites rise on either side from the desert floor. Wayne Newton has a ranch there where he breeds Arabian horses. Cordoba at his own place bred and trained polo ponies; when the Argentinian polo team finished their American tours they inevitably ended up at his home; so did many of their ponies.

Cordoba had left the gate open and all the lights on, inside and out. He filled a bucket with ice, and put the whiskey bottles and two glasses on top of the bar in the living room, where red stone, redwood, and Persian rugs, and paintings of horses, cattle, and vaqueros had been put together in a spectacular display of good taste that was singularly lacking in the city that Cordoba had left earlier that evening.

Mort Granville arrived ten minutes later, and as he walked through the door and into the living room he was all smiles and good cheer. "What's the good news, Eddie?"

"Let me pour you a drink first."

"Oh oh," Granville said. "I hope it's not that kind of news."

Cordoba handed him his drink and took a good shot out of his own glass. "It is. That fucking Lehman has pulled it off again. He's working out a deal with Mercier Frères, *Mercier-fucking-Frères,* worth at least a couple of hundred million!"

"You sure?"

"I got it straight from Mercier Frères' girlfriend no more than five hours ago."

"How soon?"

"It doesn't matter how soon. When the word gets out that an outfit like that is going partners with Lehman, forget everything. The banks will never play ball with us."

"What do I tell my principals?"

"Don't gimme that goddamn 'principals' crap one more time Granville. Just tell your pals that they can take their money somewhere else. The Palace deal is dead. *Morte.* Finished."

For the next couple of minutes the two men stood in silence at the bar. Then Granville broke the silence. "You know something. You've got to hand it to Lehman. That guy has more luck than anybody on the face of this earth. First he gets that casino handed to him as a gift—and handed to him by *me* of all people. And now, when it looks like he's going to blow it, in comes this fairy godfather from New York with a freight car full of money."

"Let's not totally revise history, my friend," said the Argentinian.

"What's that crack supposed to mean?"

"You handed him *nothing*. I've heard the story. You sold him a place that was run by a bunch of hoods who wouldn't even let him in the front door, a door, by the way, that was about to be closed permanently by the gaming commission, leaving Lehman out about sixty million dollars. I hope you never do *me* any favors like that."

The ex–Hollywood agent decided to let that pass. Cordoba spoke again. "Who blew the whistle anyway?"

"What whistle?" Granville's voice was now low and sullen.

"The whistle that put the FBI onto that counting-room scam."

"How should I know?"

"Just asking."

"You never 'just ask' anything, Eddie." Granville's interest had returned.

"It's just an idea that suddenly occurred to me."

"Ask Bill Smith. He was the chief honcho at the local FBI office at the time. If anybody knows, he should."

"Naw. Can't ask him. He still thinks Lehman can walk on water."

Granville was thinking. "I'll tell you who has no doubt been asking the same question every day during the past ten years or more."

"Who?"

"Lenny De Niro."

"Who's he?"

"One of those hoods you referred to. He and a guy called

Roberto Salgo ran the old Raffles. They and the chief auditor, I think his name was Downey, yeah, Rupert Downey, had organized the scam."

Cordoba did not particularly like the drift this conversation was suddenly taking. Salgo was a name he had totally blotted from his memory. When you have a guy killed, it's not smart to even allow the subconscious to retain the fact. Be careful how you handle this, he thought. If Mort Granville gets even the faintest whiff of something, he's just stupid and greedy enough to start turning over the soil looking for pay dirt. The problem was that the process would lead him to Beirut and Lehman, which would be the end of Lehman, but unfortunately it would also lead to Eddie Cordoba and his Corsican friends. That approach was very definitely out!

"Is this De Niro fellow still around?" he asked.

"No. Left town eleven years ago and has never been sighted since. Somebody made his pal Salgo disappear permanently, and I guess he got the message. But if he's still alive, I'm sure there would be ways to find him. What do you think?"

"Naw. Look, Mort, I think it's getting too late to think. Let your people know that The Palace is out. Maybe they should be looking at the Aladdin. I hear things are pretty unsettled over there."

Ten minutes later Mort Granville's car disappeared into the darkness of the Valley of Fire. Eddie Cordoba turned off all the lights, except one by the fireplace. He got himself a new glass of whiskey, lit a cigar, and stretched out on an easy chair. He was still there an hour, two whiskeys, and another Partagas later. He was thinking.

Sandra Lee was true to her word: she turned up in a white Swiss lace dress that was spectacular enough in itself, but it was the hat, flowers and all, that made her appear like a bridesmaid headed for a wedding or, in another time and place, a young lady on her way to tea at Claridge's, the Ritz, or the Hassler with some of her ex-classmates from Katherine Branson, Smith, or Mills who were also touring Europe. To Sandra Lee's delight, Natalie Simmons had taken the occasion equally seriously and, although *sans chapeau,* was dressed in a Chanel suit and was the picture of Fifth Avenue elegance abroad for the season. Natalie had arranged a menu that began with champagne and ended with more champagne, interrupted by onion soup, then oysters on the half shell, and then a selection of pâtés, accompanied by a baguette, cornichons, and mustards.

Sandra Lee completely dominated the conversation. She knew at least one juicy detail about the sex life of almost every major entertainer who had done his or her stuff at The Palace during the past decade. And she had no qualms about discussing even the most graphic details of what went on on a regular basis "in this very suite." It often involved "stuff that even I would not have dreamed of doing," Sandra Lee said, adding, "before I retired from that particular line of activity."

Natalie sat there and drank it all in—in absolute awe. At three-thirty the phone rang, and it immediately produced a look of disappointment on Sandra Lee's face.

"Don't worry, it's probably only Henry checking in," Natalie said.

It wasn't. It was Danny Lehman announcing that he was going to drop in for a few minutes, if she didn't mind.

"I'll just leave quick," said Sandra Lee when she heard the news, immediately reverting to Southern patois.

"Please don't. I'd prefer not to be alone."

Sandra Lee seemed to have trouble figuring that one out, but decided to stay put, at least until the next act got under way. When Danny Lehman walked into the suite behind Natalie he was chattering like a little kid, until he spotted Sandra Lee.

"Surprise, surprise!" she said. "Didn't expect to see the help up here, did you?"

Danny's face broke into a grin. "It figures," he said. "But how the hell did you two meet?"

Natalie intervened. "We were both working hookers' corner."

"Yeah," Sandra Lee continued, "and now we're both staying with this high roller that lives up here. Henry's his name."

For just a second Danny was caught off guard, then: "Come on. Henry's in New York." He paused, thinking. "However . . ." He stopped. Then he continued, "I've got an idea. Now before either of you say no, please hear me out. Okay?"

They nodded.

"I came up here to say goodbye because I'm leaving for Atlantic City again in a couple of hours. We're going to have a board meeting there later this week. You probably know why, Natalie. Anyway, I just thought of something. Sandra Lee, you've never even seen our new place there, have you?"

"No."

"And, Natalie, I'm sure you haven't been there either."

"No, I haven't."

"Well, how about both of you paying us a visit. You could fly out tomorrow morning. It'll all be fixed from this end tonight. I'll have our people pick you up at the airport in Philadelphia." Then to Natalie before either could reply: "I'm sure that not only would Henry not mind, but I think he'd be interested in hearing about what you see there. And I'd love to show it to you. And to you, too, Sandra Lee," he added. "Be a bit like old days. That is, if you still . . ." And now Danny Lehman seemed to revert physically to the boy from Philadelphia, way out of his depth in a place like this in the company of women like these two.

"You're on," Sandra Lee said. "We'd love to go, wouldn't we, Natalie?"

"Absolutely," she answered, without the slightest hesitation. Her two visitors soon departed, so it was she alone who finished off the third bottle of Dom Pérignon, ending up rather tipsy. But she went to bed early, rose at dawn, packed, and even sang while she packed. "This is getting to be fun," she said to nobody in particular as she stepped out of The Palace's limo at the airport to check in for United's nine o'clock flight to Philadelphia. Sandra Lee, it seemed, had been even less affected by the indulgences of the previous day: she was already standing at the United counter waiting.

17

The Palace East limo driver was waiting at the baggage carrousel in Philadelphia. The drive south to Atlantic City, through what seemed to be endless growths of spindly pines, took almost two hours. When they got to the outskirts of Atlantic City and then the city itself, neither woman said a word for a while. Then: "Pretty crappy-looking place, if you ask me." It was Sandra Lee.

"Very crappy-looking place."

"Very crappy place in many ways," Sandra Lee continued.

"I thought you'd never been here?" Natalie asked.

"I haven't. But that doesn't mean I haven't heard a few things. After all, I'm in the business."

"So tell me a few things?"

"All right. Part 1: Introduction to New Jersey in general. The history of New Jersey is absolutely *studded* with congressmen and other elected, and appointed, officials who have been indicted, been convicted, and served time for every conceivable type of behavior, the least of which is accepting bribes."

"Really."

"Where have you been? Look, New Jersey is the black-belt constituency in the world for corruption."

"Are you sure?"

"Well, in the *developed* world. Christ, Natalie, you can

hardly expect me to include the Congo or Nigeria. Those are run by black folk."

Natalie giggled. "How do you know all this?"

"Eddie Cordoba, I'm sorry to say. An endless fount of knowledge where what he terms 'Danny's folly' is concerned."

"Why folly?"

"He says that in the end they're going to get Danny. 'Crooks cannot abide other crooks invading their territory.' "

"He says that about Danny?"

"Of course. I've been sitting in hookers' corner when he said almost exactly the same thing to Danny's face. Cordoba knows he can get away with murder with Danny. So naturally he pushes it to the limit."

"And what did Danny say?"

" 'We're the best of the best. They *need* us. We're the bellweather. We come and then everybody comes.' Can't you hear him?"

"And?"

"Danny's been right. So far."

"What could go wrong now?"

"I don't know, honey, but I've got a feeling . . ."

"But then why does he do it?"

"Greed. Simple greed. He's got everything already, hasn't he? But not in his mind. He always wants more."

"More what?"

"Money. Just plain money."

At that moment the limo pulled up in front of The Palace East. And within minutes the two women had been whisked out of the car and up in the elevator and installed in a large, though hardly elaborate by Vegas standards, two-bedroom suite. The place was full of flowers, there were two buckets of champagne; two boxes of Godiva chocolates; two bathrobes, with their names embroidered on them, of course; two bottles of Joy perfume; two . . .

"This is ridiculous," Natalie said. "Furthermore, it's a terrible waste!"

"Of course it is," Sandra Lee replied. "But, honey, this is vintage Danny Lehman. For him this"—and her hand went from the champagne buckets to the chocolate boxes to the godawful chintz sofas in the room—"this is what life is all about." She paused. "But he means well."

"You still like him a lot, don't you?"

The black woman nodded and disappeared into her bedroom.

Their invitation to dinner was extended in the usual intimate Lehman manner: through the telephone message service. A section of the gourmet restaurant of The Palace East had been cordoned off, and screened. Natalie and Sandra Lee were apparently the only women who had been invited. Danny Lehman introduced them to the half a dozen men already gathered there as the fiancée of Henry Price of Mercier Frères and her traveling companion. The man from the governor's office and his sidekick, the man from the New Jersey Casino Control Commission, with his flunky, and two members of The Palace Inc. board, Mort Granville and Danny's old attorney from his Philadelphia days, Benjamin Shea, made up the rest of the guest list. Natalie was placed between Danny and the governor's man; Sandra Lee was apparently considered safe between Granville and Shea.

The talk over dinner was that of old cronies, men who knew one another well, allowing them to joke about balding heads, to gossip about mutual acquaintances not present, and to reminisce about the good old days in New Jersey and elsewhere. The only time it got serious was when Shea mentioned the subject of the casino's temporary license: not just that of The Palace East, but also those of Bally, Caesars, Resorts, and Playboy. The whole situation involving a "temporary" versus a "permanent" license had arisen because while on the one hand New Jersey wanted to get the economic benefits of the introduction of legalized gambling to the state as soon as possible, on the other hand it did not immediately have the legal machinery in place to process the licensing. So, in the interim, only temporary licenses could be granted, with no guarantee that a permanent one would automatically follow. Caesars got its temporary license on June 26, 1979; The Palace, Bally, and Playboy, six months later, on December 29 of that year.

"Together we've put almost a billion dollars into this town," Shea said to the commissioner, although the whole table was listening, "and you guys still have us operating on a temporary basis. This has got to change, and quickly. When we went into Vegas, the state of Nevada had us cleared, permanently, within sixty days with no fuss or muss. I know, since I handled it personally for Danny. In Nevada they understand that nobody can afford to put up that kind of money without security, permanent security."

"You've got security," the governor's man interjected.

"I don't see it," the attorney answered.

"You see it right at this table," the politician answered. The commissioner nodded his agreement.

"How about dessert?" Danny asked. After dessert he announced that he wanted to show the ladies around; he thought the rest of the guys might want to stay for cognac and cigars. The men all rose, Danny and the ladies left, and the boys got back to business.

Once they were safely out of the restaurant, Sandra Lee grabbed Natalie's arm. "See what I mean?" she said in a loud whisper. "How blatant can you get? And they don't even care who knows!"

Danny was plunging ahead of them, through a crowd that was much denser than either woman had ever seen at the sister casino in Las Vegas. But it was a different crowd: seedier by far. The women were fatter; the men were sloppier. The whole group had an unwashed quality to it, Natalie thought. Sandra Lee must have had precisely the same thought, since she glanced over at her new friend and pinched her nose between her thumb and index finger. Danny kept plunging through the crowd. They were now passing by bank after bank of slots. Again there was something new: people were actually *lined up* to get at them!

"Heh, not so fast!" Sandra Lee yelled at Danny.

He waited for them.

"Where are the baccarat tables?" she asked.

"Table," he answered.

"One table?" Sandra Lee asked in amazement.

Danny shrugged. "Different town. Come on." They finally emerged out of the back of the casino onto the Boardwalk. Danny stopped. The women joined him.

"Now look," he said. There must have been two hundred people lined up *outside* the casino, waiting to get in.

"Why?" Sandra Lee asked.

"Fire regulations," Danny replied. "We usually hit the limit around seven o'clock already. After that, nobody gets in until somebody goes out." He turned to Natalie. "That should interest Henry.

"Now let me show you one of the greatest places on earth," he said. His right arm encircled Sandra Lee's waist. He offered his left arm to Natalie Simmons. She took it, and down the Boardwalk the threesome strode. It was a marvelous evening: warm, almost hot; the moon was shining brightly; the Boardwalk was jammed with strollers. "I used to come here as a kid," Danny said, "every summer. With my mother. Atlantic City is an island, you know. The Indians used to call it *Abse-gami,* meaning 'little sea water.' The white people shortened it to Absecon Island. Then some guys from Philadelphia discovered this place and built a railroad between here and Philly. First they bought most of the island for ten dollars an acre. Changed the name to Atlantic City to hype it as a vacation place. Three years later they were selling the land at three hundred dollars an acre." They kept walking.

"I bought the property where the casino stands for two hundred thousand dollars seven years ago. Know what it's worth now? Just the land?" He answered his own question. "Ten million at least. Us boys from Philadelphia have done all right here in Atlantic City, and Atlantic City has been good to us.

"You know what Teddy Roosevelt once said about this place?" This question was, naturally, addressed to Natalie Simmons.

"No idea," she answered.

" 'A man would not be a good American citizen if he did not know of Atlantic City,' " stated Danny. "How do you like that? It was true then and now it's true again. And you know why?"

"Why, Danny?" answered Sandra Lee rather sarcastically. But Danny didn't notice; he was on a roll. "This may sound immodest," he began, causing Sandra Lee to roll her eyes, "but I brought the casino business here and it's going to change this town as much as that railroad did."

They kept walking and nobody spoke for a while. Then: "There's the pier," Danny said, pointing at the run-down pile of steel and concrete jutting out into the water. "John Philip Sousa played the pier every single summer for years until he died in 1932. Then Paul Whiteman took over. Everybody used to come here. One of the things I remember best was going with my Mom to see Amos 'n' Andy when they did a show here the year of the World's Fair, 1939. That day they pulled in eighty-four thousand customers! Boy, it was really something." He kept on walking and talking. "Mom and I used to come down for Easter. Just for the weekend. Because there was nothing, anywhere on earth, like the Easter Parade on the Boardwalk in Atlantic City. You know how many people would come? *Half a million!*"

"Then what happened?" Natalie Simmons asked.

"The do-gooders took over and ruined the place. Stopped the gambling, closed the brothels, banned the horse parlors.

Since there was no fun here anymore, all of a sudden everybody stopped coming. After the war you could have bought the whole *town* for ten million dollars." He looked at his watch. "The show's starting in ten minutes. Want to go?"

When Liberace came onto the stage, it was apparent that fun had returned to Atlantic City, and with it so had the crowds. The place was jammed. The show was stunning. Nowhere—whether in Paris or London or Tokyo—was there entertainment that was even remotely comparable to that offered night after night by The Palace and The Palace East. Danny Lehman's philosophy in this regard had been clear from the beginning and he had never wavered from it since: get the best, and once you've got them, keep them, and don't ever worry about what it costs.

Of course, there was champagne again. Then more champagne when Liberace joined their table after the show, explaining that he had come over to say hello to "the boss," as he called him. At one o'clock the party started to break up. "I've got one more idea," Danny said as they left the nightclub. "A nightcap!"

The women, both a bit wobbly, thought that though it was not an original idea, it was a terrific one.

"My place or yours?" he asked.

"Yours," Sandra Lee answered. "The whole place is yours, isn't it?"

Danny's apartment embraced the entire top floor of the eastern wing of the hotel. When one walked directly out of the elevator into his living room there was no doubt that one had left the tacky atmosphere of the casino behind. Whoever the interior decorator had been, he or she had done a magnificent job. The air-conditioning had the place chilled down almost to shivering point. But no sooner had they entered than a butler appeared from nowhere to light the fire and take their orders for drinks.

"Absolutely the last one," Natalie said, moving on to scotch.

Danny installed himself on the immense sofa next to the fireplace and when the drinks arrived waved the women over. "Well, what shall we drink to?" he asked, as they settled on either side of him.

Natalie, with some difficulty now, answered, "To Atlantic City."

"The greatest place on earth," Danny Lehman echoed. Their glasses clinked in celebration. Then Sandra Lee added, "Just to show that we don't take you for granted, Mr. Atlantic City, I for one am going to give you a big good-night kiss." It was the chastest of kisses on the cheek.

"Well, I think I could manage that, too," Natalie said, and did so immediately.

Then the three of them settled back on the sofa in silence, Danny's arms now firmly around the waists of both women. Diana Ross's voice filled the room from the background hi-fi.

"Nice," Sandra Lee said.

"Yeah," said Danny, moving just a little, and cupped Sandra Lee's breast from behind with his left hand. The strap on Sandra Lee's gown seemed to have slipped. Danny drew Natalie closer and caressed her leg. After a few moments the entire front of Sandra Lee's gown was down, and the entire bottom of Natalie's skirt was up, and—

"No," she said. "I simply can't." And, just as abruptly, Natalie Simmons was on her feet.

"Honey, take it easy," Sandra Lee said, her gown now also back in place. "Everybody just got a little carried away."

"Time for us to go, lover boy," she said to Danny. "Thanks for the evening. And no hard feelings, okay?"

Natalie, who was in front of the elevator, waiting, turned to look back at him. "I'd like to second that, if I may."

Danny grinned. The elevator arrived. Five minutes later the two women were back in their suite, where both immediately went to their separate bedrooms. It was now well past two in the morning in Atlantic City and Natalie Simmons, if not smashed, was half-smashed.

Peculiarly, it was the sight of Sandra Lee's magnificent breasts that had set her off much more than had Danny's hand. "I wonder what would have happened if it had been Henry instead?" she giggled. But Henry Price doing it with two girls, one black and one white—that was about as remote a possibility as one could conjure up. So maybe she should have taken advantage of what might have been the one and only chance she would have to see if she . . . And then she pulled back. "No. Time to get away from this world. In fact, maybe it's what they mean when they say the 'nick of time.' "

She stopped talking to the room and went to sleep, her mind made up.

The next morning the two women went to the airport in Philadelphia together, neither of them referring to how the previous evening had ended. Sandra Lee got a plane back to Vegas; Natalie, one to Washington. They promised to keep in touch.

18

An hour after Natalie Simmons returned to her Georgetown town house, Henry Price called. "I was in Atlantic City," she blurted out the moment after he had said hello.

"And?"

"It's terribly tacky. But did you know they actually line up every evening outside the casino, desperate to get in?"

"No. Interesting. Anything else?"

"Henry, I don't know anything about finance or about the casino business, but I must say I overheard something at dinner there that did not sound especially good."

"What was that?"

"You apparently need a license from the state to operate a casino. Is that right?"

"It is."

"Well, the license that they have in New Jersey is just a temporary one. Did you know that?"

"Indeed we do know that. All the licenses granted thus far to casinos in Atlantic City are temporary."

"Well, isn't that dangerous? For you and your bank, I mean?"

"We've taken account of it."

"Oh well . . ."

"I'll be meeting with their board tomorrow. Then I think I'll be off to Europe right away, assuming everything works out, which I'm sure it will. Should be back in a week. Are you all right? You sound a little . . ."

"I'm fine, just fine, Henry. Just a little worried for you, that's all. You're sure you're doing the right thing with those people?"

"You mean Lehman?"

"Yes."

"I think so. Why? Is there something else?"

"No, nothing. It's just that they are all so . . ."

"So are a lot of people who run oil companies. And brokerage houses. And more than a few governments that we deal with south of the border. Lehman's certainly no better, but he's probably no worse. Anyway, we're big boys here. You worry about your art gallery, Natalie. I can handle the Danny Lehmans of this world. By the way, is everything all right with your business?"

"I haven't had time even to call in during the past few days, but I'll be going over right away tomorrow morning."

Three days later Henry Price was in Zurich at the Baur au Lac. He was talking with Lothar Winterthur, one of the managing directors of the General Bank of Switzerland.

"I assume you or your people have gone through the financial data," Price asked.

"Looks fine, but tell me, why are we being so blessed?"

"SEC registration would take too long."

"How did you arrive at a share price of twenty-four dollars where the conversion rights are concerned?"

"It's not fixed yet. The actual conversion price will be set on the day of the closing and will be based upon the last trade in New York on that day. We'll take that price and add on a 20 percent premium."

"So you are assuming that that last trade will be twenty dollars. How can you know that now?"

Henry Price put up his right hand and pulled down some thin air. But then he added this: "I was hoping, Lothar, that you might help nudge it in that direction by a little judicious last-minute buying or selling in New York. Whatever's needed."

The Swiss banker smiled. He knew that such practices were illegal in America, though hardly in Switzerland. *"Ja,* we do that often. We call it *Kurspflege.* It should be no problem provided the whole deal comes together."

"Good. Our client and his board have already agreed to the deal. But they will expect a conversion price of at least twenty-four dollars, since that's the figure I've been using all along."

"I understand. Now tell me, Henry, who else do you expect to come in on this?"

"Why don't you just take a minute and read the memorandum. It covers everything you need to know, Lothar." He handed him a three-page document. Mercier Frères stood at the top of the list as the sole lead manager. The borrower was to be The Palace S.A. of Luxembourg. The guarantor was The Palace Inc. of Delaware. The amount was two hundred and fifty million dollars. The term was five years. The holders of the notes would have the right, at their option, to convert, starting one year from the day of closing, their note or any portion of its principal amount into fully paid-up, nonassessable shares of The Palace Inc. stock at the price to be set on the day of the closing.

The list of potential participants in the syndication, all of whom had already expressed firm interest, included two Dutch banks, one Belgian, three German, two French, and one Japanese bank's subsidiary in Luxembourg. That was where Price was headed next. But it was important to get the General Bank of Switzerland in first—firmly, and with a lot of money. Then everyone else would fall into place without hesitation.

"Is this man Lehman clean where the authorities are concerned?" the Swiss banker now wanted to know.

Henry Price shrugged. "A William Tell or Winkelried he's not. But he's an interesting fellow, even charismatic in his way. Knows the business better than anybody in the world; no doubt about *that*. And I think you will agree that this is what counts." Winterthur nodded. "But clean?" Price continued. "Nobody is clean in that world according to normal standards, Lothar. Certainly not if judged by Swiss moral standards."

Lothar Winterthur liked that. There were no moral standards on earth that could even remotely approach those of the Swiss, and this American knew it. That's why the General Bank did business with him: Henry Price was known as a good man of good stock, from a distinguished family in the best American tradition. He was not just another one of those Jew peddlers from New York who forever pestered them, trying to ingratiate themselves with a Swiss bank, hoping that some of the polish might rub off on them. Henry Price didn't need that.

"We checked him out. Came up with a few rather fishy-smelling episodes in his past. But they occurred a long time ago, and nobody in the present government seems to be even remotely concerned with them or him. He's got a real money machine there, Lothar."

Again the Swiss banker nodded. They liked money machines in Switzerland. "Tell me," he then said, "is it all true what they say about Las Vegas? That you can get almost any kind of amusement you want?"

"Probably so."

"I hear there are girls there from all over the world."

"I'm sure you've heard correctly."

"You know, Henry, I can tell you now: we'll take thirty-five million of those notes. You have our word on that, and, as you know, that's all you ever have needed from us." Price made a mental note to have somebody from his office in either London or Paris obtain confirmation in writing the next day; or if not really in writing, at least by telex. Winterthur took a few more glances at the memorandum and then tossed it back on top of the coffee table.

"I see you'll be going on the board, Henry."

"Indeed yes."

"I wonder if you might do me a slight favor in that capacity."

"Certainly. Just name it, Lothar."

"Well, I must go to Mexico City next month. To look into the Alfa Industries situation. Doesn't look good. In fact, the whole Mexican situation bothers us. They've borrowed much too much. Or perhaps, more accurately, you Americans have lent them much too much."

"Better Mexico than Poland, Lothar."

"*Ja.* Something to that. But don't exaggerate our position in Poland. It's the Germans who have their necks stuck out there, not us Swiss."

Henry Price decided to remain silent.

"Anyway, I will be going to Guadalajara, and since Las Vegas is more or less on the way, and since we are going to encourage some of our very best clients to invest in your deal, do you think that perhaps . . ."

"Everything will be arranged. They have a system there where they put people like you on a basis they term 'comp,' " Price said.

" 'Comp'?"

"Short for 'complimentary.' The Palace will take care of everything, Lothar."

"That was not the reason I asked."

"Of course not. But I am sure that Mr. Lehman would certainly have it no other way. Please let me know now the exact dates; Mr. Lehman will certainly want to meet you. One more thing: how many will there be in your party?"

"Two."

"I'm sure your wife will enjoy it. Nothing like it in Zurich, you know."

True, although Winterthur's wife was not to find out. Lothar was planning on taking along a girl from the typing pool.

Business done, Winterthur rose. "Where to now, Henry?" he asked.

"Luxembourg. I'm taking the Trans-Europ-Express, in about an hour."

"Eat at the Grand Hotel Cravat. Best veal in Europe."

Price discovered that the veal was truly magnificent. Then he moved on to Brussels, where the stuffed quail at the Villa Lorraine was also superb. So, too, was the Indonesian Rijst-tafel at the Bali in Amsterdam. By the time he arrived in London a week later to complete his rounds, he had placed the entire $250 million of five-year convertible notes, and had gained six pounds in weight. Usually he gained only five on such trips.

Getting older, I guess, he thought to himself during the Pan Am flight back to New York. He never took the Concorde; it made him feel claustrophobic. Furthermore, Pan Am was a client. He spent two hours in the office, bringing his partners up to date, and then flew commercial down to Washington, D.C. He had phoned Natalie Simmons in advance, and she was at the gate at National Airport, waiting for him.

"Nice trip?"

"The usual."

They drove to her town house in Georgetown for a drink. He suggested that they drive out to the farm; she said she would prefer to stay in town, so they did. Neither thought it necessary to even mention casinos, Atlantic City, Danny Lehman, or the quarter of a billion dollars that Price had put together in ten days flat. In their scheme of things, neither the amount, nor the client, nor the business of the client really held any more significance for them. It had all just amounted to a mildly distracting, and appropriately short, interlude that was now over.

PART FOUR

1982

19

The problem started with the Abscam investigation at the beginning of the 1980s. A man by the name of Alvin Malnik was videotaped by the FBI. *The Wall Street Journal's* description was: "The tape discloses Mr. Malnik trying to convince a federal agent posing as an Arab sheik to secretly buy into the Aladdin Hotel and Casino."

When Eddie Cordoba saw the article, all this hardly came as a surprise; he had already known about the unsettled conditions at the Aladdin casino when trying to divert the attention of Mort Granville and his "principals" away from Danny Lehman and The Palace a year earlier.

There was more: "A portion of the tape seems to offer additional evidence of Mr. Malnik's role with Caesars World. The Malnik-FBI conversation has Mr. Malnik saying, 'What you do is, like what we did with Caesars. We always, we never made any money, because we bet it back into the joint. We always added 200 rooms here, 300 rooms there, so that we have 2,000 rooms there.' "

The *Journal* pointed out the significance of all this by describing Mr. Malnik as a "Miami Beach businessman" who was "an alleged associate of organized crime figure Meyer Lansky."

There was another tape that the *Journal* had not gotten hold of from the FBI. Again it featured two men: this time a certain Saul Meyers of Miami, Miami Beach, Fort Lauderdale—it was never quite clear exactly where he was domiciled—and a certain Daniel Lehman, formerly of Philadelphia, now of Las Vegas and Atlantic City. The tape showed Mr. Meyers picking up Mr. Lehman at the airport in Fort Lauderdale. The same car was then shown as it approached a guardhouse in front of a very imposing building, either a hotel or a condominium complex. In any case, you could see the ocean in the immediate background. Armed guards checked them out and waved them in. A digital clock was running across the tape. Six hours almost to the minute later, according to the digital information on the tape, the same car was driven out of the same gate and went back to the same airport, where Mr. Lehman was seen disappearing into the terminal.

On a second tape, taken exactly eighteen days later, the same scene was repeated; there was never any sound, just black-and-white pictures.

There was a third tape and one that had been secured in a totally illegal manner; to get it, the FBI had blatantly infringed the sovereign rights of the Commonwealth of the Bahamas. There was no sound and in fact there was not much video either; it had a running time of no more than fifteen seconds. It showed a yacht docked at Paradise Island. Mr. Meyer Lansky and Mr. Saul Meyers were seen standing facing each other as they leaned over the railing. Both held glasses, both wore sunglasses. They appeared to be in discussion.

The date of the first taped Lehman/Meyers meeting was May 9, 1969. The date of the second Lehman/Meyers meeting was dated May 27, 1969. The tape of the Lansky/Meyers rendezvous in the Bahamas was dated June 4, 1969. The FBI had obviously had Meyers and Lansky under close surveillance for well over a decade.

The hearings in Atlantic City to determine whether or not The Palace East would receive a permanent gaming license from the state of New Jersey began on June 23, 1982. At these hearings the Casino Control Commission would also

make a determination regarding the "fitness" of each and
every member of the board of directors and senior manage
ment.

The first week involved skirmishing by the lawyers. But
on July 1, it quickly became serious; dead serious. Danny
Lehman was scheduled to appear and, according to commis
sion practice, would continue to appear until he had com
pleted his exhaustive testimony. Danny Lehman was ner
vous, very nervous, about the whole thing, in spite of having
sailed through the initial hearings, over two years earlier
cursory hearings that had resulted in The Palace East's be
ing granted its temporary operating license. The difference
was that *then* the chairman of the Casino Control Commis
sion and his sponsor in the governor's office had dined a
The Palace East the night before the hearings, as well as the
night after, and the night after that. Unfortunately, tha
same chairman had been caught up in the Abscam web and
had dragged the governor's man down with him.

That was bad enough. Worse still was the fact that The
Palace East was the first casino to come up for permanen
licensing in New Jersey, and Danny Lehman was the firs
principal of such a casino who would be judged as regard
his "fitness" to run such an establishment. They would se
the precedent for the state's future rulings on such impecca
ble establishments as Bally's Park Place, Inc., a subsidiar
of Bally Manufacturing Corporation, a maker of slot ma
chines, or the Playboy Casino, a sister casino of a string o
gambling establishments in England that had just been or
dered either closed or sold by the British gaming authority

Worst of all was the appearance of Randolph Stinson o
the New Jersey scene as attorney general. He was in th
process of preparing his run for the governorship as Mr
Clean, using the same ploy that had been successfully use
in Illinois and Maryland by the successors to Otto Kerne
and Marvin Mandel, governors who had both been con

victed on criminal charges related to their granting of horse-racing licenses to the wrong people in the wrong way.

Randolph Stinson, unlike *The Wall Street Journal,* was in possession of both Meyers/Lehman tapes as well as the fifteen-second study of that same Mr. Meyers in the company of Mr. Lansky on that boat in the Bahamas. Some of his people said he should have introduced that evidence at the very beginning of the hearings. Others had serious misgivings concerning the illegality of the FBI tapes. Mr. Stinson, thirty-six years old, a Mormon, and a wearer of brown shoes, flatly refused even to listen to them.

And it was he who personally confronted Danny Lehman in the hearing room of the New Jersey Casino Control Commission. Even the room—small, dingy, the paint peeling from the walls—was depressing. Danny entered it flanked by four attorneys, the best that money could buy in New York, including a senior member of the law firm who personally represented such clients as the Kingdom of Sweden, the European Coal and Steel Community, even South Korea. Neither he, nor his three flunkies, seemed especially to like their latest money-maker, Danny Lehman.

At eight o'clock precisely, it all began.

The chairman: Would the clerk please call the roll.

He called it. All five commissioners were present.

The chairman: Would the clerk please swear in the witness, Mr. Daniel Lehman.

The witness was sworn in.

The chairman: Good morning, sir.

The witness: Good morning, sir.

The chairman: We want to make this as easy as possible for you, Mr. Lehman. We shall also seek to make it brief.

The witness: I certainly appreciate your courtesy.

The chairman: Mr. Randolph Stinson, who is our state's attorney general, will now please proceed with his questions.

Q. Good morning, Mr. Lehman.

A. Good morning, Mr. Stinson.

Q. Mr. Lehman, when did you acquire The Palace?

A. In 1969. It was then known as Raffles.

Q. When did you join the board of directors of that casino in New Jersey, sir?

A. In the summer of that year.

Q. At that time, did you become familiar with the regulations applicable to the operation of a casino in Las Vegas?

A. I would say I did, yes.

Q. Mr. Lehman, are you familiar with regulation 5.011 of the Nevada Casino Control Commission?

A. I am not familiar with it by number, no, sir.

Q. Are you familiar with a regulation that makes it grounds for a disciplinary action against a licensee should the licensee be found "catering to, assisting, employing, or associating with, either socially or in business affairs, persons of notorious or unsavory reputation, or who have extensive police records, or persons who have defied congressional investigative committees, or other officially constituted bodies acting on behalf of the United States, or any states, or persons who are associated with, or support subversive movements through the country, either directly or through a contract of any means with any firm, or any individual in any capacity where the state of Nevada or the gaming industry is liable to be damaged because of the unsuitability of the firm or individual, or because of the unethical methods of operations of the firm or the individual?" Are you familiar with that regulation?

A. Yes, in general I am.

Q. Would you then say that in 1969 you were familiar with that regulation?

A. I would say so.

Q. Do you know a Mr. Saul Meyers?

A. I've met him.

Q. In what capacity?

A. Socially.

Q. Do you know where Mr. Saul Meyers resides?

The attorney for The Palace: Mr. Stinson, I object, in fact strenuously object to the line of questioning, since in no way has its relevance to the purpose of this hearing been established.

The chairman: Mr. Stinson—why don't you include the relevance in your questioning?

Q. When you met Mr. Saul Meyers socially, were you aware of the fact that he might, in many ways, come under the category of persons described by regulation 5.011 of the Nevada Casino Control Commission?

A. Emphatically, no.

Q. In addition to your social contacts, did you also have business dealings with Mr. Saul Meyers in 1969?

A. Absolutely not.

Q. Perhaps before or after 1969?

The attorney for The Palace: I object. The question is too vague. I don't think that we want this to turn into a fishing expedition.

The chairman: Rephrase that question, please, Mr. Stinson.

Q. Did you have business dealings with Mr. Meyers in 1968?

A. No.

Q. Did you have business dealings with Mr. Meyers in 1970?

A. No.

Q. Did you have business dealings with Mr. Meyers in 1971?

A. No.

Q. Did you—

The attorney for The Palace: Mr. Chairman, I—

The chairman: I think, Mr. Stinson, that you should perhaps proceed to your next—

Q. Mr. Chairman, with your permission I would now like

to show some videotapes, and at the same time introduce them into evidence.

The attorney for The Palace: I object. What is their relevance?

The attorney general: Could I and the counsel for The Palace have a word with the chairman?

The chairman nodded his approval, which was duly recorded, and the two attorneys then approached the table where the five commissioners were seated and, after a very quick discussion, returned to their places. Daniel Lehman's five-hundred-dollars-an-hour lawyer did not look happy. The lights were dimmed. The video projection began: first, the two tapes of Lehman and Meyers in Fort Lauderdale.

Danny watched them with equanimity. He had, after all, told the truth about knowing Saul Meyers.

Then the third tape came on. It was Meyers on a boat with some old guy. So what? The lights went back on.

Q. Those first two tapes were of you and Mr. Meyers in Fort Lauderdale, were they not?

A. Yes.

Q. The dates and times indicated on the videotapes, were they correct?

A. Probably, yes. I don't recall exactly.

Q. Would you tell us about the place you visited after Mr. Meyers picked you up at what, I believe, was the Fort Lauderdale airport?

A. It was the Fort Lauderdale airport. The place we went to is a club south of Fort Lauderdale, on the ocean, as you could see. Mr. Meyers is a member there.

Q. Both times it was the same airport and same club?

A. Yes.

Q. In each instance you spent approximately six hours with Mr. Meyers?

A. I don't recall. That was thirteen years ago.

Q. Are you familiar with any of Mr. Meyers's associates?

A. No.

Q. Do you mean that you never met with Mr. Meyers when he had some of his associates with him?

A. Not that I was aware of, no.

Q. Do you recall ever having met a Mr. Montague Davies?

A. Of course.

Q. Would you tell us who he is?

A. He was one of the directors of the First Charter Bank of the Bahamas in Nassau.

Q. Have you done business with that bank?

A. Yes, sir. A long time ago when I was in the coin business. They used to handle my overseas transactions.

Q. When did that association cease, if it has ceased?

A. It has definitely ceased. In the spring of 1969.

The attorney for The Palace: Mr. Chairman, I again must ask that the relevance of this line be either established or discontinued.

The chairman: I agree. Mr. Stinson?

Q. Did you recognize the man on that yacht with Mr. Saul Meyers?

A. No.

Q. Did you recognize the yacht?

A. No.

Q. The man, Mr. Lehman, was Meyer Lansky. The yacht was that of Mr. Montague Davies.

Danny was visibly stunned and confused. His attorney asked that the proceedings be adjourned for the remainder of the day. The request was granted.

Minutes later, one of Eddie Cordoba's henchmen who had been in the hearing room went to a phone booth and, though it was not even 6 A.M. in Nevada, telephoned him at his home outside of Las Vegas, giving the man who ran The Palace's casino operations a full report.

20

___

After he had hung up the phone, Eddie Cordoba stayed in bed for a full half hour, mulling over the possible implications of this sensational turn of events. At first he could see only positives. They had nailed Lehman. But the more he mulled, the more he started to worry. What if they continued rummaging around in the past and decided to take a closer look at some other events that had occurred in 1969? That could have even deadlier consequences than their establishing the Lansky connection . . . but not just for Danny Lehman. Cordoba quickly dressed and headed for The Palace. There he waited impatiently, smoking cigarette after cigarette, until it was finally eight o'clock, when the office staff began to work. Then he called down to the payroll department and made a simple request: he wanted the names of everybody on the Palace staff who was already working at the casino at the beginning of 1969, when the place was still called Raffles.

The information arrived half an hour later and the list was not long: seventeen names in all. Apparently Danny Lehman had *really* cleaned house when he took over from that gang of three that had been robbing the place blind: Salgo, De Niro, and . . . the auditor. Cordoba picked up the phone and called down to payroll again. "Say, can you try and find the name of that guy who was the chief auditor around here in 1969?"

"Don't have to look it up," answered the payroll chief,

who was one of the men whose names were on the computer printout. "His name was Rupert Downey."

"What happened to him?"

"I don't have any idea, sir. Mr. Kelly might know, though. If I recall correctly, he was working in the audit department when Downey was still in charge."

"Thanks."

He checked the list again. Kelly, now the Palace's chief accountant, was on it. "Get Kelly and tell him to come up here," he told his secretary.

The accountant arrived in less than five minutes.

"Good to see you, Matthew," Cordoba said as he rose to greet the man, giving him a little reassuring pat on the back in the process. "Do you smoke cigars?" He did occasionally.

"They're Cuban," Cordoba said, reaching back to his desk for the open box, which he then extended to the accountant. "Let's both sit over there," he continued, walking to the sofa in the corner. "Tell me, how's the month looking?"

"We should be up maybe 45 percent from the same month last year."

"Great," Cordoba said, and then changed the subject. "Say, tell me something: some of us were, you know, reminiscing about the old days last night, and the names of Salgo, De Niro, and Rupert Downey came up. Nobody seemed to remember what happened to them. I mean, everybody assumes that Salgo must have been killed. But what happened to the other two guys? Especially De Niro?"

"Sir, I have no idea about Mr. De Niro. I don't recall ever having even spoken to him. He was not the type of person to take much notice of clerks in the audit office."

So maybe the way to De Niro was through the other guy. "But you must have known Downey."

"Of course. I worked in his department, but I had absolutely nothing to do with—"

Cordoba quickly interrupted, "No, no, Matthew. Nobody

has suggested, even in the remotest sense, that you were involved with any of that stuff. They were just wondering what happened to him."

"Well, he turned state's evidence—provided the authorities with everything they needed to nail Salgo and De Niro, I guess. They let him off in the end. Still, he had to give the tax people everything he had."

"Really."

"Yes. They even took his new house. It was a *big* place. Off the old golf course. Must have been worth a million dollars."

"Probably paid for it in cash from all that skimming those guys were doing."

"No. He'd just gotten a big loan."

Who gave a happy fuck about Downey's problems or his house or his goddamn loan? The fox he was chasing was De Niro. With those crazies in New Jersey rummaging around in the past, they might very well try to find De Niro in the hope of getting even more on Lehman, and if they found him, for sure he'd start yapping about Salgo, and maybe by now he might have put together Beirut where Salgo had been heading for when he "disappeared" and Beirut where he, Cordoba, happened to be at that same time. Then, just when it was finally starting to happen to Lehman, just when this whole fucking place was about to fall into his lap, who knows what they might discover. If they could nail Lehman, the world's most careful guy, for hanging around with Lansky and his pals, for Chrissake, how safe was anybody? So if De Niro knew anything, or had found out anything in the last thirteen years, he, Cordoba, wanted to be the first to hear. Right?

But first he had to find the fucker, if he was still alive.

The accountant was still blabbering about his old boss. "In fact, all three of them had big loans. From the same bank in the Caribbean. Mr. Downey used to have me send the payments every quarter."

A bell rang in Cordoba's head. "Where in the Caribbean?"

"Some place in the Cayman Islands."

"What happened when the IRS grabbed Downey's house? Or did they grab everybody's house?"

"I really don't know, sir."

"I mean, they still owed the bank the money, right?"

"Yes."

"How big were those loans?"

"All in all, at least a couple of million."

"Banks don't walk away from that sort of money, do they, Kelly?" And Cordoba let out a laugh.

"I'll bet they know where De Niro is if anybody does, right, Kelly?"

"I really can't say, sir."

"Just for the hell of it, do you think you could check back and find out the name of that bank?"

"That might be possible. I arranged the transfers through the First National right here on the Strip. Banks, as you know, have to keep records forever. But to go this far back will take them a couple of days."

"Matthew, let's do this: first, all this is between you and me. Right? Second, we keep more money at the First National than anybody. Tell them to get the name of that bank real quick. Like in a couple of hours, not days. Okay?"

"Yes, sir."

Cordoba rose. "Say, if you like cigars why don't you take the box. I've got plenty more."

Exactly one hour later, Kelly came up to Cordoba's office with a slip of paper. On it was a name and an address: The First Charter Bank, 38 Front Street, Grand Cayman. Cordoba took one look at it and, after thanking the man, told him he could leave.

"Unbelievable!" Cordoba exclaimed when the accountant had closed the door behind him. He picked up the phone and called The Palace East in Atlantic City. His man would have just returned from the hearings. "What was the name of that bank in the Bahamas again, the one that came up in the hearings?" Cordoba asked. "Was it by any chance the First Charter Bank?"

It was. He hung up. It *had* to be the same outfit. Now think, he told himself. Lehman had dealt with that bank before 1969. That bank dealt with Salgo and De Niro before 1969. Coincidence that simply could not be. Somehow Lehman, as absolutely crazy as it might sound, had to be linked to that skimming operation. If that could be determined, there was no way that Lehman could stay on. It would make the Lansky business look like nothing. All they had there was circumstantial evidence. This was the real thing. Lehman could go to jail!

This would provide the basis for a very serious negotiation between Daniel Lehman and Eduardo Cordoba. Why bring in those crazies in New Jersey? If Lehman simply stepped down voluntarily, that would be the end of the investigation, wouldn't it? And De Niro, wherever he was, could further rest in peace. Then another thought occurred to him: why risk dealing with Lehman? He might just fire him on the spot, and once out, it might be goddamn hard to get back in. That fucker Granville would want it all for himself. So maybe the guy to engineer the whole thing—the graceful retirement of Mr. Lehman and the natural ascendency of Mr. Cordoba—would be that outside money man from Mercier Frères. Hell, they had two hundred and fifty million dollars to protect and they would hardly want it to go down the drain with Danny Lehman. That guy Price must be worried sick by now.

He was. When Henry Price had arrived at his office in New York that day at his usual hour of eleven, no less than three of Mercier Frères' partners were waiting for him.

"You've heard about your Mr. Lehman?" was the initial question one of them put very quietly to him.

"No. What has happened?"

"He's been tied in with Meyer Lansky."

"Perhaps we should all go to my office to discuss the situation," Price suggested.

After all had taken their seats around the coffee table in his office, Price asked the next question. "When did this happen?"

"It came out in the licensing hearings over two hours ago. The wire services picked it up right away."

"And what's the nature of the tie-in?"

"Through a mutual acquaintance."

"Who?"

"I forget. Sid knows. He's been on the phone all morning." All eyes focused on one of the other partners.

"Yes. His name is Montague Davies. He was with the First Charter Bank of the Bahamas. They closed up shop about five years ago. That was when a lot of banks down there did the same, if you recall."

Henry Price recalled. For many years almost anybody could, and did, form a bank in Nassau. The local rules made it absolutely impossible to get any information about a bank there, especially its officers and directors. This handy arrangement was the brainchild of the Bay Street Boys, that small group of whites who had run the island for decades almost exclusively for the benefit of themselves, and for the very large number of crooks who hid under their wings and their laws. In 1967 a reformist black government came in, and in the 1970s it passed a very simple new bank law. It merely required annual publication of the names of the officers and directors of any bank on the islands, and the amount of resources that the bank had. Rather than do that, almost one hundred banks went out of business voluntarily, First Charter among them, even though it had been gener-

ally regarded as one of the more reputable institutions in the
Bahamas.

"Any idea where this Davies chap is now?" Price asked.

"Nobody I talked to seems to know."

"I'll find out," Price stated.

"The exchange suspended trading in The Palace's shares
at the opening this morning, and it was just resumed half an
hour ago. The stock's down six dollars, Henry."

"Doesn't surprise me."

"There are quite a few unhappy people around here."

"Understandable."

"This is going to hurt the firm very badly in Europe,
Henry," continued the most senior of the Mercier Frères
partners, pouring it on.

Price said nothing.

"What are you going to do?"

Price took his time before answering and then said, "I'll
take care of it, and then you can have my resignation. Or
perhaps you would prefer it the other way around."

"We'll leave it up to you, Henry."

Immediately after his three partners had left his office,
Price went to his desk, picked up the phone, and dialed the
thirteen digits that would connect him with Lothar Winterthur's home on the Kilchberg above the Zürichsee. "It's
Henry Price," he said. "Hope I'm not interrupting."

"You are, but go ahead," was the gracious response.

"We've got trouble with The Palace. They stopped trading it on the New York exchange at the opening this morning, and when it was reopened, the stock was down six dollars. Apparently that man Lehman who runs the place may
be denied a license to continue operating in Atlantic City. It
seems he might have indirect links to Meyer Lansky,
through a man by the name of Davies, Montague Davies.
Davies apparently used to be with the First Charter in Nassau before it closed down."

"*Ja.* We know him. He's in Holland now. With the Zuider

Handelsbank in Amsterdam. What do you want to know from him?"

"The Zuider Handelsbank? I know them, too: they came in on the syndication of The Palace."

"I'm fully aware of that. No doubt one of the reasons they did was because we already had our name on it."

Price remained silent. Then the Swiss banker spoke again. "What do you want to know?"

"What kind of business this Davies fellow had with Lehman. Especially before and during 1969."

"How badly do you need it?"

"Very."

"Well then, I'll have to talk to Kordaat. He's their chairman."

"I'd appreciate it, Lothar."

"What are you going to do about all this?"

"It depends upon what we learn from Mr. Davies. That will tell us whether or not we can save Mr. Lehman's neck."

"And if we can't?"

"I'll take care of it."

"I certainly hope so. We came into this because of you, Henry. I think everybody over here will look to you to get us out," said Winterthur. "In one piece," he then added.

Twenty-one hours later, Winterthur called back and Price had his answers. Davies had "brokered" an arrangement whereby a group of individuals, Americans, had provided the funds, thirty-one million dollars to be precise, that had been lent to Lehman via the Zuider Handelsbank and one of its companies in the Netherlands Antilles—because of the tax treaty it has with the United States—to finance the takeover of that casino in Las Vegas in 1969.

"Who were these 'individuals'?"

"Well, let's put it this way, Price: we wouldn't accept a dollar from any of them even if they paid *us* interest." Strong words from a Swiss banker.

"Anything else?"

"Not only would they not pay any American taxes on the
money they hid in the Caymans, but they would be able to
deduct the interest costs arising from the loan-back of their
own illegal funds from whatever taxable income they did
declare in the United States."

"What's that got to do with Lehman?"

"Lehman was the man who asked Davies to set it up."

"Who knows all this, Lothar?"

"So far the chairman of the Zuider Handelsbank, Montague Davies, you, and I. But who knows for how long? Of
course, the whole Bahamian–Cayman Islands' operation
was shut down years ago, but the Bahamas is not Switzerland. If some of your American authorities find the right ex-
employee of that bank and pay him enough, for sure they
will nail Lehman right down the line, from beginning to
end. Then they'd probably close the casino in New Jersey
the next day, and no doubt they'd have to do the same in
Nevada the day after. Let me tell you Henry, we're worried.
Look what the British did to Playboy. Those casinos that
they had in England were valued at a quarter of a billion
dollars. When the authorities moved in and forced either a
closure or a quick sale, do you know how much they got for
them?"

"No," Price answered, and he truly did not.

"Thirty million dollars. They got back just over one
tenth."

Price made no comment.

"My advice to you is very simple," the Swiss banker continued. "Get rid of Lehman! Right now."

"The board's meeting the day after tomorrow in Las
Vegas. I'll keep you informed."

As soon as he had hung up on the Swiss banker, Price's
secretary came in to tell him that Natalie Simmons was
waiting on another line. He immediately picked up the
phone and punched the blinking light.

"Natalie. What a surprise!" he said.

"Hope I'm not disturbing you," she said, "but I was wondering if you're coming down this weekend."

He said nothing for a few seconds and then answered hesitantly. "I'm not sure."

"You sound funny," Natalie said. "Is something wrong?"

"To put it mildly," Price replied. "I feel like Hugh Lord le Despenser."

"Who, pray tell, was he?"

"He was accused of some dastardly crime and then hung, drawn, and quartered. All this happened way back in 1326."

"What reminded you of him?"

"My last phone call. Hugh Lord le Despenser, you see, having already had his balls cut off, then felt the executioner rummaging around among his kidneys, and thereupon spoke his famous last words: 'Jesus, yet more trouble.' "

"Danny Lehman?"

"You guessed. And I know . . . you warned me."

The chairman called the board meeting to order at two o'clock. All members were present, as well as the general manager of The Palace's casino operations, Mr. Eduardo Cordoba.

The meeting was held in the room designated for such occasions, located in the executive wing of The Palace—no peeling paint there; the walls were all oak, and well-oiled and polished oak, too. The atmosphere in that boardroom in Nevada was, however, no less poisonous than that of the hearing room in New Jersey just a few days earlier. You could almost hear the hum of the knife sharpener. You could almost sense the board members flinch when Danny Lehman entered the room last, bringing with him an aura of contamination, bearing a plague that would infect all unless the disease was cut off at the source.

These board members, each and every one, had been appointed by Danny Lehman. And except for Mort Granville, who, after all, had brokered the deal that had enabled

Danny to take over the casino, and Benjamin Shea, Danny's personal attorney and vice-chairman of The Palace, who had arranged for Danny to be licensed in Nevada, not one of them had ever contributed a thing to the success of The Palace. To a man, however, they had accepted perks on a scale that was mind-boggling, almost amounting to a full-time occupation in some cases, and all at Danny Lehman's company's expense: the yachts, the villa in Palm Springs, the jets, the girls, the fights, the races—all on top of board fees that ranked right up there with those of General Motors.

Then just one whiff of trouble and, boom, Danny Lehman was suddenly a stranger who had entered their casino, uninvited and bearing the stench of the unclean. "All right," Danny began, "you all know why we're here. Let me tell you here and now, once and for all, that the story about Lansky and me is an absolute, total fabrication. I have never done business with the man; I have never met the man; I have never spoken to the man. I don't even know what he looks like, for Chrissake."

Silence in the room.

"You've got a classic case here of guilt by association, but not even direct association: association twice, three times, ten times removed. It's a goddamn outrage! Not only that, but on top of it you have the FBI, who are supposed to be protecting our liberties, sneaking around trying to entrap anybody who is in a business they don't approve of."

Still silence.

"What do you intend to do, Danny?" The question came from Mort Granville.

"Do? What should I do? I've not been either charged or convicted of anything in my entire *life*. Not even a speeding ticket! Now, because of some young jerk who's running for governor of the most corrupt state in the union at my expense, who intends to win by ruining me, by spreading malicious out-and-out lies about me, I'm supposed to *do* something? Like what?"

"Maybe take a leave of absence, Danny," Granville replied. "Some of us have been discussing the matter prior to the meeting and concluded that we simply cannot escape our moral responsibilities. After all, the jobs of 3,600 employees in our casino in New Jersey are threatened. Ultimately the jobs of the 5,200 here might be. Then there are the outside shareholders. The price of our stock is now down to eighteen dollars, as you know. That's down eight from where it was before trading was suspended and then reopened. If the gaming commission closes down The Palace East—and we've heard that this decision might be imminent in spite of the fact that the hearings have been suspended for the moment—it will drop at least another eight dollars. You're the biggest shareholder, Danny: you'd be hurt worst." All heads in the room seemed to be nodding collectively at every word.

"What we thought is that you might take a leave of absence, Danny, and, as a matter of further goodwill, put your stock in the corporation in trust, maybe allowing some member or members of this board to exercise the voting rights in your absence to make sure that no outsider could come in and take advantage of this crisis situation. I think that I, as company secretary, would probably be in the best position to guard your interests in that respect."

Danny just sat there.

"I think, too, that it would be to your advantage if the impression was given to both the authorities in New Jersey and the financial people in New York that you'd decided to completely neutralize yourself as an operating officer. So I think it would be prudent if this board were to designate Eddie Cordoba as acting chief executive officer."

There it was: the blatant, greedy, open takeover-from-inside laid right out in front of Danny in the full knowledge that he had no choice but to accept. For thirteen years he had coddled this group of men, made some of them rich, asked nothing in return. Now, within just three days, they—and collectively they owned less than 1 percent of the fucking place—were throwing him out. *He,* who owned over ten million shares, was being forced off his own board and out of his own management. Next they would throw him out of his office.

That was, in fact, the next suggestion that Mort Granville was about to make. But Price, the outside money man from New York, the person who thus far had never said a single word, not one word, at a board meeting of The Palace even though he had been a member now for almost two years, suddenly intervened. "I beg to disagree with the suggestions that have been made by the company secretary. Matters are anything but clear. This is no time to make precipitous decisions. I would like to move that this meeting be adjourned."

Danny Lehman was almost as stunned by these words as he had been by the revelation that the old man in the picture with Meyers on that yacht had been Lansky. But not Mort Granville. "I'm afraid, that this board's primary responsibility is to the shareholders, not the debtholders. I'm afraid you and your group fall into the latter category."

"Wrong," said Price. "I can convert our debt into equity tomorrow morning. That would give us, with or without Mr. Lehman, absolute control of this company. I can guarantee you that if we are forced to take that route, all of you, with the exception of the chairman and vice-chairman, gentlemen, all of you will be off this board just as soon as I can convene an extraordinary shareholders' meeting."

All completely stunned, none of the board members now chose to challenge the investment banker.

He continued, "I would like it to be on the record that the chairman continues to have the confidence of this board. Now I again propose adjournment." Vice-Chairman Benjamin Shea seconded it, and the meeting ended.

"Mr. Price," said Eddie Cordoba, in a low voice, as they

ll filed out of the door and toward the elevators. "Could I
ave a word with you? In private?"

"Certainly."

Cordoba led him down the stairs rather than wait for the
levator and then directly to hookers' corner, which, since it
vas only two-thirty in the afternoon, was almost deserted.
Both the Argentinian and the New York banker ordered
cotch. Then: "You made a big mistake up there, Mr.
Price."

"Really? Why?"

"Danny Lehman has been involved with the mob from
the very beginning."

"Oh?"

"I've got the proof. And it goes far, far beyond what came
out in the hearings."

"If you think you know something, spell it out."

Cordoba proceeded to do just that. Lehman's pre-1969
association with the First Charter Bank in Nassau. The subsequent association of Salgo, a felon who never went to jail
because no doubt somebody had murdered him first, with
the same bank. Then there were De Niro and Down-
y—both guilty of skimming millions from this very casino—receiving loans from the First Charter Bank in the Cayman Islands. What the exact connection was, what scheme
they were all involved in, that had yet to be determined, but
there could be no doubt that Lehman was working in collusion with the mob from day one. Lansky had probably mas-
terminded the whole thing, using a coin dealer from Philadelphia as his front.

"That's all you've got?" asked Price.

"All? All?" countered Cordoba, incredulously. "What
more do you want? Canceled checks proving Lehman
bought this place with mob money? Well, you'll get them.
I'll make sure of that."

"Hardly. The First Charter Bank in Nassau, you see, as
well as the First Charter Bank in the Cayman Islands—both

were liquidated in 1977. Not a scrap of paper was left behind."

Cordoba looked as if he were on the edge of cardiac arrest.

Price looked at his watch. "I've changed my mind about that drink. I must be off. Goodbye, Mr. Cordoba."

21

One hour later, Henry Price took a Delta flight to Dallas. He stayed there for three days. On Friday he flew directly from Dallas to London and connected there with a flight to Amsterdam. Kordaat, chairman of the Zuider Handelsbank, came to Schiphol Airport on Saturday to meet him. From there they went to the Amstel Hotel in the center of the city. Lothar Winterthur of the General Bank of Switzerland was sitting in the lobby when they arrived, drinking an Amstel beer. Kordaat suggested they go over to his bank, which was just across the canal; Winterthur preferred to stay in the hotel, where he knew he would be able to get another beer or two should he feel the need. So after Price had checked in, the three of them rendezvoused in the Swiss banker's suite.

"The reason I imposed on both of you on a weekend," said Price, starting the proceedings, "is that time is of the essence. It always is, I know, but in this instance there is an acute urgency. We and our colleagues mutually have two hundred and fifty million dollars in that casino, and if we do not act swiftly and decisively we are at the very least going to lose all semblance of influence or control over that operation; at the very worst we are going to see the New Jersey casino closed down, and have the parent company default on its interest payments immediately.

"After what you people have gone through with Poland,

and with AEG in Germany, and with Alfa Industries in Mexico, I don't think you need any more trouble."

"*Ja,*" said Kordaat, "these are sad times. Our Dutch banking commission is getting very nervous about these things."

"So is ours," admitted Winterthur. "I'm surprised we're in this mess, frankly." He then faced Price square on. "You told me this man Lehman was clean. I specifically asked you, Henry."

"I told you he was as clean as anybody in that business. I stand by that. The problem is that he is getting hanged for a crime he didn't commit. All that stuff about him and Lansky being partners simply does not wash."

"Don't be too sure," said the Dutch banker. "As you know, I have been having a few words with Montague Davies about this matter. It might not be Lansky, but suffice it to say that the less said about Lehman and some of his transactions, the better."

"Where is Davies, by the way?" asked Price.

"We sent him to Indonesia at the beginning of the week. He will stay there for a while, and not in Jakarta either."

Both of the other bankers grunted their approval.

"Well," continued Kordaat, addressing the American, "what have you come to offer?"

"First, let me tell you what we *don't* want to do. On the one hand, we don't under any circumstances want to let the Palace board dump Lehman. If they do, some of the insiders are going to take over, rob the place blind, and laugh at us when we try to get our money back. On the other hand, we don't want to exercise our rights to convert the debt into equity in order to take control because under the terms of the convertible note that's only possible at twenty-four dollars a share, and the price is already down to sixteen dollars and my guess is that, since it's been sinking steadily, the price is going to be down in the range of ten to twelve dollars within a week."

"Klar," said Winterthur.

"Second, what we don't want to do is let the gaming commission in New Jersey continue with its investigation of Lehman. If it does, it is going to turn up some very nasty things—leaving Lansky aside—that could force it to close down the Atlantic City casino. With that cash flow gone, once again the parent company is going to be forced to default on the note, as I mentioned at the outset."

"Damned if we do something and damned if we do nothing," the Dutchman said.

"Precisely," Price commented, "except . . ."

"Except what, Henry?" asked Winterthur, now alert.

"Except if I arrange for a leveraged buyout of the whole company, which would include its casinos in Atlantic City and Las Vegas, as well as the other properties it owns."

"You mean Mercier Frères," the Swiss banker stated.

"No, I mean Henry Price, and, if you are interested, also Jan Kordaat and Lothar Winterthur. As silent minority partners."

Now the Swiss banker was *really* interested. "What does 'leveraged buyout' mean precisely?" he asked.

"Very simply, it is a method allowing a few individuals to buy a company with other people's money, Lothar. Normally, institutional money. It involves almost all debt and virtually no equity."

"I still don't get it."

"Okay, let's say somebody—somebody you don't like—tries to take over your bank, Lothar, by offering the bank's shareholders 25 percent more than the price they can get on the stock exchange. To stave off this hostile takeover, you and some of your colleagues in the bank's senior management get together, set up a shell company, capitalize it by putting in whatever cash you can scrape together, and then borrow whatever is needed to finance a more attractive offer to the shareholders. If it works, you and your colleagues end up both managing and owning the bank. In the

United States, that's the new hot thing, since everybody makes out like bandits. The shareholders get a windfall gain. The managers end up owners. And the investment bank which put the deal together, and arranges the financing, makes millions of dollars in advisory fees. Sometimes tens of millions. That's why American investment bankers are the highest-paid people on earth. And that's also why every other kid who graduates from Harvard Business School wants to become an investment banker."

"All right," the Swiss banker then said, "I understand everything, except for one point. Why should anybody lend all that money to what is essentially a shell company with almost no equity?"

"The lenders don't look at the acquiring company. They look exclusively at the assets and the cash flow of the company being taken over. Its earnings stream goes right through the shell company directly to the lenders."

"Big cash flow, big loans," said the Dutchman.

"Precisely, plus big interest: normally 15 percent," said Price.

"How much more debt can The Palace operations support at that rate?" asked Winterthur.

"Lothar, as usual, you asked *the* question. I checked with the chief accountant at The Palace. He said that receipts at Atlantic City are a full 45 percent ahead of their projections and gaining every month. In Nevada, revenues are up 1 percent. Tahoe was plagued by bad weather last year, but this year all the casinos on the lake are on the rebound and The Palace's Tahoe revenues are expected to set a record."

"So how much more debt can it reasonably support?"

"Another hundred and fifty million. If one stretches things a bit, two hundred million."

"How many shares does The Palace Inc. have outstanding?"

"Twenty million."

"Ten dollars a share, then," said Winterthur. "You said

is sixteen dollars now. That's out of the question. Nobody's going to accept a tender bid *below* market."

"I said it will probably head toward the ten-to-twelve dollar range within a week in any case. A little judicious short selling could nudge it down to eight dollars easily. Look what happened to Caesars stock when those New Jersey people started to go after them: from thirty-six dollars down to four dollars. Everybody on the Street knows that. So when they realize what's coming down on The Palace, a lot of people are going to want out, and quickly."

"Where would you seek the loans?"

"Here in Europe."

"That's not going to be easy. People here don't understand what you call 'leveraged buyouts,'" Kordaat said.

"It depends on who puts their name on it first," Price countered.

"We put our name on that convertible note," said Winterthur, "and look at the mess we are all in now."

"You're going to be in a bigger mess if they default on it," answered Price. That made an impression. "But there's more," continued Price. "I came directly from Dallas, Texas. There is a family there that Mercier Frères has been very close to for years. They would be willing to pay fourteen dollars a share for The Palace stock, provided they would not have to deal in any way, shape, or form with Lehman and his crowd, provided I can get The Palace East its permanent license, and provided they could get the whole thing."

"Wouldn't it bother them if we got it for ten dollars?" asked Winterthur.

"That's what investment bankers are for, Lothar. We put ourselves, our good names, and our money, at risk on this takeover. Nobody can really argue about four dollars a share differential for our trouble. They recognize that in Texas just as they do in New York."

"How sure is their offer?"

"As sure as such things ever get," answered Price. "I'd say if we can produce one hundred percent of The Palace, with the permanent license, there is at least a 99 percent chance of their coming through. They shook hands with me on it. That still means more than a written contract in Texas."

"What's your Mr. Lehman going to think about all this?" Kordaat then asked.

"He'll get a hundred million dollars for his ten million–odd shares instead of maybe nothing if he tries to tough it out alone. I suspect he will need very little convincing."

For a minute they just sat there in silence. The Dutchman then looked at the Swiss banker. Winterthur nodded his assent.

"Let's discuss the terms and conditions of the borrowings, Henry," Kordaat then said. "Don't you think we could cut back a bit on the interest rate? I have the feeling that 14 percent, maybe even 13½, should do it."

The three bankers stayed in that suite at the Amstel Hotel until the early hours of Sunday morning. When they parted, they had a deal.

Short selling of The Palace stock, most of it apparently originating in Europe, started in earnest at the first uptick on the New York Stock Exchange on Monday morning. The downward movement of the stock was accelerated on Monday afternoon when the Enforcement Division of the New Jersey Casino Control Commission announced that it was going to resume hearings in two weeks to determine whether or not Daniel Lehman and The Palace East would be licensed to continue operations. By Wednesday the stock was down to 10½. At closing on Friday it was 7⅞. On Saturday morning Henry Price called Danny Lehman and suggested that they meet in private in New York the following day. They met at the Carlyle at noon. By three o'clock Danny Lehman had agreed to sell his complete holdings in The

Palace Inc., exactly 10,312,000 shares, for exactly
$103,120,000 to Casino Properties Inc., a Delaware Corpo-
ration, the chairman of which was Henry Price. The sale
was conditional, however, upon the success of the tender
offer that Casino Properties Inc. intended to make for the
rest of the outstanding shares of The Palace Inc. residing
with the general public. It was lock, stock, and barrel or
nothing. Such is the nature of a leveraged buyout.

On Monday morning very shortly after nine, Henry Price
phoned the attorney general of the state of New Jersey and
sought to arrange an appointment with him in Trenton at
his earliest possible convenience.

The meeting was fixed in the late afternoon of that same
day. Initially, the attorney general was extremely disappointed when he was told that the unsavory situation at The
Palace East, particularly that relating to its chairman, was
in the process of being taken care of by Mr. Price. His disappointment was assuaged when he was led to believe that
substantial financial support would be forthcoming from
Mr. Price and his friends should he seek higher political
office, for instance the governorship, in 1985. Mr. Price requested two things: first, that the hearings of the Casino
Control Commission related to The Palace East be post-
poned a further two weeks, but that this decision be made
public only at the last moment. Second, that the attorney
general immediately initiate his investigation of Mr. Price to
determine his acceptability as far as the state of New Jersey
was concerned. With the results of the attorney general's
investigation to hand, it seemed likely, he thought, that the
commission would be in a position to grant a permanent
license to The Palace East and its new owner in rather short
order. The attorney general agreed, both with his logic and
to the requests.

The tender offer for the ten million–odd shares of The
Palace Inc. in the hands of the general investing public was
handled by Mercier Frères. The organization of the syndi-

cated loan which would provide the two hundred million dollars which would be needed to buy out both Daniel Lehman and the public was organized jointly by the General Bank of Switzerland and the Zuider Handelsbank of Amsterdam. The acquiring company, Casino Properties Inc. of Delaware, had been capitalized at ten million dollars, and the financial communities of New York and Europe were given to believe that the funds involved were the personal assets of Mr. Henry Price. The financial communities of New York and of Europe were also led to believe, and they believed it, that if this buyout of The Palace Inc. was not successful, The Palace East would be closed by the New Jersey authorities within a month, which would, inevitably, lead to a default on its outstanding convertible debentures in Europe, and a total collapse of its parent company's stock on the New York Exchange.

Thus the eager American sellers of The Palace Inc.'s shares (ten dollars a share was a hell of a lot better than next to nothing), and the equally eager European lenders of the funds necessary to provide the ten dollars each for such shares (lending another $200 million at 13.5 percent, secured by the complete underlying assets of The Palace Inc. in both Nevada and New Jersey, and the name of Henry Price, was a hell of a lot better than seeing their first loan in the form of those convertible debentures going into default), were quickly and easily lined up for the closing that was scheduled for August 1.

On July 25 Eddie Cordoba telephoned Henry Price in the offices of Mercier Frères in New York. He said he had to see Price immediately.

They met an hour later in the coffee shop next to the St Moritz Hotel, where Cordoba was staying. Eddie Cordoba came right to the point. Through his Corsican friends in Paris, he had determined that the infamous Mr. Montague Davies, owner of that yacht upon the deck of which Mr Lansky had been standing as he chatted with that man from

Fort Lauderdale, the one who was also seen so regularly in the company of Danny Lehman, was still alive and well. He apparently now worked for the Zuider Handelsbank in Amsterdam. According to what he had just read the previous day in the New York *Times* it was this same Zuider Handelsbank that was the co-leader of the banking syndicate that was financing the takeover of The Palace by Mr. Price.

This could hardly be yet another coincidence, could it? All that was happening really was that the "friends" of Montague Davies were in essence buying themselves out, this time through Holland instead of the Caribbean. And they were essentially just changing their front man from Daniel Lehman to Henry Price, were they not? *"Plus ça change, plus c'est la même chose, n'est-ce pas, Monsieur Price?"* was Cordoba's flippant way of summing up the situation.

Cordoba's final question was this: when the Enforcement Division of the New Jersey Casino Control Commission found this out, as indeed it would because Eddie Cordoba would see to it *that* it did, did Mr. Price think it likely they would grant him the permanent license that they were certainly going to deny to Danny Lehman because of his links with the same Montague Davies and his pals?

Henry Price was faced with an impeccable line of reasoning based on irrefutable facts. So he asked, "What exactly do you want of me, Mr. Cordoba?"

Cordoba, of course, had his answer ready: "Not that much, considering; say five million dollars in an account at that Dutch bank, plus job security at The Palace, permanent job security . . . I believe they term it 'tenure' in university circles."

It *wasn't* that much, considering the personal and financial devastation Price would face if the Casino Control Commission decided not to license him. "How soon do you require an answer?"

Cordoba parried, "How soon are the hearings schedule
to resume?"

Price did not reply.

"The day before, whenever that may be, should do," th
Argentinian said, after which he simply got up and walke
out.

On exactly the same day, although it was evening an
three time zones to the west of New York, Lenny De Nir
walked into The Palace in Las Vegas. After just a few step
he stopped in his tracks, stunned, dazed by the opulence c
it all. When he resumed walking he constantly scanned th
casino floor, looking anxiously for a familiar face. He foun
none. Small wonder; after all, it had been almost thirtee
years ago that he had left not only the casino but also th
town. More accurately, he had been *forced* to leave in di
grace, broken by the same man who, it had been reported i
the San Francisco *Chronicle,* was now going to get over or
hundred million dollars when he sold the casino that thi
teen years ago he had taken away from De Niro and h
friend Salgo for not one red cent.

Having half circled the main casino floor, he saw a bar c
the left that came as close to the bars he frequented in Sa
Francisco as anything he had seen thus far in the place. Th
maître d' didn't even look in his direction as he mounted th
two steps up to the drinking area surrounded by a bra
railing. Then he remembered: this was the old hookers' co
ner. And sure enough, since it was ten o'clock, there was
whole gang of them sitting at the bar. And there was th
big baccarat area he'd heard about. What he hadn't hea
was that they now had black women, for God's sake, dea
ing in the casino.

Sandra Lee saw him about thirty seconds after he sa
her. She then kept watching him. As the minutes passed sh
determined with relief that he apparently wasn't watchin
her. Then again, she reasoned, why should he recognize he

he had been twenty-two then, and a hooker. He must now
e sixty-five at least, she thought, but he looked as big and
ough, and as mean, as he did then.

There was only one reason he would come back: Danny
ehman. Danny Lehman and his one hundred million dol-
ars that had been plastered all over the papers; the Danny
ehman that had been revealed as an associate of Meyer
ansky and who was thus now fair game, even for De Niro.

Cordoba was out of town, she knew, and from what she
ad heard wouldn't be back until the following day. So if
ne went to the bar during her break there was no risk that
e would come and make another big scene over her drink-
ng in the company of the hookers. "Do you mind?" she
sked, standing beside the small table where De Niro was
eated.

"Naw, sit down." She did.

"What'll you have?" he asked.

"Just a glass of white wine" was her answer. Then:
"Don't you remember me, Lenny?"

His head moved back as if she'd threatened to slap him.
"Who are you?" he demanded in a low voice.

"Sandra Lee. You must remember me. We all used to sit
ere in the good old days—you and Roberto Salgo and Mort
ranville and all the guys from the counting room and the
ealers. We were all here almost every night before every-
ody went home."

It dawned on him. "You were that gorgeous black
hore!"

"That's right."

"I'll be goddamned!"

"What're you doing here?"

"Nothing. Just looking around."

"Looking for the boss?"

"Maybe."

"Better be careful."

"Of Lehman, that crooked little bastard from Philadel phia?" He actually sneered.

"No. Of Eddie Cordoba."

"Who's he?"

"He manages this place. Lehman is out. Cordoba's als the guy who killed your partner, Salgo."

De Niro sat there as if poleaxed. "How do you kno somebody killed him? How do you know he's even dead? he finally asked.

"I know. Look, you better get out of here fast. Meet me a my place in an hour." She wrote her address on the drin napkin and handed it to him. "Go on," she said, "I'll tak care of the drinks."

He left immediately. She pleaded illness and left the ca sino half an hour later. When she got home, she began e plaining what had happened thirteen years ago in Beiru revising history as she told it. Danny, according to her, ha intended to be as conciliatory toward Salgo as he had ult mately been toward De Niro. But Cordoba, driven by amb tion, had instead eliminated Salgo. Three months later th Argentinian was running The Palace. De Niro listened i silence, downing one scotch after another. Finally she wer to bed, leaving De Niro to sleep in the living room. At eig the next morning she woke him, and an hour later sent hi on his way. But before he left he returned to the subject Danny and Cordoba, asking her advice about where ar when he might have a word with them. Again she stress that he was wasting his time where Lehman was concerne He was out of the casino business, and, for all she knew, h already left town. As to Cordoba, she knew he was comi back from New York that afternoon, and there was no re son to doubt he would then proceed to do what he alwa did: spend a few hours walking the casino floor, checki everything out. When did he usually show up? Arou seven o'clock, before the big action started, allowing him t opportunity to talk to his employees before they got t busy. She suggested that he stay away from The Palace in the meantime. He said he would, but she didn't believe him.

So as soon as he had left, she called Danny Lehman in the executive wing of The Palace. He was cleaning out his office in preparation for leaving later that day for the East Coast. Henry Price had invited him to stay at his country place in Virginia overnight. Then on Friday morning the two of them would proceed together up to New York for the closing.

The phone call prompted a radical change of plan. Lehman left the casino just an hour later. And he did not leave alone; he was accompanied by William Smith, who, since 1969, had been the head of security at The Palace. When they got to the airport, the other originally unscheduled traveling companion, Sandra Lee, was outside waiting for them.

"Thanks," he said to her while Smith was helping to stow their luggage into the Gulfstream III.

"I'm glad you've got Smith with you."

"So am I. And both of you are going to stay with me for a while. At least for as long as that maniac is on the loose."

On the flight east neither of them even remotely referred to the subject of Lenny De Niro, even though he was the man who had brought them together so unexpectedly.

Three hours before The Palace's Gulfstream III came in to land at National Airport in Washington, D.C., United Flight 297 took off from Dulles International Airport, bound for Los Angeles, with a stopover in Las Vegas. Eddie Cordoba was sitting in first class, and by the time the 747 had reached cruising altitude, he was already into his second bloody Mary. He was celebrating.

Cordoba had spent most of the day in New York looking at properties. He had always wanted to have a place in that city, but had never been able to afford what he wanted there: a luxury apartment in midtown. Now, with a windfall gain

of five million dollars a sure thing, compliments of Henry
Price, nothing stood in his way. In the early afternoon he'd
been shown a co-op on Park Avenue that he had liked, really liked, and had spent so much time looking and relook-
ing at it that he'd almost missed his flight. Cordoba's last act
had been to write out a check for seventy-five thousand dollars. That would hold it for at least thirty days.

After dinner, Cordoba decided to take a nap. He needed
some rest, since he intended to spend a lot of time walking
around the casino in Vegas that evening for a special reason:
to assure his key employees that, despite everything they
had been reading in the papers, The Palace was definitely
going to stay in business and he, and he alone, was going to
remain in charge.

The United flight pulled up to the gate at McCarran Airport at 6:15 P.M. West Coast time, and twenty minutes later
Cordoba stepped out of his limousine in front of The Palace.
He went directly to the elevator that took him up to his
office. There he checked out the messages his secretary had
neatly lined up on his desk, and then took the elevator back
down to the casino floor. He proceeded directly to the baccarat tables, for it was at these tables that the big action
always took place in The Palace, and here were where the
big profits were made; consequently, it was extremely important that the baccarat pit bosses and dealers be the first
to receive his reassurance that all was now well.

Except for *one* dealer. He was going to fire *her* on the
spot. With Lehman gone, she'd finally lost her protection.
And she was the only link left to Salgo.

"I want to have a word with all of you," he said to the
man in charge of the baccarat area during the early evening
shift, "but first, tell me: where's Sandra Lee?"

"She went home sick about ten-thirty last night."

"When was she due in tonight?"

"About an hour ago."

"Go call her. And tell her to get her lazy ass over here.

Now! Then come back here. Like I said, I want to talk to you about something else." The dealer immediately plunged into the crowd, and headed across the casino floor in the direction of the nearest phone with an outside line.

Out of that same crowd at exactly that same time appeared a bull of a man in his late sixties. He went directly to the bar that overlooked the baccarat area, approached the maître d', and asked a question. The maître d' nodded his head affirmatively and pointed in the direction of Eddie Cordoba. Then the stranger left the bar and approached Cordoba, who was still standing on the edge of the baccarat area, watching the action on the casino floor. The old man stopped about six feet in front of him, and just stood there. Soon Cordoba noticed him.

"Are you Eddie Cordoba?" the old man asked.

"Yes."

"I've got something for you, compliments of Roberto Salgo."

As De Niro reached inside his jacket, Cordoba started to recoil. A second later two shots hit Cordoba's chest and slammed him to the carpet. De Niro then stepped forward, put his .44 magnum a foot from Cordoba's skull, and fired four bullets into it.

The time was exactly 7:16, West Coast time, on Thursday, August 12, 1982. The chief baccarat dealer never got to deliver his message to his boss, which was that nobody had answered the phone at Sandra Lee's home.

After a late dinner in the main house of Henry Price's farm, he and his guests had retired to the living room for coffee. Price, Danny Lehman, and Sandra Lee sat together on the sofa. Natalie Simmons sat off to the side, chatting with Bill Smith. Since investment bankers like to keep in touch the TV set had, as usual, been turned on in the far corner, tuned to the NBC affiliate in Washington. At eleven they aired the late news. The Israeli siege of Beirut was at its

peak, and everybody stopped talking for a moment to watch
the carnage. Before the commercial break, a scene flashed
onto the screen showing still more bodies, though this time
only two, and this time in black-and-white. It was accompanied by a voice-over teaser by the anchorman, suggesting
that the audience stay tuned, since after the break they were
going to see some remarkable footage taken just one hour
ago inside the famed Palace casino in Las Vegas.

The effect of these words on the select audience of five in
the Virginia farmhouse was immediate. All conversation
stopped. Then, after the commercial, the anchorman came
back on camera with these words: "We are about to show
you some scenes shot in rather primitive black-and-white
video. Please do not attempt to adjust your sets for the next
couple of minutes. The tape was taken by cameras which,
for security reasons, are installed behind mirrors in the ceiling above the casino floor at The Palace in Las Vegas. They
constantly monitor all activity taking place below."

The tension in the living room of the farmhouse was almost palpable as the grainy black-and-white tape began to
run, and the action was shown once at normal speed and
then in agonizing slow motion, not unlike the scenes when
President Reagan was shot. The first sequence depicted
Eduardo Cordoba having words with someone who appeared to be one of The Palace's dealers. The dealer then
disappeared, and another figure came on camera, Lenny De
Niro. Slowly, calmly, and with terrifying deliberateness, he
approached Cordoba and then paused about six feet away
from him. When Cordoba turned toward him, the two appeared to exchange a few cordial words. Then in one swift
motion De Niro drew a gun from inside his jacket and,
judging by the little puffs of smoke which were the viewers'
only evidence of gunfire, since, of course, the video security
film has no sound, fired two shots at Cordoba's heart, slamming him backward and down. As he lay there, Cordoba's
face was turned up toward the camera, and he was obvi-

ously still alive. De Niro then stepped forward, put his gun to Cordoba's head, and fired four more rounds which, at that range, caused Cordoba's skull to disintegrate and, in appalling slow motion, literally to fly apart.

In the same eerie silence, a posse of The Palace's security guards suddenly appeared on camera and, as De Niro started to flee, opened fire and seemed almost to cut the man in half.

When this grisly video clip had ended, the anchorman calmly identified Cordoba as an Argentine national and a key figure in the management of The Palace. He went on to report that his slain assailant, reported to have no less than eighteen bullets in him, was one Lenny De Niro, apparently a resident of San Francisco and believed to have been a disgruntled former employee of the casino.

Natalie Simmons was the first to find her voice. "How absolutely horrible! That poor man Cordoba! And who was that man who killed him?"

Henry Price, who had gotten up to turn off the TV set, said nothing. Danny Lehman and Sandra Lee just looked at each other. So it was William Smith who answered the question. "He was an evil man, believe me, Miss Simmons. But no doubt he had a reason for doing what he did. As crass as this might sound, I say good riddance to both of them."

If it had been a church instead of a farmhouse, this statement would have been greeted by a chorus of "Amens." But instead Henry Price finally said, "I don't think any good will come from us dwelling on this any further this evening. Danny and I have to leave for New York in about seven hours. The closing is scheduled for 9 A.M. So let's all go to bed."

Bill Smith went to bed in his cottage, but it took a while before he found sleep. His mind kept circling the events not only of that evening, but also of the last thirteen years, and it kept coming back to Sandra Lee. It had been a woman who had placed that call thirteen years ago, that anonymous phone call, which had put the FBI onto Salgo and De Niro in the first place. He had no doubt now that it had been Sandra Lee. And who had been in Beirut with Danny when Salgo had disappeared? Sandra Lee, of course. And now here she was with Danny in Virginia, three thousand miles away from where the killings had just taken place, as a result of a hurried departure from Las Vegas which, no doubt, she had engineered.

His final thought was that he had better get back to Las Vegas first thing in the morning. There would be a lot of questions asked by the authorities, including his former colleagues at the FBI. It was better that he be there personally to give the answers, and to ensure that this entire matter was closed as quickly and quietly as possible.

The next morning, Natalie Simmons was up at dawn to prepare breakfast for Henry Price. Despite all that had happened, the look of worried preoccupation that she'd noticed on the investment banker's face the day before seemed to have disappeared. And when Sandra Lee arrived with Danny Lehman—who had also been so uncharacteristically subdued the previous evening—he was once again his usual cheerful self. William Smith was the last man to show up for breakfast. He immediately had a private word with Danny, who subsequently asked Price if Smith could ride with them to National Airport. Smith now planned to return immediately to Las Vegas on the first available commercial flight. Sandra Lee, upon hearing that, said that she'd return to Vegas with Smith. She wanted to get back to her job.

The sale of The Palace Inc. was consummated at the New York office of Mercier Frères at 9:15 A.M. that day. Danny Lehman received a cashier's check in the amount of $103,120,000.00 in exchange for his delivering 10,312,000 shares of The Palace Inc. The remaining ten million–odd shares that had been in the hands of the public had also been tendered, to Casino Properties Inc., so that when the closing was completed, Henry Price and his two European silent partners now controlled 100 percent of The Palace.

When Danny walked out onto Wall Street fifteen minutes later, alone, he had absolutely no idea what he would do next, not even where he would live. He decided to stay in New York for a while and checked into the Pierre. After a week of moping around, while eating a room service hamburger all alone in his suite, he suddenly came to the conclusion that what had happened to him was probably inevitable.

Furthermore, Danny realized that although he had lost the battle, he might still be in a position to win the war. After all, when he added up everything he had stashed away during his thirteen years as the proprietor of the greatest casino on earth, he now had a net worth well in excess of one hundred million dollars. And how had he done it? By emulating success. By following the example of Cliff Perlman and Caesars Palace, and by going one better. Who was setting the pace now? It was obvious: the Wall Street gang and investment bankers like Henry Price. That was the route to go.

But how? After everything that had been in the papers, he was a pariah on Wall Street, and probably everywhere else in America. Then he had an idea. Last time around thirteen years ago, it had all started to come together when he and Sandra Lee had gone to Europe. Maybe it would work again. In Europe nobody would know, or if, by chance, they knew, care about the notorious past of Danny Lehman.

He picked up the phone and called Sandra Lee.

22

When they checked into Claridge's this time, they were shown the utmost courtesy and given one of the finest suites in the hotel. Sandra Lee immediately went apartment-hunting, and, early on the second day, found what she wanted just around the corner from the hotel: a seven-room flat, fully and exquisitely furnished, with maid service and, most important, ready for immediate occupancy.

They found out right away that what Danny had suspected was correct: when he mentioned his name in a restaurant, nobody knew him from Adam. And nobody gave Sandra Lee any funny glances either. He finally began to grasp what it meant when London was described as the most civilized city on earth.

As to his plans to get back into business, well, as Sandra Lee had pointed out, he didn't have to do a thing. When the realization sank in that he had, at a very minimum, $100 million of idle cash, and when the vultures found out where he was, the phone would start ringing of its own accord. It did, with proposals for investments in everything from gold mines in Peru to perpetual-motion machines in Texas. He ignored them all, since he had decided to put most of his money into tax-free municipal bonds, and then to move it progressively into real estate. So Sandra Lee took over the phone, screening the calls, and, more often than not, just telling the parties on the other end to forget about it without even asking Danny.

One morning in late September 1982 when a call came through from Amsterdam, she wasn't quite sure what to do, so she asked the caller to hold and went into the bedroom, where Danny was eating breakfast and reading the papers. "There's a man on the phone who says he's with the Zuider Handelsbank. He refused to give his name to me. Do you want to talk to him?"

Danny hesitated. Was the tranquillity he had found in London about to go down the drain? If so, he might as well find out right away. He picked up the phone on the bedside table.

"This is Danny Lehman," he said tentatively.

"Mr. Lehman, this is Montague Davies. Remember me?"

Although it had been over thirteen years ago, he could hardly forget *that* name.

"I do indeed," he said warily.

"I hear you've become a man of leisure," said Davies. He then continued, "However, something came up yesterday here at the bank that I thought might interest you. It has to do with making money, using a new approach."

Danny immediately relaxed: this was apparently not to be an attempt at blackmail.

"I'd like to explain further, but would prefer to do it in person," Davies went on. He had obviously maintained the aversion to talking business on an unsecured telephone line that he had developed when working for the now defunct First Charter Bank of the Bahamas. "I could manage to fly over to London today, if it is convenient."

At 3 P.M. Montague Davies was shown into the drawing room of Danny's London flat. He was deeply tanned and immaculately dressed and had entered carrying an attaché case and an umbrella—every inch the merchant banker. Danny suggested tea, and after the maid had served them, Davies got right down to business.

"Perhaps I should first explain how I got your number here in London. It was through the chairman of our bank,

Jan Kordaat. He and Henry Price are very close, and Price got the number for him."

Price had no doubt gotten it from Natalie Simmons, Danny thought. For he knew that Sandra Lee and Natalie had stayed in contact.

Davies then continued, "While I'm on that subject, you might be interested to hear that Mr. Price has already resold The Palace."

That surprised Danny. "I've read nothing about it in the papers," he said, rather skeptically.

"No, you wouldn't have. It was a strictly private transaction. Price sold out to a family partnership, some people from Dallas, it seems. Furthermore, from what I hear, he got a rather good price: the equivalent of fourteen dollars a share of the old Palace common stock."

Now Danny was really shocked. He'd sold out at ten dollars just six weeks earlier!

Montague Davies could not help but sense what was going through Lehman's mind. "That works out to Price making about forty million dollars on the deal. Not bad, eh? Then do you know what he did? Resigned from Mercier Frères. Apparently his whole involvement with you had resulted in an estrangement between Price and the other senior partners at his bank, so now that he'd taken them completely off the hook, and made forty million in the process for himself, he took the opportunity to tell them to bugger off."

The maid returned to refill their teacups. After she left again, Montague Davies resumed. "I learned all this the day before yesterday, when one of the partners at Mercier Frères paid us a visit in Amsterdam. He was delegated to replace Price as their contact man with our bank and came over to introduce himself. I take it the bank gave him this job more as a perk than anything else. Which brings me to the purpose of this visit. His main activity is heading up the M&A—mergers and acquisitions—activities at Mercier

Frères, advising clients, for a fee, on leveraged buyouts, like the one Price pulled on you, as well as straight takeovers of one corporation by another, including hostile takeovers.

"Now to the point," continued Davies. "He advised me that Litton Industries is going to buy Itek Corporation. He thinks it will take about three, maybe four, months before the deal is finalized. The takeover price will be forty-eight dollars a share. Itek is now selling at twenty-one dollars a share. Follow me?"

Danny followed him completely. "Is Mercier Frères handling the deal?"

"No. Another investment bank in New York. But apparently these M&A types, at least some of them, talk to each other."

"And why has this successor to Henry Price talked to you?" Danny asked, and then added, "By the way, what's his name?"

"I think it best we leave names out of this. As to the reason, I think it probably best you also don't ask me that."

"But I prefer to."

"All right. He'll get a commission of 5 percent of all profits generated by his 'suggestions,' which I guess is standard practice. But do you know how he insists upon being paid? Would you believe an attaché case full of cash to be hand-delivered on a yet-to-be-determined street corner in New York?"

Danny was stunned. "But why would a partner of a prestigious bank like Mercier Frères . . . ?"

Davies just shrugged. Then he said, "Greed. Tax-free greed." He immediately continued. "I'm putting together a little investment syndicate for the purpose of investing in such situations. I was assured that there are more, many more, to come. I've set up an Anstalt in Liechtenstein, which will trade through the General Bank of Switzerland, through either their Zurich office or one of their branches in the Bahamas or the Cayman Islands." Obviously Montague Davies was going full circle.

"But isn't that illegal?" Danny asked.

"Merger arbitrage? Hardly, it's the new art form on Wall Street."

"That's not what I meant? I'm referring to the use of insider information."

"It's not illegal in Switzerland. They do it all the time. Same goes for Liechtenstein. But it always pays to be as prudent as possible. If you decide to participate in our syndicate, my suggestion would be that you transfer the funds to our bank in Amsterdam. We will treat it as a time deposit giving you full documentation to that effect. The funds will however, go immediately to Liechtenstein, and proceed from there to accounts at the General Bank of Switzerland either in Zurich or at their branch in the Bahamas. The trades will be made in the bank's name. Follow me?"

"Perfectly."

"Are you interested?"

"Maybe. Can I call you tomorrow?"

"Yes. I'll be back in Amsterdam. Here's my number." Davies handed him his card. Then he reached down into his briefcase and pulled out a long yellow envelope. "And here are the papers you would have to execute to open up that deposit account at the Zuider Handelsbank. I don't think you would want to get involved in any paperwork beyond that point. I'm afraid you will simply have to trust me. But can assure you that when we take our profits in Liechtenstein, your share will be immediately deposited back to your account in Amsterdam."

Montague Davies rose and said, "Then I'll be hearing from you. By the way, the minimum amount will be one million dollars. If I were you, however, I would make it two. After all, it's about as close to a sure thing as you wil probably ever get." Montague Davies then shook hand with Danny, picked up his attaché case, collected his brolly at the door, and left.

The next day Danny deposited two million dollars with the Zuider Handelsbank in Amsterdam. On January 17, 1983, Litton Industries bought Itek for exactly forty-eight dollars a share. Danny had turned his two million dollars into almost five million. It had taken just over four months. He hadn't done as well as Henry Price had done with The Palace. But he was learning.

In the three years that followed, it was one sure thing after the other. Gulf + Western bought out Esquire at $23.50 a share in 1984. The Liechtenstein "syndicate" prebought the stock at $17. American Stores made a tender offer for Jewel Companies at $70 a share. Four months earlier Montague Davies had inaugurated a purchase program for Jewel's shares: his average price was $49.50. And so it went.

Davies always kept Danny informed, via cryptic phone calls from Amsterdam, Zurich, and Nassau. Cryptic, because Davies adhered strictly to a "need to know" policy. From that point of view, all that Danny needed to know was the results—not how they were made possible, nor who else was sharing them. Davies's mode of operation was very simple: every informant and every client was put into a separate compartment, and the only person who was able to connect them up was Davies himself. In this sense, the M.O. of the world of international investment banking closely resembles that employed by the world's intelligence services. In fact, they often complement each other. Thus the CIA is a regular customer of the Crédit Suisse, using the Swiss bank's airtight compartments, known as numbered accounts, to protect its informers and clients when money changes hands.

Danny understood this and had no problem with it . . . as long as the profits kept rolling in. And they did, month after month, year after year. But he did try to keep himself more fully informed independently. He had bought a country home in the Buckinghamshire village of Chalfont St. Giles, and had installed his office there.

Then in February of 1986 Danny received an urgent call from Montague Davies at his country place. Davies was phoning from a public booth at Schiphol Airport and about to board a plane for London. He told Danny that it was imperative that they meet at Danny's flat in three hours. Danny assured Davies that he would be there, and, accompanied by Sandra Lee, left for London an hour later.

Davies's first words were "I'm afraid that the last transaction, which involved FMC, is going to be just that: our last transaction, Danny. Our friends at the General Bank of Switzerland have heard that somebody else has been playing the same game, using the facilities of the Bank Leu in the Bahamas. The SEC is onto them, and the Bank Leu, to protect itself, is in the process of finking on the guy. His name's Dennis Levine. He does M&A for Drexel Burnham Lambert and he's a friend of our friend at Mercier Frères. This thing is bound to spread, with everybody finking on everybody else. I've heard that Ivan Boesky, the king of arbitrage, is the next guy in line to get it. Who knows where it will all end? I've already closed down all of our trading accounts in Zurich and Nassau and liquidated the Anstalt in Liechtenstein. I've also suggested to our friend in New York that he take a long vacation, preferably on a beach in Romania." He paused. "Here's the final accounting where you're concerned."

He handed Danny a single piece of paper. The accounting was handwritten. It showed that between September 1982 and February 1986 Danny Lehman had made $47 million dollars, plus change. This did not include the interest he had earned on his deposit account at the Zuider Handelsbank in Amsterdam on the profits that had accumulated there over time.

After Danny was done reading it, Davies held out his and. "If you don't mind," he said. Danny returned the iece of paper. Davies then walked over to the fireplace in)anny's drawing room, reached into his vest pocket for)me matches, lit the piece of paper, threw it into the fireace, and watched it burn.

"That's the end of the paper trail," he said, with a grin. Now, Danny, I've got a new idea. Japan. The Japanese are a the process of accumulating the biggest cash hoard in istory. As a result, the stock market over there is about to xplode on the upside, and the yen is bound to go through ie roof. A double whammy. And strictly legit, meaning iat it is no longer a sure thing, but close to it. What do you iy?"

"I'll think it over."

"No hurry on this one. But in the meantime, I do suggest iat you shift from dollars to either yen or DM in your ccount at our bank. We would put the funds on threeionth deposit and keep rolling them over until you tell us ifferently. The dollar's a goner, you know."

"Sure. Go ahead, Montague. But I think I'll pass on Jaan for the moment."

An hour later, Sandra Lee returned from her shopping. s that man gone?" she asked.

"Yes. Permanently."

"Good, I'm glad. Now what are you going to do?"

"I really don't know. Any ideas?"

"No."

"Remember all the times we've been in Seabys and in oinks?" he asked, referring to the two most prestigious oin stores in the world, where he often made purchases, lding to his personal collection. "What if we opened our vn store?"

"That's pretty stiff competition. Anyway, where would ou put the store?"

Danny didn't hesitate. "Bond Street. And by the tim
we're done they'll look paltry by comparison."

"You're always saying 'we.' Do you mean it?"

"Are you willing to take on a partner?" he asked.

"Anytime, anywhere, Danny," she replied.

"All right. It's a deal. I'll be back at one and we'll hea
over to the Savoy to celebrate."

An hour later, they walked into the Savoy Grill. All eye
turned to Sandra Lee. Nobody noticed the middle-age
short, pudgy man at her side. Danny didn't mind. He ha
just retired from a brief but highly successful career as
merger arbitrageur. Now he was about to go back, full ci
cle, to the business he had always liked best: the coin bus
ness. Now that all the world was becoming a gambling c
sino, it felt good to be back in real money again. As coff
was being served, he reached into his pocket and handed
small velvet-covered box to Sandra Lee. She opened it an
took out an American double eagle gold coin. "Thank
partner," she said and leaned over the table to kiss Dann

Every man in the Savoy Grill who watched them felt th
same thing: pure envy.

Life *was* fair.

ABOUT THE AUTHOR

PAUL ERDMAN is the author of five bestselling novels: *The Panic of '89, The Silver Bears, The Crash of '79, The Billion Dollar Sure Thing,* and *The Last Days of America.* Also an economist and former international banker, he lectures widely to business and political audiences. Mr. Erdman lives in California.

BANTAM BOOKS
GRAND SLAM SWEEPSTAKES
Win a new Chevrolet Cavalier . . .
It's easy . . . It's fun . . . Here's how to enter:

OFFICIAL ENTRY FORM

Three Bantam book titles on sale this month are hidden in this word puzzle. Identify the books by circling each of these titles in the puzzle. Titles may appear within the puzzle horizontally, vertically, or diagonally . . .

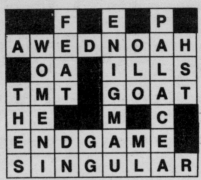

Bantam's titles for November are:

THE PALACE

SINGULAR WOMEN

ENDGAME ENIGMA

In each of the books listed above there is another entry blank and puzzle . . . another chance to win!

Be on the lookout for these Bantam paperback books coming in December: THE BONFIRE OF THE VANITIES and TIME FLIES. In each of them, you'll find a new puzzle, entry blank and GRAND SLAM Sweepstakes rules . . . and yet another chance to win another brand-new Chevrolet automobile!

MAIL TO: GRAND SLAM SWEEPSTAKES
                  Post Office Box 18
                  New York, New York 10046

Please Print

NAME _____

ADDRESS _____

CITY _____ STATE _____ ZIP _____

OFFICIAL RULES

NO PURCHASE NECESSARY.

To enter identify this month's Bantam Book titles by placing a circle around each word forming each title. There are three titles shown on previous page to be found in this month's puzzle. Mail your entry to: Grand Slam Sweepstakes, P.O. Box 18, New York, N.Y. 10046.

This is a monthly sweepstakes starting February 1, 1988 and ending January 31, 1989. During this sweepstakes period, one automobile winner will be selected each month from all entries that have correctly solved the puzzle. To participate in a particular month's drawing, your entry must be received by the last day of that month. The Grand Slam prize drawing will be held on February 14, 1989 from all entries received during all twelve months of the sweepstakes.

To obtain a free entry blank/puzzle/rules, send a self-addressed stamped envelope to: Winning Titles, P.O. Box 650, Sayreville, N.J. 08872. Residents of Vermont and Washington need not include return postage.

PRIZES: Each month for twelve months a Chevrolet automobile will be awarded with an approximate retail value of $12,000 each.

The Grand Slam Prize Winner will receive 2 Chevrolet automobiles plus $10,000 cash (ARV $34,000).

Winners will be selected under the supervision of Marden-Kane, Inc., an independent judging organization. By entering this sweepstakes each entrant accepts and agrees to be bound by these rules and the decisions of the judges which shall be final and binding. Winners may be required to sign an affidavit of eligibility and release which must be returned within 14 days of receipt. All prizes will be awarded. No substitution or transfer of prizes permitted. Winners will be notified by mail. Odds of winning depend on the total number of eligible entries received.

Sweepstakes open to residents of the U.S. and Canada except employees of Bantam Books, its affiliates, subsidiaries, advertising agencies and Marden-Kane, Inc. Void in the Province of Quebec and wherever else prohibited or restricted by law. Not responsible for lost or misdirected mail or printing errors. Taxes and licensing fees are the sole responsibility of the winners. All cars are standard equipped. Canadian winners will be required to answer a skill testing question.

For a list of winners, send a self-addressed, stamped envelope to: Bantam Winners, P.O. Box 711, Sayreville, N.J. 08872.

DON'T MISS
THESE CURRENT
Bantam Bestsellers